THE
WRECKED SERIES

Wrecked
Palace

CATHERINE
COWLES

Editor: Susan Barnes
Copy Editor: Chelle Olson
Proofreading: Julie Deaton and Janice Owen
Paperback Formatting: Stacey Blake, Champagne Book Designs
Cover Design: Hang Le

For Monica.
Thank you for your support from that very first email. Your kindness, generosity, and championing of my words have meant the world.

Wrecked Palace

Prologue

Caelyn

PAST

THE SOUND OF A PHONE RINGING PULLED ME OUT OF A deep sleep. I groaned and blinked against the darkness. The only light in the room came from the glow-in-the-dark stars peppered all over my dorm room ceiling. I fumbled around on my nightstand, trying to find the ringing device.

"Turn off your freaking phone before I toss it out the window," Bell called from across the room. Our other roommate, Kenna, let out a mumbled moan.

"I'm trying." My fingers found the charger cord, and I tugged the phone onto my bed. Glancing at the screen, my chest squeezed. 1:13 a.m., and Will was calling. I hurried to hit accept. "Will? What's wrong?"

I'd given my little brother a phone before I left for college. I kept the low-budget mobile topped up with minutes because I needed a way to get in touch with my siblings, and for them to be able to reach me. Our house phone hadn't worked in years, and my parents weren't exactly keen on us kids using their cells.

"I don't know what to do—"

Will's voice was cut off by a cry. Sobs that could only be coming from my one-year-old sister, Mia, sounded over the line, followed by someone pounding on a door. "You owe me a fucking score, asshole. I paid. Give me my shit!"

I sucked in a sharp breath. "What's going on? Where are you guys?"

"I'm in the girls' room. I put a dresser in front of the door, but there's a guy in the house. He won't leave."

The light flicked on, and Bell and Kenna were by my side in a flash, hearing the distress in my voice. I motioned for Bell to grab her phone. "Where are Mom and Dad?"

"They're not here. They haven't been in days."

More pounding cut in. "Give me my fucking score or I'll gut you when I get in there."

My heart hammered against my ribs in a painful rhythm. "Bell, call the sheriff. Someone's in the house. Will has himself barricaded with the girls in their room."

Bell blanched but immediately began dialing. As soon as someone picked up, she started recounting the situation. Kenna eased down next to me on the bed and rubbed my back.

I turned my attention back to Will. "Stay calm, buddy. The police are on their way." But how long would it take for them to get there? Our small island off the coast of Washington state didn't have its own dedicated police force. We shared access to a sheriff's department with the rest of the chain of islands. That meant in an emergency like this one, deputies had to take a boat before they got onto the island.

"I'm scared."

The tremble in Will's voice broke something deep inside me. "It's going to be okay. I'm with you." More pounding rang out in the background, and Mia started crying harder. "Is Ava holding Mia?"

"Yeah, I put them in the closet."

My hand fisted in my sheets. My ten-year-old little brother was savvy enough to know he needed to hide his little sisters away. What the hell had my parents been doing since I left for my junior year four months ago? "You're so smart, Will. And so freaking brave. What's in front of the door again?"

"I pushed the dresser and then a bed."

"That's great. That will keep him out."

"I hope so."

God, I did, too. If something happened to my tiny terrors...I tried to force out the horrendous images taking over my mind.

Bell waved a hand at me. "There are two deputies already on Anchor. They're heading to your place now."

I gave her a tight nod. I wanted to feel relief, but I couldn't. Not until I knew, with one hundred percent certainty, that the kids were okay. "Did you hear that? There are deputies coming now. They're already on Anchor."

Will sniffed. "Okay." There was more yelling and pounding, then a cracking sound. "I think the door's breaking."

I squeezed my eyes closed, sending up a thousand silent prayers. "Get in the closet with Ava and Mia."

"I can't. I have to fight him if he gets in. I have my bat."

My sweet, brave boy. Tears leaked from my eyes. "He's not going to get in. Just hold on."

Shouts sounded across the line. I heard someone yelling that they were from the sheriff's department and to get down on the floor. There was more screaming and then a shot. The crack of the bullet was so loud, Kenna jerked beside me. All of my muscles locked. "Will, are you okay? What's happening now?"

"I'm okay. I don't know."

"Will, it's Deputy Raines. Are you okay in there?"

My shoulders sagged in relief. Will answered the deputy in a shaky voice. "We're okay."

I heard a door opening, and Mia's cries got louder, but it was

Ava who spoke. "I want Cae Cae." The sound of her pleading shattered the last piece of my heart still holding itself together.

"I'm gonna be there soon, Ava."

"Did you hear that, Avs? Caelyn's coming soon."

The deputy began speaking again. "We need to take the bad guy out to the patrol car. Then we'll come back for you."

"Okay." Will's voice sounded stronger now. "I have to move the furniture, Caelyn."

"Don't hang up!" I was desperate. This was my one lifeline to my siblings, and I couldn't let it go. "Put the phone on speaker and lay it on the bed."

"All right." Something rustled, and then Will spoke again. "Can you hear me?"

"I can hear you."

The sounds of furniture being pushed across the carpet, and Will grunting, came over the line. I held my breath until I heard a knock.

"It's Deputy Raines. Can I come in?"

A door creaked in the background.

"Are you guys okay?" Deputy Raines asked.

"Yeah, we're okay," Will answered.

The slight tremor in his voice had me fisting the sheets even tighter. I never should've left Anchor. I should've simply found the cheapest apartment possible and worked at a bar or a restaurant on the island. But instead, I'd been selfish, desperate to use the scholarship I'd worked so hard for.

Ava's voice cut into my thoughts. "Can you take us to Cae Cae?"

"Who's Cae Cae?" Raines asked.

"My sister. She's on the phone," Will said.

"Is it all right if I talk to her?"

"Sure."

The phone beeped as he took me off speakerphone. "Ms.

O'Connor, we've got them. They look scared but are perfectly safe."

I burst into tears. Through my sobs, I managed to get out, "Thank you. Thank you so much."

"Of course. We're going to take them to the sheriff's station on Shelter."

"Okay. I'm in Seattle. I go to college here. But I'm going to get over there as fast as I can. Will you take this phone so that you can update me if anything changes?"

"I'll keep the phone with me. Take a deep breath. They're going to be fine."

But that wasn't completely true. Sure, physically, they were okay. But emotionally? The kids were traumatized. And I didn't know the first thing about how to heal those wounds. But like with everything else, I'd simply have to find a way. I just had to get to my siblings first.

"Cae Cae!"

Ava hurled herself at me as soon as I crossed the threshold of the staff lounge at the sheriff's station. I caught her, lifting her into my arms and rocking her back and forth. "I'm here now. You're okay."

She pressed her little face into my neck. "I was so scared."

I held her tighter against me as I squeezed my eyes closed. "I'm so sorry, Avs." As her small body trembled against me, I vowed that she would never feel scared like that again.

I scanned the room, my gaze catching on Harriet, Kenna's adoptive guardian. She'd been the one to arrange a boat for us from Seattle to Shelter Island and had immediately headed to the sheriff's station herself. She rose, little Mia fast asleep in her arms.

I blinked back tears. "Thank you so much, Harriet. I don't know what I would've done…"

"Oh, hush now. You know I'd do anything for you girls."

Kenna crossed to the older woman, pressing a kiss to her cheek. "Thank you."

"I'm happy to help however I can."

"Where's Will?" I asked.

Harriet inclined her head to the hallway. "Deputy Raines was getting him a soda and a snack. I think the adrenaline was wearing off. He was getting a little shaky."

My eyes fell closed again as if I could will away the nightmare of the past few hours. I had so many questions, but I didn't want to ask any of them in front of little ears. I pressed a kiss to Ava's head. "Can you go to Bell? I want to find Will."

Ava nodded and went easily into Bell's arms. Bell snuggled her close. "I missed you like crazy."

The small smile that Ava gave Bell had my shoulders easing a fraction. "I'll be back in a minute."

I headed back into the hallway, looking for any sign of the vending machines. After a couple of wrong turns, I spotted a head of floppy brown hair. "Will."

His head snapped up at my voice, and he shoved the soda at a deputy who looked vaguely familiar. Will charged, hitting me with a force that had me stumbling back a step. *When had he gotten so big?* I wrapped my arms around him as more tears filled my eyes. "I love you."

"Love you, too," he whispered, a catch in his voice.

The deputy made his way over to us. "Hi, Ms. O'Connor. I'm Deputy Raines."

"Please, call me Caelyn. Thank you for all you've done."

"I'm happy to help." A pained smile curved his lips. "The sheriff wants to chat with you whenever you're ready."

I wanted to chat with the sheriff, too. But first, I had a few questions for Will. I brushed the hair back from his eyes; he was in desperate need of a haircut. "When's the last time you saw Mom and Dad?"

Will released me and winced. "On Friday."

Blood roared in my ears. It was early Monday morning. "Why didn't you call me?" I'd given Will the phone for a reason. Our parents had never been overly attentive. Why my mother hadn't just gone on birth control, I'd never know, because she certainly wasn't interested in raising her children. She did the bare minimum, which often consisted of a single bag of fast food for dinner and using the television as a babysitter. But they'd never left us alone for days on end before.

Will nibbled on his bottom lip. "I didn't want you to come back from college."

"Why not?" I couldn't hide the hurt in my voice.

He squared his small shoulders. "You need to finish school and get a good job so you can get us out of there."

"Oh, Will." I pulled him into my arms, the tears I'd been trying so hard to hold back since I arrived at the station, sliding down my cheeks. I should've been embarrassed that this was all coming out in front of some deputy I barely knew, but I couldn't find it in me to care. All I cared about was wrapping my tiny terrors up in hugs and taking them somewhere safe.

"What's gonna happen to us?" Will whispered.

God, I wished I had an answer for that, but I knew I'd never let these kids go into foster care. "We're going to figure it out together. But I'm not leaving you. You're not alone."

Will sagged against me. "I'm sorry I didn't call. I should've when they started getting worse."

I stiffened. "What do you mean getting worse?"

Will released me, looking from me to Raines and back again. "They're doing drugs."

My jaw tightened. My parents had always been heavy drinkers, and I knew my dad smoked pot, but I'd never seen any hints of anything harder. The fact that my ten-year-old little brother could see the signs of drug use and knew what it meant… It shattered what little naïve hope I had left that my parents would get their acts together. "You don't have to go back there. Not ever again." I turned to Deputy Raines. "Right?"

"Correct," he agreed. "Child Protective Services has already been here. The children have been placed in Miss Harriet's care until a more permanent decision can be made."

The roaring in my ears quieted a fraction. Harriet was a godsend, a true angel. Not only had she taken in Kenna when she needed a place to live; now, she was giving us safe harbor, as well. "Thank you."

I gave Will's shoulder a squeeze. "Why don't you go hang with the rest of the crew while I talk to the sheriff? I know Kenna and Bell want to see you."

Will nodded stoically. "You're not gonna leave, right?"

My heart clenched. "Not without you."

"'Kay." He headed down the hall towards the lounge.

I couldn't bring myself to look away from his small form until he disappeared from sight. I inhaled deeply, steeling myself for what was to come. I turned back to Raines. "How bad was it?"

Raines grimaced. "House was a wreck. Everywhere but in the girls' room. It looked like Will had been sleeping in there, too. He'd moved his mattress between Ava's bed and the crib." I was going to kill my parents. For what they'd put these kids through, the fires of hell would be too kind. "There wasn't a lot of food left in the house either."

I swallowed against the bile rising in my throat. "Please tell me that means they don't have a chance in hell of getting these kids back."

"It's not gonna happen. The sheriff wants to fill you in on why exactly that's the case."

There was an ominous tone to Raines' words that had my stomach twisting. "Lead the way."

The deputy guided me down a maze of hallways before stopping in front of a door and knocking.

"Come in," a gruff voice called.

Raines pushed the door open. "Sheriff, this is Caelyn O'Connor. Caelyn, this is Sheriff Spaulding."

I stepped forward. "Nice to meet you, sir. Thank you for taking care of my brother and sisters."

The man, who looked to be in his late fifties, inclined his head to a chair opposite his desk. "Have a seat."

I did as instructed, and Deputy Raines took his leave. I couldn't help twisting a loose thread on my jeans as Sheriff Spaulding took my measure, seeming to assess every weakness and flaw in a matter of seconds. "You're in school at Seattle University."

"Yes, sir."

"You working? Taking out loans?"

He must've known my parents weren't helping me in any way. They'd just been happy to have one less mouth to feed. "I have a full academic scholarship. I work part-time to cover my room and board."

Spaulding nodded, seeming pleased with my answer. "Your parents…"

"Are total and complete wastes of space?" I offered.

"I'm afraid it's worse than that."

I gripped the loose thread on my jeans tighter. "Will said he thought they were using drugs."

"Your father has gotten mixed up with a bad crew. We had suspicions before, but tonight confirmed it. He's dealing, and I'm not talking pot."

The string popped off my jeans. "Dealing? He was bringing those people into the house? With the kids there?"

Sheriff Spaulding's gaze hardened. "I'm afraid so. In and out of the house."

"I'm going to kill him."

"You'd have to find him first. And we can't seem to do that."

I stiffened. "What do you mean?"

Spaulding leaned back in his chair. "We found your mom holed up in a motel room, high as a kite, needle by the bed. But no sign of your dad."

Needles. We weren't even talking prescription pills. "I was home this summer. They were neglectful, yes, but Mom was still caring for Mia. They drank too much, but I saw no sign of drugs."

"A lot can change in four months, Caelyn."

Apparently, a whole life could fall apart. "What about the guy who broke in?"

Sheriff Spaulding laced his fingers together and rested his hands on his desk. "Dave Herbert. Arrested on a slew of charges. He won't be breathing free for a few years, at least."

It wasn't enough. He'd scared my siblings to death, probably would've hurt them or worse. My stomach roiled at the thought.

"That's not all," Spaulding continued. "Your brother gave us a cell phone. I think he thought it might help us find your folks because it belonged to your dad. What was on that phone…it's going to lead to a lot more arrests."

"That's good, right?" I wanted all of these assholes off the streets and far away from my family.

"It is good. But while all this is shaking out, I want you to be cautious."

All of my muscles seemed to seize at once. "You think they'll come after the kids?"

Spaulding's jaw went hard. "I'd like to think not. But desperate people do stupid things. They could think going after the kids might shake your dad loose. Or that the kids know where your dad is. Miss Harriet has assured me that she has a state-of-the-art security system. I think you'll be safe on her estate, but I want you to be careful when you're out around town. Maybe give the kids' schools a heads-up."

My mind swam with all of the possible risks. I hated that we might bring trouble to Harriet's door. But what other option did we have? "Thank you. We'll be careful. Will you keep me up-to-date on the arrests?"

"I'll keep you in the loop as much as possible."

"I don't need to know the ins and outs of the cases. I'd just like to know when I can take a deep breath again."

Spaulding's expression gentled. "I understand. We're going to put Harriet's estate and the kids' schools on the drive-by loop so there will be a police presence. That should discourage anyone from doing something stupid."

"Thank you." It should've made me feel more at ease, but the fact that the sheriff thought it was necessary just ramped my anxiety up another level.

Unease slid over the sheriff's features. "We'll need Will to testify about the phone and the people he saw coming and going from the house. Possibly Ava, as well."

"What? No. That can't be safe."

Spaulding met my gaze dead-on. "If we want this Herbert clown and your mother to get the maximum sentences, we need that testimony."

I closed my eyes, letting my head fall forward. For Will, Ava, and Mia to be truly safe, to heal, anyone involved needed to go away for as long as possible. "They'll testify."

"Good—"

I held up a hand, cutting the sheriff off. "But I need you to do something for me in return."

His eyes grew shrewd. "And what would that be?"

"Help me get custody of my siblings."

Caelyn

PRESENT

"COME AND GET IT, TINY TERRORS," I CALLED FROM the kitchen.

Will appeared, shaking his head. "You know I'm not actually tiny anymore, right?"

I clutched at my chest in an overdramatic move. "Don't remind me. You're forever eight in my mind." But it didn't change the fact that my little man was now sixteen years old. He had a driver's license. And was shaving. I didn't even want to think about all of the girls who made googly eyes at him.

I shook myself out of the downward spiral I was rapidly descending into. "Where are the girls?"

"I just finished Mia's braids and she was looking for the right bracelet to go with her outfit. Ava was packing her backpack. What do you need in here?"

God, my brother was the best kid on the planet. Too good. But no matter how much I tried to get him to cut loose, it never happened. "Can you pour some OJ for everyone?"

"You got it."

While Will got everyone glasses of juice, I slid the rest of the scramble onto plates. The toaster dinged, shooting up the bread in a little hop. I quickly buttered the slices. "Girls, the countdown is on."

"We're here! We're here!" Mia huffed. "Look at my braids. Will gave me ribbons."

I turned to take in my little spitfire. "You look beautiful. And I love your outfit."

Mia was into anything brightly colored or that had glitter of some sort. Today it was a white t-shirt with a sparkly rainbow, pink pants, and gold glitter slip-ons. The pink, polka dot ribbons and a wrist full of bracelets just completed the look. "Thank you." Her face scrunched. "You can still see my string, right?"

The worry in Mia's expression had me crouching so that I was eye-to-eye with her. "Let's see." She held up her arm for my inspection. There was an array of jelly bracelets, some beaded ones, but peeking out between the bangles was a rainbow-colored friendship bracelet.

Two years ago, these fancy bead kits had become all the rage with Mia's and Ava's classmates. They were ridiculously expensive, and we didn't have a lot of extra money for that kind of thing. So, as an alternative, I'd taught the girls how to make simple friendship bracelets with string. They'd become obsessed, and Mia had made us all matching rainbow bracelets. Even Will wore one.

I held up my wrist, touching it to Mia's. "Rainbow power in full effect."

She beamed at me. "Good."

Ava appeared in the doorway. "Morning." Her voice was soft, just like the rest of her. My girl was the most sensitive of souls. The therapist I'd taken both Will and her to for the first year I'd had custody of them had told me that she might always be this way. Growing up in such an unstable home had made her constantly take the measure of those around her, always cautious to avoid any volatile situations. As much as it hurt my heart, I knew that Ava's empathy and sense of others' emotions could also be a superpower.

"Morning, Avs." I wrapped an arm around her for a quick hug. "All right, get settled. It's time for food."

"Pancakes?" Mia asked hopefully.

Will chuckled. "You ask that every day."

She turned hopeful eyes to me, and I couldn't hold in my laugh. "It's not a weekend." I tried to reserve the super-sugary stuff for special occasions.

She slumped in her chair. "Vegetables?"

I tried to reel in my laughter at her dejected expression. "You'll survive. I promise."

"I like the veggie patch scrambles," Ava offered.

"I'm glad." I'd come up with the name because when we first moved into our small rental house, I'd planted a vegetable garden in the backyard. The kids loved helping tend to the plants, and I thought it would make them keener to the idea of eating the vegetables on their plates. It was hit or miss most of the time. But Ava was always a trooper.

"*I like the veggie patch scrambles,*" Mia parroted in a whiny voice.

My gaze cut to her as I took a seat. "Mia Renee, we don't make fun in this house."

She slumped lower in her seat. "Sorry, Ava."

It wasn't exactly heartfelt, but it wasn't sassy either so I let it slide. Everyone dug into their breakfast, and my lips twitched when Mia was the first to finish hers. When she caught my smile, she shrugged like someone way older than her seven years. "It wasn't so bad."

"I'm happy to hear it." I took a sip of orange juice, glancing around the table. "Okay, hit me with the good stuff. Three things." I pointed to Ava.

"Um…" She thought for a moment. "I got a ninety-seven on my spelling test."

I held out a hand for a high-five. "That's awesome! Proud of how hard you studied." I turned my attention to Will.

He only rolled his eyes a little bit. "Mr. Harmon was sick yesterday, and we got to watch a movie during history."

I broke off a piece of my toast. "That definitely qualifies as a good thing. And what about you, Miss Mia?"

She beamed. "Coach Hughes wants me to practice with the big kids next week!"

I straightened in my chair, letting the piece of toast fall from my fingers. "She does? Why didn't she talk to me?" I was going to kill that woman.

Mia shrugged. "She said she was going to talk to you today."

I did everything I could to make sure my siblings got to do whatever activities their hearts' desired. And pretty much from the time Mia could speak, she had been asking for gymnastics. I'd put her in a pre-K tumbling class when she was four, and Mia had taken to it like a fish to water. The coach of the program had told me that Mia had real potential. But elite gymnastics programs, even the one on our tiny chain of islands, were expensive.

It was nearly killing me to send her three times a week. If she started the elite program, that three would jump to five. I wasn't sure I could swing it. All I could think about was the letter I'd received from our landlord the day before about our rent increase. That would be hard enough, but adding gymnastics on top of that? It would most likely be impossible. And there went any chance at the culinary class I'd had my eye on for the past few months.

"I can do it, right?" she asked.

I swallowed against my suddenly dry throat. "Let me talk to Coach, and we'll see."

"Okay." Mia smiled in a way that said she had all the faith in the world in me. It was a smile that socked me right in the gut. And I knew I'd simply have to find a way. Maybe I could look into selling a kidney on the black market.

"Nope, nope, nope." Kenna waved her hands in front of her face. "Don't open that within a twenty-foot radius of me."

I slowly put the packet of bacon back into the fridge under the counter. "I thought you were loving bacon lately."

Kenna's hand went to the small curve of her belly. "Something changed this week. It's so bizarre. Now, I can't stand the smell of it. It has me puking my guts up in seconds."

Bell scrunched up her face as she slid onto a stool opposite us at my kitchen station. "Thanks for that mental picture right before we eat lunch."

Kenna shrugged. "I figure you'd rather have the warning than me barfing in your purse."

I bit back a chuckle. My job at The General Store had many perks, but one of the highlights was cooking for my best friends when they stopped by. "Okay, bacon's off the table. What'll it be, Barfy Magee?"

Kenna scowled at me for a moment before turning her gaze to the chalkboard above my head, taking in the array of salad and sandwich offerings. "How about the kale and apple salad with chicken?"

"Coming right up. Bells, you want the vegan BLT?" I glanced quickly at Kenna. "That's not gonna make you upchuck, right?"

"No, your weird health nut fake meat should be fine."

I shook my head as I started pulling out ingredients. "No weirder than your fake sugar, fake hazelnut, fake milk coffee concoctions. How is that decaf treating you these days?"

Kenna pointed her fork in my direction. "That is cruel and uncalled for."

Bell let out a snorted laugh. "She knows how to hit you where it hurts."

Kenna gave a pitiful moan. "I miss real coffee."

"It'll be worth it. You don't want that baby popping out jonesing for its next hit of caffeine." I poured some chopped kale into a bowl and reached for the dressing.

"You sound like Crosby. Do you know he's read all of those baby books already? He's even joined Mom forums. Every time I even look longingly at his coffee, he starts listing off all the potential side effects. He even tried to limit my chocolate intake."

My chest gave a painful squeeze, but I kept my smile firmly in place. The last thing I wanted Kenna to know was that jealousy had made a home somewhere in the vicinity of my heart. It was a mixture of joy and pain. Over-the-moon happiness for my friend, who deserved a happy ending more than anyone else I knew. But also, a searing ache, because I so deeply wanted what she had—a true partner who would support me through all of life's ups and downs. Someone who would be there for Will, Ava, and Mia. Who would see the kids as the treasures they were.

Bell waved a hand in front of my face. "Hello? Earth to Caelyn. Please don't chop off a finger."

I forced my smile wider. "Sorry. Lost in my own world." I quickly focused on slicing the chicken once more before placing the vegan bacon strips in a skillet.

"You look tired. Is the new manager position a lot more hours?" Kenna asked.

I'd recently taken over as manager for The General Store. It meant that I not only ran the kitchen but the rest of the grocery, as well. It was a lot more responsibility and hours, but it also meant a bit of a pay raise. Unfortunately, it still wasn't enough to cover both my increased rent and Mia's gymnastics. Not even close. "The job's good. You know me, I just lose myself in another world sometimes."

Kenna and Bell shared a worried look that had me biting back a curse. "I swear, I'm fine."

"Okay," Bell started. "Ford and I wanted to know what night would be good to take the kids to Rocco's."

I knew both Bell and Kenna adored my siblings, but I also knew they tried to take them off my hands once a week so I had a night to breathe. They hoped I'd used the time to do something for myself, but I typically used it to catch up on whatever I'd fallen behind on during the week—laundry, meal prep, bills. It wasn't exactly a glamorous life, but it was rewarding in many ways. "I think Thursday would be good."

"That should work for us. I'll make sure Ford has someone to cover at the bar."

"Sounds good to me." I plated the sandwich for Bell and then lifted both meals onto the counter. "Lunch is served. Can I get you guys drinks?"

"I'll take an iced tea," Bell answered.

"Just water," Kenna grimaced.

Her pout had me grinning. "Coming right up." I grabbed two bottles from the drinks fridge and passed them to my friends. "Here you go. I'll be right back. I need to make sure no one's ready to check out up front."

Kenna waved me away. "Don't worry about us. We'll just be here stuffing our faces."

I chuckled and wove my way through the aisles, greeting a couple who looked to be tourists and telling them to flag me down when they were ready to check out. I rounded another corner and almost collided with a hulking form. "Oh, schnitzel! I'm so sorry. I wasn't looking where I was going and—" My words cut off as my gaze met ice-blue eyes. "Griffin." His name came out a bit breathy.

I cleared my throat. "Did you need to check out?" I glanced in his basket and frowned. A stack of frozen meals—like always. "You really should mix in some fresh produce with those."

He grunted. "Been eating the same thing for years, haven't died yet."

The voice was exactly what you'd expect from a man with a six-foot-six frame and shoulders so broad, I was surprised he fit through most doorways. It was low and rough, and made me want to lean in a little closer, even though everything about Griffin screamed: "*Go away!*"

I gave my head a shake to clear it. "Want me to make you a sandwich or salad before you go?"

His expression gentled the slightest bit, or maybe I simply wished it did.

"Sure. Surprise me." His eyes narrowed. "Sandwich. No weird vegetables."

I rarely got more than twelve words out of Griffin at a time. But it had become a game of sorts for me to try and get as much out of him as I could. But the days where I made his lips twitch or eyes brighten were the ones I really felt on top of the world. "One surprise concoction, coming up."

I turned on my heel and left Griffin to his shopping. I wasn't sure why I got such ridiculous pleasure from providing the man one rounded meal a few times a week, but I did.

I froze at the end of the aisle as my gaze caught on Patti Jenkins. She stared at Griffin as he reached out to grab something from a shelf. I could practically see her gossip-hungry mind whirling. When he caught her stare fixated on him, she muttered something under her breath and tugged her toddler down the aisle and away from Griffin. He tensed but didn't say a word, simply studied the chips in front of him with intense focus.

I fought the curse that wanted to surface and headed back towards my cooking station. That woman was a nosy and judgmental jerk-face. She had a daughter in Mia's grade and was always condescendingly offering me advice and *help*. But seeing her cast that same judgment towards Griffin had me seeing red.

"Was that Griffin?" Bell asked as I rounded the counter.

I cut a sharp look in her direction. Too many folks on this island talked about the mysterious man behind his back, and I didn't want my friends adding to it.

She held up both hands. "He helped drag my fiancé out of the ocean after someone tried to kill him. I'm team Griffin all the way."

Kenna scooped up a forkful of salad. "He gave Grant a black eye, so you know I'm a fan." Her expression sobered a fraction. "Just be careful."

I growled in her direction. "He's a good man." I didn't know with one hundred percent certainty, but everything pointed that way. He was polite if a little gruff. But that prickly exterior was understandable given everything he'd been through.

Bell grinned. "And it doesn't hurt that you want to climb him like a tree."

My face turned bright red. "Shhhh! He'll hear you." Yes, Griffin Lockwood was incredibly handsome. Gorgeous in a way that stole your breath and made you stupid. But he wasn't for me. I simply felt a sort of kinship with the broody man. I knew what it was like to have the majority of our small island judge and whisper because of your familial history.

Griffin seemed to take it all in stride, though. He stuck to himself and his big, dilapidated farmhouse on the far side of the island. He only ventured into town with a purpose, never to sit and eat at a café or grab a beer with other locals. He was in and out, leaving only questions and whispers in his wake.

"Sandwich ready?"

The rough voice made us all jump. I was sure my face was the shade of the tomato I was about to slice. "Um, I'm, uh, just deciding what I should put on it. We got some really nice Roma tomatoes in, and the spinach is super fresh. Maybe I'll do a tomato mozzarella deal with some balsamic and prosciutto." My mouth kept right on spewing nonsense while Kenna and Bell struggled to hold back their laughter.

"It'll be up in just a second," I hurried to put an end to my runaway mouth disease. Right after I locked myself in the walk-in fridge and never came out.

Griffin

I HEAVED ANOTHER PILE OF WHO KNEW WHAT OUT THE window and into the dumpster below. When I first returned to the farmhouse, I'd been a hell of a lot more meticulous as I went through each room. Now, if it looked like garbage, out it went.

The pile of detritus landed with a satisfying *thunk*. I turned back to survey the room, a muscle ticking in my jaw. The rose wallpaper my sister had loved so much was yellowed and peeling after years of age and the time it had been exposed to the elements. But that's what happened when you left a home vacant for over a decade. Kids threw rocks at windows. People broke in and stole everything of value. They vandalized for the hell of it.

My stomach turned as I took in the graffiti on the wall— ugly words cutting across the roses my little sister had considered her private garden. I'd been back on the island for a few years now, but it was too late. The damage had already been done.

Sheriff Raines had been the one to finally get in touch to tell me that my family's refuge was being destroyed. It was no easy task getting through to me. I'd made an art of running, and another of hiding. Raines had tracked me through lawyers and shell corporations until he finally found a cell phone number that only three people had.

I'd seen his call as a sign: time to return home and restore the home I'd once seen as a palace and had ruled as a prince. We'd called it *the farmhouse*, our family getaway from the hectic craziness of our normal lives. It sat on ten acres of pristine land on the far end of the island, away from curious eyes.

Beth and I had run wild in the forest and to the pond on the property. I remembered begging our parents to move to Anchor Island permanently, but they'd always forced us to return to our lives in Northern California. Ones that required uncomfortable school uniforms and society parties.

And when I lost them, the people I'd loved most in this world, I'd let the farmhouse fall away. I'd been so young. But even after I'd come to my senses, I hadn't been able to face this place or the memories it held. And in doing so, I'd let my favorite sanctuary almost be destroyed. It was a miracle the house hadn't been burned to the ground.

Sheriff Raines had met me here the first day I returned. I'd nearly lost my lunch in the bushes when I saw the place. He'd offered to recommend some quality contractors to help with the vast number of repairs, but I'd politely declined. Instead, I'd done something insane. I'd vowed to do all the work myself.

It was part atonement, part grieving process. And I'd grown to love the work. A small shop space sat a few hundred feet from the main house and had gone mostly untouched. After a thorough cleaning, I'd made the space my home for the first year I was back on Anchor. It had taken longer than I'd hoped for the permits and to make sure there were no structural issues.

Now, I was living in the main house. I'd gone room by room,

starting with the master suite. I'd hauled garbage, repaired walls and windows, refinished floors, and painted so many things I'd lost track. But I now had the master, kitchen, office, and one other bedroom in livable condition.

The kitchen was my greatest feat. I wasn't sure why I'd poured so much time and money into a space I only used for coffee and frozen meals. But it looked like a dream. Maybe it was because my mother had loved the space so much. When we were in Marin, our family had a chef. But here on the island, my mother had always done the cooking. She loved seeing the smiles on Beth's and my faces when she would call us in for a slice of berry cobbler or to sample a fresh batch of cookies.

I gave my head a shake, trying to clear the onslaught of memories. I had known this room would be the hardest. I focused back on the trash strewn across the hardwood floors. Some of the boards would need to be replaced, having swollen from being exposed to the sea air for such a long time.

As much as I tried to focus on the tasks at hand, I couldn't stop the visions from swamping me—the brown-haired little girl sitting on this very floor, begging me to play Barbies with her. I squeezed my eyes closed, willing the images away. It was too much.

I tore off my work gloves and strode out of the room. I needed to get out and away—anything to distract me from the ghosts that haunted me here.

⌒◎

I climbed out of my truck in the parking lot of The General Store. Why was it that I always ended up here? There was just something about the brown-haired beauty who worked at the kitchen inside. Normally, people who shined with that life-is-beautiful kind of positivity made me want to punch something. But with Caelyn, I was fascinated.

I started towards the store when a man called my name. I

stiffened and turned, expecting to see a stranger, maybe one of the reporters still holding out hope that I'd share my story with the world. The set of my shoulders eased a bit when I saw that it was Ford Hardy, owner of The Catch Bar & Grill. I said nothing but waited for the man to make his approach. He wasn't a stranger exactly, but I had no desire for idle chitchat.

"I've been hoping to run into you," he greeted.

I stayed silent.

Ford chuckled. "Not too talkative, are you?"

"Not much to say, I guess."

Ford's expression grew serious. "I just wanted to thank you for your help a few months back."

"I didn't do anything anyone else wouldn't do." Ford had been attacked by someone sick in the head. He'd been jumped from behind and knocked unconscious. I'd just come along at the right time.

"Either way, thank you." He held out a hand, and I took it for a shake. "Come into the bar sometime. I'll treat you to a beer and a meal. It's the least I can do."

I fought the wince that wanted to surface. The last thing I wanted was to sit around at the island watering hole. People whispered, thinking they were being discreet when they were anything but. Even worse, they sometimes thought it was completely acceptable to approach and ask me a million intrusive questions. "I'll try and come by."

Ford grinned. "I'm taking that as a *fat chance in hell*."

My lips twitched. "You're not a stupid man."

"Thank God for that. Well, if I can ever do anything to repay you, just let me know. My brother's a contractor. We could give you a couple of days on that house of yours if you'd like."

My jaw tightened. "I'm good. But thanks for the offer."

Ford nodded and gave me a wave before heading back towards The Catch. "There's no expiration date on that."

I wouldn't take Ford up on his offer of help unless I got desperate. I needed to do this on my own. I started towards the store. Pulling the creaking screen door open, I walked inside. It was still a bit early, but when 4:00 a.m. was your usual wakeup call, 4:30 p.m. was just about perfect for dinner. Plus, I could avoid the after-work crowd.

I made my way towards the kitchen at the far end of the grocery but stopped in my tracks when I heard Caelyn's voice.

"Is there any way you could give me more hours? Or more of the bookkeeping to do?"

Mr. Walters, the owner of the store, chuckled. "You're doing it all already, deary. I barely show up here anymore."

"Well, do you know of anyone else who might be looking for some help for things I could do from home?" she pressed.

"Are the two jobs you have not enough? You're gonna work yourself to the bone. And you need to be home for those kids."

"I know." Caelyn's voice seemed to deflate on the words. "But Mia got accepted into this gymnastics program, and it costs an arm and a leg."

Walters' voice gentled. "I'd be happy to loan you the fees—"

"No," Caelyn cut Mr. Walters off. "You've done more than enough for us."

A foreign feeling invaded my chest. A twisting sensation that burned. I'd heard the talk around the island that Caelyn had taken in her three younger siblings after their parents had been involved in some sort of drug bust. I couldn't imagine taking all that on when she must've been barely more than a child herself.

I cleared my throat, stepping around the end of the aisle. Caelyn looked up, the frown marring her gorgeous face quickly turning into a bright smile. "Griffin. It's good to see you. Have you finally given in to trying one of my salads?"

I gave my head a shake. "I think I'll stick with the sandwich."

Walters grinned. "I don't know, Caelyn can make kale pretty tasty."

I didn't try to fight the twisting of my face. "No, thank you."

Walters chuckled. "Maybe another day. All right, I'm off." He turned to Caelyn. "You let me know if you change your mind."

Caelyn reached up on her tiptoes, pressing her lips to the old man's cheek. "Thank you."

Walters headed out of the store, and just Caelyn and I were left. I slid onto a stool at the counter. It was rare that I waited here for my food, but I couldn't seem to resist the temptation today. I had this undeniable urge to make sure she was okay.

"So, what'll it be? Some version of meat and cheese?"

I almost chuckled. *Almost.* "Sounds good to me. But I know you'll sneak some vegetables on there somehow."

"Gotta keep you from getting scurvy."

I almost choked. "I thought that was from not enough vitamin C. I drink my orange juice."

Caelyn shook her head and started pulling things out of a fridge below the counter. "There's vitamin C in vegetables, too. And lots of other nutritious things you need."

"Good thing I come in here a few times a week then."

"Good thing."

An idea was forming in the back of my mind. One that just might be the answer to helping Caelyn out of her predicament and giving me some nice benefits, as well.

The screen door banged open. "Cae Cae!" a young girl's voice called out. Soon, there was a flash of movement past me.

Caelyn stepped around the counter and lifted the little girl into her arms as she hurled herself at Caelyn. "How was your day?"

"So good. I taught cartwheels at recess, and you left me my favorite cookie in my lunch."

Caelyn laughed. "Sounds like a good day to me. Where are the rest of the tiny terrors?"

The little girl beamed up at Caelyn. "They're coming, but they were being too slow, so I ran when I got to the parking lot." Her gaze caught on me. "Whoa. Are you a giant?"

I wanted to laugh but seeing the easy affection between the girl and Caelyn stole my ability to speak.

"Mia, this is Mr. Griffin. Griffin, this is my little sister, Mia."

The girl looked so much like Beth had at that age, I struggled to find words. "It's nice to meet you, Mia." My voice came out rougher than before, and I tried to force my lips into a smile, but the action felt foreign.

"Hey, sis," a male voice called.

I turned to see a boy who looked to be about sixteen or seventeen. As soon as he caught sight of me, wariness filled his features. He quickly crossed to his sisters, tugging another girl behind him. "Who's this?"

Caelyn pressed her lips together as if holding back a laugh. "This is Mr. Griffin. Griffin, this is Will and Ava, my other two siblings. I hope you don't mind, but they usually hang with me for thirty minutes before Molly takes over. Kids, you can go hang out in the office while I get Mr. Griffin's sandwich ready."

"I wanna stay with you and help," Mia whined.

"I'll go into the office," Ava offered. She had taken a step behind her brother as if hiding from me.

"They can stay." The words were out before I could stop them. Awkward and a little gruff, but Mia beamed.

"See, Mr. Griffin wants me to help make his sandwich."

Caelyn shook her head. "Well, if that's the case, we better wash our hands."

Ava headed for the back office while Will took a seat next to me at the counter, eyeing me carefully. Caelyn helped Mia up onto a little stool by the sink, and they washed their hands, Mia singing some sort of song that counted off the seconds.

"All clean," she called. "No germies can last to thirty."

I couldn't hold in my chuckle this time. "I guess they can't."

"I never thought I'd see the day," Caelyn started, putting a hand over her heart. "I do believe you laughed, Griffin Lockwood. Who knew all it took was a seven-year-old singing about germs?"

Chapter Three

Caelyn

I THOUGHT GRIFFIN'S LIP TWITCHES PACKED A PUNCH, BUT they had nothing on his chuckle. It was a little bit gruff as if coated in sandpaper, just like his voice. The tone seemed to skitter across my skin and sent a pleasant shiver down my spine.

"I like his laugh," Mia chimed in.

Redness crept up the back of Griffin's neck, and I felt a bit guilty for putting him on the spot. Mia held out her arm to me. "Can you dry my rainbow bracelet? I don't want it to stay wet and fall off."

Mia's protectiveness over her bracelet sent a mixture of warmth and worry through me. I loved that she was so attached to what she had made a symbol of our family, but I feared the day she outgrew the thing. It was already looking a little tight. We'd just have to make some more soon. "Of course." I carefully rubbed a towel over her wrist.

She held it up for Griffin to see. "This is my rainbow. Me and Ava made them. Caelyn helped. And we all have one. Even Will."

Will stared Griffin down as if challenging him to find it odd for a sixteen-year-old boy to wear a rainbow friendship bracelet. Griffin nodded. "Uh, pretty."

Mia beamed. "Thank you."

"Come on, Mi," I said, trying to shift her focus elsewhere. "Up on your stool. I need you to put the salami on the sandwich."

She climbed up onto the stool and eyed Griffin. "You like salami? It's my favorite."

"It's one of my favorites, too."

I'd never heard so many words out of Griffin on one visit before. I sent him a grateful smile for putting up with Mia's chatter.

"Do you like cheddar cheese or American?" she asked.

"Cheddar."

"Me, too." She beamed. "Cats or dogs?"

"Hmmm..." Griffin took an exaggerated amount of time considering the options. "Dogs. Definitely dogs."

Mia shook her head. "I want a cat. I've been asking forever. She'd sleep with me, and I'd dress her up, and we'd be best friends."

A ghost of something that looked a lot like pain flashed across Griffin's features. "You've got it all planned out."

Mia's shoulders slumped. "Except we can't have pets at our house. The mean landlord says."

"Mia," I chided. "The landlord isn't mean. She just doesn't want animals on her property." Pinpricks of guilt seemed to dig into my skin. I'd worked so hard to give these kids a normal childhood—one full of all the things I'd never had. But pets hadn't been something I'd been able to make a reality. Ava always looked longingly at the dogs at adoption fairs. And Mia full-out begged for a cat regularly. But when I could barely keep my head above water on the bills we already had, saving for a house of our own wasn't exactly on my radar. "Maybe one day."

"One day is so far away," Mia whined.

Griffin met her disappointed stare. "But think about how much you'll appreciate it when it finally gets here."

"Kinda like how I only get pancakes on weekends?" Mia asked.

Griffin grinned, and it was truly devastating. "Exactly like that."

Mia nodded and got to work laying pieces of salami on slices of rustic sourdough. Griffin's gaze shifted to mine, and I mouthed, *thank you*. Who knew? Apparently, Griffin was the child-whisperer.

"About ten more minutes on the steaks," Crosby said as he picked up his beer from the picnic table and took a pull. The table was one Bell had helped me haul from a garage sale and refinish so it was no longer a splinter-filled mess but instead a smooth, warm-hued masterpiece.

Kenna leaned back in a deck chair. "Good, because I'm starving."

Crosby bent and pressed his lips to her slightly rounded belly. "Brown Eyes, you're always hungry these days."

Her gaze narrowed on him. "Are you saying I'm eating too much?"

Crosby straightened, holding up both hands in surrender. "No way. I think you're perfect."

Ford chuckled. "Retreat now, man. You're fucked."

"Language," Bell chastised.

Ford winced. "Sorry, Caelyn."

I waved him off. "They're playing. They can't hear a thing we're saying." Mia was forcing Will to play spotter as she worked on some of her tumbling. And Ava had gotten sucked into playing judge for each move.

I looked around at my friends, my *family*, and a rush of warring sensations flooded me. Warmth at this amazing community I had found myself a part of. One that was always willing to lend a hand and support. And yet those little flickers of jealousy ate at the warmth. I hated it. Wanted to shove the feelings away, but they wouldn't be budged.

The tender caresses Crosby gave Kenna's stomach. The kisses Ford pressed to Bell's temple. I wanted that for myself. But as soon as those thoughts entered my mind, I'd give myself a mental smack. These were my two best friends in the world. The only people who had been there for me, no matter what. And I was happy for them—over-the-moon. I didn't want to poison any of that with my jealousy.

"Hellooooo? Caelyn?"

I snapped back to the present at Kenna's voice. "Sorry. What?"

She straightened in her chair. "What is going on with you lately?"

I forced a smile. "You know me, I'm just thinking of the million and one things on my to-do list."

Bell reached over and rubbed a hand up and down my back. "Well, quit it. Now's the time to relax. It's Friday, and it's family dinner time. Turn off the worry."

I loved Bell as if she were another limb, but she didn't understand the kind of worry I felt. The endless list of things constantly swirling around in my mind. An increase in rent, Mia's gymnastics, whether I should take Ava to another therapist, how I was going to pay for Will's college in a year and a half... I forced myself to keep my tone light even though what I really wanted to do was scream. "I'll do my best, taskmaster."

Ford grinned at his fiancée. "I'd do what she asked. The woman can be vicious."

"Don't I know it," I agreed.

Bell scowled at both of us. "You guys are mean. I'm not that bad."

Kenna let out a snorted laugh. "You might as well be a drill sergeant."

"I'm pretty sure that's you," Crosby argued. "You nearly made one of Hunter's men cry yesterday."

"I did not," Kenna protested.

"What are you doing to my brother's construction crew?" Ford asked, amusement filling his tone.

Crosby couldn't hold in his laughter. "When they were taking all of the furniture out of the downstairs—"

"The priceless antique furniture," Kenna interrupted.

"Kenna didn't feel they were being careful enough. She barked orders at them so loudly, one of the younger guys got tears in his eyes. I swear."

Kenna groaned. "He did not. Don't listen to Crosby, he lies."

"How is it being back in the guest house?" After a vicious court battle, Kenna finally had all of the legal rights to the estate Harriet had left her. But the fight had ended in a brutal attack that had almost cost Kenna her unborn child.

Kenna's fingers searched out Crosby's. "It's good. Harriet had been putting off a lot of upkeep in the main house. It makes sense to just do it all at once before the baby comes. And it's been good reclaiming the space that was my home for so many years. I'm not going to let one asshole ruin it for me."

Bell raised a glass to Kenna. "Good for you."

"Proud of you, Ken," I echoed.

Crosby squeezed Kenna's hand and then walked back over to the grill to check the steaks. "We're just about done."

I swung my legs out from under the picnic table and stood. "I'll get the salad. Kiddos, time to wash up."

Mia stood from a back handspring. "Steak!"

Will shook his head and pulled Ava to her feet. "We're coming."

I headed for the kitchen. Pulling the salad out of the fridge, I shook the homemade dressing I'd made earlier. Carefully pouring it over the greens, I tossed it together.

"Will said that Griffin was hanging around when the kids got to the store today."

Kenna's voice made me jump. "Make some noise when you enter a room, would you?"

"But then I'd lose my ninja status." She sidled up next to me at the counter, staring me down.

I sighed. "He was getting a sandwich. Is there something wrong with that?"

Kenna's lips pursed. "Of course, there's nothing wrong with that. Just as long as you're careful."

I turned to face her fully. "Careful about what exactly? Practically everyone on this island treats Griffin unfairly. They either stare and whisper, morbidly curious about him and his family, or they try and get something out of him. He's kind and honorable. And Will might not have told you, but he was also *wonderful* with Mia today."

"Caelyn, I don't think badly about Griffin. He obviously has a strong moral compass. But I also know that he's wounded in a way that means he's not going to let anyone into his life in a real way. His entire family drowned in front of his eyes, the press hounded him for years, and people have sold him out left and right. That marks a man. I just don't want you to get your hopes up…"

Kenna let her words trail off, and I winced. Of course, Kenna had seen past all my pithy comments about Griffin the Greek god. She saw beneath the surface. Saw that my crush ran deeper than finding the man handsome and intriguing. There was something about his wounds that called to my own. A pull of attraction and understanding. But I knew that meant we could only ever have a friendship.

I'd always been one to fall for the wounded birds. Thinking I could fix things for them and then we'd be one big, happy family. It never ended well. All through high school and college, I'd had one disastrous relationship after another. But I'd learned my lesson. And once I'd gotten custody of my siblings…I could count on one hand the number of dates I'd been on.

I turned back to the salad, giving it one more toss for good measure. "You don't have to worry. I'm not going down that road. All I'd like from Griffin is to be his friend. It looks like he could use one."

But that wouldn't stop me from trying to earn his lip twitches and chuckles. Because they felt like the brightest light shining down on me, and I wanted to stand in that sun.

Chapter Four

Caelyn

"No, no, no." I banged my head against the steering wheel with each word. This wasn't happening. Maybe if I closed my eyes and wished hard enough, I'd end up on a sunny beach somewhere. A place where handsome pool boys would bring me endless drinks and snacks.

I cracked an eye open. No sand and surf. There was only smoke billowing from my SUV's hood. I let my head fall back to the wheel. It had been overheating more and more recently. I knew what was wrong, but I'd put off taking it to the mechanic. The thought of one more unexpected bill had tears burning the backs of my eyes.

I'd had a long talk with Coach Hughes today, and she wanted Mia in the gym five times a week. Mia was begging to go. And there was even a family willing to let her carpool with them to Shelter Island so I didn't have to haul the other kids with me to take Mia to practice. I wanted so badly to find a way to make it happen for her. Hell, I'd sell plasma if I had to. If she had what it took to get a college scholarship, it could change everything for her. Not to mention, nothing lit Mia up like when she was tumbling.

I let out a sigh and watched the smoke continue billowing from my engine. Eventually, it would stop. Then I would deal with it. One thing at a time.

The sound of a vehicle approaching had me checking my rearview mirror. A familiar truck pulled to the side of the road behind me. Tipping my head heavenward, I silently begged the Universe to swallow me whole. Why did this man have to witness so many of my embarrassing moments? The burn at the backs of my eyes grew stronger as Griffin climbed out of his truck.

I watched as his long legs ate up the distance separating us. Everything about him said he was in control and command. I took a deep, steadying breath, willing my emotions to go on lockdown. I unbuckled my seat belt and pushed open the door. "Hey," I greeted as I slid out of the SUV.

Griffin scowled at my older-than-dirt SUV. "What happened? Are you okay?"

"I'm fine," I said, forcing levity into my voice. "Big Bertha here just decided to overheat on me."

I didn't even get a flicker of a smile with my *Big Bertha* comment. Instead, Griffin rounded the vehicle to get a better look at the smoke. "I'll call a tow."

"No!" I tempered my tone. "No. Thank you. I just need to wait for it to stop smoking before I can open the hood. I've got antifreeze in the back."

Griffin's expression hardened even further. "It's not safe for you to drive like this. Or for you to open the hood without work gloves. You got some of those?"

I licked my lips, cursing the fact that I didn't even have a towel in my SUV. "No. But I can just wait."

"Or you could call a mechanic," Griffin argued.

I bristled at his tone. "Look, I've dealt with this countless times before. I know what to do. It's not a permanent fix, but it'll work good enough for now. I'll get the heater hose repaired when I can."

Griffin tipped his head back as if praying for patience. "I have gloves in my truck."

"We still have to wait for it to stop smoking. You'll be late for whatever it is you were going to do. There's no need for you to sit around here with me." Because I couldn't take Griffin's probing stare—the one that seemed to see everything. I already knew that my life was a mess, that I was barely hanging on by a thread. I didn't want anyone else witnessing my disaster.

"I'm not leaving you on the side of the road alone," he growled.

"Okay, then." Apparently, that finely tuned moral compass didn't allow for damsels in distress. The thing was, while I was in distress, I was far from a damsel.

Griffin strode back to his truck, each step an attack on the ground. He wrenched open the cab door and rustled around for something. After a minute, he slammed the door closed and walked back in my direction, a pair of gloves in hand.

I swallowed hard, forcing my gaze away from his broad shoulders and scowling face. Instead, I chose to survey my still-smoking vehicle. The white billows were a little less now. But Big Bertha showed no signs of stopping altogether.

"Where are the kids?"

I looked back at Griffin. It was the first question he had ever asked me. I'd been making his sandwiches and trying to pry smiles out of him for years, but this was the first thing he'd ever actually inquired about. I had a hunch it was a self-protection thing. If he didn't ask questions of anyone, maybe they'd return the favor. "Will's at football practice. Mia has gymnastics. And Ava is hanging with Kenna at her office. I was just on my way to pick her up, actually." I threw a glare at my SUV, mentally cursing it six ways from Sunday.

Griffin nodded. "Busy family."

"Two-thirds of the tiny terrors really like their activities."

"How'd they earn that name?"

Griffin's lips twitched on the question. God, I was a sucker for that flicker of movement. I cleared my throat, forcing my gaze away from his mouth. "I started calling Will a tiny terror from the day my mom brought him home from the hospital, and he kept me up half the night. The nickname just kind of stuck."

"How do they feel about it?"

I turned to face Griffin fully. "What's with all the questions all of a sudden?"

He gave a careless shrug. "We've got time to kill."

I stole a quick glance at the hood of my vehicle. Smoke still seeped out a bit. "Fine. Question for a question." Griffin stayed silent for a moment, and I raised a brow in challenge.

"Fair's fair, I guess."

I did my best to hide my grin. There were only about a million things I wanted to know about the mysterious man who ventured into my store a few times a week. But I knew I had to choose carefully. If I got too personal too quickly, he'd shut this down in a flash. "What's your favorite vegetable?"

Griffin blinked a few times. "That's what you're going with?"

I shrugged. "Inquiring minds want to know."

"Corn, I guess."

I let out an exasperated sigh. "Corn barely counts as a vegetable."

Griffin's eyes narrowed. "It's a vegetable."

"Fine. Give me another one."

He rolled his eyes heavenward. "Asparagus. That counts as two questions, by the way."

I was suddenly thinking of all the ways I could work asparagus into the menu at The General Store, planning on researching recipes, pulling out old favorites. I gave myself a mental shake. I did not need to be planning anything around this man. "All right. Your turn. Ask away."

"How old were you when you got custody of your siblings?"

I did my best to keep my smile firmly in place. "Twenty-one." Still a baby myself in so many ways. I'd had no idea what I was getting myself into. If it hadn't been for the Shelter Island Child Alliance, I would've been up shit creek without a paddle. They helped me with parenting classes and a million other kinds of support.

Griffin let out a low whistle. "So young."

"I was all they had left."

"They're lucky to have you."

"They are." I wasn't the perfect guardian, but I also knew that no one would've tried harder than I did to give the children in their care a good life. I eyed the man in front of me. A faint scar bisected one eyebrow and his cheek, but somehow, it only added to his beauty, made it more *real*. "How's the house coming along?"

Griffin blinked a few times as if surprised that I knew he was working on the massive farmhouse on the opposite end of the island. But everyone knew. There had long been hushed conversations about what a shame it was that the home had fallen into such disrepair. When Griffin returned to Anchor, everyone had expected him to hire a contractor to get the place in shape. Islanders had been shocked when word got around that Griffin was doing the work himself. No one else had set foot in the home since the first few months he was here.

Griffin twisted the work gloves in his hands. "There are a lot of things I love about this island. Everyone knowing your business isn't one of them."

"Is the fact that you're restoring the farmhouse really a state secret?"

A muscle in Griffin's jaw ticked. "It's not that. I just…I like my privacy."

It made sense. I vaguely remembered that various people had sold stories to the tabloids about Griffin and his family. Photos, too. His name had been splashed across headlines off and on for years. My voice grew quiet. "You don't have to tell me anything you don't want to."

The last thing I wanted was to push Griffin into something he was uncomfortable with. I understood better than most how people could be perversely interested in your pain, your tragedy. After I'd taken custody of my siblings, there had been lots of *well-meaning* visitors to Harriet's estate. Those who offered support but really just wanted all the nitty-gritty details of what my parents had done. Harriet had finally started refusing to let anyone visit. But that didn't stop them from approaching me in town. Worse, they didn't even bother guarding their words around the kids.

A hand eased down onto my arm, the heat of it seeping through my long-sleeved shirt. "Are you okay?"

I gave my head a little shake. "Yeah. Sorry. Just…woolgathering, I guess."

Griffin's brows pulled together as he let his hand fall away. I missed the touch instantly. The warmth of it. The weight. Like a thick security blanket. He searched my face, looking for what exactly, I didn't know. "The house is coming along. But it's pretty damn slow when it's just me."

I had the sudden urge to offer to help, but I knew it wouldn't be received as the kindness I intended. "You'll get there." It might take a decade given the size of the home and the property, but somehow, I didn't think Griffin would mind.

"I will." He glanced over to the SUV. "I think we can open the hood now."

I reached out a hand for the gloves. "I've got it."

"I can do it—"

I cut Griffin off with a shake of my head. "Really. It's my SUV."

Hesitantly, he handed me the gloves. A spark of something flared when our fingers brushed—an astute awareness of the first time we'd made skin-to-skin contact. I sucked in a breath and forced my attention to the vehicle. But all I could think was that I didn't want our stolen roadside moments to end.

Chapter Five

Griffin

I PULLED OPEN THE SCREEN DOOR OF THE GENERAL STORE, and it slapped back into place behind me as I stepped through. I hadn't been able to stop thinking about my run-in with Caelyn. Our conversation and the one I'd overheard with Old Man Walters had replayed over and over in my mind. Caelyn needed a break. She'd devoted her life to three kids who would've been put into foster care without her, and she couldn't even afford to get her SUV repaired.

A whole slew of images assaulted my brain, each one worse than the previous. They all painted a vivid picture of what could happen if something really went wrong with Caelyn's vehicle. I swallowed back the bile that crept up my throat and forced myself forward. I made my way down an aisle until I reached the little kitchen at the back of the store.

Caelyn looked up from where she was sorting an array of supplies. "Hey. You're earlier than usual."

"I wanted to talk to you about something."

Caelyn's expression became guarded. "I swear Big Bertha is fine. All she needed was some coolant."

That was far from all that death trap needed. It probably needed to go to the junkyard, but telling Caelyn that would get me nowhere. "I have a job proposition for you."

Her green eyes widened a fraction. "A job?"

"Yeah. I was wondering if you'd be interested in some private chef work?" The idea had been running around in my mind since I'd first overhead Walters and Caelyn talking, I just hadn't been able to figure out how to make it feasible.

"But I work here…"

"This would be something you could do on the side. I was thinking you could prep food at home and then drop it off at my place once or twice a week. You know I basically live on frozen meals, so this could be a huge help if you think you have time."

Caelyn eyed me carefully. "But you swear by your frozen meals."

I pressed my mouth into a firm line to keep from laughing at her suspicious look. "I think I've hit the point where they're all starting to taste the same. I wouldn't mind some variety. And I've been working longer hours. I need more calories."

I watched as Caelyn mulled my offer over in her mind. I hoped like hell she took it. If I could've just handed her some extra money, I would've. But I'd learned a lot about Caelyn over the years that I'd been coming into the store. And one of those things was that she was incredibly proud. She needed to feel as if she had earned whatever was given to her.

"I think that could work out really well. If you're sure you really need it."

The muscles between my shoulder blades eased a fraction. "I'm sure. It really would be a big help."

Caelyn smiled—no, she *beamed*. It was the same smile that had made me feel as if I'd taken a solid hit to the solar plexus the first time I'd seen it. She did a little shimmy shake. "This is going to be awesome. I never get to plan full menus here. I'll need a list of your favorite foods and things that you don't like." She gave me a stern look. "And don't even think about putting '*all vegetables*' on your list of dislikes."

I held up both hands. "I wouldn't dream of it."

"How many meals a week are you thinking?"

"All of them, if you can manage it."

Caelyn blinked up at me. "Really?"

"It would be a huge help." One that I could pay her handsomely for. I cleared my throat. "We should also talk about pay. I was thinking twenty-five hundred a week plus gas and expenses, but we can negotiate if you need more."

Caelyn's jaw fell open, her eyes going wide. "Twenty-five hundred a week? Griffin, that's insane."

"You want three?"

"Did you get hit on the head by something while you were working on your house? That is way too much money."

I chuckled. "No head injuries. I did some research on the going rate for private chefs. Twenty-five hundred a week is pretty standard."

"Where? In New York City?"

I bit the inside of my cheek. "Lots of places." Places like New York, Los Angeles, and London.

Caelyn shook her head. "I'm not taking that much. I'd feel like I was taking advantage."

I chose my words carefully. "I wouldn't feel comfortable with you taking less than two grand a week. I want to pay you what you deserve." That much was true. Caelyn was an amazing cook. In the summers, the line for her sandwiches could be out the door. And from the bits and pieces I'd gathered about the woman, she gave and gave and was rarely fully appreciated for all she did.

Caelyn was silent for a moment before answering. "Okay. When do you want me to start?"

I grinned. "As soon as possible."

She pulled out a pad of paper and a pen from a drawer in the kitchen. "All right. I can probably make the first delivery on Sunday. I'm thinking Sunday will be the big haul and then I can stop by Wednesday or Thursday with a smaller delivery. But we can troubleshoot as we go."

"Sounds good to me." I pulled my wallet out of my pocket and slid out a credit card, handing it to Caelyn.

"What's this?"

"A credit card for expenses."

She studied the piece of plastic. "It has my name on it."

I shrugged. "I was optimistic you'd say yes."

Caelyn laughed, shaking her head. "Well, you are pretty dang convincing."

"I do my best. Make sure you track your mileage for gas. Or you can just fill up once a week and put it on the card. It's up to you."

Caelyn's eyes glistened, the restrained tears making the green seem to sparkle. "This is too much."

"No. It's fair."

She took a long breath. "Thank you. This is going to make a huge difference for us." She studied me. "But you already know that, don't you?"

I did my best to soften my expression, the feeling just a bit foreign. "Good things should happen to good people."

"You have a kind heart, Griffin Lockwood. Even if you'd rather people didn't see it."

Her words burned as if they'd been seared into my skin with a branding iron. When was the last time someone had said something like that to me? Probably before my parents had passed. They were always telling Beth and me how worthy and loved we were. But that had disappeared along with my family. Caelyn's words were a physical pain, similar to when frozen fingers first begin to regain feeling.

My family would've been so disappointed in how I'd hidden away from the world. How I'd turned away from those in need around me, too afraid to let anyone in. But maybe I was finding some pieces of myself again. The good parts that I'd left abandoned for far too long.

Chapter Six

Caelyn

I WAS GOING THROUGH MY DAY ON AUTOPILOT. IT WAS A miracle I hadn't burned myself or put real bacon in a vegan BLT. But all I could think about was the fact that I could finally breathe. The burning in my eyes was back, but I forced the tears down. Tears of happiness and joy and *relief.*

I would be able to handle the increase in rent and Mia's gymnastics. I'd be able to put something away for Will's college tuition. I might even be able to start saving for those culinary classes, after all. I gripped the edge of the counter and grinned down at the sandwich makings in front of me. I couldn't wait to tell the kids.

A flicker of movement caught my eye, and I looked up to see a slender man hovering in the aisle. His eyes darted about, this way and that, and his fingers moved in rapid, nonsensical patterns. *Shit.* I did not need to deal with this today.

I slowly pulled open my kitchen junk drawer, grabbing my cell phone and my pepper spray. Our island was small, only fifteen hundred people in off-season, but that didn't mean we were crime-free. And I was a woman who worked mostly alone until summer hit. The biggest issue on our small chain of islands was drugs. And I knew better than most all of the insidious ways it could infect your life.

I cleared my throat. "Can I help you, sir?"

The man jumped. "Uh. I need, uh, I need some smokes."

"We don't sell those here. You'll have to go to the gas station."

He gave a jerky nod and tore out of the store so fast, he almost knocked over a customer coming in. "Frick," I muttered and rounded the counter of my station to make sure the person was okay.

"Whoa," Shay said. "Shoplifter?"

I shook my head. "I think he was high. What he thought he was going to find in a grocery store to feed his addiction, I'm not sure."

Shay glanced over her shoulder with a worried look. "And you were in here with him all alone? That's not safe, Caelyn."

"Oh, I'm fine. I've got my pepper spray and the sheriff's station on speed dial."

Shay didn't seem appeased. "You should think about carrying a taser. Maybe even a gun."

My eyes widened. "No way. No guns." Too many kids came in and out of the store—mine included. I didn't want anything around them that could end in the loss of life.

"A taser, then," she pressed.

I studied Shay for a moment and saw the concern creasing her features. She'd been coming into the store for a few years now, ever since she took over as caretaker for one of the small private islands in our little chain. But I truly didn't know much about her other than that she had a kind smile and word every time she came in. I went on instinct, reaching out and squeezing her arm. "I'm fine. I promise. But I'll look into getting a taser."

The set of her shoulders eased a fraction. "Good."

"Now, I've got your order in the back. Do you need to do

some shopping? Want a sandwich?" Shay only came in once every week or so. I'd taken to placing orders from the mainland for her for whatever she needed. Books, puzzles, specialty items.

Shay smiled. "You know I can never turn down one of your concoctions. And I've got to do a grocery haul."

"You do that, and I'll grab your stuff."

Shay paused for a moment. "Maybe you should call the sheriff first. Just to give him a heads-up."

"I don't know that it's necessary." Sheriff Raines was a good man, but he didn't need to be bothered with something as small as this.

"Better safe than sorry. You don't want that guy to come back and cause trouble."

Shay had a point. I tapped on my cell phone to wake it up. "I'll just be a minute."

◡◎

I carefully balanced two pizza boxes and a bag of groceries as I shut the SUV door with my hip. First thing tomorrow, I was taking Big Bertha to the mechanic and getting that heater hose fixed. No more overheating for me.

Not even the midday creeper run-in had marred my day. Sheriff Raines had been more than kind when I called to let him know what had happened. He'd sent a deputy over to check out the gas station and then came to talk to me, but the man had been long gone by then. I appreciated the effort, nonetheless. Hopefully, now that he knew we didn't carry cigarettes, he'd avoid The General Store.

I gave my head a little shake as I made my way up the walk. The spring flowers Ava, Mia, and I had planted were just starting to bloom. Before long, the front of our small house would be awash with color.

"I come bearing gifts," I called as I pulled open the door.

"Gifts? I want gifts!" Mia shouted, jumping off the couch.

"Is that pizza? On a weeknight?"

The shock in Will's voice had me fighting a laugh. "And I've got stuff for sundaes for dessert."

Ava took in the bag from the store. "No carob chips and frozen yogurt?"

Kenna laughed. "Told you carob wasn't the same as chocolate."

I groaned. I would never live down my attempts to keep this family eating healthily. "No carob or Froyo."

Ava's eyes brightened. "Sprinkles and whipped cream?"

"You know it." My chest tightened at the smile on Ava's face. That alone would've been reason enough to bring the treats home.

Kenna pushed to her feet from her spot on the couch and eyed me suspiciously. "What happened?"

My brows drew together. "What do you mean?"

She drew a circle in the air with her finger, indicating everything in my hands. "You never bring junk home unless the tiny terrors have been begging for weeks."

Kenna had a point. It's not that I didn't think the kids should have treats, but I wanted them to have healthy food first. It was one of the few things within my control when it came to our lives, and why working at The General Store had always been so great. Mr. Walters had always given me food that would expire in the next few days. I'd made a game out of creating meals with food gifted from the grocery.

I shuffled my feet, and Kenna's eyes narrowed. "Out with it, Shortstop."

I choked on a laugh. "You haven't called me that in years."

"It's a reminder that I can still take you in a fight, and that's exactly what I'll do if you don't fess up to whatever is going on."

I'd always been petite, where Kenna was tall and curvy. She'd taken to calling me "*Shortstop*" in the third grade, and it had stuck for quite some time. I adjusted my hold on the pizza boxes. "Let me just set these down, and then I'll tell you the *good* news."

Kenna still looked skeptical but followed the kids and me into the kitchen. I set the boxes down and handed the bag of sundae goodies to Will. "Put these away?"

"Sure," he agreed.

I grabbed plates from the cabinets and a salad I'd made yesterday from the fridge.

"Spill it."

I turned to face Kenna and the rest of the gang. "I got a second job."

Lines creased Will's forehead. "You mean a third job? You already have the store and yoga."

"Yoga doesn't really count because I only have a couple of clients. And it's more fun than anything. This new job pays really well."

Kenna arched a brow. "It doesn't involve a pole, does it?"

"Kenna!" I chided. "Tiny ears."

"A pole like the firemen use?" Mia asked, her eyes going wide. "Are you going to be a fireman, Cae Cae?"

I shot an unhappy look at Kenna. "No, I'm not going to be a fireman. Kenna was trying to be funny."

"What are you going to do?" Ava asked.

"I'm going to be a private chef. My client just wants me to deliver the meals twice a week, so I can do it from home and still be with all of you. It means Mia can do her gymnastics, and Will, we can start saving for college."

Will's face hardened. "I don't want you working yourself to the bone to pay for college for me. I've been looking around town for a part-time job. I can pay my own way. You're already wearing yourself out with how much you do. You're gonna get sick."

Mia tugged on my hand, eyes shining. "I don't want you to get sick. I don't need the extra classes."

I lifted Mia into my arms, sending a stern look in Will's direction. "You guys, I'm fine. This offer is kind of my dream job. I get to create fun menus for someone. And I cook a ton around here anyway. Why not get paid for doing a little more? I'm not going to get sick, Mi."

"Promise?" she whispered, burrowing her face in my neck.

"Promise." I adjusted my hold on Mia. Soon, she would be too big for me to even lift her.

"Who's the client?" Kenna asked.

I swallowed hard, avoiding Kenna's gaze. "It's Griffin Lockwood."

"Oh, hell no," Will cut in.

"Will! Language." I set Mia down on the floor but kept an arm around her.

Will gripped the back of a chair. "He probably just wants in your pants."

"Why would Mr. Griffin want your pants? He wouldn't fit in them. He's a giant," Mia offered helpfully.

I rubbed my temples. This was not at all how I'd imagined tonight going. "You guys, stop. I want this. It's a great opportunity, and Griffin is really nice." I met Will's stare. "I would think we would know better than most not to believe island gossip about someone. He has been nothing but kind to me, and this job is going to change things for us."

Will looked down at the floor, but his tight grip on the chair remained. "Sorry."

"Apology accepted. Now, can we please, for the love of all that's holy, stuff ourselves silly with pizza and ice cream?"

"Yes!" Mia shouted, running for the dinner table and plopping down.

I glanced at Kenna. "You joining us?"

"Why not? Crosby's getting in some climbing and grabbing beers with Ford and another friend. I think I've earned some pizza with my favorite people."

I wrapped an arm around her. "I think so, too."

Dinner went off without a hitch. Every last piece of pizza was inhaled, and the sundae bar left the kitchen a disaster. The girls seemed to bounce right back, but Will was still quiet—not sulky but thoughtful. He excused himself to head to his room early, and before long, Ava and Mia were in bed. But Kenna stayed to help me pick up.

She handed me a bowl to place in the dishwasher. "You okay?"

I sighed, slipping the dish in place. "I'm fine. I just thought everyone would be as excited as I am." And I could admit that it stung a little that they weren't.

"Sorry. I'm happy for you, really."

I straightened, meeting Kenna's gaze head-on. "Are you, though?"

Kenna pressed her lips into a hard line. "I am…"

"But?" I knew Kenna was holding something back. Somehow, from the beginning, I'd found myself as the baby of our little trio. Maybe because I was a few months younger, or because I was smaller, or because I had a more sensitive nature. Bell and Kenna had always been extra protective of me—almost mothering. But I didn't need that. I needed my friends to stand beside me.

Kenna picked up a towel and began meticulously drying her hands. "Wounded bird catnip," she muttered.

"I'm not going after Griffin. But what's the worst thing that would happen if I did? Griffin not returning my feelings? Newsflash, Kenna, I've had my heart broken before. In more ways than I can count. It wouldn't be the first time, and it won't be the last. But I don't hide away from life because there's a potential to be hurt."

Kenna took a step back as if I had struck her. I muttered a curse under my breath. "I'm sorry. I didn't mean it like that."

She held up a hand. "No. You're right. I hid from a lot in life for a long time."

"But you don't anymore." My friend had been through so much, but she was finally, truly letting people in. "And I'm so proud of you for that. I shouldn't have said it. Low blow."

Kenna pulled me into a tight hug. "Forgiven."

"Thank you," I whispered into her ear. "Love you big."

"Love you bigger." She paused for a moment, holding the embrace. "And that's why I always want to protect you. But I'm guessing it can feel a little stifling."

I chuckled. "Maybe just a little."

Kenna released me but kept hold of my shoulders. "How about I let you live your life and just support you along the way?"

I squeezed her arms. "You already do."

And I would be forever grateful for the support of these friends who were more like sisters.

Chapter Seven

Griffin

"S-s-so cold, Griffin."

I held Beth tighter against me, the salt in the air stinging the cut on my face. "It's okay, Little Bit. Everything's going to be okay."

It was a total and complete lie. But I had nothing to give my sister other than hopeful untruths. I'd heard somewhere that you could live at least a week without water. I was holding on to that fact. But something else was wrong with Beth. She'd been wheezing from the moment I pulled her into the life raft. I'd thought it was hysteria. The knowledge that we hadn't been able to find our parents in the wreckage of the boat. But now I knew it was more.

"So tired."

"No! You can't sleep. Not yet." I was scared that if Beth's eyes closed, they'd never open again.

"Hurts when I breathe."

Fuck. It had to be something with her lungs. Maybe one was collapsed? A friend on my soccer team had that happen. He'd had to have it reinflated at the hospital, and it was pretty damn serious.

The beat of my heart seemed to rattle against my ribs in a

desperate plea for help. But I had no radio. No idea where we were. Not even a damn compass to point me in the right direction. All I had were my silent prayers.

"Love you, Griff."

Emotion burned the back of my throat. "Don't talk like that. I bet we're not that far from Hawaii. The coast guard is probably looking for us. Mom got off a mayday call before the boat started taking on water."

But between then and now, a storm had blown us God knew where. The sailboat had flipped, and Mom and Dad were gone. The ocean was miraculously quiet now. Too quiet. The silence ate away at my sanity. I held Beth's hand a little tighter. "Just hold on. Help's coming."

Her cracked lips curved the slightest bit. "Such a good big brother. Even played dolls with me when I begged."

"Hey. You promised never to bring that up. It's our secret."

Beth blinked against the sun. "I don't think the fish are going to tell."

I chuckled in spite of everything. "If word gets back to my team, I know who I'm going to blame." My team. School. College visits. Junior prom. It all seemed like a ridiculous world away. I'd been so caught up in all of it. And now, all I cared about was getting Beth and myself to safety.

Beth's wheezing intensified, and I leaned over her prone body. "Little Bit, just breathe. Slow and steady. Follow me."

I tried to show her how, but it seemed impossible for Beth to follow. Her breaths had a rattling, wet sound now. She coughed, and blood sprayed the air. Panic gripped my chest and squeezed, the grip brutal. "Beth. Just hold on. Help's coming. Please hold on. Do it for me."

But she said nothing. Her body seized, her eyes wide. And then…silence. Only the lapping of the water against the life raft.

"Beth?"

There was nothing. No one. I was completely alone.

I shot up in bed, sweat dripping down my face. I threw back the covers and swung my legs over the side of the bed, trying to catch my breath. It had been a while since I'd had a dream that lasted that long. Usually, they were vicious snapshots, just enough to ruin any shot at uninterrupted sleep. But this one had been the full movie. From the storm through the aftermath. The only piece missing was the hysterical state I'd been in by the time the Coast Guard finally found me.

I pushed up from the bed, my movements shaky. I padded to the bathroom on autopilot, turning the shower on cold. I shucked the t-shirt and boxers stuck to my skin with sweat and stepped into the stall. The jolt of the ice-cold water was just the ticket. I let the spray beat down on me, cooling my overheated skin. Slowly, I increased the temperature, hoping the water would wash away the remnants of the dream. It never did, but that didn't stop me from trying.

Eventually, I turned off the spray. Stepping out of the shower, I grabbed a towel. Quickly drying, I donned clothes for the day. It was only 3:30 a.m., but I knew there was no more sleep in my future. I wouldn't risk meeting the ghosts that lay in wait there.

Slipping on the work boots that waited just outside my door, I headed down the stairs and towards my office. It was one of the first rooms I'd completed on the entry level. Expansive windows would let the light pour in once the sun was up. I had so many memories of visiting with my father while he sat behind a desk in this space. That desk had been damaged beyond repair, but I still had it out in the shop, unable to part with it.

I eased down into the chair behind the new desk that I'd bought. It didn't seem to fit the room as well, but then again, nothing would. I tapped on the desktop keyboard, and the screen came to life. Keying in the password, I clicked on an icon on the bottom of the screen. Instantly, eight camera views popped up. I took a moment to study each one. Nothing out of the ordinary. Only a little nocturnal critter scampering across one of the views of the back of the property.

I hit a key, and another eight views popped up. Nothing out of the norm coming up here either. I was well aware that my obsession with the security of the farmhouse was bordering on unhealthy. I could hear the shrink my uncle had forced me to see in my head. "*It's understandable to have safety concerns. Just don't let them dictate your life.*"

I'd tried to go on like normal for a while. I'd applied to college. I'd even attended for two years. But nothing would ever be *normal* again. The press had hounded me, so eager for the inside scoop of what had happened during the week the Lockwood family was lost at sea. They were desperate for an account from the sole survivor.

And everyone around me had been eager to make a buck. A Coast Guard official had snuck photos of my bruised and battered body and of my sister's dead one. Tabloids had splashed them across their covers. *America's Favorite Family Destroyed.*

Classmates at the new school I'd been forced to attend when I moved in with my uncle cashed in, as well. Most of what they'd given the news outlets had been out and out lies. That I was doing drugs. That I'd knifed a teacher. Each tale had gotten more and more ridiculous.

I'd thought college would be a fresh start. And for a while, it was. I'd chosen a small school in the northeast. I'd met a girl. And for the first time, life had felt worth living again. But that had all come crashing down, too.

After that, I'd only wanted to disappear. I'd gotten pretty good at it, too. I grew a beard. Paid for everything in cash. I bought a new car and drove all over the country. I'd stay in a place for a few months, sometimes longer, but never more than a year. I didn't know it at the time, but I was subconsciously making my way back to Anchor. Slowly but surely heading west.

By the time Sheriff Raines had gotten in touch with me about the farmhouse, I was ready to be home. And Anchor would always be more of a home than the modern monstrosity of a house in Marin. The farmhouse on Anchor had been the heart and soul of our family. Restoring it meant bringing my family back to life in the only way I could.

I exited out of my security software and tried to force old memories from my mind. I clicked on my email icon. There were at least a dozen messages since I'd checked it a few days ago. I groaned, seeing my lawyer's name. Opening the message, my chest constricted. The house in Marin had sold. It was the last piece I'd been holding onto for no real reason. And now, it was gone. There was an ache at the news, but no true pain. It wasn't like I ever wanted to return there. My home was on Anchor now.

I moved onto another email, this one from an unknown sender. I guarded my email and phone number like they were nuclear launch codes, never giving out either unless absolutely necessary. Skimming the first few lines of the email, my jaw hardened.

Mr. Lockwood,

This is Marcy Roberts with Celebrity Weekly. *I've been trying to reach you for some time. I would love to do an in-depth feature on you and your family in honor of the twenty-year anniversary of their passing. Please call me at the number below.*

I quickly blocked the email address and reported it as spam. What was with the fascination with other people's pain? Did it make someone feel better about their own lives to focus on others' tragedies? Or was it simply the car-wreck phenomenon—people couldn't help but watch and stare?

The whys of it all didn't matter. I wanted nothing to do with having my family's name splashed across print and screen. I had enough reminders with my nightmares.

Chapter Eight

Caelyn

"**A**RE YOU SURE YOU WANT TO GO?" I ASKED WILL AS I loaded a bunch of the meals into a cooler.

"I'm sure. We can all go to the beach afterwards."

I studied my not-so-little brother. Will didn't seem like he was judging or worried, but he did seem determined to accompany me to Griffin's for my first delivery. "What's this all about?"

Will leaned a hip against the counter. "What you said the other night. It got to me. I know what it's like to have people judge me because of my past, to talk about me behind my back. I shouldn't have turned around and done the same to Griffin. It's not like they say anything really bad. Mostly that it's weird how he stays at his house by himself all the time. But I'd like a chance to get to know him a little better for myself."

I pulled Will into a hard hug. "You know you're the best kid in the history of kids, right?"

"You're suffocating me."

I released him on a laugh. "Suffocating you with love."

Will groaned and shook his head. "So, can I come with you?"

I glanced out the kitchen to the living room where Ava and Mia were coloring. "We'll all have to go. I don't have anyone else to watch the girls."

"I'll keep an eye on them when we get out there, make sure they don't get into trouble."

I closed my eyes for a brief moment, picturing Mia swinging from some sort of machinery. "Girls." They looked up from their drawing. "Can you be on your best behavior when I drop off the food at Mr. Griffin's?"

Ava nodded, and Mia beamed. "We're going to visit the giant?"

Will choked on a laugh, but I fought the curse that wanted to surface. "Please don't call him a giant."

Her little brows pulled together. "Why not?"

"It might hurt his feelings."

"I don't want to hurt his feelings." She looked down at her paper. "I'm gonna bring him this drawing. He'll like that."

I gave her a wobbly smile. "I'm sure he will." Though I had no idea what Griffin would do with a drawing of a rainbow and a unicorn that looked more like a colorful blob.

I turned the wheel of my SUV to round the curve of the island road that led to Griffin's house. I hadn't realized it, but he must drive past my home every time he went into town. I couldn't help but wonder if he knew that the little, sunny yellow house was mine.

I glanced in the rearview mirror. Ava looked out at the rolling landscape around us, but Mia stared intently at her drawing as if searching for imperfections. I swallowed down my chuckle and returned my eyes to the road. Everyone knew where the farmhouse was. There had been countless parties there when I was in high school, but I'd never been to one. More of the hard-partying crowd had frequented them. I had been more of a bonfire-at-the-beach kind of girl.

I pulled to a stop at the electronic gate. There was a keypad and what looked like an intercom with a small camera mounted above it.

"He's not messing around," Will remarked.

"A lot of people invaded his home while he was away. It makes sense." I could only imagine what a betrayal that must have been.

"That sucks."

"Big time." I searched for the right button, finding it under what looked like a speaker. I pressed it, and a buzzer sounded.

Griffin's rough voice came across the line. "Hey, Caelyn. Just follow the main road up to the house."

"Okay." My palms dampened as the gates swung open. I felt like I was about to go on a first date. Ridiculous. This was a job. A kindness Griffin had given. Nothing else.

"Coooooool. How'd Mr. Griffin know it was you, Cae Cae? Is he magic?" Mia asked.

Will snorted. "There's a camera."

Mia sent a scowl in her brother's direction. "He could still be magic."

I eased my SUV up the drive and towards the farmhouse. "You're right. He could have all sorts of magic. We wouldn't know."

Mia beamed, twisting her paper in the air as if it were dancing. "Then he's gonna loooooooove my magical unicorn."

I bit my lip. Poor Griffin had no idea what he was in for. Hopefully, an overly energetic seven-year-old wasn't a fireable offense. I pulled to a stop at the apex of the circular driveway, parking in front of the massive house that had seen better days. The paint was peeling, and a couple of the shutters dangled from one hinge.

Will let out a low whistle. "This place is almost as big as The Gables."

He wasn't wrong. The estate Harriet had left Kenna was larger, but not by much. There was something about the farmhouse, though. A sad song that seemed to pull at me. A bone-deep knowledge of what the house could be.

The front door swung open, and Griffin appeared. He wore jeans that hugged his muscular thighs and a t-shirt that clung to his broad shoulders. His close-cropped hair only accentuated the angular planes of his face. I swallowed, my throat suddenly dry.

"He's totally a magic giant," Mia whispered.

"Don't say that, remember?" Ava chided.

Mia threw up her hands. "I *know.*"

"All right, girls. Best behavior." I met their eyes in the rearview mirror, and they both nodded. I sent up a silent prayer that we'd make it through this food handoff without any major disasters.

I climbed out of the SUV, stopping at the passenger door behind me to pull it open and help Mia out of her booster seat. As soon as she was down, she ran towards Griffin.

"Mia," I called, but it was too late.

She came to a skidding halt in front of Griffin and held out her drawing. "I made this for you. It's an apology drawing. Sorry if I called you a giant, and it hurt your feelings. But I still think you're a giant and you have magic. But that's cool. You should be proud of that. Cae Cae always tells me that it's the things that are different about us that are the most special."

I sucked in a sharp breath, frozen to my spot. Griffin's mouth curved, and my lungs released. He squatted down so that he was at eye-level with her. "Can I tell you a secret?" Mia nodded silently. "I am a giant."

She smiled so widely I worried her face would crack in two. "See?"

Griffin leaned in a little closer. "And I have magic, too." He made a quick motion behind her ear and pulled out a quarter, depositing it in her open palm.

Mia let out a shriek that would've sent all dogs in a hundred-yard radius running. "Did you see? Did you see? Mr. Griffin is magic!" She looked back to him. "Do I get to keep it?"

His blue eyes twinkled. "It came out of your ear."

"I'm gonna put it in my unicorn piggy bank."

"A saver. I like it."

She slid the quarter into her pocket. "I'm saving up for some mats so I can practice more tumbling at home."

Griffin straightened from his crouch. "Tumbling, huh?"

"Yup. I'm gonna go to the Olympics one day."

"I believe it."

My heart gave a painful squeeze. At Mia's hope. At Griffin's sweet encouragement. It was all too much. Tears stung my eyes as I tried to force them back.

"Don't cry now," Will whispered.

"I can't help it. It's so freaking sweet."

Will shook his head and looked heavenward. "You need to get plugs in your tear ducts or something."

It wasn't a bad idea. I cried at *everything*. Sad tears. Happy tears. Overwhelmed tears. Angry tears. It was as if whenever I had an emotional overload—which was often—the release valve was my eyeballs.

"Hey, are you okay?" Griffin was suddenly in front of me. "What's wrong?"

"Nothing, I swear. It was just sweet. You and Mia."

Griffin's forehead wrinkled. "It was sweet?"

Will stepped closer. "Don't even try to understand it. She cries at the drop of a hat. The other night, she was full-on sobbing at a humane society commercial."

I turned to Will. "That song gets me every time."

Griffin let out a choked laugh. "She has a point there."

My cheeks heated as I looked back at Griffin. "Sorry about the mass delivery service, but nobody wanted to stay home."

"It's no problem." He looked around at the kids before turning back to me. "You can bring them whenever you need to."

Mia's fist shot into the air. "Yes! I want more magic."

"You might have opened a can of worms with that one," I whispered. Mia's zest for life was unparalleled, and when she discovered something she liked, she was all in. My gaze traveled back to Ava, who still hovered near the car. My other girl was more cautious. She needed time to test the waters before diving in.

"Don't worry about me," Griffin said. "I can handle a few magic tricks. It'll give me an excuse to brush up on my skills."

Even though there was warmth in Griffin's expression, there was also an underlying pain in his eyes. I couldn't help but wonder if it was somehow related to his family. If his dad had taught him those tricks. Why was it that the good ones were lost too soon, but the bad ones seemed to hang around far past their expiration dates? "She'd love that."

Will straightened next to me. "You've got a great place here."

Griffin looked up at the house. "I've got a long way to go. But it'll get there."

"I don't know much about repairs, but I can paint and do basic stuff. Let me know if you need any help."

Pride filled me at Will's words as I battled tears for the second time in a matter of minutes. He was such a good kid. And he would grow into an incredible man.

Griffin met Will's gaze, seeming to assess him in a different light. He hesitated for a few beats; the silence just shy of awkward. "I've been thinking I could use a second set of hands around here. It's tough work and it can get tedious, but I'd pay you for your time."

"That would be amazing. I've actually been looking for a part-time job so I can start saving for college."

"I'd be happy to have the help if it's okay with your sister."

Will glanced at me with a pleading look. "What do you think? Is it okay?"

I tugged on a loose string on my jeans. I wanted Will to have whatever would make him happy, but I couldn't help but notice that Griffin was coming to our rescue all over the place. If things didn't work out for whatever reason, the rug would be pulled out from under not only me but also the rest of my family. "How are you going to get out here?" Will had his license, but we didn't have an extra car.

"I'll ride my bike," he offered instantly. "It's only two miles."

"I can give you a ride home when we're done at the end of the day." Griffin looked to me. "If you're comfortable with that."

I sighed. "Why not?"

Will gave me a quick one-armed hug. "Thanks."

"I want to help, too," Mia whined. "I can paint."

I rubbed at my temples. If Mia *helped* paint, Griffin's house would look like a rainbow-colored Pollock painting. "You know what would probably be a huge help?"

Mia looked at me doubtfully. "What?"

"If you drew lots of pretty pictures for when the house is done."

She mulled it over for a moment. "Unicorns?"

"Of course," I answered.

"I'm definitely going to need a lot of unicorns in this house," Griffin said. "Rainbows, too."

Will choked on a laugh. "Just don't say anything about glitter. That shit will be in your house forever."

Griffin's eyes widened a fraction. "Duly noted."

As we stood there laughing and planning all of Mia's artwork for the farmhouse, with even Ava throwing in a few suggestions, I couldn't help the warmth that took root in my belly—the sweet simplicity of it all. But I did my best to let the feeling flow through me and not grab hold of it with both hands.

Because this wasn't my home, and Griffin wasn't my man.

Chapter Nine

Griffin

I GRINNED AS THE ALERT SOUNDED ON MY PHONE, HITTING the button for the gate to open without saying a word. We'd developed a routine over the past few weeks. Caelyn dropped off Will and food a few times a week. Sometimes, she and the girls would hang around for a little bit and see whatever project we were working on.

I couldn't deny that the moments I got to bask in Caelyn's light were the best of my week. She radiated this positivity that was miraculous for someone who had been through what she had. I'd gotten a few more pieces of the puzzle the more I saw her, and the longer I worked side by side with Will. He'd been cautious at first, but he'd let a few things slip as we hauled trash and stripped floors.

As I stepped outside, Caelyn's SUV crested the hill. I ignored the jump in my pulse as it did. As soon as the vehicle was in park, Mia climbed out of her booster seat and slid out of the SUV. She took off at a dead run, a paper flopping around in her hand as she did. At three feet away, the girl launched herself at me.

The move took me by surprise, and I hurried to catch her, resting her on my hip. "You taking flying lessons now, too?" My chest tightened on the words, a vision of Beth launching herself at my dad in a similar fashion.

Mia giggled. "I love to fly."

I ruffled her hair. "Well, you're pretty good at it."

"Mia," Caelyn warned.

"Uh-oh," I whispered in Mia's ear. "That tone means trouble."

Mia scrunched up her face. "I know."

Caelyn crossed to us. "What's the rule about getting out of the car?"

"I have to wait until you let me out," she answered in a defeated voice. "But I had to give Griffin his new picture. I was too excited."

Caelyn did her best to keep her expression stern, but the little quiver in her lips gave her away. "You're just going to have to rein in that excitement."

Mia sighed. "I'll try."

"Thank you." Caelyn looked up at me, a gorgeous pink hue hitting her cheeks. "Sorry about that."

"Not a problem. I like an enthusiastic greeting." I was shocked as hell to realize the words rang true. For the past decade, I'd only wanted space. I didn't want to be reminded of everything I'd lost. But the more I was around the O'Connor family, the more I felt the urge to let them into my world. There were painful moments for sure, but I still wanted more.

"Hey, Griffin," Will greeted. Ava hovered just behind him but offered me a smile and a small wave. My chest ached for the girl. She was painfully shy. But we were starting to make progress. Will's gaze zeroed in on the drawing in Mia's hand. "She made you magic kittens today."

I studied the paper Mia held out for my examination. "Are those gemstones?"

She nodded enthusiastically. "My favorite stickers. And the diamonds give the kittens magic powers."

"Of course, they do." I set Mia down on the ground and took the picture she offered. "Let's go find a spot for this one."

I made my way to the back of Caelyn's SUV, pulling the back hatch open and going for the cooler. Caelyn grabbed the drawing and a tote bag full of what I was sure were more delicious concoctions. "Just let me know when it gets to be too much. I'll try and temper Mia's creativity."

I glanced over at Caelyn as I lifted the cooler. "I don't mind, really."

"Your entire house is going to be covered in rainbows if you're not careful."

I chuckled. "There are worse things." So many worse things than a little girl showering me with rainbows and magic. And it wasn't like anyone but the O'Connors and I would be present inside these walls anyway. The drawings gave the farmhouse life, something that hadn't been present for a long time.

Our ragtag crew made our way into the house and towards the kitchen. Caelyn let out a sigh as we entered. "I'll never get over how gorgeous this kitchen is." The light in her eyes seemed to dance as she turned my way. "You've never made a single meal in here, have you?"

I rubbed the back of my neck. "I heat up what you make me in the oven or the microwave."

Caelyn laughed, the sound punching through my chest. "Such a waste."

I shrugged, thinking of all the time my mother had spent within these walls, the joy it had brought her. Maybe I needed to try baking cookies or something. The kind you got premade and just put on a cookie sheet.

Caelyn's laughter intensified. "You're looking at the oven like it's going to come to life and attack."

I glanced her way. "It might."

"You're a giant. You can defeat it," Mia said with complete confidence.

I gave her hair a ruffle. "Thanks, Mi. Now, let's find a spot for that drawing." I turned to the already crowded refrigerator. I'd gotten some magnets at the store, but soon, I would have to find another space for them. Maybe in the office.

"How about there?" Mia pointed to a small uncovered spot on the left side.

"Looks perfect to me." I picked up the paper from the counter and stuck it to the surface.

Will straightened from where he leaned against the counter. "What are we working on today? Besides the rainbow wall decorations, I mean."

The kid loved to give me shit. But the one-liners gave me a weird sense of pride—something about him feeling comfortable enough to give me a hard time. "It's gonna be boring, but it's something I need two sets of hands for."

Caelyn's interest was piqued. "I can stick around and be a third set. The girls can play in the yard while I help, if you don't mind."

"I don't mind at all. But you sure you don't have anything you need to be doing?"

"I'm sure." She looked to the girls. "You okay hanging out here?"

Mia beamed. "I love it here. The yard has way more room for tumbling."

Caelyn sobered. "Nothing too crazy. You don't have a spotter or mats."

"I won't. Promise."

"What about you, Ava?" Caelyn asked.

"I don't mind." She paused for a moment, looking at the window. "It's peaceful here."

"Looks like you've got yourself an extra set of hands, Lockwood."

I grinned. "Well, let's put them to good use." I led our crew out the back door. The girls headed for the yard, Mia immediately throwing herself into cartwheels and more complex tricks that I didn't know the names of. Ava made a beeline for the bench that had been a favorite of my mother's. She pulled a book out of a bag I hadn't noticed she was carrying.

A flicker of worry lanced through me. "Will they be all right here? We'll just be in the shop over there, and the gate's locked."

Caelyn started towards the shop. "They'll be fine. Ava won't move from that spot now that her book's open. And Mia could keep herself busy flipping back and forth for hours."

Will chuckled. "I'm kind of surprised she doesn't do back handsprings in her sleep."

I took a quick peek over my shoulder and, sure enough, Mia was springing from one move to the next. "How the hell does her body twist like that?"

Caelyn snorted. "I have no idea. I sure as heck didn't get that tumbling gene."

I frowned, worry gripping me again. "She's not going to hurt herself, right?"

Caelyn paused and turned to face me, her expression gentle. "Mia's been scaring the wits out of me since she was able to walk. But I swear she knows her limits. She won't get hurt."

I still wasn't completely sold on the idea of a seven-year-old girl throwing her body into the air and just hoping she landed on her feet. But it wasn't my place to argue. I forced myself to keep walking towards the shop.

I pulled open the door and hit the button for the oversized garage door. Light spilled into the space from outside as it opened. When I flicked on the overhead fixtures, Caelyn gasped. "There's so much furniture."

I surveyed the space around us. "A lot of the stuff was damaged beyond repair. But there was a fair amount I just couldn't force myself to part with. It's time to do a real inventory. I've got someone coming to pick up the things I want to get rid of tomorrow morning. We just have to pull it outside so they can have access." I wasn't going to let anyone inside to wander around, even just in the workshop. I didn't trust strangers not to have sticky fingers or go looking for things of note from my family to sell.

Caelyn wove through the crowded space, her fingers dusting over furniture pieces as she passed. "Bell would love this place. You know, she might be able to help you fix some of this stuff up if you want. I could call her and have her come out here—"

"No." The single word came out more harshly than I'd intended. And the hurt that flashed across Caelyn's face had me kicking myself. "I don't have people I don't know at the farmhouse."

Sympathy filled Caelyn's expression but the echoes of hurt still danced in her eyes. "Fair enough."

I nodded and focused on the task at hand, trying to ignore the reminder that typical relationships, ones that entailed friendliness with neighbors and acquaintances, weren't for me.

And that included brown-haired beauties who'd brought light into my world for the first time in years.

Chapter Ten

Caelyn

I COULDN'T STOP THINKING ABOUT GRIFFIN. WHICH WAS WHY I was currently baking banana chocolate chip muffins for him on my rare free morning instead of taking care of the ten million other things I needed to do. I kept seeing the pain laced with what almost looked like fear in his eyes when he told me he didn't let strangers into his home—even the outbuildings of it. I hadn't realized what a big deal it was that he'd allowed me and the kids inside the walls he'd built for himself, what an incredible gift of trust it had been. But I couldn't let go of the image of Griffin's face as he spoke the single word, "*no.*"

I hated the picture wreaking havoc on my mind and heart. The thought of how alone he had been over the past years. I'd heard the whispers, of course, but I'd been young when the Lockwoods had embarked on the sailing trip from Japan to Hawaii, with their final destination being Anchor Island. A massive storm had sent them off course, flipping the sailboat and flooding it with water. Only the two children had made it to a life raft. But Griffin's sister had died from a collapsed lung as he watched.

The Lockwood family had been a society favorite for

generations. They had senators and even a president in their family lineage, but Christopher Lockwood had been a man determined to go his own way. He'd started a software company that had made him a fortune, a large portion of which he gave away each year. The loss of the family had sent ripples of pain throughout the world.

I remembered people on the island talking about it when it happened, worrying about the boy who had spent so many summers here. But the rest of the world seemed to be even more curious—no, rabid—for information on what had happened. A Coast Guard officer had been dishonorably discharged for selling pictures of Griffin and his sister's body to a sleazy tabloid. And the uncle who had gotten custody of Griffin had ended up in jail for trying to steal a large portion of the money the Lockwoods had left to Griffin.

No wonder the man had trust issues and kept people at arm's length. And I knew the stories I was familiar with were only the tip of the iceberg. I was sure there were countless more tales of betrayal and manipulation.

The last thing I ever wanted was for Griffin to feel as if I were using him. But here he was, giving me a job I desperately needed, and another to my brother, who was coming alive under his new purpose. Will had fallen in love with restoring the old house. He'd brimmed with pride when showing me the calluses starting to take shape on his palms. I didn't want him to lose what he was gaining, but I couldn't live with myself if Griffin felt at all like we were taking advantage.

I pulled the oven door open to check the muffins. Perfect. I slid the two trays onto the stove to cool. I'd doubled the batch because Ava would never forgive me if I made her favorite and didn't save some for her. Just as I slipped off the oven mitts, the doorbell rang.

I crossed the short distance from the kitchen to the entryway and pulled open the door. "Callie! What are you doing here?"

I pulled the woman into a hard hug, and she laughed. "Your hugs are always the best."

I released her and stepped back. "Come in. I just took some banana chocolate chip muffins out of the oven. They should be ready to eat in a few if you want one."

"You know I'll never turn down whatever it is you're making."

I ushered Callie towards the kitchen. "Coffee? Tea?"

"Anything with caffeine."

I eyed her more thoroughly. The dark circles rimming her eyes were more pronounced than usual, and she was a bit pale. "You're working too hard." Callie was beyond dedicated to the children and families she helped at the Shelter Island Child Alliance—sometimes to the detriment of her own health.

She smiled as she shook her head. "Takes one to know one."

I pointed at the kitchen table, gesturing for Callie to sit. "Fair point."

"Kenna said you got yet another job."

I couldn't help the scowl that stretched my face. "Don't listen to that gossip. This is a job I can do from home, and it's hardly any extra work."

Callie pulled out a chair and sat. "Why don't I believe that?"

My back teeth ground together as I poured two cups of coffee into mugs. I added a dash of soy milk to mine and cream and sugar to Callie's. "Why is it that no one seems to believe that I can handle my own life?" It was really starting to grate on me. I'd been taking care of myself and these kids since I was twenty-one. I knew what was too much on my plate and what wasn't.

Callie was suddenly at my side. "It's not that at all. You tackle more than just about anyone I know. You are incredibly strong and brave, and you love those tiny terrors with a dedication I wish every child that came through the Alliance had."

Tears gathered in my eyes. "Why do you have to go and make me all emotional?"

She grinned. "Because I'm an evil heifer. Or because you cry at the drop of a hat."

I smacked her with an oven mitt. "I can't help it that every emotion I have comes out my eyeballs."

"No, you can't." She picked up her mug and inclined her head towards the table. "Let's sit."

The combination of her words and tone said that our joking time was over. It had worry pricking at my insides. I crossed to the table and quickly sank into a chair. "What's wrong?" A million different possibilities flew through my mind, none of them good.

Callie's expression was gentle, but her grip on the mug was so tight, her knuckles bleached white. "Your mother was granted early parole. I got notified since the kids went through one of our programs."

My jaw went slack. We hadn't heard from Chrissy O'Connor once since her arrest. She never tried to get in touch with me or make amends with the kids. She never once sent a birthday or Christmas card. I'd always had a mixture of relief and pain at the lack of contact. It saved me from having to decide whether or not to allow it, but I knew it had hurt Will and Ava. Mia had no memory of the woman.

I cleared my throat. "She's supposed to have a twelve-year sentence. It's been less than seven."

Callie winced. "The prisons are crowded, and my source says she hasn't made trouble during her time there. The parole board thought she was a good candidate for early release."

I vaguely remembered the prosecutor of the case telling me that I had to register with the board if I wanted to be notified of hearings or her release. But I honestly hadn't thought there was any way she'd get out before her twelve years were up—definitely not after less than seven. But apparently, that was just my naïve belief in the system. My head snapped up. "She's not coming back to Anchor, is she?"

Callie shook her head. "I talked to her parole officer. She's going to be moving to Shelter Island. The motor court on the northside."

I nodded woodenly. At least there was a little distance. And it wasn't like she'd given any indication that she wanted anything to do with the children she'd left to the wolves. "Do you know if there's been any sign of my father?" I checked in with Sheriff Raines every so often to see if he'd heard anything, but it had been a while.

"I called Parker on my way over here. There's still been no sign of him. But once your mom's out, they'll be keeping an eye on the motor court. Maybe he'll show."

I could only hope. Then maybe he would finally pay for all the pain he'd brought on his children. My blood heated as I thought about how Will tried to be perfect, taking on so much more than a sixteen-year-old should; how withdrawn and fearful Ava could be, and how Mia was determined to hold us all together with her rainbow string.

Sean had scarred his children and brought evil into their lives. When the sheriff at the time had dug deeper into the network my father's actions had exposed, it had been far darker and more vast than anyone had expected. The state police had been called in, and then the FBI. A few foot soldiers had ended up getting jail time, but it hadn't been the huge bust the cops and feds had hoped for.

I'd just been glad it was over. That the kids and I were safe to move out of Harriet's and into our own little house. From there, we'd begun to build a life. Soon, we had a routine. And we'd been happy. We didn't have every material thing we wanted or needed, but we had each other, and we were safe.

I traced invisible designs on the side of my coffee mug. "Chrissy hasn't said anything about wanting to see the kids, right?"

Anger lit Callie's features. "Not a word."

I blew out a breath, leaning back in my chair. "As much as that makes her a heartless bitch, I'm glad for it."

Callie's expression softened. "You're allowed to be relieved that someone who hurt your siblings doesn't want to come back into their lives."

I glanced up at the ceiling as if it held all the answers I was looking for. "Do I tell them?"

"That she's out?"

I nodded, bringing my focus back to Callie. "It feels dishonest not to, but they never talk about her. They don't ask about either of their parents."

"That's because you've created such a stable and loving home for them. It's more than they ever had living with Chrissy and Sean. You know them best. What does your gut say?"

"I need to tell them. At least Will." It was the right thing to do. If I were in his shoes and someone hid something like this from me, I'd be pissed as hell.

Callie took a sip of her coffee. "Then make some time for just the two of you and tell him. If you decide you want to tell the girls later, you can. I think Will would appreciate you telling him first. It'll give him the space to react how he needs to."

She was right. If I told them all together, Will would want to hold everything inside to protect his sisters. He'd only worry about Ava and Mia instead of processing however he needed to. I met Callie's gaze. "What would I do without you?"

"Be lost and adrift in the world?"

I balled up my napkin and tossed it at her. "Thank you. I mean it. You and the Alliance…you've done so much for us." Callie had still been in college when I first came to the Alliance, but she'd already been an intern, and now she ran the show.

"It's stories like yours, the ones that have a happy ending, that make all the long hours and heartbreak worth it."

I could only imagine everything Callie had seen and heard. I knew it had to have marked her profoundly. "Every kid and family that comes through those doors is lucky to have you."

She reached over and squeezed my hand. "Thank you." Glancing at her watch, she pushed to her feet. "I need to get back to the office, but call if you need anything at all."

"I will."

Callie glanced at the stove. "Think I can take one of those to go?"

"You can take *two*."

She gave me a quick squeeze. "You're too good to me."

I sent Callie off with two muffins and set to work putting the rest into plastic containers. My mind whirled as I moved, a mix of anger, sadness, and fear circulating. I knew I could put off dropping the muffins by Griffin's, but I wanted to see him. In the midst of the upheaval of the past hour, I wanted a lip twitch or one of those rare chuckles that warmed me to my core.

That alone should've kept me away. But it didn't.

Chapter Eleven

Griffin

I GRUNTED AS I TOSSED THE BROKEN CHAIR INTO THE additional dumpster that had been delivered to the property. Between that and the two guys who had just loaded up a truck with furniture, the workshop would be mostly empty for the first time in years. Guilt swirled in my gut, the same words haunting me for the past twelve hours. The way I'd snapped at Caelyn. The hurt on her face.

She'd been off for the rest of the afternoon as she helped Will and me haul furniture out of the space and into the yard for the movers to pick up. And Will had given me a dirty look or two. This morning, I'd made a call to Second Chances and asked Bell Kipton if she'd like to take a look at the pieces before they went to Goodwill. She'd jumped at the chance. The movers were going to let her peek around the truck before they returned to the farmhouse for a second load.

I wasn't sure if Bell would tell Caelyn about my call. Who was I kidding? I hoped like hell she did. That maybe if she did, everything would return to normal, and I wouldn't lose this breath of fresh air I'd found.

I threw the next piece of broken furniture with a little more force than necessary. I didn't need to be thinking about how some woman made me breathe easier. The last time I'd gotten lost in how a woman brightened my world, it had ended in disaster and my secrets being laid bare. And so much worse. I needed to focus on restoring the farmhouse and nothing else.

The sound of tires crunching gravel came from the front of the house. It wasn't heavy enough to be the truck returning. I muttered a curse and headed towards the driveway. I'd left the gate open for the movers to return, thinking it was rare for anyone to head up the private drive. I should've known better.

I strode around the house and took in a sedan coming to a stop in front of the farmhouse. I scanned the plates. Washington, but with a car rental company frame. My eyes narrowed as a woman climbed out of the vehicle.

"You're on private property. I'm afraid I'll have to ask you to leave."

The woman had light brown hair that was curled in waves that framed her face. Her smile was practiced, fake. "The gate was open."

I crossed my arms over my chest. "That doesn't change the *No Trespassing* sign or the fact that you're not welcome here."

"You don't even know who I am. Maybe I could be welcome."

The sliminess to her words and expressions meant I knew exactly who she was. Sure, I didn't know her name or her employer, but she had *reporter* written all over her. I slid my cell phone out of my back pocket. "I guess I'll be calling the sheriff, after all."

"Wait. Please. Just give me ten minutes. I've been emailing and calling your lawyer. No one ever returns my inquiries. Don't you want your story out in the world?" She crossed in front of the car, invading more and more of my space.

My skin bristled at the action, as if each step she took grated against my flesh. "If people don't return your inquiries, take the damn hint. I'm not saying a word to you other than to get the hell off my property. After this, I think I'm going to have a damn good case for harassment. Possibly a restraining order, too."

The woman, who I assumed was the Marcy Roberts who'd been filling my spam folder, froze. A hardness slipped over her features as her true nature came out. "That would be a mistake, Mr. Lockwood."

The sound of another vehicle filtered through the air. I glanced down the drive, muttering a slew of curses. Caelyn's SUV crested the hill, and my muscles stiffened. She didn't know how to handle reporters. Hell, she might let something slip without even realizing it. Her vehicle came to a stop behind the rental, and she slid out. Her brown hair was in two braids tied with colorful bands. I couldn't help the flicker of a smile, knowing that Mia must have demanded as much.

Caelyn grabbed a basket from the SUV, her gaze going from me to Marcy and back again, uncertainty filling her features. "I'm so sorry to interrupt. I just wanted to drop these muffins by."

Marcy's expression morphed into one of welcome in the blink of an eye. Gone were the shrewd offers and conniving threats. "You're not interrupting. I'm Marcy Roberts. And you are?"

I could see story ideas, ones full of lies and conjecture, brewing in her head. "Don't answer her," I barked.

Caelyn jumped, and Marcy's head snapped back to me. "That's not very nice. It would be unfortunate if I had to write an article about how abusive you were to guests in your home. Want to rethink that statement?" She turned to Caelyn. "Maybe you'd like to share your story about Mr. Lockwood? We pay well for exclusives."

The muscles in my back and shoulders tensed. All the lies that had been printed about me over the years. All the gossip and speculation. These vultures never wanted to just let my family rest in peace. Let *me* rest in peace.

Caelyn's jaw went slack, her gaze jumping from Marcy to me and back again. As all the pieces came together, she strode forward and stepped between Marcy and me, her face going red. The picture she made was both hilarious and adorable. She looked as if she would defend me against any attack, a basket of baked goods on her arm. "You need to leave."

"Interesting." Marcy pulled a notebook from her pocket and began scribbling.

Caelyn stepped forward. "If you don't leave on the count of three, I'm going to bean you with this basket. You're on private property and acting in a threatening manner. I'd be well within my rights."

Marcy looked up from her notepad. "So similar to the man you're defending. Did you know he put a reporter in the hospital? The guy was in a coma for three days."

My gut twisted as I stared at the gravel, unable to look at Caelyn, afraid I'd see fear or disgust. I'd been young and stupid, at my wit's end and going just a little bit crazy. And the reporter in question had made my life a living hell for years. He'd somehow been able to turn any person I'd gotten close to.

"Well," Caelyn began, "if they were anything like you, I can see why."

My head jerked up, and I took in Caelyn backing Marcy towards her car, using the basket of baked goods to do it. Caelyn gave her another little shove. "Get lost." Pulling out her phone, she snapped a photo. "This is going to the sheriff." She glanced back at me. "Should I take her driver's license, too? Give it to Raines?"

"Get off me, you crazy bitch. You can't touch me or my wallet," Marcy blustered.

Caelyn's eyes narrowed. "That's where you're wrong. I can do whatever I want as long as you're on this land. It's your choice whether you stay or go. But I'll warn you now, the sheriff here doesn't take kindly to outsiders bothering his citizens."

Marcy's eyes widened a fraction. "You hick island people are insane."

"You remember that before you think of coming back," Caelyn called as Marcy climbed into her car.

Gravel flew as Marcy tore down the drive. I yanked Caelyn away from the vehicle. "Shit! Are you okay? Gravel didn't get you, did it?"

The tension went out of Caelyn. "I'm fine." She looked down the drive and then back at me, her eyes widening. "Did I just threaten her with my muffin basket?"

A grin split my face. "Honey, you scared the crap out of her with that basket."

A small giggle escaped Caelyn. Then another. And soon, she had dissolved into laughter. "I just threatened someone with baked goods. Who am I?"

I watched Caelyn carefully, unsure if she just thought it was funny or if she was losing it. "Are you okay?"

She straightened, the tears from her laughter brimming her eyes. "This has been one seriously messed-up day."

I stiffened. "What else happened?"

Caelyn shook her head and wiped at her eyes. "Nothing."

"It doesn't sound like nothing." A mix of anxiety and something like fear gnawed at me. Worry, I realized, for a woman I shouldn't be growing to care about.

"You have enough to deal with." Her gaze traveled back to the driveway. "Is she going to write a story about you?"

I bit the inside of my cheek. I wanted to force Caelyn to tell me everything that was wrong, not talk about some idiotic reporter. "She'll probably write something that is completely full of lies, and people will believe it hook, line, and sinker."

Caelyn nibbled on her bottom lip. "Has it always been this way for you?"

"Worse." I searched her face for any signs of deception. There was nothing but openness and honest empathy. "You didn't look me up?"

Her eyes widened. "No." She blushed. "I mean, I've heard talk about you and your family around town. I'd have to live under a rock not to. But I didn't search the internet or anything. I wouldn't." Her gaze locked with mine. "I know what it's like to have the island think your life is open for discussion and gossip. I wouldn't do that to someone else."

I sank to the stone steps in front of the house. Of course, she understood better than most. "I'm sorry. I just…"

Caelyn crossed to the stairs and lowered herself to the slate. "You're just used to people looking at you as something other than human. They don't realize how painful it is."

I looked up into Caelyn's green eyes full of so much under-standing. In the past, at best I'd gotten sympathy that made my skin crawl. But Caelyn was different. She truly understood what it was like to live under a microscope, your most painful memories fodder for gossip. She knew what it was like to have to constantly have your shields up because someone could carelessly toss out something that would remind you of your darkest days at any moment. "How do you do it?"

Her brow wrinkled. "Do what?"

"You're so…positive."

Caelyn chuckled. "I'm not some Pollyanna. I have my share of rough days. Today was one. But as much hardship and pain as there is in the world, there's also endless beauty. Do you know what I ask the tiny terrors every morning? Tell me the good things. There is so much of it all around us, even amidst the hard stuff. You just have to take a moment to recognize it."

I took in the simplicity of Caelyn's words, but also the power in them. She was right. But because I'd been so focused on locking myself away from the world, avoiding any chance for betrayal or pain, I'd missed out on a lot of those opportunities. "You're a wise woman."

She grinned. "Why thank you, kind sir."

I shook my head. "You gonna tell me what happened today?"

Caelyn sighed and looked out over the rolling hills and forest surrounding us. "My mom's getting out of prison."

"Was this expected?"

She bent, picking up a piece of gravel and rolling it around between her fingers. "She was supposed to have twelve years. It's only been half that."

I bit back a curse. Our justice system was beyond broken. The people who deserved the harshest sentences often got a break, and those who deserved a second chance often paid for way longer than they should. "Can you fight it?"

"It's too late."

"I'm sorry. Do the kids know?"

She shook her head. "I just found out this morning while they were at school. I have to tell Will soon. I'm not sure about the girls."

It made sense. Will was more adult than teen, but Ava and Mia still had that innocence to them. "You'll know when the time is right to tell them."

Caelyn tossed the stone into the air, catching it in her palm. "I hope so."

We were silent for a long moment before I spoke. "The reporter I punched… It was a long time ago. He'd broken into my apartment and—"

Caelyn reached over, her palm coming to rest on my forearm. "You don't owe me any explanations. You've shown me time and again how good your soul is."

Her touch, her words, they seeped into my bones. The warmth of them was so hot it burned. And I never wanted to forget the feeling.

Chapter Twelve

Caelyn

I HUMMED TO MYSELF AS I WIPED DOWN COUNTERS AFTER the lunch rush, paying careful attention to each nook and cranny. There was something cathartic about cleaning. It was one of the few things where you could see your progress in black and white.

I wondered if Griffin felt the same about his house. I loved seeing the concrete changes each time I visited. And it seemed like progress was happening a little faster now that Will was helping out.

My chest warmed as memories of yesterday filtered through my mind. It was the first time Griffin had truly let me in. I knew it was scary for him, terrifying, but he'd done it anyway. And sitting on the stone steps, I suddenly hadn't felt so alone.

It was a hard thing to describe, to even truly wrap my head around, but I'd felt alone since I'd taken custody of the kids. Yes, I had Bell and Kenna, Callie and the Alliance, Harriet before she passed, but the real weight of it rested on my shoulders. And as much as those amazing women in my life loved and supported me, they couldn't understand what it felt like to have everyone on the island whispering about you, knowing that your parents had brought drugs into the community, into a home with children. They couldn't understand how terrifying it was to know that the well-being of the siblings you loved more than life was up to you and you alone.

In a completely different way, Griffin understood it all. But his wounds were so much deeper. He'd lost his entire family, including the sibling he'd tried to save. And instead of an island prying into his life, the whole world had. I couldn't imagine the kinds of scars that left behind.

I felt a pulling sensation in my chest, a deep tugging. I wanted to be the one to help ease those hurts for him, tend the marks left behind. I closed my eyes for the briefest of moments. I could be there for Griffin, be his friend and his sounding board, but I needed to hold that deepest part of my heart back. Because if I let that piece free, I would fall. And Griffin wasn't in a place to catch me.

A throat cleared, and I looked up. "Patti."

"Daydreaming again, are we?" she asked, brows raised.

Straightening my spine, I forced a smile. "Just thinking as I clean. What can I help you with? Would you like a sandwich or a salad?"

"Neither. You know I make my own meals."

I held back the eye roll I wanted to set free. Patti said it as if she deserved a medal for cooking her own food "Anything else I can help you with?" Mentally, I was screaming, *why are you here?*

She straightened the purse on her shoulder. "I wanted to see if Mia would like to come over and play with Mallory this weekend."

I did my best to keep my expression pleasant. "That's kind of you to offer, but we have plans this weekend." Patti's daughter, Mallory, was too much like her mother: a know-it-all and a tattletale. Mia was not a fan.

Patti raised a brow. "Oh? What are you up to?"

The gleam of interest in her eyes had me going on alert. "Mia has gymnastics, and we're spending some time together as a family on Sunday."

"At Griffin Lockwood's? I've heard you've been spending quite a bit of time out there."

I stiffened. The gossip mill was working overtime apparently, and of course, Patti was at the center of it. "Have you now?" I wasn't going to give her anything. It was none of her dang business, and it pissed me right off that she was talking about Griffin behind his back.

Patti's expression sobered. "Is that really wise, Caelyn? I know you're not a mother yet, so your instincts might not be as finely tuned as the rest of us, but he has a violent history."

I counted to ten in my head and then let out a long breath. Nope, still too furious to speak. I counted to ten again and met Patti's gaze. "I've had just about enough of your high and mighty BS. You sit and judge and gossip, never once thinking about the ugliness of your own heart." Patti gasped, but I kept right on talking. "Griffin Lockwood is a kind and decent man who has been through hell. You and your cronies only make that worse by stirring up sensationalized rumors. And you don't know me, Patti. Not one real thing about me. I may not have birthed those children, but I love them as if they were my own. I'd do anything to protect them. And that means I'll do whatever it takes to shield them from the venom you spew."

Clapping sounded from down one of the aisles, and Shay stepped into view. "Amen." Her gaze hardened on Patti. "You're a nosy bitch who needs to get a life. Get out of here and don't come back."

Color rose in Patti's cheeks as she seemed to struggle for breath. "Well, I never. I guess I should expect this kind of behavior from an oddball like you. You hide out on that little island and rarely come to town. You're probably a criminal."

Shay's face went pale for a moment, but she recovered quickly. "Even if I was, I'd still be a better human than you."

Patti uttered something very unladylike under her breath and then turned back to me. "I'm going to be calling Child Protective Services to report my concerns."

I froze. I could only imagine the kind of story Patti would weave. One that I was sure would end with a visit from a social worker. I had permanent custody of my siblings, but with enough lies and manipulation, that could change. I willed my wildly beating heart under control. Everything would be fine. I'd call Callie and see what her advice was. She'd know what to do.

I took a slow, deep breath. "You do whatever you need to. But karma's coming for you." At least I hoped it was.

Patti glared at me and then took off down an aisle and out the front door. I slumped against the counter. Without a word, Shay rounded the bar and came into the kitchen space. "Are you okay?"

I nodded and then shook my head. "What is wrong with that woman?"

"She's crazy. And a bitch. That's what." Shay gave my arm a squeeze. "People like that…they're deeply unhappy. It's not about you."

I gave Shay a watery smile. "I'm sorry you got caught up in the middle of it."

She snorted. "Please, I'm happy to deal a smackdown when it's warranted." She glanced towards the door. "Guess she's going to have it out for me now, too, huh?"

I winced. It was not fun to be the center of Patti's focus. And it was even worse if you'd done something that she found offensive. "The least I can do to make up for it is make you lunch."

Shay's lips quirked. "I take it that means I need to watch my back around the nosy B."

I chuckled. "It wouldn't be a bad idea."

"Then cook me something delicious. But make yourself something, too. You're looking a little pale."

I was feeling just a little bit wobbly on my feet. I took a sip of my juice that was on the counter. "Two delicious concoctions coming up."

After some food and conversation with Shay that centered around nothing too serious, I felt a lot better. As Shay got to her feet, I pulled her in for a quick hug. "Thank you. I know we don't know each other all that well, and it means a lot that you stepped in for me."

Shay looked a bit taken aback by the hug and my sentiments but squeezed my shoulders. "Anytime. You're a good egg, Caelyn O'Connor, and no one should be treating you poorly."

"Thank you. And we should do this again sometime. Maybe you can come over for dinner, meet the tiny terrors."

Shay's mouth opened and then closed, a hint of wariness flitting across her features. "That's really kind of you. Maybe one of these days when I get some time off."

I knew a brushoff when I heard one. I just wasn't sure why. "It's an open invitation. But no pressure either."

The set of Shay's shoulders relaxed a fraction. "Thank you."

"I'll see you soon."

"See you."

I waved Shay off and went about cleaning up my station. I glanced up at the clock just as Molly came running into the store. "I'm here! I'm here! I'm so sorry I'm late, Caelyn."

I grinned at the young girl. "You're five minutes late. Don't sweat it."

"Thank you. You're an angel. Get going. I'll finish cleaning up."

I grabbed my bag from under a cabinet. "Appreciate it. Just text me if you run into any issues."

"I know."

I pulled out my keys. "And Mr. Walters will be here to help you close up."

Molly chuckled. "Yes, Mom. And I promise, I won't have any boys over."

I stuck out my tongue at her as I passed. "Make good choices!"

"Hugs not drugs!" she shouted as I left.

I chuckled as I headed out into the sun and the parking lot. I slipped my sunglasses out of my bag and put them on as I made my way towards my SUV. Big Bertha had gotten quite the make-over at the mechanic's last week. Sure, she looked the same, but her insides were all shiny and fixed up. I beeped the locks and went to open the door, but a piece of paper fluttered from where it was caught under the windshield wiper.

I leaned forward and plucked it up, giving its contents a cursory glance. I froze. In large, block letters it read: *YOU'RE GONNA PAY.*

Chapter Thirteen

Griffin

Y ET AGAIN, I FOUND MYSELF IN MY TRUCK, MAKING MY
way towards town. Taking the route that took me past
Caelyn's sunny yellow house and The General Store. A
route I didn't need to take. What excuse had I come up with this
time? I needed milk. So what if I barely drank the stuff?

I needed to get a grip. I'd almost convinced myself to just go
around the block and head home when I caught sight of Caelyn
standing next to her SUV in the parking lot. She was frozen to
the spot, her gaze locked on a piece of paper, her face pale.

I didn't think. I simply pulled my truck to the side of the road
and hopped out. I jogged towards her, and the closer I got, the
more my chest tightened. She looked…terrified.

"Caelyn," I called.

Her head snapped up, eyes darting around.

"What's wrong? What happened?"

She shook as she reached out to me, paper in hand. "This was
on my car when I came out of the store."

I took the note from her and scanned it, letting out a litany of
curses. "How long ago?"

"I—I just came out. I've been in there since this morning."

I pulled out my phone and dialed one of the few contacts in my cell. It rang a few times, and then a gruff voice answered. "Sheriff Raines."

"It's Griffin Lockwood."

"Hey, Griffin. What can I do for you?"

I looked down at the letter, trying to figure out how to best explain. "I'm outside The General Store with Caelyn O'Connor. Someone left a threatening note on her SUV."

Sounds in the background quieted. "What kind of threat?"

I read him the note.

"I'm at Island Sports right now responding to a theft. Try not to touch the note any more than you have already. I'll be there in ten."

"Thanks." I hit end on my phone and turned back to Caelyn. "Sheriff Raines will be here in ten."

She nibbled on her bottom lip. "Maybe it's just kids playing a prank. We shouldn't worry him."

I met Caelyn's stare. "Kids are in school right now."

Her eyes widened. "School. I'm supposed to pick up the kids in fifteen minutes." She started fumbling through her bag, searching frantically for something. "I'm not late. Never. Not once. I know what it's like when your parents forget to pick you up time and time again."

I set the note back on the SUV and took Caelyn's shoulders in my hands. "It's okay. They'll understand."

Caelyn took a slow, steadying breath as if trying to rein in all of the emotions running through her. "I'm going to call the elementary school and tell them I'm going to be late. Can you call the high school and have them tell Will to go wait with the girls? He knows how to look out for them."

I squeezed her shoulders. "Of course." I released my hold on Caelyn, even though it was the last thing I wanted to do, and pulled out my phone again. After a quick search, I found the number for the high school and explained the situation to the school secretary. She needed to speak with Caelyn to verify the story, but once that was done, the woman agreed to let Will know that Caelyn was running late and to meet her at the elementary school.

I shoved my phone back into my pocket just as Caelyn was wrapping up her own call. She gripped the device so hard, her knuckles were white. "Mia's teacher is going to wait with them until I get there."

"They're going to be fine. Completely safe."

Caelyn let out a shuddering breath. "I just don't want them to be scared."

"You've made it so they won't be."

Caelyn nodded but didn't seem assuaged. She had a jittery quality to her now, as if she couldn't stand still.

A sheriff's department SUV pulled to a stop behind my truck, and Parker Raines stepped out. I nodded in greeting. Caelyn gave an awkward little wave. "Sheriff."

He smiled warmly. "I've told you time and again, call me Parker."

"I know. It's just weird because the old sheriff was all about formal titles. But that doesn't matter. From now on, you're Parker. You know my friends and I call you Sheriff Hotstuff." She let out a little squeak. "I can't believe I said that out loud. When I'm nervous, I ramble. And this note has me really freaking nervous. I'm just gonna shut up now."

Caelyn clamped her mouth closed as her cheeks reddened. Parker and I looked at each other and then we both barked out a laugh. Caelyn's face got even redder. "It's not funny," she hissed at me.

I grinned. "Come on, it's a little funny. Do you guys have a nickname for me, too?" I couldn't help but ask.

Caelyn's gaze jumped around, anywhere but at me. "No. No nickname for you, sorry."

She was lying, and now I was curious about what that nickname was.

Parker finally got his laughter under control. "I've been called a lot of things on the job, but I'm not sure Sheriff Hotstuff is one of them."

Caelyn covered her face with her hands. "I'm never going to live this down."

Parker knocked Caelyn's arm with his. "Trust me, of all the things I've had happen on a call, this doesn't even rate on the embarrassment radar."

Caelyn's hands fell away from her face. "Thank you."

"All right," Parker began. "Tell me what happened."

Caelyn immediately sobered, a hint of fear entering her features. I had the sudden urge to pull her into my arms. To shield her from anything that would put that kind of look on her face. She glanced at the store and then looked back at Parker. "I was working my normal shift, and when I came out, I saw a piece of paper under my windshield wiper. I thought it was just a flyer or something. But it wasn't."

Parker pulled a pair of gloves out of his back pocket, along with a plastic bag. "Let's take a look." He snapped on the gloves and picked up the note, his jaw hardening as he read. Carefully, he slipped the paper into an evidence bag. "Any idea who would leave you a note like this?"

Caelyn's face paled. "None at all. Do you think maybe someone put it on the wrong car? Or it's just a sick prank?"

I didn't think that someone who had gone to the trouble of writing a note like this would put it on the wrong vehicle. But I understood why Caelyn wanted to hope that it might be true.

"It's possible…" Parker started. "But it's probably unlikely. I'll see if the bank's security cameras caught anything, but I don't think they reach quite this far. Has that guy come back to the store? The one you called me about before?"

"What guy?" I growled.

Caelyn flinched. "A man came into the store. Seemed like he was on something. Tweaking probably. When I told him we didn't carry cigarettes, he took off." She looked at Parker. "He hasn't been back. And, honestly, I only called about him because another customer was freaked. She wanted me to call the sheriff's department and let them know."

"She was right to have you call me," Parker said.

All I could think about was some guy jonesing for his next high, skulking around The General Store. Worse, he could've been casing the place for money to pay for that next fix. I turned to Parker. "You have officers doing drive-bys?"

Parker rubbed the back of his neck. "After everything that's happened this past year, the county approved me to hire more staff. We now have someone on island at all times. I'll have them put the store on their regular route."

I turned to Caelyn. "You have something to protect yourself with? A knife? Taser?" I hated the image of Caelyn having to fight anyone, but the idea that she might not have anything to defend herself with was even worse.

A small smile curved her mouth. "You sound like Shay."

"I don't know who the hell that is, but if she's telling you to be cautious, I like her."

Parker chuckled. "Me, too." His expression grew serious. "There *is* a longshot we need to consider."

Caelyn began twisting the strap of her bag. "What?"

"That this could be related to your parents."

I didn't know much about Caelyn's parents, other than that they had been charged with drug-related offenses and had lost custody of the kids. But Parker's tone had my entire body stringing tight.

Caelyn's eyes went wide. "Mom's out of prison."

Parker nodded slowly as if trying to put together invisible pieces in his mind. "Hadn't thought about her as an option. I haven't been in touch with her parole officer since she was released, but I'll remedy that."

Caelyn shivered even though the sun shone brightly, and I had another urge to pull her in close. When would the world give this woman a break? She nibbled on her bottom lip. "She's shown zero interest in me or the kids. Not once has she initiated contact. Do you really think that after all of these years, the first thing she does is leave me a nasty note?"

Parker rolled off his gloves and pulled his cell phone out of his pocket. "I'm honestly not sure. But you were an integral part of putting her away for as long as you did. Your testimony, allowing Will to testify, it's why her sentence was the max."

"But she's out. And it's not like she can be mad about my dad. He never even saw the inside of a jail."

Parker shook his head. "Some people have bitterness in them that even years won't lessen. And speaking of your dad, you haven't heard anything about him, have you?"

"No." Caelyn looked out towards the ocean at the end of the street. "I used to call the state police and my FBI contact every couple of months or so to see if they'd heard anything, but I haven't in a while. And it's not like he's showing up on our doorstep with presents for all of the birthdays and Christmases he missed." She looked back at Parker. "What about the people he was mixed up with?"

Parker's expression hardened. "They got smart after Sean almost blew their operation sky-high. We know drugs still come through the islands, but whenever we bust a single player, they're locked up tighter than a drum. Anything on their cell phones is in a code we haven't been able to decipher."

"Sean's your dad?" I asked.

Caelyn nodded, her fingers wrapping tighter around her bag. "So the people he worked for…they're still here?"

"I don't know if it's the same people or a new crop. They've never made a move against you, so I doubt this is them now. Not really their style, either. They're more of the burn-down-a-building type."

"Parker…" I warned. Caelyn did not need that kind of shit in her head. And neither did I. I was already two breaths away from losing it.

Parker winced. "Sorry. I didn't mean to freak you out. This is just way out of their wheelhouse. I think you can take a breath. Chances are it's your mom getting in a pot shot. I'm going to talk to her parole officer and make a personal visit to her residence. In the meantime, I'll drop this note off at the lab and see if anything pops."

"Thank you, Parker. I really appreciate your help with all of this. You always seem to be the one who steps in when my life is falling apart."

I looked between the two of them, wondering if there was something a little more personal going on. Parker caught my look and gave a small shake of his head. "I was on call the night someone broke into the O'Connors' home."

Caelyn's expression went stony. "He's being polite. Parker responded to the call as a deputy when Will, only ten years old at the time, called me in a panic because my parents had disappeared for days and someone had just broken into the house. He barricaded himself in a bedroom with Ava and Mia. I could hear the man pounding on the door and screaming for his drugs. I was in college in Seattle then." Her voice hitched. "I couldn't get to them, wasn't there to protect them. Luckily Parker got there in time."

Her words for Parker made sense now. As did the rage burning in her eyes. Caelyn loved her siblings fiercely, and I knew what it felt like to fear you were going to lose someone you should've been able to protect.

"I was just doing my job. And you know I'll do anything I can to help you and those adorable hooligans."

Caelyn shook her head, tears filling her eyes. "It's not just you doing your job. Not to me."

Parker cleared his throat, looking a little uncomfortable. "Well, then I'll just say I'm happy to do it. And I'll keep doing that job, starting with getting this processed." He held up the bagged paper.

I reached out a hand to shake Parker's. "Let us know what you hear."

"Will do. Keep an eye out for this one, will you?"

I swallowed, my throat suddenly feeling like sandpaper. The last person I was supposed to look out for had taken her last breath in front of my eyes. "Will do."

Parker headed for his SUV, and I turned back to Caelyn. "Are you okay?"

She looked so damn lost. When her gaze met mine, it was almost empty. "This is extremely unprofessional, but I could really use a hug right now."

I didn't think. I just moved. I wrapped Caelyn in my arms the way I'd wanted to from the moment I saw her staring down at that damn piece of paper. She was so tiny, her face burrowing into my chest as I held her tightly. But as small as Caelyn was, she seemed to curve to the harder planes of my body perfectly. How long had it been since I'd touched someone in this way? College, maybe?

God, that was a million years ago. But the absence of touch only made the feel of her heart beating against my flesh that much stronger; the warmth of her skin radiate that much brighter against mine. I held her tighter against me with only one thought reverberating in my mind.

I never wanted to let go.

Chapter Fourteen

Caelyn

I FORCED MYSELF TO RELEASE MY HOLD ON GRIFFIN. IT WAS the last thing I wanted to do. His sheer size alone made it feel as if he could shield me from the world. And his heat fought back the cold that had taken root in my bones.

I felt my cheeks warm as I stepped back. "Sorry about that. I just..." I didn't have a clue how to finish that sentence. I was losing it. And I needed someone to hold me together for once.

Griffin gave my shoulder a squeeze, letting his fingers trail down my arm before they fell away. "You're allowed to need someone, too."

I swallowed against the sudden dryness in my throat. My eyes burned with the force of tears wanting to be set free. But if I let them loose now, I'd have a breakdown for sure. "Thank you. I, uh, better go get the kids. Thanks again for, um, everything."

"Give me your keys."

I blinked up at Griffin. "Why?"

He held out his hand. "You're not driving right now. You've had a scare. I'll take you to get the kids."

"How are you going to get back to your truck?"

"I'll take a cab or walk."

There was only one cab on the entire island, and the driver, Shorty, took more days off than he spent on. "You don't have to do that. Really. I'll be fine. Promise."

Griffin kept his hand extended. "Keys."

I sighed, pulling my keys from my purse. "How quickly we return to one-word sentences and grunts."

Griffin plucked the keys from my hand. "Get in, smartass."

"Ooooooh, three words. Maybe all isn't lost."

Griffin climbed into my SUV and pushed the driver's seat way back. "I speak when I have something to say. I don't waste words."

I buckled my seat belt as we backed out of the parking space. "That's actually pretty profound. You should think about writing poetry."

"I think I'll pass."

"I'm shocked."

I drummed my fingers against my knees as Griffin drove, as if the action could make Big Bertha go faster. Griffin reached out, resting a hand over my overactive fingers. "They're fine."

I licked my lips and nodded. "I know. I just need to lay eyes on them."

"I get that. But dial back the panic, or they'll be freaked."

He was right. I closed my eyes for a brief moment, doing a yoga breathing exercise. As my eyes opened, Griffin squeezed my hand. "There you go."

When his hand slipped away, I felt the loss instantly. I cleared my throat. "I'm still going to hug them extra tight."

Griffin's lips twitched. "That's fair."

As we pulled into the elementary school parking lot, I caught sight of my tiny terrors waiting with a teacher. Mia was dancing around, Ava had her nose in a book, but Will... he was on guard. There were no other words to describe it. His gaze worked in a constant pattern, surveying his surroundings. When he caught sight of the SUV, his already tense posture straightened even more.

Crap on a cracker. Will had been worried. I let a slew of colorful curses fill in my mind. The last thing I wanted to do was give the boy one more thing to worry about.

Griffin pulled to a stop in front of our crew, and we hopped out. As soon as Mia saw Griffin, she flew at him. "Griffin!"

He caught her as she launched herself at him. "Hey, Little Bit."

"Miss Shepard, this is my giant, Griffin. He has magic."

Miss Shepard's eyes twinkled as she smiled at Mia. "You were lucky to find him then, weren't you?"

She nodded enthusiastically. "The luckiest."

I stepped forward, wrapping an arm around Ava. "I'm so sorry I'm late. There was an issue at the store, and I got held up."

Will's eyes narrowed at my words, but Miss Shepard waved me off. "Not a problem at all. You let me put off some paperwork for another few minutes."

"Thank you for sitting with them."

"Anytime." She looked back at Mia and Griffin. "See you tomorrow, Miss Mia. You can tell me all about your magical giant."

Heat crept up the back of Griffin's neck as Miss Shepard walked away. I couldn't help the chuckle that escaped. "You might have a whole new reputation around town now."

Griffin looked up as if praying for patience. "Heaven help me."

"I'll help you, Griffin," Mia offered. "What do you need?"

"Hmm. I think I need a trip to the park and some pizza. What do you say? Will you guys go with me?"

"Yes!" Mia shot her fist into the air and then twisted in Griffin's arms so she could see me. "We can go, right?"

"I think that sounds like a great plan."

As Griffin helped Mia into her booster seat in the SUV, and Ava climbed into the backseat, Will tugged on my arm. "What happened at the store?"

I blew out a long breath. "I'll fill you in later. But everything's fine."

Will didn't look like he believed a word coming out of my mouth. "I'm not a kid anymore, Caelyn. I can handle whatever's going on. I deserve to know."

"You might be wise beyond your years, but you're not an adult. Not yet. Don't wish away your teenage life."

"I don't give a crap about that. I want to know what's going on."

"Language," I warned. "I will fill you in, but it's not your responsibility to handle what's going on. It's mine."

Will's eyes grew hard. But instead of saying anything, he remained silent. Without a word, he slid into the final free spot in the SUV.

I climbed into the passenger seat and gave my temples a quick rub. I could feel a monster headache coming on. Griffin cast a worried glance at me and Will. "Seaside Park work?"

"That's my favorite," Mia chimed in.

I smiled but knew it came across a bit forced. "That's great."

The five-minute drive consisted entirely of Mia chattering away, Ava with her nose still in her book, and Will glaring out the window. At least two out of three of them were happy. Griffin pulled into an empty parking spot near the swings. Mia took off running for the monkey bars, Ava putting her book down to trail behind.

Will's eyes narrowed on me. "You gonna tell me what the hell is going on now? Or you going to make up another lame excuse?"

"Will," Griffin barked. "Don't talk to your sister that way."

Will turned his heated gaze on Griffin. "You're not even a part of this family. You don't get a say in any of this."

"I might not be a part of your family, but no one talks to your sister that way in front of me. Not cool."

I swallowed as Griffin and Will faced off in some sort of silent battle of wills. I wasn't sure if I should step in or wait them out. But after a few seconds that felt more like an hour, Will backed down. All the tension went out of his shoulders, and his head slumped. "I'm sorry. It's just…I know something's up." He turned to me. "You've been tweaked the last couple of days. And you're never late on the days you pick us up. I just want to know what's going on."

I pulled Will into a hard hug. My guy was too dang insightful for me to hide anything from him. "You're right. And I always planned on telling you. I was just looking for the right time. Things have been crazy the past few days, and—"

"And you didn't want to tell me whatever this is," Will finished for me.

It wasn't that exactly. Not in the way Will thought, anyway. I didn't want to burden him with what our mom being out of prison might bring up. "It's not because I don't think you can handle it. It's because I don't want you to have to."

He nodded slowly. "I get that."

He got it because he felt the same way about Ava and Mia. He would do anything to protect and shield those girls. I straightened my shoulders as if that would help me brace for the blow I was about to deliver. "Mom got released from prison early. She's out on parole."

"What? It's only been like six years."

"I know. I guess she's been a model prisoner. I'm sorry, Will."

A muscle in his cheek ticked. "You have nothing to be sorry for. She does. Except, apparently, she doesn't have to pay for it."

I gripped Will's arms. "She'll pay for it every day for the rest of her life because she doesn't get you or Ava or Mia. She's missing out on the greatest gift she was ever given."

Will's eyes reddened as he clenched his jaw even tighter, trying to hold back tears. "She deserves more."

"She does. But we know that the world isn't always fair." I hated that it was a lesson we'd both learned at way too young an age. I wished we'd both gotten way more years where the only things we had to worry about were what toys we wanted or if we could go play with our friends. But that wasn't the case.

Will's eyes flared. "Did she show up at the store today? Is that why you were late?"

My hands fell away from Will's arms as my eyes searched out Griffin. Though I wasn't sure what I was searching for. Help, maybe? The right words to tell Will what had happened? Griffin gave me a small nod, silent encouragement.

I twisted my thumb in the hem of my t-shirt as I searched for the words. "I'm not sure if she was there or not. Sheriff Raines thinks it's possible. There was a note on my SUV that wasn't so nice."

"What did it say?" Will asked, voice low.

"I don't remember the exact wording."

Will turned his focus to Griffin. "Was there a threat?"

"Nothing explicit. But, yes, it was threatening." Griffin said it straight out, no pulling any punches, simply trusting that Will could handle the information.

"They going to arrest her?"

Griffin didn't look away from Will's angry stare. "The sheriff is going to question your mom and talk to her parole officer."

Will nodded. "If she did it, will she go back to prison?"

"I'd say that's a pretty safe bet. But they have to prove it first. It might not have been her."

Will threw his hands up. "Who else would it be? Dad's gone—probably in Canada or Mexico by now. Mom's the only one who would be mad like that."

I hoped that was the case. Because as messed up as what our mother had done was, I couldn't see her actually going out of her way to hurt me. By neglect or selfishness, sure, but not by malicious actions. But maybe prison had changed Chrissy, made her darker. I had no idea.

I gave my head a small shake to bring myself back to the present. "Parker is great at his job. He'll find out who did this." At least, I hoped he would.

"Griiiiiifffffffiiiiin!" Mia yelled from the monkey bars. "Come play with me."

Griffin looked at Will. "You okay?"

Will nodded, his cheeks reddening a bit. "Sorry about earlier. I was just frustrated."

"I get it. Just don't take your frustrations out on your sister."

"I won't. Promise."

Griffin gave him a chin jerk and headed off to Mia, who was executing some spin on the bars that made my heart catch in my throat. Will bumped his shoulder against mine as we watched Mia and Ava play with Griffin. "I'm sorry I was a jerk."

"Forgiven. I'll allow you one jerkish moment a quarter."

Will chuckled. "Thank you."

We were quiet for a moment as Griffin said something to Ava. She bit her lip, seeming to think his words over, and then she nodded. He lifted her and held her waist as she made her way across the monkey bars.

"He's really good with them," Will said.

"He is." And every time I saw a tender moment like this one, Griffin wormed his way into my heart a little more.

Chapter Fifteen

Griffin

"THIS IS SOOOOOO GOOD."

I could barely make out the words that came out of Mia's very full mouth as she chowed down on her pizza. I bit back a chuckle. "I'm glad you like it."

She grinned, her teeth red from the sauce. "Pizza's my favorite. Well, not as favorite as pancakes, but close."

Will shook his head, laughing. "There is nothing on this Earth you love as much as pancakes."

Mia looked thoughtful for a minute. "Nope."

"It is really good," Ava said softly from the opposite side of the booth where she sat next to Will. "Thank you for taking us."

My heart cracked a little more at the softly spoken words. Ava's quiet way meant that every sentence I got from her was precious. "You're welcome. We might have to make it a weekly tradition."

Mia's eyes grew wide. "Really? That would be amazing. Can we, Cae Cae? Can we?"

Our entire table turned to face Caelyn. She threw up her hands. "Fine! You're all going to turn into little pizzas."

Will smirked. "At least it's not that whole wheat crud you try to pass off as pizza night at home."

Caelyn's cheeks pinked. "You can't taste the difference between whole wheat dough and regular."

Ava smiled down at her plate. "You really can."

Caelyn let out an exasperated sigh. "Fine. I know when I'm losing a battle."

"I'm not so sure about that," Will said. "You held onto those carob chip things for a long freaking time."

"What's carob?" I asked.

"Gross chocolate," Mia offered.

Will shook his head. "You can't call it chocolate. There's no sugar."

"I give up, you guys. I promise never to make cookies or anything else with carob again. Just cut me some slack already," Caelyn moaned.

I grinned at her. Caelyn was the most adorable health nut I'd ever encountered, and I'd spent most of my formative years in California. "I don't think you've tried putting carob in anything you made me." Everything Caelyn had prepared for my meals was delicious. Even if she did try to hide vegetables in everything. I'd bitten into a meatball the other day to find carrots and zucchini mixed in. I'd still eaten every bite.

"I know better than to try carob on you," she muttered.

I pressed my mouth into a hard line to keep from laughing. "You know what I think we need after this?"

Mia licked her fingers clean. "What?"

"Ice cream."

Caelyn groaned while Ava and Mia cheered. Will couldn't hold in his laughter. "Oh, man, it's so good to have an adult on the side of a good junk binge."

Caelyn's eyes narrowed on Will in a mock glare. "You know, I've been kindly ignoring your stockpile in the garage. But I could get the sudden urge to do a little spring cleaning…"

Will's mouth dropped open. "You know about that?"

"Know about what?" I asked.

Caelyn, very primly and properly, folded her paper napkin into a neat square. "Will has a trunk full of junk food in the garage that he thought was a secret." Her gaze turned back to him. "But big sisters know all."

Mia nodded solemnly. "That's because they're magic."

I ruffled her hair as I looked at Caelyn, her green eyes shining with mirth. "You're not wrong about that, Little Bit. Not wrong at all." The first time I'd called Mia the nickname I'd used for my sister, it had just slipped out. It had shocked the hell out of me when it had, but now it just seemed...*right*. Something about the little girl reminded me so much of Beth. It was painful and yet warmed those dark places in my chest all at the same time.

As the kids continued to laugh and give Caelyn a hard time, something in the air shifted. Some sort of sixth sense borne of years living under a microscope let me know that there were eyes on me. I looked up to see a large table of women and kids. The children were busy talking amongst themselves, eating and laughing, but the women seemed to be stage-whispering to each other, their eyes every so often drifting towards our table.

My entire body locked. The sneers on a couple of their faces had my gut twisting. I'd been a fool to think I could venture into town with Caelyn and her siblings and not gain any attention. But I honestly hadn't considered it. I'd only been thinking about how I could distract Caelyn from her nightmare of a day. How I could keep the kids' focus on something other than their sister being late to pick them up and what might be wrong.

But, of course, people would talk. They would whisper about my history. Wonder why I was with the O'Connors.

A warm hand landed on my knee, searing the skin there. "It's not about you," Caelyn whispered.

"Of course, it's about me." It always was. And if she were seen with me, people would start talking about her, too.

Caelyn's fingers dug into my flesh. "It's not. I had a run-in with their supreme leader earlier today. They're pissed at me and gossiping."

My gaze jumped to Caelyn, searching her face. "What kind of run-in?"

Caelyn nibbled on her bottom lip. "Patti Jenkins. The one with the ugly sneer on her face? She's always found it necessary to inform everybody of all of the ways I'm falling down on the job of guardian."

"Seriously?" I asked. Caelyn was an incredible guardian. It would be impossible for the kids to be in better care.

"She's just one of those miserable humans who needs to make herself feel better by trying to break others down. But when she told me I didn't have good instincts because I wasn't a *real* mother, I nearly lost it."

"What?" I growled.

"I told you. She's a real piece of work."

I studied Caelyn carefully. "Tell me the truth. Did any of this have to do with me?"

Caelyn's lips formed a hard line. "She mentioned you, yes. But plenty of other things, too."

My stomach sank. It was starting already. The last thing I wanted was for Caelyn to have more on her shoulders simply because she had a friendship with me. "We can go."

Her head snapped up. "Are you kidding?" My eyes widened. "We do not let ignorant, cruel people win. That's a rule."

Will looked at us, picking up on the tail end of the conversation. "She's right. It's a rule in our family, and if you hang with us, you have to follow it."

I swallowed against the burn in the back of my throat. "Well, I can't go breaking rules that would get me kicked out of the cool-kids club."

"Dang straight." Caelyn's eyes locked with mine. "Don't you

dare listen to any nonsense or whispers coming from people who don't know you. Or I'll—I'll—I don't know what, but it'll be bad."

Will choked on a laugh. "When she's really flustered or mad, she can never think up punishments on the fly."

The tension running through my shoulders eased as I took in Caelyn's flushed face. "I promise I won't listen."

"Good." She slapped her hands down on the table. "Now, let's go get some freaking ice cream."

Ava giggled at the ferocity of Caelyn's tone. "You really want that ice cream, don't you?"

She smiled at Ava. "I might get two scoops."

"Careful. You could end up in a sugar-induced coma," Will warned. "Your body's not used to all those sweets."

She stuck out her tongue at Will, and he laughed. Mia held her arms out to me, and I picked her up. She burrowed into my shoulder. "Griffin?"

"Yes?"

"Will you come over after? I know it's not Friday, but maybe we can watch a movie?" she asked, eyeing Caelyn hopefully.

I glanced in the same direction, unsure if I'd overstayed my welcome. But the truth was, I wanted any excuse not to leave her or the kids. I hoped the note had been left by her spiteful mother, but I didn't want to risk leaving them alone tonight.

She threw up her hands. "We only live once, right? Movie night it is."

Mia took her movie nights very seriously. After an intense discussion over what film to watch, we'd landed on an old version of *Swiss Family Robinson* that Mia and Ava could practically recite by heart. When the pirates attacked, Ava covered her face with a pillow while Mia mimed sword fighting as if she could defeat them herself.

Will was a trooper through most of it but finally called it quits halfway through to go and finish up some homework. By the time the credits rolled, Mia had passed out from her sugar high, and Ava rubbed her eyes.

"All right." Caelyn climbed to her feet. "Time to get you party animals to bed so you're not falling asleep in class tomorrow."

Ava nodded sleepily. "Thanks, Cae Cae. Thanks, Griffin. Tonight was really fun."

I grinned as the girl wobbled to her feet. "Anytime." I bent to pick up a dead-to-the-world Mia.

"Oh, you don't have to do that," Caelyn said.

"I don't mind." Mia weighed about as much as a sack of flour. "Can you point me in the right direction?"

Caelyn nodded, leading me down the same path Ava had taken. We stopped at a small room that had two twin-sized beds. Above each was a rainbow with their names painted on them in a glittery script. My gaze swept over the space, taking in as many details as possible. The small table littered with arts and crafts projects. A dresser with gobs of play jewelry on top. The photos of Caelyn and her siblings that dotted the various surfaces. It was warm and homey and though small, everything a little girl could want.

I laid Mia carefully on her bed as Caelyn pulled back the covers. I grinned at the brightly colored unicorns dotting Mia's PJs. "I guess you were smart to make them change before the movie."

Ava crawled into her own bed. "We always get too sleepy to change after."

Caelyn pressed a kiss to Mia's forehead and then crossed to Ava to do the same. "Got Scooter?" Ava held up a stuffed dog and nodded. "Got your nightlight?" She looked at the outlet beside her bed and nodded again. "Love you oodles."

"Oodles and poodles," Ava whispered back, her eyes growing heavy.

I silently followed Caelyn out of the room. "They are pretty damn adorable."

She grinned over her shoulder. "Most of the time. But when they fight…" She let out a low whistle. "It can get very high-pitched around here."

I chuckled. "I can imagine."

We came to a stop in the small living room, Caelyn shuffling her feet. "Any chance you want a really horrible night's sleep on our couch? You totally don't have to if it's weird. I work for you and—"

"I'd like to stay." I'd already been wondering what the chances were of me getting arrested if I slept in my truck outside the O'Connors' house.

She let out a whoosh of breath. "Thank you. I'm trying not to let myself get freaked, but I am a bit."

I reached out and squeezed her arm. I wanted to pull Caelyn into my arms, to hold her and tell her that everything would be all right, but that wasn't my place. "I'm happy to stay. And it's understandable that you're feeling unsettled right now. Cut yourself a little slack."

"Thanks. I'm going to get ready for bed and I'll grab you a blanket and a pillow."

"Thanks." I surveyed the couch that would be my bed for the night. It was decent-sized but the lumpiness factor might make things interesting. I tried plumping up one cushion after the other, but it didn't seem to do much good. But I could deal with anything for one night.

"Here you go."

I turned at Caelyn's voice and froze in my tracks. She wore a baggy t-shirt and minuscule shorts that had the air in my lungs suddenly disappearing. Somehow, even though Caelyn was petite, her legs still seemed to go on for days. Endless planes of creamy white skin. I couldn't help but wonder what it felt like. If it was as smooth as it looked.

I gave myself a mental shake. "Thanks." My voice was gruffer than I intended as I took the proffered pillow and blanket.

Caelyn toyed with the hem of her t-shirt. "Thanks again…for everything. It means more than I can say."

My ribs constricted at her words. Caelyn deserved someone looking out for her. Someone who made her life easier instead of the other way around. "I'll do whatever I can to help."

She nodded. "Well, I'll see you in the morning. Hope you sleep well."

"You, too."

Caelyn turned and headed for a ladder that led to a loft space over the living room.

My brows pulled together. "Where are you going?"

She turned, a smile teasing her lips. "To bed, in my loft."

"You don't have a room? You sleep in the loft?"

Caelyn's cheeks pinked, and I wanted to kick myself. I hadn't meant to embarrass her. She cleared her throat. "When we were looking for a place to live, this was by far the best neighborhood. I'll take safety and good neighbors over my own bedroom any day."

"That's smart." I couldn't imagine how terrifying it would've been for a twenty-one-year-old to be searching for a home and having to consider the safety of her young siblings as she did so. "You amaze me."

Caelyn's body gave a small jerk. "Why?"

"Because you've handled more than most adults and did it while making sure three kids feel safe and loved."

Her cheeks grew redder. "Any sibling—"

"No." I cut her off. "Not any sibling would."

Tears began gathering in her eyes. "Don't you make me cry. I'll be really mad at you."

I chuckled, crossing to Caelyn and pulling her into a hug. "Don't cry. You know I don't handle the tears well."

She sniffed through a laugh. "Not scared of much, but tears do you in, huh?"

When it came to Caelyn, they certainly did. I reluctantly released her. "Get some sleep."

"I will."

I watched as she climbed the ladder, thoughts about how easy it would be for her to slip and fall filling my mind. Thoughts about everything Caelyn had given up, to give her siblings the best possible life she could. I crossed to the couch, lying down and pulling the blankets up around me. The light from above clicked off, but I didn't find sleep for hours. The woman with the green eyes haunting me each fitful hour did find me, though.

As dawn crept in, I groaned and rolled over. When I did, I jerked back, my heart hammering in my chest. A grinning face met me, just inches from mine.

Mia's little legs swung back and forth as she sat on the coffee table. "I was waiting for you to wake up. Want to do gymnastics with me?"

I rubbed at my bearded cheek. "What time is it?"

"Almost six. I tried to stay in bed, but I was really excited."

I chuckled and pushed up, swinging my legs over the side of the couch. My back screamed in protest. That couch was not sleep-friendly. "I think we'd wake people up if we did gymnastics."

Mia shook her head. "We'll go outside. Then we won't wake anyone up. I'm not allowed to go outside by myself unless I have permission, but no one is awake. You'll go with me, right, Griffin?"

Of course, I'd go with her if she asked. Because this little spitfire had me wrapped around her finger just like her big sister.

Chapter Sixteen

Caelyn

I WALKED DOWN THE STEPS OF THE BACK DECK, THE DEW-covered grass tickling my flip-flop-clad feet. I couldn't help the ridiculous smile that spread across my face at the sight in front of me.

Mia flew from a cartwheel into a back handspring. As she finished, Griffin applauded. "That's incredible."

"You could do it, too. I can teach you." She began tugging on his arm.

He chuckled, shaking his head. "Sorry, Little Bit, I don't bend that way."

Griffin's chuckles and smiles were coming a lot easier these days, but I didn't take a single one for granted. They still had the ability to sucker punch me right in the belly in the best possible way. He was truly letting my little brood in. The kids were good for him, and I hoped I was, too.

"Okay, crazy gymnasts, time for breakfast," I called.

Mia jumped in the air. "Pancakes?"

"Smoothies first." I held out two smoothies.

Her face scrunched. "Not the green ones."

Griffin looked suddenly wary. "Green…smoothies?"

"She puts vegetables in them," Mia complained.

I tried my best to hold back my laughter, but a little escaped at the look of complete horror on Griffin's face. "You'll like it. I promise."

"I don't like eating salad. I sure as hell don't want to drink it."

Mia turned to him. "You said a bad word. You have to do extra chores."

He winced and covered her ears. "Don't listen to me." He mouthed *sorry* to me.

"Don't worry about it. You'll just have to clean up the kitchen after breakfast."

Griffin grinned. "Fair enough."

I held out a smoothie to him. "And you have to try this."

He looked less enthused about that prospect but took the drink. Cautiously, he took a sip. His eyes widened. "This is… good."

I rolled my eyes. "Vegetables are not evil."

"Not evil, but they usually taste like…a word I'm not allowed to say around tiny ears."

Mia giggled and tugged on Griffin's free hand. "Come on. Let's chug them so we can have pancakes!"

He shook his head as he let Mia lead him up the steps and into the house. I followed behind. Will was already at work stirring the pancake batter, and Ava was perched on one of the chairs reading a book. She looked up when we entered. "I got everyone water. Should I do juice, too?"

"Why don't you ask everyone what they want?"

Ava looked up a little hesitantly at Griffin. "Do you like juice with your pancakes?"

He gave her a gentle smile, one that twisted something inside me in an almost painful way. "No OJ for me, thank you. I'm good with water."

"I want milk," Mia called.

We proceeded in the breakfast-making that looked a little more like semi-controlled chaos. But somehow, all managed to get seated around the kitchen table with a plate of pancakes.

I took the platter Will handed me. "Okay, hit me with the good stuff. Three things."

Mia practically bounced in her seat. "Can I have more than one? I have so many."

My chest warmed as I unloaded a pancake onto her plate and then mine. "You can have as many as you want."

She beamed and held up one finger. "Griffin played on the monkey bars with me. We had the best pizza ever even though it was a school night. We got to watch my favorite movie. And I'm teaching Griffin gymnastics." With each point, she held up another finger.

Will snorted. "How are your splits coming along, Griffin?"

Griffin gave Will a wan smile. "Better than yours, I bet."

Will arched a brow. "We might just have to put that to the test."

I held up a hand. The last thing we needed was this turning into some weird, macho competition. "I really don't want to have to take either of you to the hospital when you tear a muscle." I turned to Ava. "What's your good thing?"

She thought for a moment. My girl took everything seriously, even deciding her best thing from the day before. "We were all together. And it was a really fun day."

My eyes burned and began filling with tears. Will groaned. "Seriously? You're crying at that?"

I glared at Will through my tears. "It was really sweet."

Griffin looked slightly panicked. "Are you happy or sad?"

"Happy," I said, trying to get myself under control. "Very happy."

The set of Griffin's shoulders eased, some of the anxiety

slipping from his features. Will chuckled. "You're just going to have to get used to the tears if you plan on hanging around."

Griffin rubbed his bearded jaw. "Tears aren't my strong suit."

Mia leaned closer to him. "Why? They're just letting the feelings out."

I'd tried hard to instill the belief in my siblings that no feeling was bad or wrong. And neither was expressing those feelings, as long as you weren't hurting someone else. Mia let her feelings fly, no matter the situation. Ava was quieter about hers, but whenever we had our time just the two of us, she'd let them free. Will was more bottled up. Too many years with parents who didn't give a crap, and a father who judged him for any tears shed.

Griffin shifted in his seat, seeming to search for the right words. "I hate the idea that one of you might be hurting."

Mia reached out and laid a hand on his arm. "Everybody has hurts sometimes. But they don't last forever."

So wise for such a little one. I felt my eyes filling again.

"Oh, geez," Will complained. "Someone distract her, quick."

Ava reached over and tickled my side. I squealed and squirmed away. I gave her my best *I'm serious* face. "That is not allowed."

She grinned. "But you're not crying anymore."

"Fair enough." I turned my focus to Will. "It's your turn, and you better make it good."

He smirked. "Just not too good, or you'll flood the table with your tears." I shook my head and motioned for him to get on with it. "We got pancakes on a school day, and my chemistry test got moved to next week."

I placed my hands on the table. "Thank you."

"Wait," Ava chimed in. "You and Griffin should do one, too."

My face heated. "We don't need to make Griffin—"

He cut me off. "I had amazing pizza, a green smoothie that didn't taste half-bad, and I learned how to do a cartwheel."

If you would've told me two months ago that this man would be sitting at my breakfast table playing along with our family's silly traditions, I would've said you'd taken an extra hard hit to the head. But here Griffin was, and it was like he belonged with us in that extra seat at our table. My mind kept catching on one tiny fact, though. "You learned how to do a cartwheel?"

He chuckled. "It wasn't pretty."

"You'll get better," Mia offered. "You just have to practice."

I did my best to hold back my laughter. "I need to see this."

Griffin winced. "Maybe another day. I think I might've pulled something."

I snorted. "I can get you an ice pack before you leave."

"I might need it."

"What about you, Cae Cae?" Ava asked.

"This breakfast. You guys are good for my soul. And no one makes me laugh harder than my tiny terrors."

"And Griffin," Mia added. "He makes you laugh, too."

My gaze locked with Griffin's across the table. "Yeah. He makes me laugh, too."

Chapter Seventeen

Griffin

CAELYN AND I WATCHED AS THE KIDS CLIMBED ONTO the school bus. Apparently, the island was so small that the schools shared buses. There was a phantom squeeze in my chest as they disappeared aboard. I couldn't help the worry, the million *what-ifs*, swirling around in my mind. I fought the urge to ask how safe it was to let them ride the school bus alone, knowing Caelyn wouldn't appreciate the question.

She bumped me with her shoulder. "Thanks again for everything."

I looked down at her—rosy cheeks, green eyes blazing in the morning sun. "Anytime."

She grinned. "Be careful what you offer. Mia could have you living on our couch permanently."

A part of me would've happily agreed to the arrangement. I hated that there would be no one looking out for Caelyn and her siblings tonight. No one to stand between them and someone who might want to take things further than a threatening note.

"What's with the scowly face?" she asked.

I did my best to ease my expression but knew I was only partially successful. "We should talk about precautions."

The amusement fell from Caelyn's face. "I guess you're right. I talked to Will, and he's going to keep a closer eye on the girls. He'll be extra careful when he walks them to the store from school those couple of days a week. I'm going to ask Parker for an updated photo of my mom to show Will so he can be on the lookout."

Annoyance pricked at my gut. "And what about you?"

"Me?" She honestly looked surprised that I'd asked. As if it were ridiculous for me to be concerned about her, as well.

"Yes, you," I growled. "The note was left on your SUV. It was directed at *you*. I want to know how you plan on keeping yourself safe."

Her expression hardened. "I've been taking care of myself and those three kids for years. I'm not a moron. I have pepper spray in my purse and Parker on speed dial. We don't have an alarm system, we can't afford it, but we do have good locks. It's not fancy, but it works."

I let out a slew of curses in my mind. "I didn't mean it that way. I know you take amazing care of those kids and yourself. But this isn't exactly your everyday safety issue. I'm just worried."

Some of the stiffness eased out of Caelyn's muscles. "I'm sorry. I'm just a little sensitive when it comes to people thinking I can't take care of myself and my family."

"Understood. But I don't think that."

"I know," she whispered. "I'm just strung a little tight."

"I think that's understandable." There had been a ton thrown at Caelyn over the past few weeks, and she'd had no time to herself to process. "Why don't I pick the kids up from school? I can take them out to the farmhouse. They can run around, and then you have a little time to yourself before you come pick them up. Get a coffee, go for a walk."

Caelyn was silent for a moment. "I don't know."

"I like having them around. And Will's supposed to work with me today anyway. I don't want him riding his bike out to my place alone until we know what's going on."

"You're sure you don't mind? It'll be two hours or so until I'm done with work."

I squeezed her shoulder. "Take a little longer. Give yourself a break. Some time to process this week."

She nibbled on her bottom lip. "I wouldn't mind sneaking in a quick yoga practice."

"Do it." Caelyn needed time and space for just her, and I'd do whatever I could to help her get it.

"Okay. And I'll bring my pepper spray."

I chuckled. "Glad to hear it."

"Thank you… Again."

"No thanks needed." I shoved my hands into my pockets. "What time do you have to be at work?"

Caelyn glanced down at her phone. "Shoot. I need to open in ten minutes."

"Let's go, then."

Caelyn locked the front door, and we headed for the SUV. The trip to The General Store was quiet, my brain taking the time to come up with every possible thing that could go wrong in the next eight or so hours.

Caelyn pulled into a spot at the back of the parking lot, but I paused before climbing out. "Call Parker and then me if anything out of the ordinary happens. Anything at all. Better to be too cautious."

"I will, oh overprotective giant."

My eyes narrowed on her. "I think the term giant is reserved for Mia."

Caelyn grinned. "Fair enough. I'll see you a little after five."

"See you then."

We climbed out of the SUV, and I waited until she was safely inside the store before heading for my truck. I stopped just shy of the driver's side door and glanced across the street. My gaze caught on Ford and his friend, Crosby. I made a split-second decision and crossed to them.

Crosby wore a wide grin. "Did you just get out of Caelyn's SUV? At eight in the morning?"

It took me a second to get the insinuation. But Ford beat me to any retort. He slapped Crosby on the back of the head. "Not cool, man."

"It's not what you think." The back of my neck itched, and I fought the urge to rub it. "Caelyn ran into some trouble yesterday. I was just looking out for her and the kids."

All traces of humor fled from Crosby's face. "What kind of trouble?"

I knew that Caelyn hadn't had time to fill in her friends regarding what had happened, but I also knew that when she did, she'd likely downplay the entire thing. I wanted the people around her, especially those who worked nearby, to keep an eye out for anything suspicious. "Someone left a threatening note on her SUV yesterday."

"What the hell?" Ford muttered.

"Her mom just got paroled, so Parker thinks it might be her. But unless fingerprints come back on the note, we won't know for sure."

Ford's eyes widened. "Chrissy got paroled? She was supposed to have years left on her sentence."

I grimaced, thinking of how much it had hurt Caelyn and Will to know she wasn't serving her full sentence. "Overcrowding and good behavior, I guess."

Crosby let out a low whistle. "What can we do?"

"You're both close. Keep an eye out. Maybe find reasons to drop by the store more than usual?" Ford's bar was just across the street from the store, and Crosby's law office was right next door, so it wasn't out of the norm for either of them to frequent the shop. I could only hope that Caelyn wouldn't catch on to being looked after. I glanced at the empty parking lot across Main Street. "I hate that she's there alone for most of the day right now."

Ford nodded. "That'll change in a couple of weeks. Tourist season is already picking up. Old Man Walters will get her some help soon."

"If you know him, maybe you could have a quiet word? Suggest that he bring someone on now?" I asked.

"Not a bad idea," Crosby agreed. "I can call him now. And I'll make sure to keep an eye and ear out. I'll tell my assistant, Penny, what's going on, too. We'll stop by at least once a day."

The vise that had been gripping my chest since I'd first thought of leaving Caelyn alone this morning eased a fraction. "Thank you."

Ford studied me carefully. "What's going on between you two?"

His tone wasn't threatening, but I still bristled at the question. I'd had too many years of people prying into my private life. I took a slow breath, giving myself time so I didn't bite his head off with my answer. "We're…friends."

"I know you think it's none of my business, but Caelyn means something to me." He motioned to Crosby. "To both of us."

"She means something to me, too. Caelyn's a good woman. And those kids are special. They've had a shit hand dealt to them and they deserve better than that. I'm just helping out where I can."

Crosby grinned and clapped me on the back. "I'm glad you're looking out for her. She deserves that and more. Maybe—"

"Crosby…" Ford said in a low, warning tone.

"All right, all right." He held up both hands. "I won't interfere.

And I'll keep an eye out for Miss Caelyn. Now I have to get going, or Penny is going to have my hide for being late for this meeting."

Crosby jogged across the street, and Ford shook his head as he went. "Ignore him."

"Happy to."

Ford chuckled. "I'll have my brother keep an eye out, too. Hunter's working on a construction project down the block. They're framing so they'll have a clear view of the store."

I held out a hand for Ford to shake. "Appreciate it."

Ford's hand gripped mine and held. "She's been through a lot, and her heart is as tender as they come. Tread carefully."

I met his stare and didn't look away. "I'm not going to hurt her."

Ford released his hold. "I'm glad to hear it. Call me if you hear any updates or if Caelyn needs anything."

"I will."

I felt more at ease as I crossed to my truck and climbed in. But as I started it up, it was still hard as hell to drive away.

Chapter Eighteen

Caelyn

"FOR THE LOVE OF TRIPLE FUDGE ICE CREAM." I let out a groan as I picked up the third pan I'd dropped today.

"Uh-oh. That sounds serious."

I jumped as I straightened, letting out a muffled squeak. The note left on my SUV yesterday had worked its way into my head. I'd sworn to myself that I wouldn't let it, but the words had snuck in and were now wreaking havoc on my brain. The idea that someone, most likely my mother, wished me harm had me jumping at my own shadow.

I did my best to smooth out my expression as I took in the man in front of my station. He was tall with dark hair and features. Handsome with a bit of an edge. "Sorry about that. It's just one of those days. What can I help you with?"

It was just a bit early for the lunch rush. Usually, the time when Griffin would've snuck in to avoid the lunch crowds. Just the thought had a little pang pinging in my chest. Even though I saw him several times a week now, I missed his surprise visits to the store. The demand for veggie-free sandwiches.

"I saw the *Help Wanted* sign in the window and thought I'd see if you're looking for anyone part-time. I've heard great things about your sandwiches. I live over on Shelter, but word has made it that far that this is the place to get lunch on Anchor."

The man's deep voice snapped me out of my musings. "I'm glad to hear we're making a name for ourselves. But if you live on Shelter, are you sure you want to commute over here for part-time work?" It was a bit of a haul. I didn't think we needed the extra help yet. But Mr. Walters had shown up a couple of hours ago insisting that he wanted two people working at all times.

"I really need the extra hours. I've got a kid I'm trying to get joint-custody of, and lawyers don't come cheap."

There was little that would've made me want to hire someone more. Maybe because my parents had never fought for my siblings and me a day in their lives. "Do you have any grocery experience?"

The man smiled. "Bagging and stocking shelves in high school. But it's been a minute since I've run a cash register. I'm Max, by the way."

"Caelyn." I reached out to shake his hand. "Sorry I didn't make introductions."

"No big."

"What's your availability?"

"I work nights at a bar on Shelter so I'm available for any day shifts here."

It was exactly what we needed. And I had to admit, it would be nice not to have to run back and forth between the register up front and my kitchen in the back. "Looks like this might be a good fit. Why don't you pull up a stool, and we can talk details while I make you a sandwich?"

"Really? Just like that?"

I shrugged. "Why not? It's not a marriage proposal. If things don't work out, we'll go our separate ways. Now, what sandwich can I get you?"

Max glanced up at the chalkboard menu. "It all sounds really good. Why don't you just give me your favorite."

"Trusting. Is there anything you don't eat?"

"I'm pretty adventurous."

Not another veggie-phobic, at least. I smiled down at my cutting board as Griffin's face filled my mind. "I'm going with a prosciutto concoction that's a fan favorite."

"Sounds amazing." Max slid onto the stool. "So, how long have you worked here?"

"It feels like forever." I'd worked at the store since I was in high school. I was lucky enough that when I needed a job after taking custody of my siblings, Mr. Walters had given me my old one back. He'd also been more than understanding about all the millions of emergencies that had popped up in my first few years as a guardian. And he'd let my responsibilities grow with time. "The prepared foods piece is new, though. Only a year or two old."

"So, you're a born and raised islander?"

I slid the sandwich into the panini press. "That I am. What about you?"

Max toyed with a paper napkin by his placemat. "Grew up on Shelter and doubt I'll ever leave."

"And why would we want to? This is one of the most beautiful places in the world. I mean, not that I've seen a lot of other places, but just based on pictures…"

He chuckled. "I agree. We're damn lucky to be where we are. Your family still here, too?"

I lifted the top of the press and used my spatula to slide the sandwich onto a plate. "All the family that matters."

"Sounds like there's a story there."

"Isn't there always when it comes to family?"

"Ain't that the truth?" Max took a bite of the sandwich, and his eyes widened. "Holy shit. This is amazing."

I laughed. "I guess your friend spoke the truth, after all."

"I guess he did. I feel like I owe him at least a beer now."

"Sounds like fair payment to me. Or you could just pay it forward and tell someone else to come eat here." As busy as tourist season was around here, we could always use more word of mouth. At some point, maybe Mr. Walters would expand our operation, and we could start a true café. I caught myself before I got lost in all the possibilities. "Do you want anything to drink?"

"I'll take a Coke if you have it."

"That I can do." I bent and grabbed one from the small fridge under the counter. "Here you go."

"Thanks. This really is one of the best lunches I've had in a while."

"I love hearing that. Most of the time, people take things to go, so I don't get the reaction."

"Shortstop!"

Kenna's voice rang out through the small store, and I stiffened. "I'm back here, but I have a customer." I glanced at Max, blushing. "I'm so sorry. That's one of my best friends, and her manners are just a bit lacking." I sent a pointed stare in Kenna's direction as she appeared.

Max stood, gathering the remains of his sandwich and his freshly cracked Coke. "Don't worry about it. I'll get out of your hair. But do you need me to fill out any paperwork?"

"You can do it on your first day. How about tomorrow at noon?"

"I'll be here. Thanks, Caelyn."

I watched as Max made a hasty exit from the store and then I turned my glare on Kenna. "Seriously? You're going to scare away my new employee now?"

She looked just the slightest bit sheepish. "Sorry. I didn't think anyone would be back here." I didn't say a word, just kept my gaze leveled on Kenna. Her eyes narrowed. "Don't give me that stern *mom* look. Do you remember all the times you and Bell came over to my place the past few months and gave me a hard time for not letting you in on what was going on in my life?"

"Um, I think that was more Bell than me, but sure."

Kenna had kept us both in the dark one too many times as she tried to fight a past that had reared its ugly head. Her hands went to her hips. "Doesn't that feel a little hypocritical now?"

Kenna let her words hang in the air, but it took me a minute to catch her meaning. My eyes widened. "How did you hear? Parker?"

"No." She paused for a moment, making my brain spin in circles. "Griffin talked to Crosby and Ford."

"Griffin? My Griffin?" I hated how much I wanted that little bit of ownership to be true.

Kenna's brows rose. "*Your* Griffin?"

"You know what I mean. The Griffin that I'm friends with, not some other random Griffin running around." My cheeks heated with every word. Why couldn't I control my mouth when I got flustered? It was like it grew legs and ran away each and every time.

Kenna smirked. "Suuuuure. Anyway, he talked to the boys this morning and told them that someone left a threatening note on your car. Why wouldn't you tell us what was going on?"

"I wasn't *not* telling you."

"The lack of incoming calls from your number says otherwise."

I let out a groan. "I swear. This is not me hiding something from you. It's just—Griffin was driving by when I saw the note. He called Parker and then stayed with me." Hot tears began to build behind my eyes. "He went with me to get the kids. Took us to the park and for pizza. He slept over on the couch. He made me feel safe."

God, how long had it been since the safety of my little family hadn't rested solely on my shoulders? Probably never. And knowing you were responsible for making sure no harm came to three of the most precious beings on the planet? It was exhausting. Totally and completely worth it but tiring in a way that seeped into your bones. For the first time since I'd taken custody of my siblings, I'd relaxed last night. I'd slept so deeply, I hadn't even heard Mia come out to the living room and wake up Griffin. I'd been at total peace.

Kenna watched me carefully, her mental wheels turning. "He's good to you."

"We're friends, Ken. That's all."

"I'm not trying to judge or control, I swear."

I took in her expression, one that was completely open and accepting. I loved my best friend, but open and accepting wasn't her usual M.O. She was constantly worried that someone would hurt the people she cared about. But falling in love with Crosby had worked miracles in her life. And it seemed she'd taken our conversation a couple of weeks ago to heart. My shoulders relaxed a fraction. "Thank you. He's really kind. He's been great for the kids. And I think we've been good for him, too."

I thought about how much more open Griffin had become over the past weeks. It was as if he'd been in this state of suspended animation, existing but not fully living. My tiny terrors and the chaos they created brought real life back to Griffin's existence. And I hoped I did, too.

"I'm glad. I really am," Kenna said.

I rounded the counter and pulled her into a hug. "Thank you."

"If you start crying on me, I'll pick up on my overprotective big sister kick again."

I chuckled as I let her go. "I'll try to keep it in check."

Kenna brushed her hair back from her face. "Thank you. Now, tell me about this letter."

I grimaced but recounted what had happened from finding the note to Parker's arrival and everything that came after. Kenna let out a low whistle. "Do you really think it's your mom?"

"Who else would it be? It's not like I regularly piss people off to that degree. I lead a pretty boring life." My mind flashed to the scene with Patti. Okay, maybe I pissed people off occasionally.

"What's with that look?"

"What look?"

Kenna let out a little growl of frustration. "The one that says there's something else you're not telling me."

This was the problem with having friends that knew you so well. They could read every single micro-expression on your face. "I had a run-in with Patti yesterday."

"What did that nosy B want?"

I smiled at the intense scowl on Kenna's face. "The usual, to make her disapproval of my parenting skills known."

"Someone needs to put her in her place. Want me to do it? Please let me do it. These pregnancy hormones are making me extra vicious, and I need an outlet."

I choked on a laugh. "Actually, I handled it."

Kenna was silent for a moment. "You handled it? How? By buying her a coffee and a muffin?"

"No. I told her she was a venomous gossip, and then Shay told her to get lost." I was pretty damn proud of myself. But the reminder of Patti's threat to call Child Protective Services sent dread pooling in my stomach.

"Damn, girl. Being friends with Griffin seems to agree with you."

I forced a smile as I met Kenna's gaze. "I think we're good for each other."

Chapter Nineteen

Griffin

"FOR REAL?" MIA SQUEAKED.

I chuckled as I buttoned one of my old shirts around her to protect her school clothes. "For real. You guys go crazy. Will and I will be just across the hall working in the other bedroom."

"This is amazing! I'm going to paint a rainbow and a unicorn and kittens…" Mia continued with her list as she started surveying her paint and brush options.

"What do you think, Avs?" I asked.

She nibbled her bottom lip as she fastened the last button on her makeshift smock. "Are you sure? Isn't it going to damage the walls?"

My chest tightened at the uncertainty in Ava's voice. She was so careful to play by the rules, to not get into trouble. I hoped doing something a little crazy, but in a safe environment, might get her out of her shell a bit. "There was some damage to the walls, so we have to redo them completely. You can go wild in here because we'll be covering it all up with plaster and paint in a couple of days."

Mia turned to face Will and me. "You're going to cover up my unicorn?"

I forced down my laugh. "We are. But your unicorn's magic will still be under all that paint. And we'll know it's there."

She thought about it for a moment and then nodded, picking up a brush and getting to work. Ava was still for another minute and then slowly moved forward and selected a small brush. Instead of going for the brightest colors in the bunch, she chose a few muted shades of green.

"They'll be good," Will whispered.

I nodded. "We'll be right across the hall if you need anything."

Mia waved a hand, not stopping her bold strokes on the wall. Ava sent a small smile my way. "Thanks, Griffin. This is really cool."

Why did that simple statement make me feel as if I'd won the damn lottery? These kids were worming their way into my heart one day at a time. I shoved down that faint voice that said it was a risk to let them into my life, to let myself *care* for them. Because I knew just how easy it was to lose it all.

"So, what's on the agenda for today?" Will asked, shaking me out of my spiraling thoughts.

"Paint, paint, and more paint."

Will let out a groan. "Why do I feel like we do more of that than anything else?"

The kid wasn't wrong. "It's paint and hauling shit." I froze, meeting Will's gaze. "Don't tell your sister I swore."

Will barked out a laugh. "She's got you running scared, huh?"

"She does have some epic punishments. And I'm worried she's going to start doubling my vegetable intake as one of them."

Will grinned and headed for the rollers against the far wall. He bent, examining the can of paint. "Pink? Kind of a surprising color choice."

I looked around the room that no longer looked quite as familiar. The rose wallpaper had been stripped, and the warped floorboards replaced. But I still somehow wanted to pay homage to the girl whose room this had once been. "This used to be my sister's room. Her favorite color was pink, and this somehow just feels right."

Will was quiet for a moment. "I'm really sorry about what happened to your family."

We hadn't ever talked about it, he and I. But I knew he had to know some of the broad strokes. It would be impossible to live on this island and not know. "Thanks. I am, too."

Will was silent as he mixed the paint and poured it into the pans. I'd already taped off the crown molding, doors, and newly placed windows. Before long, we were working in an easy rhythm.

"So, how's spring conditioning for football?" I asked. Caelyn had shared that Will was one of the top players on our islands' team. And they took it seriously. That meant a year-round program to make sure team members stayed in shape.

"It's fine. Boring as hell mostly."

I studied him from across the room. In the hours we had worked together, Will hadn't shared anything about football. He talked endlessly about his sisters. All the ridiculousness they got up to. The funny stories and adventures they went on. He talked a lot about music—bands he'd recently discovered or songs he was learning on the piano or guitar. But never football.

I cleared my throat. "You don't like it, do you?"

Will's eyes went wide. "What do you mean?"

The slightly panicked expression on his face had all sorts of alarm bells going off in my mind, but I kept my voice even and casual. "You just never talk about it. If you loved the sport, you'd talk about it."

Will returned his focus to the wall, rolling the pink hue in practiced, even strokes. "It's not my favorite thing to do."

"Then why do it?"

He shrugged. "I'm good at it. And if things keep progressing the way they are now, I might be able to get a scholarship. If I can even go."

I kept my own roller moving across the wall, trying not to make Will feel as if he were on the spot. "Why wouldn't you go to college?" From everything Caelyn had told me, Will was a prime candidate for a full-ride somewhere.

A muscle in his jaw worked. "Someone has to help Caelyn. I'm not going to leave her alone to handle everything herself. Maybe I can work for a few years and then go to school. Or take online classes or something."

A burn started in the back of my throat. This kid. Mature beyond his years and so damn selfless. I wanted to fix it all for him in that moment. To promise that I'd be there for Caelyn and his younger sisters. I swallowed the words down. "Your sister, she knows what she's doing. And she has an amazing support system. Bell and Ford, Kenna and Crosby. You know they'll all step in if she needs them. I will, too."

Will's strokes on the wall became a bit more forceful. "She won't tell them if she needs help. She never does."

My grip on my roller tightened as I thought about Caelyn suffering in silence. I knew she was proud, wanted to do things on her own, but if Will could see her struggling, it had to have gotten bad in the past. But Will couldn't take this on. He was too young, and he had a bright future in front of him—if he could only reach for it.

I paused my painting and turned to face him. "If you could do anything, what would it be? No rules, no holding yourself back, anything."

Will kept his attention on the task at hand. "Maybe something with music. I'm honestly not sure."

I adjusted the brush in my hand. I wanted Will to have whatever dream he settled on. And I'd do whatever I could to help him figure out what that might be.

Chapter Twenty

Caelyn

"**Y**OU DIDN'T HAVE TO DO ALL OF THIS, YOU KNOW."

I forced my gaze away from Will chasing Mia and Ava across the lawn and looked back at Griffin. The twilight glow seemed to make his eyes almost sparkle. It was no hardship, looking at this man. "It's the least I could do. Thank you again for keeping the girls busy."

Griffin scowled. "You don't have to thank me for that. I like spending time with them."

I forced my laugh back. "Good to know the scowl isn't completely out of commission."

Said expression on Griffin's face only deepened. "I don't scowl."

I couldn't hold in my laughter any longer. "What's so funny?"

"The first year you came into the store, I think you scowled every time. I made a game out of trying to get you to smile."

"Seriously?"

I shrugged. "You were scowling, but I could tell it was a front."

Griffin shook his head, looking out at the yard as Mia let out an especially high-pitched shriek. "I guess I'm not as much of a badass as I thought."

"That's not such a bad thing. I like the real you better." I snapped my mouth closed. The words had just slipped out without me meaning to release them. They revealed a little too much about how closely I watched Griffin, how much joy I got from him coming out of his shell, letting us in.

Griffin was silent, but his gaze had drifted back to me. I could feel it on me without even looking his way. It seemed to heat each place it touched. I cleared my throat, trying to dissipate whatever energy was gathering between us at the picnic table. "The kids really love it here."

"I'm glad. It's been nice having some life back in the place. And it doesn't hurt that you provide feasts to accompany it."

I surveyed the table in front of us, my cheeks heating. I might've gone a little overboard. But I wanted to do something special for Griffin, for him to share the food I made him with people who cared about him and not with his empty kitchen.

I'd gone with an Italian theme since we'd gotten in our first heirloom tomatoes of the season. I'd made a bruschetta to start, an array of salads, and a caramelized tomato pasta for the main course with garlic bread on the side. Dessert had been fresh berries and vanilla ice cream.

Griffin turned slightly on the bench. "Can I ask you something?"

His voice jarred me from my spiraling thoughts. "Sure."

"Why cooking?"

"What do you mean?"

He drummed his fingers against the wood of the table as if searching for the right words. "You love it, right?" I nodded. "Why?"

No one had ever asked me that before. It had always been just an accepted truth. But Griffin, he always looked just a little deeper than the rest of the world. I toyed with the edge of my napkin. I didn't share a lot of my childhood with anyone. Embarrassment usually held me back. But some pull in me wanted to share the truth of my *why* with Griffin.

"Growing up, if I wanted food that didn't come from a fast-food dollar menu or a Cup of Noodles, I had to make it myself. Sometimes, my parents forgot to feed us altogether. It just became my thing. I started doing the grocery shopping and cooking for myself and the tiny terrors. Eventually, Mr. Walters gave me a job and would always send me home with produce that was about to go bad in a couple of days. It became kind of a game. What could I make with what I had?"

I glanced out at Will, Ava, and Mia, my chest warming. "I love being able to take care of them in that way. And it just grew from there. It still feels like a game in a lot of ways. Figuring out which unexpected flavors complement each other. I just wish I knew more."

"What do you mean?" Griffin asked. "Your cooking is amazing. Some of the best I've ever had, and I've eaten at Michelin-starred restaurants."

His praise swept over me in a wave of warmth. "I think you're biased because you're friends with the cook."

Griffin scoffed. "I'm a tough grader when it comes to my stomach. I don't care who the chef is."

I chuckled. "Good to know."

"So, what is it that you want to learn?"

I took in the array of dishes in front of us and imagined all the possibilities. "It's endless, really. I'm completely self-taught, so it's almost like I don't know what I don't know. I'd love to learn from a teacher who could critique my technique. I'd love to learn different cuisines. My dream is to go on a trip around the world and take cooking classes along the way. Learn the quintessential dishes of each place I went."

"That would be quite the experience."

"From the guy who's terrified to turn on his oven."

He tossed his napkin at me. "Hey, now. I reheat the food you make me, and sometimes I do that in the oven."

I held up both hands in surrender. "What was I thinking? You're a master chef."

"Thank you. I appreciate you acknowledging my reheating prowess."

I grinned down at my napkin. Who was this man? He joked and played. Let my siblings run wild through his house. Allowed me to take over his kitchen. I looked up at Griffin, at the beautiful planes of his face. My fingers itched to run over his stubbled cheeks. Instead, I tightened my hold on my napkin. "What about you? Is there something you're dying to do? Somewhere you'd love to visit?"

Griffin shifted on the bench, going quiet for a moment before answering. "I want to be here. Finish this house. That's what I want most of all."

My chest seized at his words. There was so much pain and longing in each one. "You've already made incredible progress. And now it's going even faster."

"Will's been great. He has a real knack for this stuff."

A glowing pride slid through me. "He's such a good kid. And he works so hard."

"Thanks to him, we've gotten another two bedrooms on the second floor fixed up."

My eyes widened. "That's incredible. Were you able to salvage any of the furniture?" He'd gotten rid of so much that he'd been storing in the shop, I wasn't sure if there was anything left to put back into the rooms.

Griffin rubbed the back of his neck. "I'm sorry about that."

"About what?"

"Snapping at you when we were cleaning out the shop."

My fingers began to itch again. This time, I couldn't resist reaching out. I let my hand briefly squeeze Griffin's knee, the rough denim burning into my palm. "You don't have to apologize for having boundaries."

Griffin grunted. "But I do need to apologize for being an asshole." He held up a hand before I could speak. "Please don't punish me for cursing."

I laughed. "You're safe since it wasn't in front of the kids."

"Thank God." He began picking at the label of his beer. "I've had a lot of people sell me out. My stories, my photos. The only way it didn't happen was if I was alone, and no one knew who I was. But when I erased myself, I let my family go, too. I lost them and myself all over again. But this time, it was my own damn fault. Our favorite place, the one where I felt closest to them, was almost destroyed—family heirlooms damaged beyond repair."

"Is that what was in the shop?" I asked. Griffin nodded. It all started to make even more sense. Of course, he'd been on edge. He'd been facing all the damage that people had inflicted on one of the few pieces he had left of his family.

"The worst was losing my dad's desk. It was in our family for generations. My sister and I used to sit under it like it was our own personal fort while he told us about all the people who had sat at it before. Beth thought it was magic."

My eyes burned. It was the first time he'd spoken of his sister. "She sounds like someone else I know."

Griffin grinned, a smile that was still sad around the edges. "The first time I saw Mia, she reminded me so much of Beth, it nearly stole my breath."

I latched my fingers together, forcing them to stay on my lap so I wouldn't throw my arms around Griffin. "Is it too hard for you? To be around her?"

He shook his head. "It's a good kind of pain. Mia reminds me of all the good memories I have of Beth. I've been too focused on losing her for too long."

"I'm glad it helps in a way. You can talk about her if you want. Beth. I'd love to hear more about her."

Griffin stared out at the kids rolling around in the grass, but it was almost as if he couldn't see them, as if he were lost in another time. "I'm not used to talking about her. But maybe one day."

I couldn't help the flicker of disappointment. I wanted to know it all, everything he would share with me. I wanted him to be able to bring his sister and his parents out into the light again. But I couldn't force it. I knew better than most that sharing those secret parts of yourself couldn't be rushed. "Open invitation."

"Thank you."

"But I'm glad you're sticking around. I'd miss your scowls and grunts. And it would break Mia's heart not to have her giant around."

Griffin shook his head. "I told you, I don't scowl."

"Whatever you say, Mr. Magic Giant. You know I can't wait for the local rumor mill to start spreading that around. The magical giant who only comes out of his castle once a week."

That familiar scowl stretched across Griffin's face. "You're way too amused about this."

I shrugged. "It is a little funny."

"I'll show you funny."

Before I knew what was happening, Griffin lunged, plucking me off the bench and hauling me over his shoulder. I let out a squeal that had all the kids running our way.

"I wanna do that!" Mia begged.

I pounded on Griffin's back. "Let me down. I swear to God I'll put cayenne pepper in all your food for a week if you don't."

Ava appeared upside down in my line of sight. "What'd you do, Cae Cae?"

"She's being an instigator," Griffin answered.

"What's an insta-grator?" Mia asked.

Will chuckled. "An instigator. It means she's causing trouble."

Griffin started striding through the backyard. "And trouble-makers should take a dip in the pond, don't you guys think?"

The girls cheered, dancing around us as I began to twist and flail. "Don't you dare, Griffin Lockwood."

"I'd be careful if I were you," Will warned. "Caelyn's revenge is epic."

Griffin slowed as he reached the edge of the yard. "I guess I don't want to do anything to risk my supply of food."

"Aw, man," Mia complained. "It would've been so fun to watch you throw her in the pond."

I laughed as Griffin slowly began lowering me to the ground, but my breath stalled as we came face-to-face, our lips the barest brush apart. It would hardly take any movement at all for them to meet. To taste Griffin on my tongue.

"Why are you guys staring at each other?" Mia asked.

Will let out a cough that sounded more like a strangled laugh.

I snapped out of the haze Griffin's lips had me in and wiggled to be let free. "Griffin was just making sure I wasn't going to poison his food."

Mia looked suddenly worried. "You're not, right?"

I gave Griffin a mock assessment. "Not if he's on his best behavior."

Mia gave him a sympathetic look, one borne of years of getting in trouble. "That happens to me a lot, too."

Griffin held up both hands in surrender. "Best behavior. Scout's honor."

"Were you a Boy Scout?" I asked.

Griffin shook his head, a twinkle in his eye. That mischievous glint had my eyes dropping to his mouth again. And I couldn't help but wonder what it would be like to forget the world around me and lose myself in the taste and feel of everything that was Griffin.

Chapter Twenty-One

Caelyn

"REMEMBER WHAT WE TALKED ABOUT?" I ASKED AS I headed down the street with Ava and Mia in tow.

"Don't touch anything and keep our voices low," Ava answered instantly.

"That doesn't sound like very much fun," Mia groused.

I paused, turning to face my tiniest terror. The one who was a whirling ball of energy and who could, I was sure, destroy Bell's new shop in a matter of seconds. "Mia Renee…"

She let out a harrumph. "I know, I know. Sometimes we have to do stuff we don't want to do."

I forced my laughter down. "And if we get through this in one piece, we get to go to the park afterward."

"But only if you don't break anything," Ava added helpfully.

"I'm not gonna break anything! Maybe you'll break something. And then you'll be in trouble. And then I'll go to the park, but you'll have to have a timeout."

"Girls." I held up a hand. It had been one of those mornings. The kind where everything was a struggle. The shirt that Mia wanted to wear was dirty. Ava had left the book she wanted to read at school. And Will was trying to rush us all out the door so we could drop him at Griffin's for work. Mia had been pitching a fit since we left the farmhouse because she wanted to stay with the boys. I took a deep breath. "I need five minutes to talk to Bell. That's it."

They nodded and kept mostly silent for the rest of the walk to Second Chances, though I did catch them sticking out their tongues at each other. I ignored it. An antique bell tinkled as I pulled open the door to Bell's shop. It had only been open a couple of months, but business was already booming. A local interior designer who worked on several high-end homes had discovered the unique pieces Bell restored and had fallen in love. Her business alone could've kept the shop afloat.

"My favorite people," Bell called from the back of the store. "This certainly brightens my morning."

"Sorry to drop by unannounced."

"You know you're welcome anytime." Bell did a quick assessment of my face and turned to the girls. "Ford's in the break room, and he has muffins from The Mad Baker. Why don't you go get some?"

Mia and Ava both perked up immediately. They shot me a quick glance, and as soon as I nodded, they took off in search of the treats. I let out a breath.

"What's going on? You look exhausted," Bell asked.

"It's just one of those mornings. Everyone's unhappy." What I needed was a solid week on a sunny beach. One of those resorts that had activities that kept kids busy all day long so you could lay by the pool and have someone bring you drinks and food.

"You've got a look on your face that I honestly can't read."

I grinned. "I'm picturing myself at one of those fancy resorts where handsome men bring you fruity drinks with little umbrellas in them."

Bell chuckled. "It's good to have a Zen zone."

"I go there often."

Bell pulled me into a quick hug. "I'm sorry it was a rough morning."

"Life happens. Mad Baker muffins should improve their moods significantly."

"They always work for me. Now, what brings you by?"

I suddenly felt nervous, like maybe the plan that had taken shape in my mind last night was a very bad idea. "Can't I just come to visit my best friend?"

Bell eyed me suspiciously. "Sure…"

She was the master of letting silences do the work for her. She'd let a single word hang in the air until you suddenly had a burning need to fill the quiet. Just like I felt now. "I need your help with something."

"Anything. You know that."

"When the delivery guys brought Griffin's stuff by here, did you take anything?"

Bell's brows rose. "A lot of stuff. Why?"

"Was a desk one of those things? It would've been pretty large."

Bell motioned for me to follow her through the store, calling out to Ford as she walked. "We'll be right back." Across the back alley was a storage facility and workshop for everything that wouldn't fit in the storefront. She pulled open a heavy door and led me to the workshop side of the space. "Something like this?"

I took in the piece. It looked like it had been through a war. The top was scratched to hell, and one of the legs was broken. But I could see how it would fit perfectly in Griffin's office. I crouched low, trying to see if I could fit under it the way Griffin had as a child. My gaze caught on something when I did. Names carved into the underside of a drawer. Probably ten in total. Most I didn't recognize. But two tucked together, I did. *Griffin* and *Beth*.

I crawled out from under the desk. "Can you fix it?"

"I'm gonna try. It's been through the wringer. But it just kind of called to me when I saw it on the truck. Not sure why. When my dad saw it, he thought I was crazy."

"I want you to fix it, and then I need to buy it from you." I was making more money now; I could afford Bell's markup.

She took my arm. "Honey, I'll give it to you. What's all this about?"

I shook my head. "I'll pay for it. Really. I can swing it. I just—Griffin needs this in his house. I think he thought it was beyond repair. But you can fix it. Just don't do anything to the names on the underside of the drawer."

Bell stilled, understanding filling her expression. "Beth was his sister, wasn't she?"

I nodded, tears gathering in the corners of my eyes. "He needs this desk."

"Then we'll get it fixed up for him."

"Thank you."

She understood better than most that some things helped you hold onto those you had lost. Items became touchpoints. She would make sure Griffin could keep hold of his.

Bell pulled me in for another hug. "I love your heart."

"Love yours, too. And those crafty hands that make miracles happen."

She let out a little snort, releasing me. "Let's not get too carried away. I've got a big enough ego as it is."

Bell had zero ego, but she did have amazing skills when it came to furniture restoration. I just hoped the desk could be saved. And that Griffin wouldn't think I was overstepping. I laid a palm on the carved-up wood as if I could urge it to heal. Laughter coming from the direction of the store had me snapping out of my thoughts. "Come on, let's go make sure my sisters aren't destroying your store."

Bell grinned. "If anyone's causing destruction, it's Ford."

We made our way back into Second Chances to find Ford holding Mia upside down as she giggled like crazy. Ava simply looked on, shaking her head.

"Ford," Bell chastised. "You could drop her."

"What? Like this?" He made a move like he was going to let Mia go, and she shrieked with delight.

"I'm never having babies with you if you keep this up."

He flipped Mia right-side-up and set her on her feet. Crossing to Bell, he pulled her into his arms. "Come on, Trouble. We're gonna have dozens of kids. Fill that house of ours with them as soon as it's renovated."

A familiar burn filled me. The one that spoke of jealousy. I forced my eyes closed for the briefest moment before opening them again. Bell wrapped her arms around Ford's neck, planting a kiss on his lips. "If you want a dozen kids, you're going to have to birth at least ten of them."

Mia giggled. "Boys can't have babies, Bell."

Bell released Ford and turned to Mia. "Then I guess Ford's just going to have to settle for two."

"I want six," Mia shared.

"Heaven help us all," I muttered.

Ford patted me on the back. "Good luck with that one."

I couldn't even begin to wrap my head around Mia having her own babies one day. They were growing up too fast. It felt like just yesterday that I was holding Mia's little fingers as she mastered walking. I gave my head a shake. "Okay, kiddos. Who wants to go to the park?"

"Me!" Ava and Mia answered in unison.

"Let's get a move on. What do you say to Ford and Bell?"

"Thank you for the muffins," Ava answered quietly.

"Yeah, thanks. They were the best. Almost as good as pancakes," Mia added.

Ford chuckled. "Anytime."

Bell gave the girls hugs, and we headed out onto the sidewalk. Mia skipped a few steps ahead, twirling something between her fingers.

"Whatcha got there, Mi?" I asked.

"A bracelet. I made it last night. It's for Griffin. Want to see?"

I stopped in my tracks. Mia turned and offered me the woven string. A ripple of rainbow colors. One that looked just like the ones my family wore.

"Think he'll like it?" she asked hopefully.

I swallowed hard against the emotion gathering in the back of my throat. Was I making a terrible mistake getting these kids involved with Griffin? What if he decided to leave the island? Or that having high-energy little ones running around his property all the time was annoying? What if he started dating someone, and she didn't want us around? I shut every single thought down, one by one, shoving them forcefully from my mind. "I think he'll love it."

"It's really pretty," Ava offered.

Mia beamed. "I can't wait to give it to him."

I sent up a silent prayer that Griffin was down with donning rainbows and wouldn't crush Mia's spirit. Maybe he could at least come up with an excuse as to why he couldn't wear it but tell her he'd keep it nearby. Hopefully, she'd settle for that.

As I handed Mia back her bracelet, I caught movement out of the corner of my eye—a figure quickly rounding a corner across the street. She was older, gray now streaking her hair, but I would recognize that profile anywhere. My mother. She was here. And she was watching.

Chapter Twenty-Two

Griffin

I TOLD MYSELF TIME AND AGAIN THAT I WAS LOSING IT, that nothing was wrong. But I couldn't shake the feeling. Caelyn had been off when she picked up Will yesterday. On edge as if she were expecting someone to jump out of the bushes at any moment. I simply wanted to make sure she was okay. Have a conversation where little ears weren't listening in.

I pulled into a parking spot at the edge of the lot and climbed out of my truck. Heading for The General Store, my steps faltered as I took in the glaring woman coming towards me, a toddler in one arm and a bag of groceries in the other. She muttered something under her breath.

It took me a moment to recognize her as the person who'd been giving me the evil eye at the pizza place a couple of weeks ago. "I'm sorry, I didn't catch that."

She huffed and raised her chin. "I've tried to set Caelyn straight. To guide her way in what it means to be a parent. But she won't listen. Those children need someone at home with them. Someone who can be dedicated to their care. Instead, she's obsessed with growing this little sandwich shop. And now, she's wrapped up in *you*. A loner with a violent streak. Probably doesn't even care that she's ignoring the children in the process."

My hands fisted and flexed, the urge to set her straight strong. But I kept my voice even. "You must have a sad life that you have all this time to cast judgment on others. Maybe it's time you focus some of that attention inward."

I kept right on walking as she gasped in outrage. Normally, I would've let it get to me. I would've felt the pull to retreat to the farmhouse, the attention and judgment making my skin feel too tight for my body. But this woman was ridiculous. The fact that she saw Caelyn as less than was all I needed to know about the ugliness of her soul.

I wasn't going to let that infect me. If people chose to believe the lies that had been told about me over the years, so be it. I would just keep living my life.

I pulled open the door to the store and was relieved to see a secondary cashier at the front of the shop. The woman gave me a smile and a wave. "Let me know if you need help finding anything."

I nodded and made my way back towards Caelyn's station. She stood in the center of her little kitchen space, staring out the window towards the docks. She looked so incredibly lost in that moment. I had to fight the urge to round the counter and pull her into my arms. To promise her that everything would be okay. Instead, I slid onto one of the stools in front of her. "You ready to tell me what the hell is going on?"

Caelyn jumped and whirled. "Geez, make a little noise when you move, would you? You're like Kenna with her ninja training."

I wanted to laugh but I couldn't because I was too focused on the dark circles rimming Caelyn's eyes. "Something happened. Tell me." I couldn't help, couldn't protect her, if she didn't tell me what was going on. "Did you get another note?"

Caelyn shook her head. "No, nothing like that. I just—I'm ninety-seven percent sure I saw my mother yesterday."

I stiffened. "Where?"

"Outside Second Chances. I was walking out with the girls and I saw someone rounding the corner across the street."

"Did you call Parker?"

Caelyn leaned against the counter. "And tell him what? That I think I saw my mother, who I haven't set eyes on in over six years? Besides, there's nothing he can do. It's not like we have a restraining order or anything."

A powerlessness seemed to radiate through Caelyn's entire body. I hated everything about the set of her frame. It was the opposite of everything that had drawn me to Caelyn from the moment I saw her in this very store. Her vitality, fire, light. All of it seemed to have seeped out of her.

I stood and rounded the counter, pulling her into my arms. I held her tight against me as if I could infuse life back into her. "Everything's going to be okay."

"But what if it's not?" she mumbled into my chest. "We both know that things don't always work out."

My ribs constricted at her words. "But this will. I'm going to call Parker and let him know you saw her. It's all information he should have anyway." As much as I wanted to hold on, I forced myself to let Caelyn go. But first, I reached up and slid a hand under her hair, squeezing her neck. "You have people looking out for you."

A flicker of light entered Caelyn's eyes. "Do you happen to know how I suddenly have a much busier store than I used to? Mr. Walters decided to bring on another part-time employee. Crosby and Penny stop by approximately three times a day. Ford is always forgetting something that he needs to come and pick up. And don't even get me started on how often my friends are here."

I dropped my hold on her neck, shoving my hands into my pockets. "Would you believe that your personality is so charming that people can't stay away?"

Caelyn snorted. "Suuuuure."

My expression sobered. "We care about you. We just want to make sure there are plenty of people around, and that you feel safe."

She reached out a hand, giving my arm a squeeze. "Thank you."

Her warmth seemed to seep into me at the small contact, a heat that spread fast and fiercely. One that left me feeling cold in its absence. I wanted more, and that made me nervous as hell. "I should go."

Caelyn's shoulders straightened. "Of course. You're sure you're okay to pick up the tiny terrors again?"

That small little action put distance between us. Distance I didn't want but that was safer for both of us. "I love having them at the house. Really."

"I do feel better not having them walk to the store alone. Especially if my mom's around."

I couldn't imagine how a run-in like that would end. Ava and Mia likely wouldn't be able to place her, but Will would. It was much better to avoid the possibility altogether. "I think it's smart, too."

Caelyn nodded, rolling her lips together. "Okay. I'll head to your place as soon as I'm off work."

"No rush." I truly did love having all of the O'Connor siblings at the farmhouse. For the first time in over a decade, they made me believe that I would truly bring life back to the place.

A throat cleared behind me. "Sorry to interrupt."

Caelyn gave a small jolt. "Hey, Max. You're not interrupting at all. What do you need?"

The man gave her a smile that was just a bit too slick for my liking. Who was I kidding? I didn't want any guys anywhere sending hopeful smiles Caelyn's way. Max moved in closer to her. "Just need to know if the produce should be unloaded now or later this afternoon."

I scowled at the guy's back. Caelyn widened her eyes at me. "See you tonight?"

Her words swallowed my scowl right up. Because they made it seem like Caelyn was mine, and a part of me, one growing by the day, wanted her to be.

I eased down onto the grass and leaned against the trunk of the tree. It had taken me a long time to settle on this spot. It was a decision I hadn't been ready to make at sixteen. It wasn't until I'd returned to Anchor, to the farmhouse, that I knew their final resting spot had to be here. I'd mixed ash with dirt and buried a family photo in honor of the bodies I didn't have to put to rest, hoping that somehow my family's souls would feed the growth around me. That they would become a part of the trees and the grass and wildflowers that grew on the outskirts of the pond. The place that had been a favorite for all of us.

As the bark of the tree bit into my back, I could almost convince myself that they were still with me. "Sorry it's been a while."

I plucked up a long piece of grass, making a small tear down the center. I could see my dad trying to teach Beth and me how to whistle through it. Beth had picked it up right away, but I'd struggled, sounding more like I was suffocating than whistling. When I finally got it, she had tackled me to the ground, happier for me than she'd ever been for herself for picking up the trick.

There were millions of those kinds of memories. Ones I'd buried in my mind because so many of them had been stolen and displayed for all the world to see. But things were changing.

I was sharing the farmhouse with Caelyn, Will, Ava, and Mia. And I found myself wanting to show them Beth and my parents, too.

I already was, even if they didn't know it. The magic trick my dad had taught me. My mom's favorite bench. The pond my sister begged me to visit daily. Little by little, I was letting my family out of the tightly guarded box I kept them in. And I didn't feel as though I'd lost them by doing it. In fact, their presence felt even stronger.

"I've been bringing some people around." I twisted the blade of grass around my finger. "Mom, you would love Ava. The two of you would probably spend hours in your garden on that bench talking about your favorite books. Beth and Mia would be hell on wheels, giving us all daily heart attacks. And, Dad, Will is your kind of kid. He soaks up everything you teach him."

My voice hitched. "There was so much you had left to teach me, and I hate that I've had to learn it all on my own. I've made so many mistakes." Because despite the vile rumors printed about me, there were ugly truths, too. They were things the press wasn't interested in. How I'd shut out the world around me. How I'd lost myself at the bottom of a bottle for at least a year. How I'd forgotten everything my parents had taught me. To be of service, to help those less fortunate. I'd turned everything around me off and lost myself in a pit of my own grief.

"I'm waking up." I grinned down at the grass around my finger. "Mom always said we had to do things at our pace. But I'm sure Dad has been shaking his head, wanting me to hurry it up already."

I released my hold on the grass and let it flutter to the ground. "Caelyn's helping. I guess she always has. Ever since I saw her, and that smile socked me right in the gut. She has this way of changing how I see things. She always looks for the good. Even when things are really hard."

My family would've loved Caelyn, her siblings, having the farmhouse be full of laughter and chaos…life. I felt the familiar anger rise, the heat that filled me when I was reminded of something they were missing. Something they should be experiencing right alongside me.

I breathed through it, letting the late spring air soothe away the burn. "I love you guys. Miss you every day."

I pushed to my feet and headed for my truck. As I made my way to the school to pick up the kids, I realized the anger hadn't stayed the way it normally did. I didn't feel it eating away at my insides, infecting everything around me.

I pulled to the end of a long line of cars and caught sight of Mia dancing as she waited with Ava and Will. There was always music playing that only Mia could hear. And the way she didn't seem to care if anyone was watching… God, I hoped she never lost that.

As I moved my truck forward, Mia caught sight of me and began waving wildly. Will shook his head but did it while smiling. Ava was oblivious to it all, lost in the pages of the book on her lap.

When I came to a stop in the designated pickup zone, Mia ran towards the vehicle. Will caught her by the strap of her backpack and whispered something in her ear. She scowled at him but slowed her movements, allowing Will to open the door to the cab of my truck and help her in.

"Griffin! I have something for you."

"It's my lucky day then."

She scooted across the seat and started riffling through her backpack as Ava climbed in.

"Hey, Avs," I greeted.

"Hi, Griffin."

It wasn't a play-by-play of her day, but it was something. Ava and I were making slow and steady progress. She no longer hid behind a sibling when I was around, she even let me help her with homework after school on occasion.

"Here!" Mia held out something in my direction as Will hopped into the front seat.

"What's this?" I took the brightly colored item from her small fingers.

"That's your rainbow. So you're a part of our family, and you never have to leave."

My gaze snapped from the bracelet to Mia to Will. He had frozen in the passenger seat. Everything was simple in Mia's world, but that didn't mean that she didn't carry with her the knowledge that her parents had disappeared from her life. She might not have any memories of them, but she knew they were gone. Probably understood more than her siblings thought.

"Mi," Will began.

"I love it," I quickly cut in. "Can you put it on me?"

Mia beamed as a teacher scowled at us for holding up the line. I didn't give a damn. I'd hold everyone up for hours if it meant Mia felt safe and secure. Her small fingers tied the ends into a very thorough knot. "I made it giant-sized."

I chuckled. "Good thing." I held up my wrist. "What do you guys think?"

It was Ava's gaze that met mine in the rearview mirror. "It looks like you belong with us."

Something in my chest cracked at her words, the simple sincerity of them. And for the first time in a long time, I *did* feel like I belonged.

Chapter Twenty-Three

Caelyn

I LEANED BACK IN THE ROCKER, THE CURVED LEGS MAKING A soothing sound as I moved. I took a sip of my wine and closed my eyes for a moment. I could hear Ava and Mia in the living room bickering over who got to pick their game piece first, and the faint strains of Will's keyboard piano as he practiced in his bedroom. Those sounds were just as soothing as the wood rungs of my chair against the porch. We were home, safe, together.

I forced my eyes back open and tapped the screen of my phone. I hit Callie's name in my contacts and waited as the phone rang. It took a minute, and when Callie answered, she sounded out of breath. "Hey, Caelyn."

I grinned out at the darkening sky. "Lost your phone again?"

Callie let out a huff. "It runs away from me, I swear." I could picture her frantically patting all the papers on her desk in search of her phantom phone. Callie was a miracle worker in so many ways, but she was overworked, underpaid, and needed about four assistants. "So, what's up?"

My smile fell away. "I need to run something by you. Or see

if you can put some feelers out for me. Or maybe just get your advice—"

"Caelyn," Callie cut me off. "Just tell me what's going on."

Callie's phone might run away from her, but for me, it was my words—and always when I was flustered or anxious. I let out a long breath, trying to center myself and organize my thoughts. "I had a particularly nasty run-in with that Patti Jenkins woman I told you about." And after I'd seen her again today, it was clear she wasn't releasing that grudge.

"The one who's always so judgy?"

"That's the one. We got into it, and she threatened to call CPS. I just…I want to make sure we're okay. I mean, they're not going to try and take the kids because I told this woman she was an awful human, right?" As the words tumbled out of me, panic tightened my ribs, squeezing my lungs.

"Oh, sweetie. No. Take a deep breath."

I obeyed, picturing the breathing I took my people through in my yoga classes. Tears stung the corners of my eyes. "I hate that I'm scared all the time. Just waiting for some other shoe to drop."

"It's hard doing this alone. And you had to fight really hard to get custody in the first place. It's completely understandable that this horrible woman has you freaked. She hit you where you're most vulnerable."

I nodded as if Callie could see me. "What do I do?"

Papers shuffled in the background on Callie's end of the line. "Nothing. I'm going to call CPS and make them aware of the situation. As sad as it is, it's not unusual for someone to make a false report out of anger or revenge. They know how to spot those. And this Patti lady's intentions are going to come through loud and clear."

I twirled the wine glass between my fingers. "The sad thing is, I'm pretty sure she thinks she's right. That I am a horrible guardian and am ruining the kids' lives."

"You know that's not true, right?" Callie asked softly. I stayed silent. I knew I cared for my siblings more than anyone else ever would, but I also knew I fell short in all sorts of ways. There were so many days where I felt like I was barely holding it together. "Caelyn O'Connor, you listen to me, and you listen good. You are an amazing guardian to those kids. I wish I could clone you and give you to every child that has walked through the doors of the Alliance. Don't let a bitter, hateful woman get in your head."

A small laugh escaped me at the ferocity of Callie's tone. "Thanks, Cal. You're the best, you know that, right?"

"I am pretty damn awesome. Even if I don't know where my phone is half the time."

"You really are." I paused for a moment. "You'll let me know what CPS says?"

"Of course. I'll call my contact first thing tomorrow morning."

"I'm bringing you brownies," I offered immediately. Nothing could ever be enough to repay Callie and the Alliance for everything they'd done for us, but I could keep her stocked in baked goods.

"Cream cheese frosting?" she asked hopefully.

"You know it."

"Can't wait. I have to go. I have another call in a few minutes. But take a deep breath and try not to worry. Everything's going to be fine."

"I will. I've got wine, a clean kitchen, and kids who aren't currently trying to murder each other."

Callie chuckled. "Sounds like a winning combination to me."

It was. As Callie and I said goodbye, I stood, stretching and filling my lungs with air that held just a hint of salt. I pulled open the front door to hear Mia moan, "But I want to be the red one."

I put on my best serious face. "Rock, paper, scissors. And if we have a sore loser, that color disappears."

Mia's eyes flashed with heat, but she nodded. The girls duked it out, and Ava was the winner. Mia held her tongue as Avs picked the red piece. I slid down next to Mia and gave her a squeeze, whispering in her ear, "Proud of you."

She beamed up at me. "Proud enough for pancakes tomorrow?"

I couldn't hold in my laugh. "You know I think you should be a lawyer one day. You're too good at negotiations."

Mia opened her mouth to speak but a shattering sound pierced the air. Everything seemed to happen in slow motion and yet super speed all at the same time. I turned my attention to the source of the sound but before I could recognize it, shards of glass sprayed, and something sliced across my temple.

The force of the blow had flashes of light dotting my vision. Screams filled the air around me, but they sounded far away, as if traveling through water. Slowly, they became more pronounced as the world came back into focus.

"Get down!" I cried, covering Mia with my body and pulling Ava to my side so I could shield her, too. There was nothing but silence, and then the screech of tires. I straightened slowly.

Ava, wild-eyed and tear-filled, searched the room in a panic. "Cae Cae," she whispered.

"It's okay. We're going to be okay." Things were about as far from okay as they could get.

I carefully eased Mia up, drops of blood dripping down her face. My heart seized in my chest. But before I could get any words out, Will appeared in the hall. "What the hell?" His eyes widened as he took in the glass all around us.

The fear and anger on his face jarred me out of my panic. "Will, get Ava. Get to the girls' bedroom."

Will pulled Ava to her feet, wrapping an arm around her as he hurried her along. I lifted a sobbing Mia into my arms and ran towards the bedroom, but not before I caught sight of what looked like a brick on our living room floor. I forced the shudder down as I gripped Mia tighter.

As soon as we reached the bedroom, I pulled out my phone

and dialed 9-1-1. The dispatcher picked up on the second ring. "Sheriff's department. What's your emergency?"

"This is Caelyn O'Connor. Someone just threw a brick through my front window. My little sister is injured. And I don't know if anyone is still out there. Can you send someone?" The tremble in my voice gave away my fear.

"Are you somewhere safe now? Can you lock yourself in another room?"

"There's no lock," I began, but as I did so, Will slid the girls' dresser in front of the door. "We've got something that will keep people out."

"Good. Stay where you are. I have deputies on the way. Can you remain on the line?"

I sat on the bed, Mia still crying in my arms. "I'm going to give you to my brother. I need to assess my little sister's injuries."

"All right," the dispatcher agreed.

I handed the phone to Will. "Can you talk to her?" He nodded, and I turned my attention to Mia. "I gotta let you go so I can look at your face, Mi." She only clung harder to me. "It's okay. You're okay. I just need to check your cut." I took one of Mia's hands and hooked her fingers through the belt loop on my jeans. "Just hold onto me here. I'm not going anywhere."

Mia's fingers tightened on the loop, and I was able to extricate myself from her hold. I quickly took inventory of Mia's face. Her cheek had a series of small cuts, but nothing looked too serious. "Does it hurt anywhere other than your cheek?"

Mia shook her head, and I let out a breath. "Okay. Ava, can you hand me a tissue from your desk?"

Ava was by my side in a flash, the box in hand. "Here you go." She was quiet for a moment before asking in a small voice, "Is she going to be okay?"

I gave Ava a smile I hoped didn't read as false as it felt. "She's going to be just fine."

"What about you?" she asked, studying the side of my face.

I realized my temple was throbbing. My fingers prodded the area, and I winced. As I brought them back, I found them sticky with blood. "I'm going to be fine, too. We just need to get cleaned up." I turned my focus back to Mia, carefully studying the nicks in her perfect cheek, making sure there were no shards of glass left behind. They'd need to be cleaned with alcohol and dressed, but I didn't exactly have access to my first-aid kit at the moment.

When I was done wiping the blood away, I pressed a kiss to Mia's forehead. "Feel better?"

She didn't say anything, just clung to my belt loop as if it were a personal safety line. I wrapped an arm around her and squeezed.

"What about you, Cae Cae?" Ava asked. "Want me to clean your head?"

I plucked a tissue from the box. "I got it." I wiped at my temple, but it just seemed to keep bleeding.

"The deputies are here," Will called. "They're approaching the house."

"Tell them the front door is unlocked," I replied. And how stupid was that? I'd come in from lounging on the porch and hadn't even thought to lock the deadbolt. I might as well have welcomed the attackers in with open arms.

Footsteps sounded in the hallway. "Sheriff's department."

"We're in here," I called.

"Stay put for now. We're going to search the house and then we'll be back with an all-clear."

"Okay." My voice was steady, but the rest of me was anything but. As my gaze swept the room, all I could think was that these kids had already been through something far too similar, and how all of this had to bring back so many terrible memories. I'd promised them and myself that I'd keep them safe.

But I'd failed.

Chapter Twenty-four

Griffin

MY PHONE RANG JUST AS I TOOK A LONG PULL OF MY beer. The sound almost had me choking on my drink. No one called me. But I'd taken to carrying the device around with me because I'd given Caelyn and Will the number. I wanted them to be able to reach me whenever they needed.

Ford flashed across the screen, and my stomach sank. I hit accept. "Hey."

"You're gonna want to get over to Caelyn's place."

My muscles pulled so tight, I thought for sure one would snap. "What happened?"

"Someone threw a brick through the window. Mia got a few cuts. We're heading over there now, but I thought you'd want to know."

I didn't hear anything after "Mia" and "cuts." I stood, leaving my dinner out on the picnic table as I moved towards my truck. I started it up and headed for Caelyn's at a speed that would get me cited for reckless driving if any cop stopped me. I didn't care. The only thing I could think about was getting to Caelyn and the kids. Mia's face flashed in my mind. So little and trusting.

I pulled to a stop behind two sheriff's department vehicles. Leaving my keys in the truck, I hopped out. If someone needed to move my vehicle, they could take it. I ran towards the house, not saying a word. When I reached the entryway, I saw two officers picking through glass and debris. A brick lay a foot away from a board game.

They'd been sitting right there. Playing. And someone had sent that brick through their window.

"Where are they?" My voice had a feral quality to it.

One of the deputies rose, his hand going to his gun. "And you are?"

"It's okay," Kenna called from the kitchen. "He's a friend." She turned to me. "Go around back, everyone's in the yard. I'm just getting the kids some juice."

I was moving before she finished speaking, jogging down the porch steps and rounding the sunny yellow house. My eyes caught on Will first. A mixture of rage and fear overtook his expression. Ava was curled in Bell's arms, her head on Bell's shoulder. Then I landed on Mia and Caelyn. Caelyn was turned away from me slightly, talking to Parker.

But Mia saw me immediately. "Griffin," she wailed. "I want Griffin."

I don't think I'd ever moved so fast. In an instant, I was taking her from Caelyn's hold. "It's okay, Little Bit. You're safe." I said the words over and over, as much for myself as for her.

"Don't leave me," she whispered.

Her words cracked something deep in my chest. "I'm not going anywhere." But I wanted to. I wanted to run fast and far, and I hated myself for it. How had this happened? And so quickly? I cared about them all. Every last one of this O'Connor brood. And if any of them were truly hurt? Worse? I would lose the little ground I'd gained.

I'd kept myself removed for so long. Not letting even a single person break through the wall that protected me from the possibility of destruction. But that wasn't the case any longer. I was linked to this family, and I wasn't sure there was anything I could do to sever that tie—even if I'd wanted to.

My gaze locked with Caelyn's, and I saw the tears streaming down her cheeks. A rage like I'd never known before lit through my veins as I took in the side of her face. A long gash curved the side of her temple. I held out my empty arm, and Caelyn immediately walked into it. I held them as tightly as I could without hurting them.

I lost all track of time as we stood there. I breathed them in. They were hurt, but they were safe. I wasn't going to lose them.

Parker cleared his throat. "EMTs are here to check Caelyn out."

I reluctantly let her go, but Mia stayed curved around me like a monkey. "It's okay, Little Bit," I whispered in her ear, rubbing a hand up and down Mia's back.

"I really don't need EMTs. I just need some alcohol swabs and a Band-Aid," Caelyn protested.

"The EMTs are going to look at you. Mia, too." I tried to keep my voice even, but there was a bite to it that I couldn't disguise.

Caelyn sighed. "Fine."

Crosby pushed to his feet. "Now that Griffin's here, Ford and I are going to go get some plywood so that we can board up that window when the techs are done."

"Thanks, Crosby," Caelyn said.

He nodded. There was no mischievous grin or smartass comment tonight. Crosby looked like someone no one in their right mind would want to mess with. He met my gaze. "You got them?"

"I got them." Nothing else would happen to this family if I had anything to say about it.

As Crosby and Ford headed out, Kenna appeared with two juices in her hands. "You want some apple juice, Mi?"

She shook her head. "Want my giant."

Kenna gave us a watery smile. "Looks like you've got him."

Mia clung even tighter to me. I picked up rubbing her back again as the EMTs rounded the side of the house. Her little fingers curled into the neck of my shirt. "No! I don't want to go with them."

"I've got you, Little Bit. They're just going to check out Caelyn and then look at your cheek." Whoever had sent that brick through the window had better hope I didn't find out who they were.

"Caelyn, you okay?" an EMT in his mid-twenties asked.

"I'm fine, Nick. Just a little bump on the head."

"That is not just a bump on the head," I growled.

She rolled her eyes at me. If Caelyn was giving me grief, that meant she would be fine. I let out a slow breath and leaned against the picnic table, keeping Mia in my arms. I glanced at Parker as the two EMTs began assessing Caelyn's injuries. "What the hell happened?"

Will edged closer to our conversation as Parker started to speak. "We're not sure. Brick through the front window, but no one saw a person on foot or in a car. We've gone house to house on this block and haven't gotten a single witness."

I looked at Will. "What did you see?"

A muscle in his cheek ticked. "Not a damn thing. I was in my room playing piano and heard a crash. I thought someone might've dropped a dish or something. But then there was screaming." Will's face reddened as he did his best to hold back tears. "By the time I got out there, whoever threw the brick was long gone. We got the girls out of there and into the bedroom and waited for the deputies."

I squeezed Will's shoulder. "You did good. You kept them safe."

"I didn't," he said in a rough whisper. "Caelyn and Mia are hurt. They—"

"No," I cut him off. "You got them out of a dangerous situation. Got them somewhere safe while you waited for help. Did you know someone was going to throw a brick through that window?"

Will shook his head. "Of course, not."

"Then there's nothing else you could've done. Don't take on what some other asshole did."

"You said a bad word," Mia whispered sleepily.

I chuckled. "I guess I'll be on kitchen duty tomorrow."

"I'll help you," she offered.

"Thanks."

I heard Caelyn suck in a sharp breath, and my head jerked in her direction. Nick the EMT was probing the cut on her head. My jaw tightened as I pushed off the table and headed in their direction. "Careful. Can't you see she's hurting?"

He sent a scowl in my direction. "I'm doing my job."

"Well, do it a little more gently," I gritted out.

Parker dropped a hand on my shoulder. "Okay, okay. Let's all dial it back a notch."

Caelyn forced a smile. "I'm fine, really. A piece of flying glass must've nicked me."

Everything about her said otherwise. Her face was pinched in pain. Her skin even paler than her normal fair complexion. And there was something below the surface...fear. I bit back a dozen curses I wanted to let fly free. "I think we should take you to the hospital. Let a doctor check you out."

"No. I don't need a hospital. I don't even need the EMTs. I just need a Band-Aid and a couple of Tylenol. That's it."

I opened my mouth to argue, but Parker got there first. "What do you think, Nick? Hospital? Or is she okay without it?"

The EMT carefully taped a bandage into place on Caelyn's head. "There's no sign of a concussion. I think she'll be fine."

"You *think*?" I barked. Who was this idiot? Had he even gone through medic training?

Bell appeared at my side, an arm still wrapped around Ava. "My dad can check her out in the morning. I think, right now, everyone just needs some sleep. Ford and I can stay here tonight."

"They're going to stay with me until Parker figures out who's behind this." The words were out of my mouth before I could consider the wisdom of them. All I could think about was having Caelyn and the kids behind my fences and cameras and alarms.

"We are?" Caelyn asked, blinking rapidly.

"I've got an alarm system, cameras. And there are enough rooms finished upstairs now for you to all have your own. You'd just have to share two bathrooms."

Ava looked up at me. "We all share one bathroom here. Two will be even better."

"I don't know," Caelyn began. "I don't want us to invade your space and—"

"Please," Mia cut her off. "I want to stay with my giant. He'll protect us."

I felt a burning sensation deep in my chest—a mixture of pride and fear. I rubbed a hand up and down Mia's back. "I'll do everything I can to keep you safe."

Chapter Twenty-five

Caelyn

I SIGHED AS I SHUT THE DOOR. "I NEVER THOUGHT THEY'D
go down."

Griffin gave my shoulder a squeeze. "They've been
through a lot today. It's understandable."

I nodded woodenly. I wanted to lean into Griffin's touch.
To let the warmth of him swallow me whole. As if he sensed it,
Griffin pulled me into his arms and simply held me. My cheek
pressed against his chest, and the steady beat of his heart calmed
something inside me.

Griffin's chin rested on the top of my head. "You're safe here.
I promise."

"I know." I never felt safer than I did when I was with Griffin.
I wanted to battle against that feeling. To hold tight to my auton-
omy as protector of my family. But I was exhausted. And scared
out of my mind. If that brick had hit one of the girls in the head,
they could've been killed.

I shivered, and Griffin pulled me tighter against him. "What
is it?"

"It could've been so much worse. The girls could've been

badly injured. Killed. And their faces. God, Griffin. I promised them that they'd never have to go through what they did when they were younger. But here we were barricaded in a bedroom. Again. I broke my promise." Tears spilled over, tracking down my cheeks and onto Griffin's shirt. He only held me tighter.

"They're strong, Caelyn. They're going to get past this. Sure, they'll be scared for a few days, but kids are resilient. And they have *you*. You make them feel safe."

I sniffed into Griffin's shirt. "I'm not so sure about that. Mia wanted her giant."

Griffin chuckled, the sound reverberating in his chest. "I guess sometimes it comes in handy to be tall. She thinks I can scare all the bad guys away."

I released my hold on Griffin and forced myself to step back. "Thank you. For everything. I'll never be able to repay—"

He scowled at me. "Quit it. You don't owe me anything."

I bit my lip to keep from laughing at the sternness in his expression. "Okay. No owing. But I can still thank you."

"If you have to."

"I do." I reached out and patted Griffin's chest, the planes of muscle a physical manifestation of how steady and strong he was. "So, you're just going to have to figure out a way to endure it."

Griffin's lips twitched. "I'll endure it." His hand captured mine, and he gave me a gentle tug. "Come on. I need to show you a few things."

Instead of releasing me when I began to follow, Griffin linked his fingers with mine, weaving them together so we were one force moving through the house. I'd wanted the feeling for so long. The deep knowledge that someone had my back. A partner who would face all the trials that life brought alongside me. I tried to shake it off. Because Griffin was my friend, not my boyfriend or partner or lover. He was simply a man with the kindest of souls.

Griffin came to a stop outside his office. "How good is your memory?"

My brows drew together. "Like can I remember what year JFK was assassinated or can I remember where I left my car keys?"

He grinned. "How are you with passwords?"

"Pretty good, I guess." There was no need for me to admit that all of my passwords were variations of the same thing.

Griffin nodded slowly as if unsure I was telling the truth. "You've already got the alarm system down, but I need to give you a couple of others." He crossed to his desk, releasing my hand as he went. I was suddenly colder and felt so very alone.

Griffin tapped a few keys on the keyboard. "It's be7mo3da26. That will get you into the system."

"I don't need to use your computer. Everything I need is on my phone." I didn't even have a computer at home. Will had a secondhand laptop he used for school, but that was it.

"I want you to be able to bring up the cameras. Come here." Griffin motioned me over next to him. "Here's the app." With a few clicks, we were suddenly looking at various views of the property. "They're equipped for night vision so you can see whatever you need to at any time."

I watched in fascination as he clicked from camera to camera. Some of the images made sense. The front gate. Entry points to the house. A few of the workshop. But there were at least a dozen others. Views of the pond. The back fence. "This is a lot…"

Griffin stiffened in his chair, and I wanted to give myself a swift kick. I laid a hand on his shoulder. "I'm not judging. I'm just wondering why you have it all. Do that many people try and bother you?"

He exited out of the camera app, hitting a button so the computer screen went black. "Want something to drink?"

His avoidance of the question shouldn't have bothered me, but it did. I hated that this man knew everything about me, and yet there was still so much he held back. "Sure. Do you have any tea?"

A small smile ghosted Griffin's lips as he headed for the kitchen. "I always keep a box. I can't stand it. But my mom loved the stuff. It just seemed wrong not to have it in the kitchen."

It wasn't an answer to what I'd asked, but it was something. A piece of his story. "What was her favorite?"

"Peppermint."

I smiled as he moved to a cabinet and pulled out a box. Grabbing the kettle, I began filling it with water. "I make the kids peppermint tea every time they have an upset stomach. That or sassafras."

"Sassafras is a real thing? I thought that was something they only talked about in old Westerns."

I chuckled, turning the burner on and placing the kettle down. "Very real, and it's magic when it comes to nausea."

"Good to know." Griffin laid a tea bag next to the stove and pulled out a glass for himself, filling it with water. "I became pretty fixated on security after college. My shrink said it was because it was something within my control. Something I could do to keep myself safe."

I sucked in a breath and couldn't seem to let it out. As if any movement, even an exhale, would stop Griffin from speaking.

He turned the glass in nonsensical circles on the counter. "You know people sold information about me. Mostly lies. Some of them were beyond ridiculous. I didn't care so much about those. It was the truths that cut. In a matter of months, the little bit of sanity I'd built for myself crumbled."

Griffin swallowed, seeming to struggle to find the right words. "First the accountant found out my uncle was siphoning off money from my trust fund. Apparently, he thought he deserved to be paid for the trouble of taking care of me."

"What a dingleberry," I muttered.

Griffin's brows rose. "Dingleberry?"

"It's become a recent favorite word of mine for jerks of the worst variety."

His mouth curved in the barest hint of a smile. "Well, my uncle was that. But even after he went to prison, I was still hanging on. I met a girl. For the first time since my family died, I felt like I had a person, you know?"

I swallowed against the sudden dryness in my throat. I could see in my mind a younger Griffin, not even yet twenty-one, and all alone in the world. I knew how that felt. It was terrifying, and it made you desperate to grab hold of anything or anyone that made life feel a little more stable. "I know."

"I thought we were happy. Maybe we were for a time. But that reporter got to her. I still don't know how, exactly. Maybe it was money. Maybe he convinced her that she'd actually be helping me deal with what happened." Griffin's eyes met mine. "Jen always wanted me to talk about my family. But I wasn't ready. I know it hurt her. *I* hurt her."

He looked away, back to his untouched glass of water. "A month after my uncle was sentenced, I found that reporter in my apartment. Jen had given him the key. I found him going through a box of mementos. I still don't know if Jen knew about the box or if the reporter had just found it by luck. But I lost it. I'd never lost it like that. He snapped a photo of me, and I decked him. He hit his head on the corner of my nightstand. Was unconscious for three days. People said I was a monster."

"You're anything but a monster," I snapped.

Griffin's gaze came back to me, and he shrugged. "Maybe I have a little monster in me. I punched that guy who was an ass to you at the store."

I grinned at the memory. Kenna's ex-boyfriend had shown up at The General Store a couple of months ago and had made a scene. He'd been cruel, and when he turned that vicious streak on me, Griffin had laid him out with a single punch. "Am I supposed to be offended by that?"

"It could've ended badly. I could've really injured him. But the look in your eyes… I couldn't let him hurt you anymore."

My breath caught in my lungs. It turned out Griffin paid attention far better than I'd thought. He could read every expression that crossed my face before I had the chance to hide it. "Maybe it makes me a little bit of a monster that I'm glad you hit him."

Griffin took a step closer. "I guess we'll just have to be a little monstrous together."

My heart rattled against my ribs as he moved in even closer. His eyes locked with mine, freezing me to the spot, burning a hole inside me. And just as he leaned in, the kettle let out a shrill whistle. I jumped a good foot into the air and scrambled to take it off the heat.

"Sorry," I mumbled. "I'll just fill this cup and take it up to bed. Thank you for the tea. And the cameras. And—and—" Griffin caught my elbow, forcing my gaze to his. "And for making us safe."

He leaned forward and pressed his lips to my forehead. "Sleep well." And with that, he was gone. The kitchen was empty, and I was alone. But my forehead burned where his lips had been, and I didn't think I'd sleep a wink.

Chapter Twenty-Six

Griffin

I STARED UP AT MY CEILING AS IF IT COULD SOMEHOW magically send me off into unconsciousness. But my ceiling had never been very good at that. Instead, I was hyperaware of every noise in the house. Every settling creak or gust of wind against the windows.

An hour or two ago, I'd heard the faint sound of light footsteps. I'd climbed out of bed to see Ava and Mia opening the door to Caelyn's room. "Can we sleep with you, Cae Cae?" Ava had asked shyly. Caelyn had, of course, welcomed them in.

Maybe I'd been wrong, and it would take a lot longer for the girls to recover from their ordeal. They'd refused to take separate bedrooms, and now they were sleeping with Caelyn. My hands fisted in my sheets as Mia's tear-streaked face flashed in my mind. The gash on Caelyn's head. The way Ava's hand trembled as she took mine when we walked down the street to my truck. The only one who seemed to be holding it together was Will. But I had a feeling he was simply locking things away. I'd taken that route before. And it never ended well.

I threw the covers back, swinging my legs over the side of

the bed and heading for the door. Lying around wasn't going to change a damn thing. I needed to move. If I stayed still in this state, my skin began to itch.

As silently as possible, I made my way downstairs and towards my office. I brought the computer to life, scanning through the different camera angles. All was quiet. I swore I could still smell a hint of Caelyn's shampoo in the air. Something floral that I couldn't identify. That smell brought it all back. How she'd felt in my arms. The silk of her skin beneath my lips.

I gave myself a good shake. It wasn't the time. Caelyn had been through too much. I needed to be a friend and support for her, nothing else.

I straightened from my spot at the computer and headed for the far bookcase. The whole back wall was covered in shelves, but one was a little different—a project that my father had installed in the house. He was by no means paranoid, but he *was* cautious. He knew people wished my family harm. Or who would've loved to kidnap one of us for ransom. So, he did everything he could to keep his family safe.

I gave the side of the shelf a little tug. It swung out. I slipped inside the small room that led to another door. Next to it was a keypad. I punched in a six-digit code and heard the lock turn. Pulling the second door open, a light automatically flickered on. The bulbs that illuminated the staircase gave off low, ambient light. Just enough to see where you were going, but not enough that it would expose its location to someone in the office if the lights were off.

I made my way down the stairs to the small basement. There were a few cots, some camp chairs, and a wall of emergency supplies. Most of the food needed to be disposed of when I came back, but I'd replaced some of it. I had a decent stash of snacks and water. And there was a secondary landline that allowed for calls out if someone ever did break in.

It had been months since I'd been down here. But everything was still in its place. And there was plenty of room for all the current residents of the farmhouse. In a few days or a week, when the kids had settled, I'd show them the safe room. Teach them to memorize the code. Show them how to use the phone.

Just having the plan helped somehow. It was another tool in my arsenal to keep them all safe. I shut off the light and climbed back up, emerging into my office.

I settled behind the computer, opening an internet browser this time. I hated when people searched for things about my life on the internet. It wasn't that I wanted to be asked about it either, but there was something about the anonymous action that felt like a violation. Yet that was exactly what I was about to do to Caelyn.

There were things I needed to know so I could be prepared for all the possibilities she might be facing, though. Details I didn't want to force her to go through again. So, I typed in her father's name: *Sean O'Connor.* A laundry list of hits appeared on my screen.

Some results had nothing to do with Anchor and Caelyn. But far more did. I clicked on an article from a Seattle newspaper. The trials had taken place there. The cases a little too big-time for our small chain of islands.

I skimmed the words. The reporter seemed to have been covering the case from beginning to end. More people were involved than I'd originally thought. More than a dozen arrests and eight convictions. Most of the sentences were in the five to ten-year range. People who had been involved in the drug trafficking ring that Sean was embedded in.

It sounded as if there were more than a few that the prosecutor hadn't had enough evidence to convict. I couldn't help but wonder what had happened to those people and to the network of cookers and distributors. They hadn't just disappeared. Maybe they'd simply gotten better at hiding their movements.

My mind couldn't help but jump to the possibility that it was one of those people making trouble for Caelyn. But it didn't make sense. If they really blamed Caelyn and her siblings for their testimony, wouldn't they have started the harassment sooner?

My gaze caught on a photo in the article. The woman in it looked more than just a little worse for wear. Her face seemed to sag with the weight of her actions. Chrissy O'Connor. Did she have enough hate and bitterness in her to throw a brick through her children's window?

It was so far from anything I could imagine. I knew people did horrible things. Hell, I'd experienced more than my fair share of it. But I couldn't wrap my head around a mother being so vicious. Maybe it was because my own had been so caring. My chest burned at the thought. With the question that always haunted me. *Why them?* My parents and sister weren't perfect, but they were good, kind, generous people. Why did we lose them when this endless list of cruel and violent criminals went on to live long and happy lives?

I clicked out of the browser. It had been a mistake to go down that rabbit hole. I didn't need the darkness of the thoughts swirling around in my mind right now. Because I'd been swallowed by that darkness before. And it had taken me years to get out.

I stood, locking the computer screen. I was still itchy, needing something, *anything* to do. Normally, I'd work on the farmhouse. Letting the physical exertion work out all the tension and anxiety. But now I had a full house of people who would wake if I did that.

I glanced at the clock. It was a little after six. The kids got up around six-thirty. Breakfast. They'd need breakfast. And that would give me something to do with my hands. An activity to beat back the monsters pounding on my door.

I strode to the kitchen, coming to a stop in the middle of the space. I didn't have the first idea of where to even start.

Ingredients. I went to the pantry, pulling out a loaf of bread. Toast was easy. I could handle toast.

I set it on the counter and went to the fridge, surveying the contents. Most of it was packaged meals Caelyn had left. But there wasn't enough for all of us. I did have a carton of eggs and some cheese.

My dad had been the master of cheesy eggs. Every Saturday morning, he'd be in charge of the kitchen. He'd turn up the oldies station and sing off-key as he cooked, Beth and I sitting on the counter and watching him work.

I had the sudden and burning urge to make those cheesy eggs for Caelyn and the kids. To grab my portable speaker and find some oldies to play. But I'd draw the line at singing. That was taking it a step too far.

Pulling out the eggs and cheese, I shut the door with my foot. I moved from cabinet to cabinet, grabbing everything I could possibly need. Pan. Cheese grater. Salt and pepper. Bowl. I pictured my dad, the steps he took every Saturday morning. But the image, the details of it, were fuzzy. I could see his face clear as day, but his hands were out of focus.

I muttered a few choice curses under my breath. Curses for losing yet another piece of him. And it was my own damn fault. Because I hadn't kept their memory alive. Instead, I'd stuffed it down for far too long. Because every time I thought of them, I'd been flooded with the pain of them being taken from me. So, I'd turned it all off. The good and the bad. And I'd learned too late that losing the good was far worse than remembering the bad.

I cracked an egg on the side of the bowl with a little too much force. Pieces of shell went flying into the bowl. "Dammit." I reached for a towel and ended up sending the whole thing crashing into the sink.

"What's going on?"

I spun at the sound of Caelyn's voice, my hands covered in

eggshell and goo. "I, uh. Hell. I was trying to make cheesy eggs, but apparently, I'm not cut out for the job."

Her lips quirked up. "Cheesy eggs, huh?"

"My dad used to make them. Every Saturday. I just thought it might be nice to make them for you guys."

Caelyn's expression softened. "I love that you had that. I bet I would've liked your dad. I happen to be a big fan of cheesy eggs."

I could see it. Caelyn in the kitchen cooking with my dad. She and my mom giving him a hard time. She would've fit right in. I cleared my throat. "He would've loved you."

She crossed to the sink, picking up the bowl and rinsing it out. "Then the least I can do is make some cheesy eggs in his honor."

And that's what we did. Caelyn walked me through her process and as she did, that picture of my dad became a little clearer. The image of his hands less blurry. Caelyn was a miracle, giving me back my family without even knowing it.

Caelyn

"**Y**OU'RE SURE YOU FEEL UP TO IT?" I SURVEYED AVA'S and Mia's faces. I had already called Mr. Walters and asked for the day off because I assumed the girls would want to stay home from school. To rest, recover. I should've known better.

Mia nodded as she ate her last spoonful of cheesy eggs. "If I don't go to school, then I can't go to gymnastics with Katie. I don't want to miss it."

Ava stood, taking her plate to the sink. "I have a book report I need to turn in."

Will eyed me from across the table. "I'll stay home."

I crossed my eyes at him. "Sorry, pal. You're stuck in boring old history today."

He shrugged. "It was worth a try."

Griffin chuckled as he stood and picked up Mia's plate. "I would've tried, too. I hated history. Always got the dates for stuff mixed up."

My eyes caught on something as he grabbed Mia's silverware. Colorful string woven in a rainbow pattern. I tried to swallow the lump of emotion. It was no use. Tears pricked the corners of my eyes.

"Oh, boy. What now?" Will asked as he looked at me incredulously. "How in the world can you be getting teary about history class?"

Griffin was in front of me in a flash. "What is it? What's wrong? Does your head hurt?"

"No. No. I'm fine." I quickly wiped at my eyes, giving him a watery smile. "You're wearing Mia's bracelet."

He glanced down at the string on his wrist. "Is that a good thing or a bad thing?"

"Good. It's good," I croaked.

"It's the best," Mia said, hopping off her chair.

Griffin gave me a wary look. "I can never tell with your tears. They're really disconcerting."

I burst out laughing, and Will shook his head. "I keep telling her she needs to get plugs."

I pointed my fork at Will and then Griffin. "You're both on my you-know-what list. I can't help when they surface." I took pity on the slightly fearful expression still on Griffin's face. "Most of the time, they're happy tears."

"Mm-hmm," he muttered.

I pushed back from the table, shaking my head. "Who knew the thing that would stop men dead in their tracks, scare them worse than anything else, was just a few tears."

Griffin chuckled. "You know how to get me."

We moved through our morning routine with ease. As if we'd all been cleaning up and getting ready for our days together for years. It shouldn't have been a surprise. Everything with Griffin always just seemed to fit. And the kids flourished under his attention. But I couldn't help but wonder what would happen when we had to leave.

I dropped off the last of my brood, making sure they knew

they could call anytime if they were worried or scared or overwhelmed. Then I simply sat in the elementary school parking lot. Mr. Walters had already asked Max and Molly to cover for me at the store. I had the day totally and completely free. When was the last time that had happened? I honestly couldn't remember. And I didn't have the faintest idea how to spend it.

The last thing I wanted was to make a nuisance of myself at the farmhouse. Griffin had already opened his home to us when he was used to solitude. I texted Parker.

Me: *Any updates?*

It had barely been twelve hours, but I kept hoping for a miracle. That they'd found the perpetrator and they were in jail. That it was a band of kids who had gotten out of hand, but after a scare, they'd learned the error of their ways. *Something.*

Parker: *Nothing yet, but we're working on it. It's going to take a while to process all the evidence. You holding up okay?*

My shoulders slumped. Time was the thing working against us the most. Because the longer this took, the more opportunities this invisible person had. I shivered, feeling suddenly very exposed in this half-empty school parking lot.

Me: *I'm fine. Thanks for everything you're doing.*

I looked like I'd been in a car accident, and my head felt like there was a marching band playing inside, but I wasn't going to share that.

Parker: *I'll update you as soon as we have anything.*

But I didn't want to wait around for evidence processing or trying to track down every neighbor in a four-block radius. I had some questions that I needed to have answered for myself. I started my SUV's engine and headed for the ferry.

Normally, ferry rides from island to island were relaxing. I'd get out of my vehicle and go sit on the top deck, taking in all the beauty around me. This time, I stayed put. I let my vision go fuzzy on the line of cars in front of me. I played the arguments back and forth in my mind. But I kept settling on one thing. I had to see her.

Parker could ask my mother a million questions, but I had a better shot of knowing if she was telling the truth. And maybe, just maybe, she'd be honest with me. If she'd been the one to throw that brick, if she were truly that angry, I didn't think she'd be able to hide that kind of rage—not if we came face-to-face.

I was tired of hiding. Of feeling scared. And no one, especially my mother, was going to hurt my siblings. They'd been through enough. This new game, it had to stop. Now.

In a blink, we were docking at Shelter Island. My hands tightened on my steering wheel as I waited for my turn to disembark. By the time I was driving down the ferry ramp, my palms were damp, and my stomach seemed to have twisted itself into an intricate knot.

I didn't need a map to find my way to the trailer park. My parents used to take us there as kids when friends of theirs had barbeques. I tried to see those memories through a new lens. Had they been using already? Dealing? I still couldn't picture it. All I could remember was being told to leave the grown-ups alone and not get into trouble.

I drove through town. Past the quaint business district, through the picturesque neighborhoods where houses boasted freshly potted flowers and pristine lawns. Soon, the landscape became slightly more rural and finally, I caught sight of a shabby sign marking the turnoff.

I pulled into the park. The trailers were close together, the yards, if you could call them that, small. Some looked nice as if the owners took pride in their surroundings. I respected the hell out of the owners of those trailers. I knew what it was to make the best out of what you had. How hard it was to stretch that dollar. Putting in back-breaking work on your home after working a long day.

But most of the trailers looked as if they had given up. Or at least the people inside them had. I stopped in front of the manager's office. As I climbed out of my SUV, a skull-splitting mixture of music assaulted me. Today, it sounded like a country fan was going head-to-head with a hard-rock groupie, trying to see who could get their stereo louder.

I pulled open the screen door. Holes dotted the mesh, and the paint was peeling in places. A woman sat behind a counter. No, she reclined. Her desk chair leaned so far back, it looked as if she were seconds away from toppling backwards.

I opened my mouth to speak, but she held up a finger for me to wait, her attention zeroed in on a small television sitting on the corner of the counter. The focus of the show was soft, and two people were locked in a passionate embrace. Just as the man deepened the kiss, another entered the room. "How could you?" Then the screen snapped to a commercial.

"Hot damn. I knew it was coming, but I still can't wait to find out what happens." The woman who looked to be in her forties turned her attention to me. "Sorry about that, darlin'. I'm hooked on that show somethin' fierce."

I couldn't help but return the woman's smile. Maybe I needed to pick up a daytime tv habit. "I'm looking for Chrissy O'Connor's trailer. Can you tell me which one it is?"

The woman's expression turned wary. "You police? The police have been bothering that poor woman like crazy. I don't get no trouble from her. The rest of these hooligans? Nothing but headaches. But Chrissy, she gives me no trouble."

"I'm her daughter." I hated even saying the words. She'd lost the right to be my mother a long time ago. But I'd say whatever it took to get this over with.

The manager's eyes widened. "I didn't even know she had kids."

"She doesn't."

"But you just said—" She waved a hand. "Oh, forget it, I got enough drama with my shows. She's in number twelve. Far back corner."

"Thank you." I left the woman to her show and hopped back into my SUV. As I wove through the park, my stomach knotted tighter and tighter. I tried my best to lock every emotion down, to hide any expression from my face. Because as long as it had been, I didn't want to give my mother the satisfaction of knowing how much she'd hurt me.

I slowed as the numbers approached twelve. I came to a stop outside a trailer that was somewhere in between the two extremes. There were no potted flowers or cute lawn furniture. But there was no trash in the yard or peeling paint either.

I shut off my engine and took a deep breath. Climbing out of my vehicle, I beeped my locks and gripped my keys so tightly the metal bit into my palm. I climbed the three steps to the home and knocked.

I didn't hear anything at first. But then again with the warring music lovers on the other side of the park, I wouldn't have. Just as I was about to knock again, the door opened.

I sucked in a sharp breath at the sight of the woman in front of me. The only word swirling around in my mind was *haggard*. She looked so incredibly beaten down. I fought back the sympathy that was taking flight in my belly. I reminded myself of that terrified phone call I'd received so many years ago. I reminded myself of the brick. The cuts on Mia's face. Everything in me hardened.

"Mom."

She blinked rapidly at me. "Caelyn. What are you doing here?"

No, "*Oh my gosh, it's so good to see you, baby girl.*" No begging for forgiveness. Just wondering why the hell I was here and bothering her.

"I need to talk to you."

She glanced around the trailer park as if looking for someone. Was it her dealer? Someone she didn't want me to know she was associating with? "All right." She stepped back into the small space. "Do you want something to drink?"

My gaze jumped around the living space and kitchenette. Everything was surprisingly clean and tidy. "No, I'm fine."

My mom eased into a recliner that looked like it had seen better days. "What happened to your head?"

I ignored her question. "Were you on Anchor last week?"

She stiffened, the slight rocking of her recliner stilling. She licked her lips. "I needed to see you guys. I wasn't going to talk to you. I just had to see with my own eyes how you were."

"You needed to see us?" I parroted. I couldn't seem to say anything else.

"Mia's so big." Tears filled my mother's eyes. "And Ava. She's almost a young lady now."

"She's still a child," I bit back. "And seeing you would confuse her. And cause her a tremendous amount of pain."

Color leached from Mom's face. "I know. That's why I didn't try and talk to you. I just needed to see."

"You haven't earned the right to see anything."

"I know I haven't. But I always was selfish."

The admission startled me into silence for a moment. I simply stared at the woman in front of me, trying to read beneath the surface, to ferret out the truth. "Did you leave a note on my car?"

Her eyes widened. "No. I swear. The cops came asking about it, and I told them the same thing."

"Did you throw a brick through my window last night?"

Mom straightened in her chair. "No, I did not. What the hell is going on? Someone threw a brick through your car window?"

If she was lying, she was one hell of an actress. I shook my head. "Through the window of our house."

My mom lurched to her feet and grabbed my hand. "You need to be careful. The people your dad was mixed up with…

They're bad news. Worse than a lot of folks know. And a bunch of them are already out. Got out before I did."

I jerked my hand out of her grasp. I didn't want anything to do with her touch. Her worry, whether it was an act or real. "What are you talking about?"

She began looking around furtively as if someone might jump out at any moment. My back teeth ground together. "Are you high?"

"What? No." Her face hardened. "I got sober in prison. Six years."

I tried to see the truth in her. Or confirmation of a lie. But I couldn't tell. I didn't know this woman anymore. She might as well have been a stranger on the street. "Do you know where Dad is?"

Her eyes shifted, staring at something over my shoulder. "No."

That was a lie. Every muscle in me hardened, including my heart. "If you care about your family at all, you'll tell Parker where he is. Let the FBI bring him in. Maybe if he's put in jail, we can finally put this nightmare to rest. Will and Ava won't worry that he'll just show up out of the blue one day."

"He's my husband," she whispered.

"He's a drug dealer who brought violent people into your children's home."

Ragged pain seemed to pour from her eyes, but she didn't falter for a moment. Didn't even consider altering her stance. "You can't change who you love."

"Then you're more of an idiot than I thought." I spun on my heel, heading for the door.

"Wait, Caelyn. Please. You need to be careful. You don't understand."

I tried to tune her out as I jogged down the steps and to my SUV. But nothing would silence the knowledge that my mother would always choose her husband over anyone else. Even if he was risking the lives of her own children.

Chapter Twenty-Eight

Griffin

I HUNG UP MY PHONE FOR THE FOURTH TIME. STILL NO answer. I was now full-on pacing in front of my truck. I'd come by The General Store to check on Caelyn, just to make sure she was hanging in there and not worrying about the kids or someone doing anything while she was at work. But Caelyn wasn't there. A woman I'd only seen a handful of times was working at the kitchen station. She told me that Caelyn had taken the day off. Where the hell was she? She'd dropped the kids off at 8:15 a.m. and now it was almost lunchtime.

I strode towards the water, scanning the shoreline. There were undoubtedly people out and about, tourist season picking up. But I didn't see Caelyn anywhere.

I tapped Parker's contact in my phone. After two rings, he answered. "Raines."

"Hey, it's Griffin. Have you heard from Caelyn today?"

"She texted me this morning to check and see if we'd made any progress. Why?"

I muttered a curse. "And let me guess, you didn't have anything for her."

"Not yet. What's going on? Is Caelyn okay?"

My gut twisted at the question. She'd better be okay. "She just isn't answering her phone, but I'm pretty sure I know where she is."

Someone had endangered Caelyn's family. The children she would do absolutely anything to protect. So she would go to the person who just might be the source. I started back to my truck. "I've gotta go, but I'll let you know if I don't find her."

"How about you let me know either way?"

"Will do." I hit end on my screen as I hopped into my truck. I made my way to the ferry just as they were loading. I beat out a rhythm on my wheel as if that would make the boat go faster. When that failed, I tried Caelyn again. Still nothing.

A million different scenarios played in my mind. Each one was worse than the one before. We had no idea who Caelyn's mom was mixed up with these days. She could've gotten out of prison and gone right back to the crew she'd left behind. Yet I would've bet my last dollar that was exactly where Caelyn had gone.

Cars began slowly unloading when we reached Shelter Island, and I pulled up the trailer park's location on my phone. She'd mentioned that her mom was staying there but I didn't have a lot or a trailer number. Hopefully, I could just drive around until I saw Caelyn's SUV.

But as I pulled down the ramp, I caught sight of the vehicle Caelyn lovingly called *Big Bertha*. For the first time in the past hour, I took a full breath. She was safe. But as I caught sight of her expression as I passed, I knew she was the furthest thing from all right. I did a quick U-turn and got in line with the vehicles heading back to Anchor.

Each second that passed, I gripped the wheel harder. As soon as I was parked in my spot on the ferry, I shut off my engine and jumped out of my truck. I was tall enough to have a decent vantage point to survey the cars. After a minute, I saw the SUV in a front corner. I strode quickly through the maze but Caelyn's vehicle was empty.

My jaw worked as I tried to guess where she'd gone. Somewhere outside but not too crowded. I stepped around gatherings of tourists and moved to the rear of the ferry. Caelyn's hair blew behind her in long, glossy waves. My pace picked up without me even thinking about it, and as I clasped her shoulder, she whirled around, fists clenched. "Griffin." She let out a whoosh of air with the word. "What are you doing here?"

"You weren't answering your phone." As if that should explain it all.

Her brow furrowed. "But how did you know where I was?"

"When I realized you weren't at the store, it didn't take a genius to figure out where you must have gone. Why the hell weren't you answering your cell?" Frustration that sounded a little too much like anger slipped into my tone.

Caelyn's expression hardened. "I didn't hear it, okay?"

"You shouldn't have been going to see your mom by yourself. Do you have any idea how dangerous that could've been? You have no idea who she's running with these days." Those same images, the what-ifs, filled my mind, and my temper spiked higher. "You could've been hurt. Killed. Then what would Will, Ava, and Mia do?"

Caelyn's eyes went glacial. "I know better than you ever will the responsibility that's on my shoulders. I'd do anything for them."

I blew out a harsh breath, trying to rein in my anger. "I'm sorry. I know. I was just—I was worried."

The fight seemed to go out of Caelyn in a flash, and tears filled her eyes. "No, I'm sorry. I needed to see her. Needed to know if it was our mom that was doing all of this."

I pulled Caelyn into my arms, holding her close, as if that

would reassure that she was safe, whole, no longer in danger. "Did you see her?" She nodded against my chest. "Was it her?"

"Yes, and I honestly don't know. I don't think so." Caelyn began crying even harder. "But she doesn't care. It's all about my dad. That's the only person she's ever really loved. But it's not even love. It's this sick addiction. She knows where he is."

I tensed. "Is he here? On one of the islands?" There were dozens in our small chain. A couple of larger ones like Shelter, some mid-sized ones like Anchor, and even more smaller ones. Lots were even privately owned. If Sean O'Connor wanted to disappear here—and he had help—it wouldn't be hard.

"I have no idea. She wouldn't tell me anything. Even knowing that someone's threatening her children, she *still* wouldn't tell me anything."

And there was the reason for the tears. I couldn't fathom the pain that carved into a person. To have a parent betray you like that. I pressed my lips to the top of Caelyn's head. "She doesn't deserve you. Never did."

Caelyn's hands fisted in my t-shirt. "She said she's sober. Has been for six years. I thought if that ever happened, she'd care. That if you took away the booze and the pills, maybe she'd be like she should've been all along. But she doesn't care, Griffin. She never did. What is it about me that's so unlovable?"

My arms spasmed at her words, flinching and tightening around her. "There isn't a damn thing about you that's unlovable, Caelyn. She's the one who's broken. And you can't take on someone else's brokenness. That's theirs to carry."

"I feel like no matter what I do, no matter how often I tell myself it's not worth it or how much evidence I stack in front of myself, I still want her love. And I hate myself for it."

I rubbed a hand up and down Caelyn's back, my fingers dancing over the ridges in her spine. "It'll probably always be there, the pain of losing what you always wanted but never had. But the hurt of it, the longing, it'll lessen. The fuller your life, the less you'll notice she's not in it."

Caelyn tipped her head back so that her chin was resting on my sternum. "How'd you get so wise?"

I smiled. "You get a lot of thinking time when you work on a house alone." Her lips were a breath away from mine. I wanted to kiss her so badly it was a physical ache. I wanted to lose myself in her mouth and steal all her pain.

"We've been keeping you from that alone time."

"Worth it." The only problem was, I never wanted them to leave.

Chapter Twenty-Nine

Caelyn

I TIPPED MY FACE UP TO THE SUN, LETTING ITS WARMTH SEEP into me.

"Whatcha doin', Cae Cae?" Mia asked, coming to a stop next to me.

"I'm soaking up all the warm and happies." Because after yesterday, I needed all of that I could get. I still felt like I had a bit of a crying hangover, and Griffin had been treating me like spun glass. But mostly, I was better. I'd just needed to let it out. All that toxic stuff I held inside and so rarely let anyone see. But after airing it, releasing it, I felt so much lighter.

She giggled. "I thought we were supposed to be helping Griffin."

I opened my eyes and looked down at Mia. "You're right." I held out a hand, and she took it. "Let's get rid of some ugly bushes."

Her face scrunched up. "They are pretty ugly."

Some sort of invasive shrubbery had made a home at the back of Griffin's property, in between the garden and the pond. And our Saturday project was to get as much of it as we could out of there. A dumpster had been delivered and sat beside the workshop, ready to be filled.

This morning before most of us had woken up, Griffin had gone to the hardware store and picked up gloves for me, Ava, and Mia. Mine had daisies, Ava's were green, and much to Mia's delight, hers were pink. It was just the thing we all needed. A sense of purpose, some good, old-fashioned hard work, and being together.

"The slowpokes are finally here," Will called as we approached.

"We were soaking up the happies," Mia defended.

Griffin's lips quirked. "And how do you do that?"

Mia flung her arms wide, tipping her face up to the sun. "Like this."

He chuckled. "Looks good to me. You got enough happies to help me clear some brush?"

Mia nodded seriously and held up her gloved hands. "I'm ready."

"Okay. You and Ava are going to be picking up all the sticks and things that have fallen to the ground. You'll put them in the bins over there, and when they fill up, we'll empty them into the dumpster. Think you can handle it?"

"Easy-peasy," she answered.

Griffin turned to Ava. "What about you?"

She smiled. "I'll make sure Mia doesn't try to run away and go swimming."

I groaned. Mia had been begging us to go swimming in the pond now that the days were warmer, and I was constantly terrified she was going to take off on her own.

"I wasn't gonna," Mia said indignantly. "You're such a tattletale."

"I'm not tattling, I'm just promising to keep you out of trouble," Ava argued.

I groaned. It was going to be a long day if we were at this point already at nine o'clock in the morning. "Girls… How about this? If we get all of the brush cleaned out and you two don't bicker, we'll go to the pond this afternoon."

Mia's face lit up, and she began dancing around in circles. "We're going swimming!"

"Only if it's a good day," I warned.

Her dancing slowed, and she got very serious. "Best behavior. I'll pick up every single stick."

Will snorted. "Who knew all it took was the promise of a pond to reel her in?"

The girls ran off to begin their tasks, and I turned to Griffin and Will, holding up my daisy-gloved hands. "Reporting for duty."

"It was either daisies or boring tan-colored ones. The daisies seemed more fitting. They're sunny," Griffin said, his gaze locking with mine.

Something about his expression had my belly warming, and everything inside me going just a little bit squishy. "I like the daisies."

Will cleared his throat. "Can we please get to work?"

I coughed, and Griffin turned away, rubbing his neck. "All right. I'm going to use a pickax to get at the roots of these suckers. Then you two can pull them out and toss them into the dumpster. Just let me know if it gets to be too much or you need a break."

I followed Griffin over to the first patch of brush. "You forget. I'm used to being on my feet and cooking all day. And I do yoga. I can handle this."

Griffin arched a brow. "Yoga isn't exactly manual labor."

"It's harder than you think," I argued. He scoffed, and I knew I was going to make him pay for that sound. "If it's so easy, then you don't mind logging a session with me one of these mornings?"

Griffin swung the pickax into the dirt, striking at the heart of the bush's root system. "I can handle some yoga."

Will groaned as he and I pulled at the brush that had come loose. "You are going to regret that those words ever passed your lips."

I grinned at Will as we dragged the shrub over to the dumpster. He knew me too well. There was nothing I loved more than proving how difficult yoga could be. When I used to teach a regular Saturday class, it was always the highlight of my month when one of the women brought in her doubting husband, and he was sweating and cursing before the class was over.

We worked for another hour or so before Griffin had apparently worked up enough of a sweat to peel off his t-shirt. I swallowed hard as I took in his broad shoulders and lean muscles. Will knocked into me. "You've got a little drool there."

I gave him a shove. "I'm just worried Griffin's going to get a sunburn."

Will rolled his eyes. "Are you going to offer to apply some sunscreen for him?"

I grabbed my water bottle and sprayed some in Will's direction. He darted out of the stream's path, laughing as he went.

"Cae Cae!" Mia cried.

I was instantly on alert, jogging towards her voice, Griffin right on my heels. As soon as we caught sight of the girls, I saw that Mia had something cuddled in her arms.

"What happened?" Griffin barked.

Mia looked up, eyes wide and full of wonder. "Baby kitty."

I froze. Mia walked closer, revealing a tiny ball of gray fur cradled in her arms. It didn't look old enough to be away from its mother yet. I glanced at Griffin and then back at Mia. "Where did you find it? Were there any others?"

"Under one of the bushes. I didn't see any more, and we looked."

Ava nodded. "For almost thirty minutes." She looked at Griffin. "Sorry we stopped our job. But that kitten needs its mom, right?"

Griffin ruffled Ava's hair. "You did the right thing."

"I'll be her mom," Mia said. "Please, Cae Cae! Can we keep her? Please?"

My chest clenched and my eyes burned. "We can't, Mi. You know what the landlord said."

Mia instantly turned to Griffin. "Will you keep her, Griffin? Please? I'll take care of her. You won't have to do anything. I've been saving my allowance, and I can pay for her food."

Griffin looked at me with panic in his eyes. "How do you ever say no to that face?"

"It pretty much kills me every time." Just as I was about to explain to Mia that Griffin couldn't keep her new friend, the kitten let out a fierce *mewl*.

"I think she wants down," Ava said.

Mia set the kitten on the grass, and it instantly made its way over to Griffin. Instead of rubbing itself on his leg like most cats did, it launched itself at him, locking its claws in Griffin's jeans and beginning to climb.

"Ow, shit," Griffin winced. "I'm naming him Lucifer."

I plucked the kitten off Griffin's leg and cuddled it to me, flipping it onto its back. "I'm pretty sure it's a she."

Griffin peeked over my shoulder. "How do you know that?"

I pressed my lips together to hold in my laughter. "No balls."

"I guess that's solid evidence."

"We can call her Luci!" Mia cheered.

Griffin looked from the kitten to Mia to me. "I guess I have a cat."

My heart did a funny flip in my chest. That this man would do anything to make my girl happy. Even sign up for a lifetime with a devil cat.

Chapter Thirty

Griffin

I FOLLOWED THE SOUND OF ADORABLY OFF-KEY SINGING. PAUSING in the doorway of the kitchen, I took a minute to drink Caelyn in. Her back was to me as she sliced what looked like strawberries, placing the pieces into a bowl beside her. As she sang, her hips swung back and forth. The motion drew my attention there, but it was the cutoff denim shorts that held me captive. They molded to her curves as if they were made for her alone.

I forced my gaze away and cleared my throat. "Hey."

Caelyn squealed, whirling around, knife in hand. "I am going to have to put a bell on you, I swear."

"Only if it's a pink sparkly one like we got for Luci."

In the past twenty-four hours, Luci had been cemented as a member of the household. She'd been to the vet, was outfitted with everything a kitten could ever dream of and had attached herself to Mia like sisters separated at birth.

"I guess I'll have to go back to the pet store then," she said with a grin.

I eyed the massive pile of strawberries behind her. "What are you making?"

"I got a steal on these strawberries at the farm stand. I'm thinking strawberry shortcake for dessert."

"Do you think you could double that recipe?"

Caelyn set the knife down on the cutting board. "Sure, why?"

I twirled my cell phone between my fingers. "Bell, Ford, Kenna, Crosby, and Hunter are coming for dinner."

Her eyes widened. "They are? We don't have enough food. And you don't like people in your house."

I winced. I'd felt like crap ever since I snapped at Caelyn about that fact. But she was showing me time and again that opening up my home and my life didn't mean that I was putting myself at risk. There were good people on this island, and Caelyn and her friends were some of them. "I want you to feel comfortable here. And I know you used to host those family dinner nights."

Caelyn's expression softened. "Griffin, you don't have to make yourself uncomfortable for us. You've already done so much."

I moved in closer, tucking a strand of hair behind her ear. "I want to. I want you and the kids to have this. And I want to get to know your friends better."

She reached up on her tiptoes and pressed her lips to my stubbled cheek. "Thank you. You might like them, you know."

"If I don't, I'll just sic Luci on them."

"That cat does know how to use her claws."

I groaned. Wasn't that the truth? The couch in my office would never be the same. "We need to figure out how to clip them."

Caelyn held up both hands, backing away. "You're on your own for that one, buddy. I like my eyes where they are."

It was only a little kitten. She couldn't be that bad. Then I looked down at my forearms that were already covered in red scratches from our trip to the vet. "Maybe I'll just get her a scratching post instead."

"Sounds like a much better plan to me." Caelyn moved to

the fridge, surveying its contents. "I think I'm going to have to go to the store if we're doubling our dinner guests."

"We made it a potluck. We're in charge of dessert, and they're covering everything else."

She closed the fridge. "Let me guess, Bell is doing sides, Crosby signed up for meat of some sort, and Hunter offered to bring the booze as soon as you said the word *potluck*."

"You certainly know your friends."

"We've been friends practically since birth. Well, everyone except Crosby."

I wondered what that would be like. I hadn't had any friends like that. Even before I'd lost my family, we'd always been somewhat set apart. Maybe it was because of the press's fascination with us. Or that my father's parents had more money than God. But we'd always been careful with who we let into that innermost circle. So careful, it was really only the four of us. But we'd liked it that way. The only problem was that once they were gone, I'd been totally and completely alone.

"Thanks for having us over." Ford extended a beer to me.

I took it, taking a healthy sip. "No problem."

His gaze met mine, a sort of understanding there. "It can't be easy to have us invading your space."

I glanced around the back deck and yard. Crosby and Hunter manned the grill, teaching Will the finer points of cooking chicken and steak. The girls were chasing Luci around the back lawn. And Caelyn, Bell, and Kenna sat huddled in chairs. Every so often, a cackle of laughter would escape their group. And each time it did, the tension that had been running through my body since our guests' arrival eased a little bit. "She needed this."

Ford followed my line of vision. "She did. Don't get me wrong, Caelyn's tough. All the girls are. But they need each other.

They've been each other's family more than their own blood for a long time."

"I'm glad they have each other." But I couldn't help a flicker of jealousy. It made no sense to be envious of the friendship Caelyn had with Bell and Kenna. But I wished I could've been there for her all along. That *I* was as woven into her life as the women next to her were.

"And I'm glad she has you now."

I turned my attention back to Ford. "I just want her to be safe. There's a better chance of that here."

He raised a brow. "That all you want?"

"Are you trying to dig gossip out of me right now?"

"That would be Crosby. He's worse than the island knitting circle. Anything you tell him will likely have made its way around to half the island's residents by morning."

I made a mental note not to tell Crosby anything important. But even as my mind filed away that reminder, my gaze traveled back to Caelyn as if she had some invisible hold on me. "All I can tell you is that I care about her. Where it goes from there, I'm honestly not sure."

"I think you're good for each other."

I watched as Caelyn's head tipped back as she laughed. Everything about it was free and unencumbered. Simply letting her joy at being with the people she loved flow out of her. I knew without a doubt that she was the best thing that had happened to me after losing my family. I just hoped I brought some of that same light into *her* life, as well. I wasn't so sure.

"What the hell?" Hunter muttered. "Who is that?"

I turned, following Hunter's stare. There, at the edge of my property, stood a photographer, telephoto lens fixed firmly on our gathering.

"You have got to be kidding me," Crosby barked. "Will, watch the steaks."

Hunter and Crosby jogged towards the fence line. I started to follow, but Ford placed a hand firmly on my chest. "Don't. This creep wants a shot of you. A story. Don't give them that."

My back molars ground together. He was right, of course. But since I was sixteen, I'd always been the one to fight my battles. No one had stood between me and whatever shitty thing was headed my way. Not until Caelyn came between that reporter and me, using her muffin basket to defend my honor. But now it seemed I had more than just her. I had what seemed like the beginnings of a community.

I gave Ford a chin jerk, and he took off to follow Hunter and Crosby. Caelyn was instantly by my side. "I'm so sorry, Griffin."

I tipped my face down to take her in, worry lining the curves of her face. "Why are you sorry? None of this is your fault."

She didn't seem so sure. "If my friends hadn't come over, they probably wouldn't have bothered you."

I hated the guilt that filled her tone. That these vulture reporters were trying to ruin our evening. I took Caelyn's hand and tugged her closer to me, locking my fingers with hers. "I'm done not living my life because of these jerks. I'll do what I can to keep them away, but I'm not hiding anymore. I'm not giving pieces of my existence away because there's a chance it might get splashed across some headline."

Caelyn's hand squeezed mine. "I could always threaten them with a muffin basket."

I let out a bark of laughter. "It seemed to work pretty well the last time."

Mia came running up to me with Luci in her arms. "What's going on? Who are Crosby and Hunter chasing? Is that the man who threw the brick?"

My gut clenched at the worry and fear in her expression. "No, Little Bit." I lifted her and Luci into my arms. "Sometimes, people try and take photos of me. They go places they shouldn't be."

Her eyes widened. "Because you're a magic giant?"

I chuckled, a little of the tension leaving my muscles. "They're curious because of my family."

"Because they died?" she asked hesitantly.

"Yeah, mostly because of that."

Mia snuggled into my chest. "I'm sorry you lost your family. But you're in our family now. That's what the rainbow bracelet means."

I swallowed hard as I met Caelyn's gaze over Mia's head. Tears gathered in the corners of her eyes, but she smiled. "She's right. I'm afraid you've been claimed."

I didn't mind one bit.

Chapter Thirty-One

Caelyn

"HEY, CAELYN."

I looked up at the sound of Shay's voice. "Hey, you. I feel like I haven't seen you in forever."

She flushed and looked over her shoulder as if expecting someone to be lurking nearby. "Sorry I haven't been by to pick up my order. Things have been busy."

"No apologies necessary. Things have been crazy around here, too." Unfortunately, the photographer at the farmhouse had managed to snap a photo of Griffin, Mia, and me. It had taken a couple of weeks, but they finally figured out my name, and reporters started making a habit of coming by the store. But after Mr. Walters put up a large sign stating: *No reporters allowed on-premises, violators will be tased,* things had calmed way down.

"I heard. How are you holding up?"

The worry in Shay's expression had me forcing my smile wider. "I really am fine. I think all the reporters are finally gone." That didn't stop Griffin from being a very grumpy goose. He might have come to terms with his name being splashed across the papers, but mine was another story. He had his lawyer pursuing every legal action in the book.

Shay twisted her fingers together. "I heard about the brick, too. You're being extra cautious, right?"

I fought the shiver that wanted to surface. "I am. But there hasn't been anything else. I'm hoping it was just kids and a prank that got out of hand." Even as I said the words, I knew they weren't true. I hated to admit that it looked like the culprit might be my mother. Why else would it all stop the day I went to see her?

Shay nodded. "I'm really glad to hear that. Now, I'll get all of the stuff you've been holding for me out of your way."

I laughed. "It's not that much, and you know I'm happy to do it. Here." I pulled out the ledger from under the counter. "Just sign this."

Shay scrawled her name across the line I pointed to. "Did you have any luck with those violin strings?"

"I did. It took me a few calls, but I got you two packets. Those puppies were not cheap."

She winced. "I know. But they're the best. Thanks for taking the time to find them."

"No problem." I pulled the stack of boxes out of the back pantry. "How long have you been playing?"

Shay was quiet for a moment, and I thought she might not answer. "Almost as long as I can remember."

"I'd love to hear you sometime."

"Maybe."

That single word might as well have been a *hell no*. But I knew what it was to hold some dreams close to your chest. I wouldn't push Shay to share hers with me. "Do you need anything else?"

"I'm going to load this up in the boat and then I'll come back for groceries."

"Sounds good. I'm about to head out to pick up Will from football, but Max will be here to check you out."

Shay nodded. "Thanks again for all of this."

"Anytime. Just call or email if you need something else."

"Will do."

I made quick work of cleaning up my station. My little family had settled into a routine of sorts, and Griffin had become a huge part of that. On the days Will had football, Griffin picked up the girls from school while I stayed at work, usually to catch up on bookkeeping. Then I would get Will and dash home to make us all a quick dinner. Weekends were all hands on deck. We worked tirelessly on the farmhouse, but everyone loved it. Mia even complained when she had to leave for gymnastics in the afternoons. Pancakes and movie nights remained a tradition. And our extended family potluck dinners had become regular occurrences, too.

Life was good. But I couldn't help but wonder if we were overstaying our welcome. Every time I tried to bring it up with Griffin, he would simply shake his head and say, "You're staying." But at some point, we'd have to go back to our regular lives. But they'd be missing such a vital piece.

I made my way up to Max at the front register. "You sure you're all right to ride solo until Molly gets here?"

Max's head snapped up, his focus going from his phone to me. "Sorry," he said sheepishly. "Yeah, I'll be fine. I've got the routine down."

I surveyed Max's face. He'd been a huge help since he came aboard. Never late and always willing to do whatever we needed. But he looked exhausted and had dark circles rimming his blue eyes. "Everything okay?"

His hold on the phone tightened, his fingers bleaching white. "My ex. She's moving Trevor to the mainland."

"Oh, Max. I'm so sorry." I reached out to squeeze his shoulder, but he flinched away, a flash of anger in his eyes. I knew it wasn't directed at me, but it had me stepping back, nonetheless.

"I'll never get to see my son now."

My heart broke for him. I couldn't imagine what I'd do if someone tried to take my siblings away from me. I'd completely lose it. "Let me know if there's anything I can do. I'm happy to be a reference whenever you have to go to family court."

Max's jaw worked back and forth as he struggled with everything that was raging below the surface. "Not sure that's gonna cut it but I appreciate the offer."

"Of course. I have to go so I'm not late picking up Will but call me if you need anything."

"Sure." His gaze met mine. "Enjoy your time with them."

The pain in Max's eyes socked me right in the gut. "I will. Promise."

Max gave me a silent chin jerk, and I headed out, coming to a stop as I saw Will jogging across the parking lot. "What are you doing here? I'm supposed to pick you up at the field."

"We got out early," he answered.

"We had a deal, Will. No walking to the store alone." We hadn't had any incidents recently, but that didn't mean I was ready to take chances.

He sighed. "Relax, big sister. Joe's mom gave me a ride."

That was better but still not great. "You have a cell phone for a reason. Use it. Or I guess I could just take it away if you don't need it."

"Caelyn…"

"Will…" I parroted.

"All right. I promise to call you with my location twenty-four-seven. Would you like to inject me with a tracker, too?"

I started walking towards my SUV, Will following. "You know, that's a great idea. Let's stop by the vet on the way home. I'm sure they can work you in."

Will threw an arm over my shoulders. "I wouldn't put it past you."

If it were safe and not morally dubious, I'd do it in a heartbeat. Anything that helped keep these kids safe.

We climbed into the SUV and started back to the farmhouse. "So," Will began.

"Uh-oh," I muttered.

"Why uh-oh?"

"Because nothing good ever started with a 'so' that hangs in the air."

Will chuckled. "This isn't bad. Promise."

"Hit me with it."

"When Griffin and I were at the hardware store after school yesterday, I saw his driver's license."

"Okay…" I began. "What? Does he have some super embarrassing middle name or something?"

Will shook his head. "His birthday's tomorrow."

I straightened, stealing a quick glance at Will. "He didn't say anything." Not even when the two of us had discussed Will's birthday that was coming up in a few weeks. Of course, he hadn't. Griffin never shined a light on himself, even when he should have.

"Do you think we can do something for him? I don't know, like get him something special?"

I slowed at a stop sign, taking a longer look at Will. "You guys have really connected, huh?"

Will's cheeks reddened. "He's cool. And a good guy. And no one else is going to celebrate with him. We should."

"You're right." A plan was already forming in my head.

"You know. I could babysit, and you guys could go out on a date."

I almost sent the SUV off the side of the road. "What? We don't need to go on a date."

Will grinned. "You guys would have fun."

"It's not like that between us." But the words felt like a lie. As each day passed, there were more lingering touches, more reasons Griffin found to take my hand. And every single one drove my hope a little higher.

Will stared in my direction. "It might not be that way now, but it could be. You deserve a life, Caelyn. You more than anyone deserve to be happy."

I pulled the SUV to the side of the road and turned to Will, studying his face. "I am happy. You and Ava and Mia make me happy. My job and my friends. And Griffin, too. I have a great life, Will."

He turned his gaze out the front window. "You gave up your life for us."

I grabbed his arm. "That is not true. You make my life better than I could've dreamed. You always will. Even when you go to college. Even when you make a family of your own one day. You and the girls will always be my greatest joy, the people I'm most proud and happiest to see."

He swallowed hard. "I just wish you could have more."

"I don't need more." But as I said it, the thought of those cooking classes, the dream of traveling the world to learn different cuisines, marriage, babies, it all flickered in the back of my mind. I cleared my throat. "You let me worry about what makes me happy, okay?"

"Okay," he mumbled.

"Now, how are you going to get Griffin out of the house tomorrow so we can throw him a surprise party?"

Will grinned. "I've got an idea…"

Chapter Thirty-Two

Griffin

"YOU'RE SURE THIS IS WHAT YOU WANT TO SPEND your paycheck on?" I asked as pavement turned to gravel. The money had already been spent, but we could always return the tools.

Will ran a hand over his brand-new toolbox. It had all the basics that he usually borrowed from me. "I'm sure. I really like working on the house." He was quiet for a moment. "I've been thinking a lot about college…you know, if I go. And I'm thinking architecture. Maybe minor in music."

Heat hit my chest—pride, I realized. I'd do whatever it took to get this kid to college. "I think you'd make a hell of an architect." Will had an eye for design and a head for numbers. Maybe it was because he'd played music for so long, but his mind just worked differently than most. He'd given me more than one suggestion on a project that I'd taken and run with.

"You think so?"

"I do. You've got an eye for it. And combine that with hard work, and no one can stop you."

He nodded, staring at the window as we approached the

farmhouse gate. I thought he was still thinking about his future but as I punched in the code, he said, "I feel like I need to warn you about something."

I glanced his way. "What's that?"

"I have a feeling you don't like surprises, and there are going to be a whole bunch of people up there."

The gate slowly opened, but I didn't move my foot to the accelerator. "Why are there a whole bunch of people up there?"

Will winced. "I might've told Caelyn it was your birthday. I thought she'd just take you out to dinner, but she has a thing about birthdays. Really wants them to be properly celebrated. So, she kind of took that information and ran with it…"

I swallowed hard. "You guys—"

"Don't be mad at her. It was my idea. I'm sorry if you hate it."

I grabbed Will's shoulder. "I was going to say that you guys didn't have to do that. But it's really thoughtful." I smiled reassuringly. "And I am kind of partial to birthday cake."

Will relaxed. "That's good because I have a feeling that Caelyn made you a massive one. That's what she's been doing over at Bell's all morning."

I shook my head. I'd wondered why Caelyn and the girls had taken off so early this morning. She'd had a slightly guilty expression as she explained that they were having some girl time. "Your sister really isn't the best liar."

Will chuckled. "She's the worst. She always blushes and looks at her feet."

"Good to know her tells." I started up towards the house.

"Park in front," Will said. "I'm supposed to think of a reason to bring you around back."

"I'll make my best surprised face."

"Let's just hope you're a better actor than Caelyn."

I pulled to a stop and switched off the engine. "It wouldn't be hard."

As we rounded the side of the house, I heard whispers and a, "*Sssshhhhh.*" I did my best to keep the grin off my face. As soon as our feet hit the back lawn, a deafening, "*Surprise!*" was shouted. My steps faltered, and all the air seemed to get sucked out of my lungs. Kenna and Crosby held one end of a banner, and Bell and Ford the other. It was clear that Mia and Ava had made it. Unicorns and rainbows and glitter adorned the letters that read: *Happy Birthday, Griffin!* Hunter held up the middle of the banner so it didn't sag as the girls danced in front of it.

My gaze caught on Caelyn. She stood with her hands clasped in front of her mouth as if praying that I'd like it all. She looked absolutely breathtaking. She wore a light blue sundress I'd never seen before that skimmed her form and landed mid-thigh. Her hair curled around her face in loose waves, seeming to highlight every feature. I couldn't seem to catch my breath.

Will elbowed me. "You're working that surprise thing a little too well."

I coughed. "How did you guys do all this?"

Mia ran up to me, hurling herself into my arms. "Do you like it? We've been working all morning. We made cakes, too!"

"I love it, Little Bit. Thank you for my sign. You and Ava made it, right?"

"We did!" She grinned at Ava. "I told you he'd like it."

Ava studied the banner. "I tried to get her to stay in the lines."

"It's perfect," I said.

The sign was placed on the grass, and there were back slaps and birthday wishes. Crosby and Hunter fired up the grill as Bell and Kenna started a game with the girls. Caelyn smiled. "Do you hate me a little bit right now?"

It was on the tip of my tongue to say that, no, I loved her. The urge shocked the hell out of me. But it shouldn't have. "Not even a little bit."

"I'm glad."

She seemed almost nervous, like a new kid on the first day of school. I took her hand and squeezed. "Thank you."

She stretched onto her tiptoes and pressed her lips to my cheek. "Happy Birthday."

As she eased back onto her feet, I caught sight of the picnic table. It was covered with a colorful tablecloth, and balloons were tied to just about every surface. "Are there five cakes over there?"

Caelyn blushed. "I didn't know what kind you liked, so I made options."

I burst out laughing. "Those kids are going to be on a sugar high for weeks."

She covered her face with her hands. "I know." She peeked through her fingers. "What's your favorite?"

"Kind of cake?" I asked. She nodded. "I'm simple. Vanilla. Chocolate frosting."

Her hand shot in the air. "Victory is mine!"

I bit back a smile. "What else did you guess?"

"I did vanilla cake and vanilla icing, fudge cake, sprinkle cake, and my personal favorite, triple berry creation."

I gave one of her curls a tug. "I'm going to have to do some scientific research to make sure I know which is my favorite."

"It's the only responsible thing to do."

Mia and Ava hollered for us to come join them in some sort of lawn game. The afternoon passed in a sea of food, laughter, and as startling as it was, good friends. No photographers popped up to ruin our day. No surprise threats or visits from the sheriff. We simply got to enjoy being together.

I eased back into one of the Adirondack chairs on the deck. As I took in the scene before me, I could think of only one thing: my family would've loved this. It was everything my mom wished this house could be. It wasn't about having the perfect restoration of the building itself. It was about the life that swirled within and around it.

"Griffin?"

I turned to see Ava approaching hesitantly, a small, wrapped package in her hands. "Hey, Avs." She hovered a few steps away, and I patted the chair next to me.

As she lowered herself into the seat, she handed me the gift. "Happy Birthday."

My chest swelled and constricted at the same time. "Thank you. Should I open this now?"

"If you want. You don't have to."

"I want to open it right now."

A tiny smile curved Ava's mouth. "It's just something small."

I met her gaze. "It's from you. Whatever it is, I'm going to love it."

She nibbled on her bottom lip but nodded. I slipped a finger under the seam of the wrapping, careful not to damage the contents. As the paper fell away, I saw a handmade book. There was a drawing of the farmhouse on the front that was incredibly realistic. "Did you draw this?"

Ava blushed. "Yeah. I couldn't get everything just right, but I tried."

"It's amazing. You're so talented." I couldn't help but wonder what else this little girl was hiding away from the world. Her siblings were so bold with their talents, putting them on display for everyone to see and not thinking twice. But Ava kept so many things just for herself.

I slowly opened the front cover. A photo of me, Caelyn, and the kids was pasted to the first page. It was from one of our potluck dinners. Will had taken me down in a game of faux tackle football, and the girls had charged, piling on top of us. We were a mess of tangled limbs and laughter.

I kept turning. A photo of Mia on my shoulders. Will and me hanging drywall. Ava grabbing Luci from mid-climb up my leg. The last one stole my breath. A picture I'd had no idea someone had taken. I had an arm wrapped around Caelyn's waist and was gazing down at her. I couldn't remember what it was she'd been saying, but I was rapt. Caught up in the pull of her.

As I stared at the photo, I realized one thing. I was in love with Caelyn O'Connor. Had been for months. A woman who I hadn't even kissed. The knowledge had me questioning my sanity a bit. But it didn't change the fact that nothing in the world could make me walk away from that bit of crazy.

"Do you like it?" Ava asked quietly.

I turned to face her. "This is one of the most special gifts I've ever received. I'm going to keep it always."

"Really?"

The hope in Ava's voice was gutting. "Yes. When the living room is done, I'm going to put it on the coffee table so that everyone who visits can see it."

She beamed. "That's awesome." Hopping up, she threw her arms around me. "Love you, Griffin."

My throat constricted. "Love you, too, Avs."

As she released me, running for her sister and Luci, my gaze locked with Caelyn's, tears filled those gorgeous green eyes. "*Thank you*," she mouthed.

I couldn't even form silent words. Because what did you say to a woman who had given you everything and didn't even realize it?

Chapter Thirty-Three

Caelyn

"Y OU'RE NOT SUPPOSED TO CLEAN UP AFTER YOUR own birthday party," I chided as I placed a stack of dishes on the counter.

Griffin followed suit with his own plates. "Well, your usual helpers are down for the count. It must have been the combination of sugar overload and running around the backyard for five hours straight."

I grinned at the mess around us. Even Will had passed out already. I'd gone to ask him if he had training tomorrow, and he'd been sprawled out face-down on his bed. "Totally worth it." I turned to take Griffin in. "Did you have fun?"

He leaned a hip against the counter. "I haven't celebrated my birthday since I turned sixteen." His words cut—realization that he'd been alone for so long. "It felt good to celebrate again. Thank you. For everything."

I could feel my cheeks getting hot. "I've got one more surprise for you."

"Are you trying to kill me? I already got choked up when Ava gave me her book, and when I saw their sign. Are you determined to turn me into a member of the frequent-crier club?"

I burst out laughing. "It's a pretty good club to be a part of."

He tugged on the end of one of the ties of my sundress. "If you're a member, I want to join."

Something about the words had my pulse thrumming a little faster. "Come on. It's in the shop." I grabbed his hand, and we headed towards the outbuilding. The moon was almost full, giving us all the light we needed to follow the path. But with each step I took, my stomach churned harder. What if this was a horrible mistake? What if Griffin was mad that I'd messed with something that had been so important to him?

I ignored the doubting voices and pulled open the door to the shop. Flicking the lights on, I gave our eyes a second to adjust. There were still a few odds and ends scattered around the space but it was mostly empty. Except for a tarp-covered something in the middle of the room.

I crossed to it, not letting myself pause to consider if I was about to cross some invisible line. My hand closed around the drop cloth, the fabric rough against the tips of my fingers. I pulled.

Griffin was utterly silent. After a few moments, I forced myself to look at him. Unshed tears glistened in his eyes. "Is that my dad's desk?" His voice was hoarse as if he'd spent the afternoon chain-smoking and shooting whiskey instead of chasing kids around his backyard.

"I asked Bell if she could fix it. I told her she had to keep the carvings underneath untouched."

Griffin moved slowly towards the piece of furniture. His long fingers brushed across the gleaming surface then dipped under the drawer to feel for the names. His gaze met mine. "How?"

"I don't know. She's a miracle worker. I knew that if anyone could do it, Bell was the one." I searched his face, looking for some confirmation that I hadn't overstepped. "I couldn't let you just throw it away. Not if there was a chance we could bring it back to life."

He moved so fast, I could barely blink before he pulled me into his arms. "Thank you. Those words aren't enough. But nothing I can think of is either. You've given me so much, and you just keep piling it on. All this goodness and light and *life*."

His breathing was ragged, his chest heaving against my cheek. I fisted my hands in his t-shirt. "You've given me just as much. And Will, Ava, and Mia. We adore you. And we want you to be happy." *Adore* wasn't the word I wanted to use. It wasn't close. *Love* was the only thing that came close. Because I'd done the thing I'd promised myself I wouldn't do. I'd fallen in love with the broody man and his heart of gold. But I didn't care anymore. I was going to let myself love him. Even if he never loved me back.

Griffin pulled back slightly, his large, callused hands framing my face. He moved so slowly, his eyes searching mine as his head bent. I couldn't breathe. The air refused to enter my lungs no matter how much my brain urged it to do so.

The kiss was so tender, a complete juxtaposition of the man who ate up the space around him. His mouth was the same, soft lips and a bite from the stubble that surrounded them. My hands gripped his shirt tighter. I needed more of everything that was this man in front of me.

Griffin's tongue parted my lips. A teasing caress mixed with insatiable hunger. My body pressed harder against his, seeking more of the fire that flickered to life between us. In an instant, I was lifted to the desk, Griffin hovering over me. He trailed kisses down my neck and across my shoulder.

As he pulled away, a heat I'd never seen in the depths of his blue eyes before shone. His hands framed my face again. "I've wanted to do that since the moment I heard you laugh. The first time I came into the store."

I sucked in a sharp breath. "What?"

His stare got even more intense, evidence of a battle I'd been blind to. "I tried to stay away. I didn't trust myself. Or anyone else. But I've wanted to kiss you since that day. Wondered what it would feel like to swallow that laugh."

Tears pricked the backs of my eyes. "Why now?" It was the only thing I needed to know. Was this simply satisfying a curiosity? One kiss, and then we would go back to the way things were? The thought burned.

Griffin trailed his fingers down the side of my neck, tracing invisible patterns across my skin. "You showed me how much I was missing by locking myself away from the world. You showed me that I could trust you with anything. But you've been showing me that from the first day I met you. In your kindness. Your care. How damn selfless you are. Everything I see in you challenges me to do better. *Be* better. To not run away from life because I was hurt in the past. I want this with you. I don't know for sure where it will lead. But I want to find out."

He was asking. Would I go there with him? Could I take that risk? There was only one answer. "Yes."

With that word, Griffin moved in again, but a voice cut through the night. "Caelyn? You out there?" Will called. "Mia needs you."

"Be right there," I called back, disappointment flaring bright and strong.

Griffin's forehead fell to mine, and we stayed just like that for one more stolen moment. And I couldn't help but wish that moment would last a lifetime.

Chapter Thirty-four

Griffin

I GROANED AS I TOOK THE FIRST PULL OF MY COFFEE. IF there had been a way to inject the caffeine directly into my veins, I would've done it. Usually, my nightmares left me blurry-eyed the next morning. But last night it had been the feel of Caelyn's lips and the taste of her skin that had haunted me.

All I could think about was that she was only a few rooms away. How easy it would be to cross the distance and slip into her bed. Then I'd remind myself that her siblings occupied the room across the hall and next to her. Not a smart move.

I grinned down at my coffee. She'd said yes to exploring this thing between us. Mia's nightmare had meant we hadn't progressed much further than that. But we had all the time in the world ahead of us.

I listened carefully. I didn't hear anything at first. And then I caught some laughter coming from the backyard. I moved towards the sound.

Opening the back door, I found the entire O'Connor clan doing some sort of yoga practice. The kids seemed to follow

Caelyn as she flowed from one position to another. Even Will moved through it with ease.

I sucked in a sharp breath as Caelyn bent at the waist, her spandex-covered ass pointing directly at me. Suddenly, I didn't need that shot of caffeine anymore. I was wide-awake.

"Hey, Griffin. You've got a little drool there."

I gave a small jerk at Will's voice, my coffee sloshing out of my mug and running down my hand. I glared in his direction, which only made Will laugh. Caelyn stood, turning to face me and suddenly seeming just a bit shy. "Morning."

I crossed to her in a few strides, pulling her into my arms and pressing a kiss to her temple. "Morning."

She squirmed. "Griffin, the kids."

I chuckled. "They're used to me holding you. And they'll get used to me kissing you, too." I surveyed her face. "Unless you think last night was a mistake…" Just saying the words had the little bit of coffee I'd drunk souring in my stomach.

"No." Caelyn gripped my t-shirt and pulled me closer. "I definitely don't think that kiss was a mistake." She rose to her tiptoes and pressed her lips to the corner of my mouth.

I fought the urge to toss her over my shoulder and take her back to the house. Will cleared his throat. "So, you two have anything you'd like to share with the class?" He was grinning so widely, it looked like his face might crack in two.

Caelyn's fingers twisted and untwisted the hem of my shirt. "I don't think there's anything the class needs to know at this juncture." She widened her eyes and tipped her head towards Ava and Mia.

"I thought there were no secrets in this family?" Will teased.

"You know a secret?" Mia asked, lifting Luci into her arms.

Panic briefly flashed across Caelyn's features but then she shook her head. "Will's just giving me a hard time." She turned her gaze to the teen. "And if he keeps it up, he's going to be on dish duty for the rest of the week."

"Keep it up, Will. I'm on dishes this week, and I'm happy to share," Ava offered, her eyes twinkling.

Her smile told me she might be more aware of things between her sister and me than Caelyn thought. I took another sip of coffee. "You guys done with your yoga? Time for breakfast?" I gave Caelyn my best puppy dog eyes as I asked.

She just shook her head. "We've got a little more to go. Why don't you join us?"

The sudden evil glint in Caelyn's eyes had me wanting to take a step back. Instead, I set my coffee down on the bottom step of the deck. "I could use a little morning snooze, sure."

Will shot me a warning look. "Don't come crying to me when this all goes wrong."

"How could it go wrong? It's basically stretching."

"Some of the stuff is actually pretty hard," Ava warned.

"Yeah," Mia echoed. "Even harder than some of my gymnastics exercises."

Caelyn gestured towards the grass. "But I'm sure with all those muscles, it shouldn't be a problem for you."

I grinned. "You eyeing my muscles, Caelyn?"

She rolled her eyes heavenward. "Just hurry and warm up. I'm not going to have a pulled muscle on my conscience."

I didn't see how the exercises I'd seen Caelyn and the kids doing could lead to injury, but I obeyed anyway. I tried to recall the different stretches my soccer coach had taken us through in high school. Moving through as many as I could remember, I kept my eyes on Caelyn as she moved into some sort of lunge.

"Why don't you try this one?" she asked, straightening.

"It's one of the warriors," Mia added. "I like them 'cause they make me feel strong."

"You are incredibly strong, Little Bit." I glanced at Caelyn. "Tell me what I need to do."

Caelyn helped position my body and showed me how to

stand, but the second I got my feet in the right spots, I started to stumble. "Shit."

"Ooooooohhhh. Bad word," Mia called.

I winced, giving Caelyn a sheepish smile. "I'll do dishes tonight."

"Let's see if you can master this pose before we talk punishments."

"I'm trying," I groused. "I think it's because I'm so tall. My center of gravity is different than the average person's."

Caelyn tried showing me the position she wanted me to emulate again. "Balance is important. Especially when you're doing all these crazy house improvement projects. You could fall off the scaffolding."

I grunted. "I'm pretty sure I'm not twisting into these ridiculous positions on my scaffolding."

Caelyn kept trying to bring me through all sorts of different poses. Ava and Mia gave up on their exercises and became an audience for mine. "That's a five-point-five," Mia chirped.

I sank to the grass, sweat dripping down my face. "Five-point-five? That was at least an eight." Ava covered her mouth as she giggled. I turned my focus to her. "I thought I could at least count on you to have my back."

She shrugged. "Will did try to warn you…"

I glared at Will. "You could've been a little sterner in your warning." At this rate, I was going to need a week of ice baths.

Will chuckled. "But what fun would that be?"

"All right, Mr. Grumpypants. You're released for the day. Just a little child's pose before you go."

Caelyn's hands ghosted over my hips as she guided me into the position. I let out a groan. "I don't know if I'll ever forgive you for this."

She bent, whispering in my ear. "Ready to admit yoga isn't some sissy form of exercise?"

"I promise never to call it stretching again."

Caelyn laughed and went to join her sisters on the grass. "Just hold that for at least sixty more seconds."

"Fine—ow, shit! What the hell?" Claws dug into my back as a paw took a swipe at my ear.

"Don't move, Griffin! It's Luci," Mia begged.

"Get this devil cat off me, please," I gritted out. The beast was surely drawing blood.

"I've got her," Ava said, lifting the creature off my back.

I sat up, glaring at the kitten. Mia threw her arms around my neck. "Don't be mad. She just wanted to do yoga with you."

I couldn't help the laugh that escaped me. And as I looked over at Caelyn, who had lifted the kitten from Ava's arms and kissed its furry head, my chest gave a painful squeeze. I hadn't realized how empty my life had been. Not until they had filled it. Even if they did bring a devil cat with them.

Chapter Thirty-five

Caelyn

I HOISTED MY BAG OUT OF THE PASSENGER SEAT AND SHUT THE
door with my hip. I let out a startled yelp as I came face-to-face
with my mother. "What are you doing here?"

She looked around the empty parking lot. "Has anyone been
following you lately?"

"Following me?" My pulse picked up speed. "No. What are you
talking about?" I took a second to survey her, checking her pupils.
They seemed normal, but I wasn't sure I even knew what they would
look like if she was high.

My mom reached out and gripped my arm, her nails digging
into my flesh. "Think, Caelyn. Have you felt like there have been
eyes on you?"

I ripped my arm from her grasp. "No. Now you need to tell me
what's going on."

Her gaze darted to the street as a truck drove past. "Someone
broke into my trailer."

"Mom, that trailer isn't exactly in a stand-up neighborhood. Did
you call the sheriff's department?"

Her focus jumped back to me. "No. I don't want them in my space."

I studied her, trying to figure out why that might be. A healthy paranoia from being locked up for so many years? Hiding a stash of drugs? Or did she have something at her place that would lead to my father? As hard as I looked, I couldn't see the truth. "You need to call Parker. Tell him where Dad is. Tell him what you're worried about."

Mom's jaw clenched in a way that said her stubborn streak was coming out to play. "I would never do that to your father. He's my husband."

"We're your *children*. But I guess you don't care about that." Just saying the words aloud stoked the anger that was always on a simmer inside me. It didn't take much to bring it to a rolling boil. And thinking about what my parents had put my siblings through would do it every time.

My mom toyed with the keychain in her hands. "I'm sorry. I know we hurt you, but I'm better now. I know I can't change the past, but I'm trying to make things right. To look out for you."

"Making things right would mean making Dad pay for his crimes. Letting the courts sentence him. Looking out for us means putting us first. Above the man who got us all into this mess in the first place."

Pain melted through her features. "I'm sorry. I can't. I love him. And he's better now. I swear to you. He's not messed up with that crew anymore—"

My entire body went rigid. "Is he here? On Anchor? Or Shelter?"

My mother's mouth snapped closed, and she didn't say another word—her silence was answer enough.

"You always did love him more than us. This is just the first time you've said it out loud." I met her gaze, staying silent for a moment, hoping she'd really hear what I said next. "Stay away from us. Until you're willing to put your children before your loser husband, I don't want to see you."

Mom sucked in a sharp breath. "I understand. I'm sorry, Kitten. I really am. I love you. I do. I just…"

"You can't give him up." My voice broke on the sentence. It was too much. Never. Not once had I ever been someone's top priority. Sure, I had people in my life who cared about me, who were wonderful friends. But not once had the people who were supposed to love me most come through on that promise. They let me fall time and time again.

I trembled as I sucked in a breath, tears filling my eyes. I hated that she still had this power over me after all of these years. That some part of me would never stop hoping that she would pull it together and love me. "You get to make that choice. But I get to make mine, too. And that's walking away."

I started towards the entrance of the store, tears falling in earnest now. Walking away was my only choice. Because if I let my mother back in, she'd take me down with her. In an endless cycle of unfulfilled promises and pretty lies. I couldn't do it. I wouldn't.

Griffin's face filled my mind. The burn of his blue gaze right before his lips met mine. The promise to see where things went between us. I'd been so excited to lean in to that exploration. But that's all it was. A promise of a maybe. I wiped at my face as I unlocked the door.

"Running a little late, aren't we?"

I turned at the sound of Patti's voice. Seemed this day was just going to keep on giving. "We don't open for five more minutes. I'm sorry, but you'll have to wait."

Patti opened her mouth to speak and then took in my tear-streaked face. Apparently, even the ice queen had a heart because she paused. "I can wait. Take your time."

My shoulders slumped in relief. I didn't have it in me to duel with Patti, too. I made quick work of opening the doors and flicking on the lights. After I had the cash register up and running, I came back to let Patti in. "We're good now. Thank you for waiting."

She nodded, moving around me and into the store. But after a few steps, she stopped and turned. "Was that your mother?"

I tried to steel what little emotional reserves I had left. "Yes."

"I'd think you'd be happy to see her," Patti huffed.

"Would you be happy to see the woman who left your siblings alone for three days while she went and got high? The woman who thinks it's more important to hide her husband than protect her children? The woman who thought you were never good enough for her to love, no matter what you did? That woman?"

Patti's mouth opened and closed a few times before she spoke. "I—I'm sorry. I didn't know."

I threw up both my hands. "Of course, you didn't. You were too busy making up stories in your head for who you *think* I am."

She licked her lips. "Your father sold my husband drugs."

"What?" The single word came out on a whisper. None of that computed with anything I knew about Patti and her family.

"He got injured on the job. Hurt his back. The recovery from the surgery was bad, and when the doctors cut him off from painkillers, he needed something else for the pain. Your father was happy to give him plenty of options." She swallowed hard. There were no tears in her eyes, but the set of her jaw told me she was fighting them. "We almost lost everything. He's better now. Sober. Working his program."

"I'm glad." I wasn't sure what else to say. Or what to do with a Patti who wasn't pretending to be better than everyone else in her orbit.

She straightened her purse on her shoulder. "I may have been harboring some anger that shouldn't have been directed at you."

I snorted. "May have?"

Patti jutted out her chin. "I'm trying to apologize."

I grinned. I might've gotten a little insight into Patti's life, but she wasn't going to become an entirely different woman in one conversation. "Thank you. I appreciate that. But I'd appreciate it even more if your snide comments about me, my siblings, and Griffin would stop."

Her lips thinned and fixed into a tight line. "He's a loner. Volatile."

"Oh, he is not, Patti. You don't know him. And he's not going to let you. You've already been nasty to him one too many times. And you know what? That's your loss. Because he's amazing."

"I'll try to keep my opinions to myself."

I tipped my face to the ceiling, calling on all my patience. Because I knew Patti would never be able to keep a damn thing to herself. "All I can ask is that you try."

She nodded and, without another word, started on her shopping as if we'd never had this weird confessional of a conversation. But her words stayed with me long after she left. As I worked, filling sandwich orders and stocking shelves, they hung in the air around me. Sometimes I forgot just how many lives my father had affected. His actions had crushed more than just our little family. How many people had he gotten hooked on substances that would destroy them? How many people had he lured into his chain of dealers?

The questions lay like a heavy blanket of grief and guilt on my chest. It made breathing just a little bit harder. And I could understand a little better why so many in this community had looked at me with disdain. Maybe they hadn't been personally affected by it all, but they knew the poison that my family had pumped into their world. And I was a reminder of it.

My phone buzzed in my back pocket. Pulling it out, I saw the name of the elementary school flash on my screen. *Crud.* I really hoped one of the girls wasn't sick. I waved to Max at the front of the store and motioned to my phone. He nodded, and I stepped back into the hall headed towards the office.

"Hello, this is Caelyn."

"Caelyn, it's Sue at the office. We have a bit of a situation."

My heart plummeted to my stomach. This sounded more like someone being sent to the principal's office rather than someone running a fever. "What's wrong?"

She cleared her throat. "Someone claiming to be the girls' father tried to take them out of school."

I froze. "What?"

"A man came in. Said he was Ava and Mia O'Connor's father and that he needed to take them out of school. That there had been a family emergency."

My mind raced. Dad was here? This wasn't happening. "You didn't—please tell me you didn't release them to him."

"Of course not. You have to be on the approved list to pick up children, and you have to show ID. Plus, I know exactly who your father is, and he's supposed to be in jail, not picking up children he has no rights to."

My muscles came unstuck, and I moved through the store. I motioned to Max. "I have to go. Emergency at the girls' school."

His eyes flashed. "What happened? Is everyone okay?"

"I can't explain right now. I have to go."

"Of course. Let me know if you need anything, okay?"

I nodded but kept moving. "Sorry, Sue. I'm on my way. Did you call the sheriff?"

"Yes. Sheriff Raines and one of his deputies are on their way."

"Can you—?" My voice began to tremble as I started my SUV. "Can you call the girls to the office? I just want to know they're in someone's sight, just in case. Wait. My dad, is he still there?"

Sue huffed. "No. He's not. He left. But not before punching Mr. Reilly in the face."

I sucked in a sharp breath, picturing our mid-fifties gym teacher sprawled out on the ground. "I'm so sorry. I'm on my way. I'll be there as soon as I can. Please look out for my girls."

"I will, sweetie. Nothing's going to happen to them. You just drive safe."

If by *safe,* she meant like a bat out of hell, then I had her covered. My lungs seized as soon as I hit end on my screen. Will. Oh, God. I hit the number for the high school. The secretary answered, and I quickly explained the situation. "Please call him to the office, and don't let him leave. No one has shown up for him, right?" What if my mother had gone to the high school? Will would've gone with her just for the opportunity to give her a piece of his mind.

"No one has been taken out of school today, Caelyn. Just take a deep breath. I'll call him to the office."

"Thank you." I was shaking now, slight little trembles I couldn't seem to stop. "I'm going to have someone pick him up. I'm not sure who, but they'll be on the list."

"No problem. And if you need anything else, you just call."

I nodded but then realized the woman couldn't see that action across the phone. "Thank you."

I hung up as I rounded the bend in the road that would take me to the elementary school. My finger hovered over the names in the favorites section of my contacts. But there was only one person I wanted to call. He answered after two rings. I kept my voice as strong as possible but knew it wavered a little. "Griffin? I need you."

Chapter Thirty-Six

Griffin

MY ENTIRE BODY LOCKED, FROZE IN THE MIDDLE OF an aisle in the hardware store. A man muttered a curse as he stepped around me, but it barely registered. "Where are you?" It was the only thing I could think of to ask.

"I-I'm driving to the elementary school. I need you to go to the high school and pick up Will. Then drive over and meet me. Can you do that?"

The tremble in her voice gave me a burning desire to thrash the row of fixtures in front of me. "What happened?"

"My dad. He showed up at the elementary school and tried to take the girls."

I was moving before she'd finished her sentence, dropping the nails in my hand to the floor without another thought. "Are they okay? He didn't get them, did he?"

"They're safe. I don't know much more. Will you hurry?"

My ribs constricted in a brutal squeeze. "I'm on my way. I'm gonna get there as fast as I can." Caelyn never asked for anything. Not a damn thing. Probably wouldn't even ask for a life jacket if a ship were sinking. She'd simply try to swim to shore all on her own. But she was asking me this. "I'll be there."

"Thank you," she whispered.

"Hang up the phone and drive safe."

"Okay." She stayed on the line for a moment longer, silent as if she couldn't let the connection lapse.

"I'll be there soon. Promise."

"See you in a few minutes."

She disconnected the call just as I climbed into my truck. I tore through town, doing my best to at least pause at the stop signs. Hopefully, the sheriff's deputies were all at the school already. Images flashed in my mind as I drove. A brutal mix of my sister then Mia then Ava. They were all calling out to me for help, but I wasn't there.

I gave my head a vicious shake, gripping the wheel harder. Now wasn't the time to lose it. Will would already be freaked. I had to lock it down for him. For Caelyn. For the girls.

I pulled up in front of the school and came to a screeching halt. I was stopped in a fire lane, but it didn't matter. I would be in and out of there in seconds. I pulled open the door and jogged down the hall to the office. As soon as I entered, Will jumped to his feet. "What's going on? They won't tell me anything. Where's Caelyn?"

I gripped Will's shoulder as I looked at the secretary. "I'm Griffin Lockwood. I'm taking Will. I'm on the list."

"I know who you are, Mr. Lockwood. You just give my best to Caelyn. Tell her if she needs anything to call me."

"I will." I steered Will out of the office and down the hall. We weren't jogging, but our pace wasn't exactly slow either.

"Tell me," Will growled.

"Your dad showed. Tried to take the girls out of school. They're fine. But we need to go be with your sisters."

Will missed a step and stumbled but caught himself. "They're sure it was him?"

I glanced Will's way as we climbed into the truck. I hadn't thought about the possibility of it being someone else, someone pretending to be Ava and Mia's father. But for what purpose? "I don't know. Let's just get over there and see what's what."

I drove the couple of blocks to the elementary school as quickly as possible. Instead of pulling into the fire lane like I wanted, I forced myself to take the time to find a proper parking spot. As soon as the engine was off, Will and I were out of the vehicle and running towards the school.

We made a beeline for the office but didn't have to open the door. Staff and sheriff's department deputies milled about, but I only had eyes for my girls. I ignored every other person in the room. Parker stopped speaking mid-sentence as I wrapped Caelyn, Ava, and Mia in my arms. Mia unlatched herself from Caelyn and hooked her arms around my neck. "I knew you'd come," she whispered.

Caelyn pulled Will into our little huddle. "You're okay? No one showed up at your school?"

He shook his head. "Just Griffin."

We all stood there for a minute in this group hug that I was sure looked ridiculous. I couldn't find it in me to care. I didn't want to release any of them. Here, together, I knew they were unharmed.

Parker cleared his throat. "Everyone's safe. That's what's important."

My gaze cut to him, and I forced myself to step back. "What's important is that you find out who the hell was here and lock them up."

Mia clung to me tighter. "He's not gonna take me, right? I don't want to go with my dad."

I rubbed a hand up and down her back, glaring at Parker. "No one's taking you anywhere but home, Little Bit."

"With you, right?"

Her voice was so small, I wanted to throttle something. "With me."

She burrowed into my neck, and I did my best to keep my hold on her light. I turned, reaching a free hand out to Caelyn. I needed to touch her, to assure myself that she was fine, too. "You're all right?"

She nodded. "We're okay. Right, Ava?"

Ava parroted Caelyn's nod, but it was in no way convincing. I gave her the gentlest smile I could muster amidst the rage flowing through my veins. "You're safe. No one's gonna hurt you. Okay?"

"Okay, Griffin," she whispered.

There was a commotion at the door, and I turned to see Kenna, Bell, and Ford. Kenna was by my side in a flash, followed closely by the other two. She held out her hands to Mia. "I'm gonna need a hug."

Mia went to her instantly. "I always have hugs for you."

Kenna laughed, but there were tears in her eyes. "Everyone's all right?"

"We're fine," Ava said quietly.

Bell held out a hand. "Can I get one of those hugs? Just to make sure for myself?"

Ava smiled and walked into Bell's open arms. Caelyn pressed in closer to me. "Would you guys mind taking the kids to that bench in the hall? We need to talk to Parker."

"Of course," Kenna answered.

"I'm staying."

My gaze locked with Will's, his expression stubborn and defiant. I cleared my throat and gave him a pointed look.

He looked down at his shoes, rethinking his plan of attack. "I mean, I'd like to stay." He looked at Caelyn. "I deserve to know what's going on."

She sucked in a breath. "Okay."

Kenna and Bell took the girls out into the hall, but Ford stayed with us as we turned our attention to Parker. I pulled Caelyn into my side. I wasn't sure if it was for her or me—maybe both of us. The feel of her body against mine reassured me that she was here. Safe. Everyone was.

I refocused on Parker. "What can you tell us?"

He scrubbed a hand through his hair. "Not as much as I'd like. A man came into the office this afternoon and asked for the girls. Said he was their father and that there'd been a family emergency." He winced as he glanced at Caelyn. "When Sue gave some pushback, said that there was a list and that he wasn't on it, he said that Caelyn had been in a car accident."

Caelyn's body gave a small jerk in my arms. "It might've worked…" Her voice trailed off as terror grabbed hold.

"No, it wouldn't have," Parker assured her. "The school has security measures in place for a reason. Photo ID and a list of approved names for pick up and drop off. He wouldn't have gotten out of here with Mia and Ava."

Caelyn nodded woodenly, but I could tell that none of this eased her mind. I pressed my lips to her temple briefly. Even her scent, that hint of vanilla and something that was uniquely Caelyn, didn't calm me as it usually did. I still kept breathing her in, hoping it would eventually ease me.

Will shuffled his feet. "Are you sure it was my dad?"

Parker turned to face him. "Sue can't say for sure. The man had a beard and wore a baseball cap. Why do you ask?"

"It's just that he's been gone for so long. Why would he come back now? It's not like he ever gave a crap about us. It doesn't make sense."

"It's because Mom's out." Caelyn's fingers dug into my t-shirt the way they always did when her emotions were heightened. "I've seen her. Twice. She still loves him. And she knows where he is."

Parker straightened. "You think they're going to try and run?"

"Maybe. I honestly don't know. She said she's trying to make things right. Maybe she wants her kids back. But she's a stranger to me, Parker." Caelyn's voice cracked. "I don't know that woman. Not sure I ever did."

Parker pulled out his phone and made a few notes. "You should've called me. Told me you had a run-in with her."

"I told her to go to you. To tell you where our dad is. She refused. You taking time out of your day to go bang on her door wouldn't change anything. She's too stubborn."

Parker's eyes zeroed in on Caelyn, his gaze hard. "I need to know all the pieces in play. No more holding back, okay?"

Caelyn tightened her hold on my shirt. "You're right. I promise I'll tell you everything from now on."

"Thank you. I'm going to send a couple of deputies out to your mom's place while we finish up here. Why don't you guys head home? Get the kids settled. I'll swing by after we've wrapped up here."

"Thank you, Parker. For everything. I'm sorry we're bringing you into this mess yet again," Caelyn said.

Parker's jaw hardened. "This is not your fault. Don't you take someone else's actions on your shoulders."

"He's right," Will said. "Our parents are assholes. But that's not on us."

Caelyn's lips curved the barest bit. "I prefer the term dingleberry. It limits the cussing."

Ford chuckled. "You girls love that word."

She shrugged. "When the shoe fits…" Caelyn stepped out of my hold to ruffle Will's hair. "Come on. Let's go home."

Something about the gesture had the first little bit of tension leaving my muscles. It was so normal. The way Caelyn and Will always teased. It said that everything was going to be okay.

Parker held out a hand to stop Ford and me as Caelyn and

Will headed out of the office. "What's the security like at your place?"

That small piece of ease vanished in a flash. "It's good." It was top-of-the-line a few years ago. But that was no longer good enough. I needed whatever the best was.

Ford seemed to read my thoughts. "I've got a buddy. He's pretty well-known, and it's made him a nut about security. I'll call him on the way to your place. See if he has any recommendations."

"Thank you," I said. "I really appreciate it. Let him know price isn't an issue, and I'll pay double if his guy can install it in the next week." Ford gave me a chin jerk of agreement, and I turned back to Parker. "You think whoever this was will try again?"

He rubbed a hand over his jaw. "I don't know. And I don't like being in the dark. Hopefully, we'll know more after the deputies talk to Chrissy. But I'd rather be overly cautious."

I would, too. The truth was, I would give anything, pay any price, if I could just keep this family safe. Because somehow over the past few months, they'd come to mean everything to me.

Chapter
Thirty-Seven

Caelyn

I LEANED BACK AGAINST GRIFFIN'S CHEST, LETTING THE sounds of the kids playing and the feel of Griffin surrounding me soothe my frayed nerves. Crosby had talked Will, Ava, Mia, Bell, and Ford into a game of soccer. Kenna was in the kitchen making us a pitcher of iced tea. The people I loved most in the world were all here, and they were safe.

Griffin pressed his lips to my temple. "They're rebounding."

He was right, of course. Few things were more miraculous than the resiliency of children. I'd seen it time and again. But the knowledge that it was possible didn't change how much I hated that my siblings seemed to need to employ it more than most. "I don't want them to ever be hurt or scared. When I took custody of them, I promised myself they would never have the kind of fear they experienced when my parents abandoned them and that man broke in. But they've been terrified twice in the past month."

Griffin pulled me tighter against him. "But you make them feel safe, even when life is scary."

I made a humming noise in the back of my throat. Not an

agreement or a disagreement. I didn't want to be just a safe place to land for these kids. I wanted to stand between them and anything that might cause them harm.

Griffin didn't try to further make his point. He simply held me and let his presence be a balm. My eyes had just started to close when he shifted, pulling out his phone. "Hey, Parker. Come on up." There was a brief pause. "Okay. We'll meet you out front."

"He's here?" I asked.

"Yeah. He wants to talk to us alone."

My stomach gave a violent twist. *Alone* meant something bad. Something he didn't want to say in front of the kids. "Okay." I hated the smallness of my voice, but I couldn't seem to infuse any more strength into it.

Griffin pulled me to my feet. "No matter what, we'll figure it out."

I searched his face, looking for that silent promise that I would come first to him. That I wouldn't be so easily cast aside as I had been by my parents, by boys and men I'd dated in the past. It was unfair to even quietly look for that vow. We barely knew each other; had only kissed. Yet somehow, it felt as if I'd known Griffin for a lifetime. That he could see inside every nook and cranny of my soul. And with that knowledge and vision came the potential for devastating hurt if he decided that I wasn't good enough.

I tried to force the thoughts from my head, to settle in the knowledge that I wasn't alone for now. It would have to be good enough. I laced my fingers through Griffin's. "Let's go."

We rounded the house, making our escape without the soccer players noticing. We reached the front of the farmhouse just as Parker's SUV rounded the drive. I gripped Griffin's hand tighter as Parker came to a stop and climbed out. He wore an expertly fashioned mask. I couldn't read a single expression on his face. And that scared me even more.

He strode towards us, stopping just a couple of steps away. "Caelyn, I've got some news."

My eyes burned in my effort to keep them open, to not look away from whatever was coming my way. "Say it quick."

Parker nodded. "Two deputies went to pay your mom a visit. There was no answer at first. But when they knocked harder, the door opened. I'm sorry. She's dead."

I stayed ramrod straight, willing all the steel I could muster into my spine. "Overdose?" I'd waited for that call ever since my mother's arrest. I wasn't an idiot. I knew there were ways to get drugs in prison. But to have it come now? I sucked in a sharp breath. "Oh, God. This is all my fault." My knees began to shake.

Griffin gripped my shoulders and turned me to face him. "What are you talking about?"

"I—I was awful to her this morning. I told her I didn't want to see her unless she turned Dad in. Oh, God. She must've gone to score after that."

"Caelyn," Parker began. "It wasn't an O.D."

"Then what—?" I stopped mid-sentence at the look on Parker's face, the brief moment when his mask slipped.

"She was murdered."

I tried to take a breath, but I couldn't seem to grab hold of the air. It just flew right through my body without actually bringing any oxygen to my lungs. My muscles cramped, and I heard Griffin mutter a curse though it sounded far away. Suddenly, I was lying down, the grass cool against my back with Griffin hovering over me. Worry, no...*panic*, etched his features. "Caelyn, I need you to breathe. Slow and steady."

He raised and lowered a hand, guiding me through the breaths. Before long, my muscles seemed to release, and the world didn't seem quite so fuzzy anymore. "I'm okay," I croaked.

Griffin scowled. "You're not okay." He slowly helped me into a sitting position. "Do you want to go to the hospital? Go see Dr. Kipton?"

"No. No doctors. I'm fine. I just…" I didn't know how to answer that. I'd just lost it.

Griffin cupped my cheeks, his large hands engulfing my face. "You're allowed to feel whatever you need to. Just know I've got you."

The burning in my eyes was back, but for a whole new reason. "I know."

Parker cleared his throat. "Should I call the EMTs?"

"No." I pushed to my feet, Griffin close by my side. "I'm fine. Really. I just…I need to know what happened."

Parker looked understandably skeptical about sharing any details with a woman who'd almost hyperventilated herself into fainting. Griffin motioned him towards some benches that were at the front of the house. "Let's sit. Then you can tell us everything."

I squeezed Griffin's hand. A silent thank you for having my back, for not allowing Parker to hide things from me out of some misguided protective instinct. We eased down onto the benches, Griffin plastered to my side and Parker on his own bench. He surveyed my face for a moment before proceeding as if checking to see if I could handle it. "She was stabbed."

I swallowed against the bile creeping up my throat. A part of me hated my mother. Some days, that piece was larger than the others. But I loved her, too. And just like the hate, that bit fluctuated. But even on the days when I hated her the most, when Ava had a nightmare about the past, or Will took too much on his shoulders, or Mia asked why her parents didn't love her… Even on those days, I wouldn't have wished her dead. I simply wished for justice to be served. This wasn't justice.

Parker continued. "So far, no witnesses. And you know that neighborhood. It's not like there were security cameras." He turned a piece of gravel over with the toe of his boot. "There was a message."

"Where?" I asked.

"On the wall. It said: *Traitor*."

I inhaled through my nose, trying desperately to keep from losing my lunch all over the drive. "My dad?" How had it come to this? Had she told him he needed to turn himself in, and he'd turned on her? As despicable as he was, I just couldn't see him doing that. But then again, I hadn't really known my parents at all.

Parker looked out at the land around us as if searching for the right answer. "Signs point that way. But it could be someone else mixed up in that crowd. A player we're not thinking about."

My breaths started coming quicker. "If that's true, the list of possibilities is endless. How do I keep the kids safe when it could be anyone? Did you know that my dad got Patti's husband hooked on that stuff? God knows how many people on this island hate us because of what my parents did."

Parker's eyes widened. "I didn't know. But that's no reason to hate you."

Griffin rubbed a hand up and down my arm. "He's right. It's not."

"People aren't always logical. It doesn't take much to breed hate or fear in someone." I'd seen it time and again, and I knew Griffin had, too. I met his gaze, silently urging him to understand.

He brushed his mouth against mine. "We're going to keep you safe."

I gave my head a little shake. "We can't be everywhere all the time. I'll be at work; the kids will be at two different schools. Not to mention Mia's gymnastics and Will's football. How is it possible to keep eyes on them at all times?"

Griffin squeezed the back of my neck in a rhythm I knew

was meant to calm. "We're going to divide and conquer. Ford and Crosby already offered to help, and you know Hunter will, too. Between us, them, and Bell and Kenna, the kids won't be alone outside of school. Not for a single second."

"I'm stationing an officer outside of the elementary school for the next few weeks at least," Parker added. "The high school already has a security guard. And I'm giving him a radio that will keep him in contact with the department. We've got the tiny terrors covered."

Many on the island had thought it was a bit ridiculous to have a security guard in a high school the size of Anchor's. But now, I was counting my lucky stars that someone would be on watch for Will. "What about recess?"

"All of the staff and teachers have been made aware of the situation. They'll keep a close eye."

I laced my fingers through Griffin's, tracing an invisible pattern on the back of his hand. "Okay."

"What about the store?" Griffin asked. "It's not like you can have someone stationed at the door asking for ID before they go inside." His hand gripped mine a little harder. "Maybe you should think about taking some time off."

My mouth fell open. "You know I can't." I already felt insanely guilty for allowing Griffin to pay me for meals when we were living here, but he'd insisted that he should actually be paying me more with all the work we were doing around the farmhouse. I wasn't sure Mia's glitter drawings could really be counted as work. But the truth was, we needed the money. I was still paying the astronomical rent on the old house, and Mia's gymnastics wasn't getting any cheaper. I'd started tucking a little bit of money away for that cooking class I was hoping to take, but if I stopped my job at the store, it would all fall apart.

"Please." Griffin squeezed my hand. "Think about it. You can get rid of the rental house and just store your belongings in the workshop here until this mess is over. You pay too much for that place anyway."

My head was swimming. It was all just a little too much. "That place is our home, Griffin."

He looked as if I'd struck him. It wasn't that we weren't comfortable here. If anything, we were too at home. But that little yellow house was where my family had made our way in the world from the moment we stepped out on our own. Out of the shadows and into the light. I wasn't ready to let it go. Especially when the farmhouse wasn't our forever. At least, not anytime soon.

I rubbed soothing circles on the back of Griffin's hand. "That house has been the kids' home for the past six years. I don't want to lose that just to try and save a little money."

Griffin's jaw worked back and forth. "I get it."

It didn't seem like he did. Somehow, I wasn't getting my point across, and I'd hurt him in the process. And I had no idea how to make it better.

Parker cleared his throat. "I'll have deputies doing regular drive-bys and stop-ins. I know your friends have been stopping by, too. Let's keep that up. And I spoke with Mr. Walters. He's going to make sure you're never on shift alone."

"That sounds like a good plan. I'm just sorry everyone has to go to all of this extra trouble."

Griffin's hand spasmed in mine, and he released me. The withdrawal of the touch, his silent support, was physically painful. Griffin stood. "I'm going to grab a beer and check on the kids. You guys need anything?"

I stayed still and silent, but Parker shook his head. "I'm good."

I watched Griffin's back as he stalked away, biting my bottom lip to keep from crying. "I messed up," I whispered.

Parker patted my knee. "You didn't. There's no more

powerless feeling than when someone you care about is in danger. Everything feels out of control. And some of us don't handle it so well."

I looked over at Parker. "I'm not sure that's all it is. He was mad that I wouldn't give up the house. Like it was an insult somehow."

A smile stretched across Parker's face. "He wants you with him. Safe. Where he can keep an eye on you."

My stomach churned. Did Griffin want *me*? Or had he just become fixated on keeping me safe?

Chapter Thirty-Eight

Caelyn

FOR WHAT FELT LIKE THE MILLIONTH TIME THAT DAY, I jumped as the screen door to the store slapped against its wooden frame. "I swear I'm going to break that door in half," I muttered.

"What did it ever do to you?"

I let out a little squeak as I caught sight of Max making his way from the back room, arms full of produce to restock. My cheeks heated. "Sorry. I'm a little jumpy today and ready to take it out on that poor defenseless screen door."

He chuckled but sobered as he took in my face. "Everything okay?"

There was something about Max's focus. It was intense and seemed as if he could read any expression like he was fluent in body language. I broke the stare. "I'm fine. Just a long few weeks."

"Well, I was going to hit up The Catch after closing with some friends. Why don't you join us for a beer or two?"

I studied Max for a moment. I couldn't tell if this was simply a friendly gesture or something else. I got asked out occasionally, but it had been a long time. Some small part of me wanted to say yes. Not because I had any interest in Max, but because I felt a burning urge to stick it to Griffin. Ever since the conversation with Parker, he'd receded into his old scowly, grumpy ways. Only now, it was worse. He'd barely said two words to me since yesterday afternoon. And when you lived in the same house and ate all of your meals with someone, that was a feat.

I blew out a breath. No matter how much of a jerky grumpy-pants Griffin was being, I couldn't do it. Because even at his scowliest and most grunty, I still loved the bugger. Falling in love with a man who might never be able to give me what I needed could be the biggest mistake I'd ever made.

"Uh, Caelyn?" Max began. "Are you all right?"

I blinked a few times. "Sorry. Got lost in outer space for a second. It's really nice of you to ask, but I have plans with Griffin and the kids tonight."

He nodded, heading for the produce section. "Maybe another time. We meet up every week."

"Sure. Maybe."

Kenna appeared right at that moment, rounding the counter and pulling me into a hug. "Hey, Cae. Was the new guy asking you out?"

I pinched Kenna's side. "Quit it."

"Ow! What was that for? You're lucky I'm not nauseous today. Something like that could get you barfed on."

I scowled at her. "Max might've heard you. Don't embarrass him."

Kenna arched a brow. "Do you want him to ask you out?"

"No. But he's nice, and he doesn't deserve to be embarrassed."

Kenna studied me carefully. "What's going on?"

"Oh, I don't know. I had a brick thrown through my window, my sisters were almost abducted, and my mother was murdered. Just a few things."

She winced. "Sorry. I know it's a lot. I didn't mean to come across like a heartless bitch."

"No, I'm sorry." I pulled Kenna in for a hug. "It's just been a very long twenty-four hours."

She rubbed a hand up and down my back as she hugged me. "You know you don't have to be here today. Nobody expects you to go on like nothing happened."

"I don't want to be anywhere else." My voice broke on the last word, tears fighting to get free.

"Hey, hey now." Kenna pulled back but kept hold of my shoulders. "What's this about? Your mom?"

I shook my head. The tears should've been over my mom, but I just couldn't summon them for her. The only thing I felt about my mom was a truckload of guilt, my last words to her playing over and over in my mind. "Things are off with Griffin. And that's really inconvenient because I'm in love with him. I'm terrified that he's just going to be done with me and throw me away."

"Come on." Kenna tugged me into the back office and shut the door. "There are lies taking root in your mind right now, and you need to yank those suckers out. Trust me. I know what it's like to think that everyone who comes into your life is a breath away from leaving it, especially those you love most. But I don't think Griffin's shown any sign of that. He seems pretty stuck on you."

I bit down on my bottom lip, trying to get my riotous emotions under control. "I'm scared all the time, Ken. Before Griffin came into the picture, I was scared that something awful would happen to one of the kids. That I would fall behind on my bills and we would end up homeless. That I'd lose custody. The list is endless. And I was so tired of carrying all that worry on my shoulders. Of having to hold everything all by myself. But then Griffin came along. And he took some of that burden without me even asking. The kids fell in love with him. Before I knew it, I was leaning on him. Depending on him. And he makes me feel so safe. I've never felt as safe as I do in his arms. But now I'm even more scared because what if he decides he doesn't want this. Doesn't want us. Me. I'm not sure I'll ever recover."

Tears glistened in Kenna's eyes, spilling over and down her cheeks. "Love is the most terrifying jump you'll ever make. But I promise you, it's worth it."

"It's worth it to you because it worked out for you and Crosby in the end. I might not be so lucky."

Kenna dug her fingers into my arms. "It'll still be worth it. Because no matter what happens, you're expanding your heart. Increasing your capacity to love. But I wouldn't count Griffin out. I think he's going to come through for you in the end."

I stared at the friend I'd known for my entire life. She'd always been more than a bit of a pessimist. Or a *realist* as she called it. I'd never heard anything like this come out of her mouth. "Who are you, and what have you done with my best friend?"

Kenna gave me a little shove. "Oh, stop it."

"You're even *crying*."

She wiped furiously at her cheeks. "It's the pregnancy hormones. They've turned my tear ducts on at full power."

I gave her a small smile. "Thanks, Ken. I love you. You know that, right?"

"I do. Now you just have to trust that some of that love you pour out into the world will come back around to you."

I took a deep breath. I couldn't lose myself now. I just needed to hold on to hope that, eventually, Griffin and I would find our way, and that what was meant to be would happen. Even if there was hurt along the way.

I moved the rag along the countertop, careful to get every nook and cranny of the surface. Something about the task soothed me.

It always had. So many things were out of my control in my life—it had always been that way. But a good, deep clean always made me feel as if I could put my world back to rights, no matter how far it had veered off path.

I took a moment to stretch my back. The minutes seemed to slow as we got closer to four o'clock. Just ten more ticks on the clock, and I was home-free.

A throat cleared, and I turned towards the sound. "I'm sorry, we're closed for the day—" My words cut off as I recognized the man in front of me. He was the one who had come into the store all those weeks ago and had practically run Shay over. But he looked...less disheveled. His hair was no longer greasy, and his clothes were clean.

The man twisted the ballcap in his hands. "I'm not here for a sandwich, ma'am. I, uh, I'm Dave Herbert."

I froze at the name. How had I not recognized him when he first came in? I'd spent hours staring across a courtroom at his face. The man who had broken into our family home and terrorized my siblings all those years ago. And he was standing in front of me now. My hand slowly reached into my back pocket for the pepper spray I'd put there this morning.

"I'm takin' it by the look on your face you remember me."

"It would be impossible to forget the man who tried to attack my brother and sisters. Who left scars on them they'll never be rid of." Dumb, dumb, dumb. The last thing I needed to do was threaten someone who had a proven track record of violence. I should've been screaming for help. But I couldn't resist the urge to try and make this man understand all the ways he'd hurt my family.

Instead of anger flashing across his face, I saw pain. At least I thought that's what it was. Dave twisted his hat into a tighter spiral. "I wouldn't have hurt them." He sighed, continuing on, almost as if he were talking to himself. "At least, I don't think I

258 | CATHERINE COWLES

would've. But who knows when I'm messed up on that stuff?" His head came up so he could meet my gaze. "I know there's nothing I can say to erase the pain I've caused, but I need you to know I'm sorry. More sorry than you'll ever know. I'm on parole now. And I'm getting help."

I searched his face, trying to ferret out the truth. Or the lie. "You were high when you came in here before."

Dave winced. "I had a slip. Thinking of coming here, facing you, apologizing… I didn't handle it well."

Guilt swirled in my belly. My mother's face flashed in my mind. The final harsh words I'd hurled her way. She had been fighting for her sobriety, but that hadn't been enough for me. Tears stung the backs of my eyes. "I can't forget what you did." I wouldn't lie to him. The terror he'd wrought on my family had molded us all into who we were now. "But I appreciate you coming here to apologize."

Dave swallowed, his Adam's apple bobbing. "I want to make things right. Maybe I could do some work around your house. Or bring you groceries. Whatever you need."

"If you want to make things right, you'll stay sober. You'll work your program, and you won't be the person who hurt my family ever again." A little of my anger lashed out, the rage that had built over the seven years I'd been soothing nightmares and reassuring fears. I swallowed it back. "That's what you can do."

Dave nodded. "I will. Promise. I got a good sponsor, and he's helping me. Please believe me. I don't want to hurt anyone the way I did those kids."

"What did you just say?" a voice growled. I turned to see Griffin stalking towards us. "Who the hell are you?"

Oh, no. This was not going to be good.

Chapter Thirty-Nine

Griffin

I TOOK ANOTHER STEP TOWARDS THE MAN. THE RAGE pumping through my veins was a living, breathing thing. I couldn't have heard him right. This wasn't the man who had terrorized Will, Ava, and Mia. He wouldn't have the audacity to show his face here. "I asked you a question. Who are you?"

"Griffin—" Caelyn began. My head snapped in her direction, and she immediately stopped speaking at the look on my face.

"I—I'm Dave Herbert. I'm not here to start any trouble. I just came to apologize."

"And what are you apologizing for?" I punctuated each word as if it were its own sentence.

The man's jaw went hard, and he lost a little of the fear in his expression. "That's between me and Ms. O'Connor."

"Oh, really, now? Well, Ms. O'Connor is my business, so I beg to differ."

His eyes widened in understanding. "I really did just come to apologize. I swear."

A hand encircled my arm, the touch firm, but the skin delicate. "He's telling the truth, Griffin. Dial it back a notch."

I glanced down at Caelyn. She looked beyond exhausted. Not the kind of tired that meant a lack of sleep, but the kind that spoke of a fatigued soul. My jaw worked. It was my own fault. I'd let my pride and fear get the best of me. When she'd refused to let go of the lease on her house, I couldn't help but take it personally. All the old doubts about letting people into my life took root in my brain. And the thought of her and the kids going back there…it turned my anxiety up to one hundred. Who would look out for them if they were alone? I knew Caelyn could handle just about anything, but I didn't want her to have to take it all on her shoulders. And there was always that one thing you wouldn't be ready for. I knew that better than anyone.

I tried to lessen the ferocity of my expression because it was by no means directed at her. That's what had messed things up between us in the first place—me acting like a grumpy asshole. But Caelyn needed a wakeup call. She always saw the best in people. No matter what. And she needed to be on alert now.

I squeezed the back of her neck. "You don't know him. He could be mixed up in all of this stuff."

"He came to *apologize*."

Caelyn's mind always looked for the positive, never considering the darker implications of someone's actions. Normally, I loved that about her. But right now, I needed her to be a little more suspicious. I turned my gaze towards the man I knew was Dave Herbert. "Where have you been the past few weeks?"

A brief flash of defiance glinted in his eyes. "You're not my parole officer."

My hands fisted and flexed instinctively. "No. But I can guarantee you that Sheriff Raines will be paying you a visit in the near future. And I'm guessing if you're on parole, you'll have to answer those questions. He might even piss-test you. That test going to be clean?"

The defiance in Dave's gaze turned hotter. "I've been here. I got a job working construction."

"You go by Caelyn's house at all since you've been out?"

"What? No. I wouldn't do that," Dave said.

I couldn't get a bead on him. It was as if he were two different people. One who truly was trying to get his life together, and another who was ruled by anger and something darker. Wherever the truth lay, whatever the shade of gray, I wasn't going to figure it out now. "You've said your piece. Now stay away from Caelyn. And don't even think about going near one of the kids."

He held up both hands, slowly backing away. His gaze went from me to Caelyn. "Thank you for listening. I mean it."

She nodded but her grip on my arm tightened, and she didn't say a word. When Dave disappeared from sight, I pulled her into my arms. "Stop taking years off my life." Caelyn was silent, her hands fisting in my shirt—the silent tell that her emotions were running wild. I pressed my lips to her hair. "I'm sorry."

She tipped her head back so that she could see my face. "For what?"

"Being an asshole. You needed support, and I was a selfish prick."

Caelyn searched my face, looking for something. "I don't handle it well when people run."

My brows pulled together. "I didn't run. I was right there."

"You might as well have been a million miles away."

My chest constricted when her voice hitched. I brushed the hair away from her face, cupping her cheeks. "I'm sorry. It's instinct. A self-protection thing. I'll try to be better about it, but I can't promise it won't pop up now and again."

Her grip on my t-shirt tightened. "Protection? From me?"

"No one has more power to hurt me than you do."

Caelyn sucked in a sharp breath. "And you think I'm going to? That I want to cause you pain?"

"No. Not after I've had some distance from it. But in the moment, all I could think about was that I'd handed you everything you would need to destroy me. I know it doesn't make sense, but you holding so tightly to your house…it felt like you were one step from running out of my life."

"Griffin…" Caelyn placed a hand on my chest, over my heart. "I'm not running away. I'm just being smart, practical."

I understood it. We'd barely started dating. But I couldn't imagine the farmhouse without the life Caelyn and the kids brought to it. "I'll miss you when you leave. All of you."

Her face softened. "Do you honestly think you'll keep us away for more than twenty-four hours at a time?" She rolled her eyes heavenward. "I can already hear the whining. *I want to go to the pond. I want to play soccer with Griffin. I want to work on the farmhouse.* I'm never going to hear the end of it. And you know I'm a pushover."

I grinned and tugged Caelyn closer to me, our bodies flush. "And what about you? Will you miss me? Will you whine?"

She stretched up onto her tiptoes and brushed her lips against mine. "I'll miss your mouth." Her fingers wove with mine. "Your hands." Her gaze locked with mine. "How safe you make me feel."

My heart gave a thundering stutter in my chest. "You have it all. And you're not going to lose it being two miles away." Hell, I'd spend every night on that blasted back-killing couch of hers if I had to. Anything so she never felt alone again.

Chapter Forty

Caelyn

"H EY, MOLLS," I GREETED AS SHE ENTERED THE store for her afternoon shift.

She made her way to the back of the store, eyeing me carefully. "Are you okay? You tore out of here with that mountain of a man yesterday before I had a chance to talk to you."

"Sorry. Things have been a bit extreme lately. I really appreciate you and Max closing." The explanation sounded lame even to my ears, but there wasn't a lot I could share with her. Parker was trying to keep a lid on my mom's murder until he had more information. And that meant I hadn't told the kids yet.

Guilt gnawed at me. Will deserved to know. He knew something was up. But I thought he'd reasoned it away as me being tweaked about someone trying to take Ava and Mia. And he wasn't wrong about that. I called the school at least five times a day to check on them. But what had happened to our mother… That terrified me to my bones.

"What's going on?" Molly asked. "Did someone leave you another note?"

I shook my head. I had to give her something. "Someone tried to take the girls from school the other day."

"What? Are they okay?"

I nodded. "They're fine. Sue didn't let him get past the office. But I'm freaked, to say the least."

Molly rounded the counter and gave me a quick hug. "Of course, you are. That's insane. Is there anything I can do?"

"I wish there was. Parker's trying to figure out who's behind all of this but so far, not a lot of luck."

"I can't imagine. Just let me know if you think of anything I can do to help. Whatever you need, okay?"

I smiled, and it wasn't even forced. Some things about living in such a small community were hard, but so many more were wonderful. Like how so many folks had your back, no matter what. "Thank you. It means a lot."

My phone buzzed in my back pocket. Pulling it out, I froze as the high school's number flashed across my screen. This wasn't happening. Not again. I hurried to answer. "Hello? This is Caelyn. Is something wrong? Is Will okay?"

"He's fine, Caelyn," the school's secretary soothed. "But I'm afraid he's gotten himself into some trouble. I need you to come down here."

"He what?" Never. Not once in the past six years had I been called to school because Will was in trouble. It simply wasn't in his nature.

"He's in the principal's office. And Mr. Henry wants to talk to you."

"Okay. Tell him I'm on my way. Thank you for calling." I hit end, my fingers trembling just a bit.

Molly looked back at me with a worried expression. "Is everything okay?"

"I have to go to the school. Will's in the principal's office."

"Will?" Molly asked.

I almost laughed. It wouldn't be unheard of for me to be called to the elementary school because Mia was in trouble. She had a fiery temper and zero tolerance for bullies. She'd put someone in their place by any means necessary. But Will or Ava? Never. "There has to be some mistake. I need to go. Do you think you can convince Max to stay on a little longer?"

I didn't think he'd object. Molly straightened. "You go. I'll get him to stay."

I grabbed my purse and squeezed Molly's shoulder as I passed. "Thank you."

"Anytime. If you need to take the rest of the day, just text me. I can handle things here."

"You're a lifesaver." I hurried out of the store and towards my SUV but paused for a moment halfway there, staring down at my phone. I didn't want to do this alone. I knew I could. I'd faced a million and one minor and major catastrophes myself. But now, I didn't want to. Instead of letting that freak me out, I hit Griffin's name in my contacts. He answered on the first ring.

"Are you okay?"

My lips curved just a bit at the genuine worry in his voice, the care. "I'm fine, but I'm wondering if you can meet me at the high school. It's okay if you're too busy and can't make it. It's not that important."

"Caelyn," he growled. "I'll be there in ten minutes."

"You will?"

"Yes," he said.

"You didn't even ask why."

"I don't need to know why. You asked me to come, so I'll be there."

Emotion, swift and fierce, clogged my throat. I swallowed it down so I could get out two words. "Thank you."

"Always. Wait for me in the parking lot."

"Okay." It was on the tip of my tongue to tell Griffin that I loved him. It was absolutely insane and would probably send him running for the hills, so I swallowed that down, too. But I held it inside me, the knowledge of that truth, the light of it. I'd hold it there for as long as I needed.

"I'll see you soon."

"Soon," I echoed.

The line went dead, and I shook myself from my stupor. Heading for my SUV, I beeped the locks and climbed inside. As soon as the high school came into view, all thoughts of Griffin fled, my mind turning to Will and an endless stream of questions.

I pulled into a parking place where I'd be easy to spot. And as I waited, I drummed an anxious beat on my steering wheel. I wished for magical psychic powers that would allow me to reach through the walls and read the principal's mind—and Will's. To know what was awaiting me so I wasn't ambushed when I got inside.

My heart clenched. What if Will was freaking out right now? Scared, or worse? I shut off my engine and hopped out of my SUV. I started towards the building just as Griffin's truck pulled in next to me. He quickly climbed out, scowling. "I thought I told you to wait for me."

"Don't turn that scowl on me. I started to worry, and I needed to get inside." I headed for the school.

Griffin jogged to catch up, his hand snagging my elbow but not bringing me to a stop. "What happened?"

"Will got into trouble. He's in the principal's office."

"Will?"

I glanced up at Griffin as I continued walking. "I know. There has to be some mix-up."

He wrapped an arm around my shoulders as he pulled open the door with his free hand. "We'll figure it out."

A pleasant warmth spread through me at his words. "Thank you."

He pressed his lips to my temple. "Don't stress."

"Easy for you to say. This kid hasn't been in trouble a day in his life. Something's wrong." Possibilities swam in my head. Each one worse than the one before until I'd come up with all sorts of ridiculous scenarios. But I simply couldn't stop.

Griffin's jaw hardened. "We'll fix it."

"Even if he's expelled?" God, what if his whole future had been ruined today?

Griffin came to a stop outside the office, framing my face with his hands. The feel of his rough calluses against my skin was oddly comforting. He locked his gaze with mine. "Will isn't going to be expelled. I promise."

Something about the ferocity of his tone had me believing every word. I reached up and pressed my lips to his stubbled jaw. Just like the calluses, they were somehow soothing. A reminder that this man had the toughest exterior but the gentlest of spirits beneath. Those three little words yearned to get out yet again. I settled back on my heels. "Let's do this."

Griffin pulled the office door towards him and held it open for me. I searched the space, finding the secretary behind her desk. "Hi, Nicole."

"Hey, Caelyn. Sorry about all of this."

"It's not your fault. Can you tell me what happened?" I'd take any hint she'd give me.

Her eyes widened as Griffin appeared behind me. "I, uh, don't know much, but Will punched another student in the cafeteria."

"What?!" I shrieked.

Griffin gripped my shoulders. "Cool it. You blowing your lid isn't going to help."

I felt as if I were in some weird alternate dimension. Will, *my* Will, punching someone? "Can we go in?"

"Sure." Nicole stood, leading us towards Mr. Henry's office. She knocked twice, and he beckoned us in. Nicole gave me a sympathetic smile and left.

My eyes went instantly to Will. He sat slumped in a chair, an ice pack across his knuckles. I hurried over, sitting next to him and wrapping an arm around his shoulders. "What happened?"

He wouldn't meet my gaze. "I'm sorry."

I rubbed a hand up and down his arm. "Will, no matter what, we're going to figure this out. We're a team, remember?" He nodded slowly. "Now, tell me what happened."

His head rose, his eyes blazing. "Is Mom dead?"

I sucked in a sharp breath. My gaze jumped from Will to the principal and back again. At least Mr. Henry was giving us a moment to talk before he jumped in. Griffin squeezed my shoulders. I wanted to sink back into his hold. Run away from the truth I had to lay at my brother's feet. "I'm sorry, Will."

"Why didn't you tell me?"

"I—I needed some time to figure out how. And Sheriff Raines didn't want people to know yet—" My words cut off as I realized someone had spilled the beans. "Who told you?"

"Drew," Will muttered.

I gritted my teeth. Drew's mom was a dispatcher at the sheriff's department. Parker was definitely getting a heads-up that he needed to have a talk with her. I refocused on Will. "And you punched him when he told you?"

"He said she was probably whoring herself out for drugs, and that's why she got killed. He said we were homeless." Will swallowed, his voice catching. "That no one wanted us, so you were forced to drop out of college and take us in."

A fiery rage lit through me so fast, I nearly toppled off my chair. I never thought I'd have an urge to be violent towards a child, but I wanted to deck Drew myself. I gripped Will's arms, making him face me. "You are wanted. There's no one I'd rather be with than you and Ava and Mia. You're my life. Not because it was forced on me, but because I love you. From the minute you were born and started terrorizing me."

Will's lips gave the faintest twitch, and I pushed on. "I'd be lost without you three. You make my life so much better. And if anyone says otherwise, it's because they're miserable. You hear me?"

Will nodded. "I hear you. I'm sorry. I know I shouldn't have hit him, but it was instinct. He started shoving me around and I just reacted."

"He shoved you?" I asked, my voice tight.

"Yeah. Tried to knock me into one of the columns in the cafeteria."

Blood roared in my ears. "He shouldn't have done that. But you're right, that doesn't mean you should've punched him." There was a grunt behind me, and I wasn't sure if Griffin was siding with me or with Will. I turned to the principal. "What are we looking at here?"

Mr. Henry gave Will and me a gentle smile. "It's an extreme situation. But we have a zero-tolerance policy for violence." My stomach dropped. "Will is suspended for one week."

I let out the breath I'd been holding. That wasn't so bad. "What about Drew?"

Mr. Henry's jaw hardened. "We also have a zero-tolerance policy for bullying. Drew is also suspended for one week, and he'll have mandatory sessions with the school counselor for the remainder of the year. Possibly to be continued when we return in the fall."

"Was anyone else involved?" Griffin asked, but it wasn't directed towards Mr. Henry; he was looking at Will.

Will shrugged. "No one else said anything, really. Just laughed."

A muscle along Griffin's jaw ticked. "You did the right thing, Will."

"Griffin," I hissed. "He should not be punching people to solve his problems."

"Sometimes, there's no other choice. They would've given him hell for the rest of the year if he hadn't stood up for himself, defended himself. Now, they'll all know to keep their mouths shut and their hands to themselves." Griffin turned to Will. "But if you're man enough to stand up for yourself, you're man enough to deal with the consequences. The ones from school and whatever your sister decides for at home."

Will nodded solemnly. "I'll do what I have to."

My head ping-ponged back and forth, looking from Griffin to Will. When had this happened? And as irritated as I was at Griffin for telling Will that punching some kid was the right move, especially in front of the principal, I couldn't argue with his reasoning.

I sighed and looked at Mr. Henry. "Sorry about…" I wasn't even sure how to finish that sentence.

Mr. Henry's lips pressed into a firm line as if he were trying not to laugh. "Don't be. You're raising a good young man there. We all have our moments where we have to take a stand."

"Thank you. We'll be back next week." I pushed to my feet, heading out of the office. "Come on. Will, you're going to have to ride home with Griffin. I have to go back to work. If I haven't been fired for bailing on them so much this month, that is."

Griffin grinned, shaking his head. "You're not going to be fired. You're too good at what you do."

"We'll see." I held my palm out and looked at Will. "Phone."

His mouth fell open. "But it's my birthday tomorrow. None of my friends will be able to call or text me."

I wavered a bit in my resolve. Will would only turn seventeen once. "You can have it for an hour tomorrow, but other than that, no tv, video games, or phone for a week. You'll help Griffin with the farmhouse this week when you're done with your schoolwork for the day, and you won't be getting paid."

I turned to Griffin. "And don't even think about paying him behind my back."

Griffin held up both hands in surrender. "Wouldn't dream of it. Why don't you head back to work? We've got it from here."

I nodded and started to walk away. Then I turned back and pulled Will into a tight hug. "I love you more than life. Don't you ever forget it." He nodded against my shoulder, and I fought the tears that wanted to surface. I released him and started for the exit. I just hoped I didn't run into Drew on the way. I wasn't sure I'd be able to stop myself from giving him a nice uppercut to the jaw.

Griffin

"**Y**OU'RE NOT GOING TO GIVE ME A LECTURE?"

I kept focused on the task in front of me, rolling a smooth line of paint onto the wall. In another twenty-four hours, the living room would be finished. With Will's help, the house would be done by mid-Fall. "Do you need a lecture?"

"I don't know," he mumbled. "I might feel less guilty if Caelyn had yelled at me."

I chuckled. "The worst is when they say they're disappointed in you."

Will paused his painting. "I don't think Caelyn's ever said that. Not to me, or Ava or Mia. Not even when Mia painted the hallway with her bright pink glitter nail polish."

Of course, she hadn't. I often forgot that these kids carried around a world of wounds invisible to most eyes. And Caelyn's tender heart would refuse to risk the addition of any more. "That's because you guys make your sister proud."

"Not today, I didn't."

I set down my paint roller. "Sometimes, you have to do

what's right for yourself. Even if that means letting someone else down."

Will gave his head a stern shake. "I never want to let Caelyn down."

"Even if that means abandoning yourself?" I'd had flickers of concern the first time Will and I had talked about his future, but the more time I spent with the teen, the more that worry grew.

His jaw flexed. "I'm not abandoning myself. I'm just making things easier for Caelyn. For Ava and Mia, too."

There was too much on those slender shoulders. Too much on the shoulders of everyone in the O'Connor family. They all carried more than their share of burdens in hopes they could make it easier for those they loved. The weight completely disproportionate because of all that had been leveled on them at such a young age.

"Come on." I motioned for Will to follow me. He set his brush down and headed after me as I wound my way through the halls and upstairs. There were two guest rooms at the far end of the house that I wanted to make into a single room. It would make for a perfect rec room. Space for a large television with overstuffed couches. And more than enough room for whatever games the kids wanted to play. Somewhere along the line, I'd started making plans for the house that revolved around each of them.

We came to a stop in the first room, and Will looked around. "We haven't worked in here yet."

"Nope."

"What are you thinking?"

I motioned to a wall. "That's coming down."

Will's eyes widened. "The wall?"

"Yep."

"When?"

"I think now's a good time." An idea was forming in my mind, circling around a memory. When I'd gotten in trouble mixing it up at school, my father had taken me to cut firewood. We hadn't even had a wood-burning fireplace in our house in Marin, but he'd known that I needed to let off some steam. A pressure release so I could finally talk things through with him.

I picked up one of the two sledgehammers and a pair of goggles and handed them to Will. I'd already checked the farmhouse's plans, and there were no pipes or wires we would disturb. "Have at it."

"You want me to swing this at the wall?"

I chuckled. Will looked as if I were trying to trick him into something. I picked up the other hammer. After putting the goggles in place, I heaved the hammer over my head and sent it flying into the wall.

"Holy shit," Will said.

I inclined my head towards the wall. "Have at it."

It took him a moment, but he finally took a swing, sending the end of the hammer into the wall. Plaster and bits of drywall went flying. "Whoa." He turned to face me. "That's awesome."

I grinned. "Let's do this." We let it fly for the next fifteen minutes, and when I thought he'd begun to work some of the energy out of his system, I paused in my destruction. "You ready to talk?"

Will launched his sledgehammer at the wall again. "About what?"

"Your mom, Drew, take your pick."

He yanked the hammer free of the wall. "She's not my mom."

I froze. "What do you mean?"

"A mom isn't just someone who shares your blood. They're supposed to look out for you, take care of you, love you. She never seemed to be able to figure that out. Caelyn is more of a mom than Chrissy will ever be." He paused, letting the tool come to rest by his side. "Would ever be. Not like she's going to get a chance to make things right now."

My heart ached for the kid. No matter how much his mom had let him down, a part of him had still been holding onto hope that she'd get it together. "You're allowed to be sad. Just because she was a crappy mom most of the time doesn't mean there isn't a part of you that won't miss her."

Will's jaw clenched, and he sent the hammer into the wall again. "I'm not sad." He wailed on the wall another few times.

"Then what are you?"

Will whirled on me. "What is this? Some messed up therapy session? I don't want to talk about it."

I considered my words carefully as if each one had the potential to set off a landmine. "You can't keep holding all of this inside." After spending the past few months working alongside Will, I'd started to realize that he stuffed everything down. He didn't want to be a burden to his sister, to worry her, so he simply kept silent and pretended that he wasn't feeling anything at all.

"Why not? Isn't that exactly what you do?"

I sucked in a sharp breath, opening my mouth to deny his accusation and then thought better of it. "I used to. And it almost killed me." Will was silent, but his eyes were intensely focused. "After my family died and so many people betrayed me, I didn't have a safe outlet for my pain. I shoved it all down. Just like you're doing now. But the thing is, pain finds a way to the surface, and it's usually ugly if you've been trying to control it."

"What happened?" he whispered.

"I started drinking so much, it's a miracle I didn't end up with liver failure. I needed six or seven drinks just to quiet the memories so I could sleep. And during the day, I was barely living." Memories of the years I'd spent just traveling the country flooded my mind. I had no purpose and was so damn alone.

"I've never seen you drunk."

"No. I have a beer now and then, but I made a promise to myself a long time ago that I'd find another way to deal. It took me a while to find it, but this house became my outlet. I worked myself to the bone so I could pass out at the end of the day. But as I was hauling trash and refinishing floors, I started to work through some of the worst of the memories. There was nothing else around to distract me. I had to face it."

Will swallowed hard. "Did it work?"

I leaned back against the wall. "It helped. A lot. But it wasn't until I let people in again that I finally felt some peace."

"Caelyn?"

"Yes." My chest constricted. "She's this soft place to land that I didn't think I'd ever have. She's unconditional acceptance and complete trust. But you and your sisters have helped, too." Will looked skeptical, and I chuckled. "You brought life back into this place. Back to me. I'll never be able to repay you for that. But I can be a safe space for you, Will. You can tell me anything. It doesn't matter how ugly or selfish or hard. I'm here."

Will's face reddened with the force of holding himself back. I pushed off the wall and started towards him. He shook his head, pulling off his goggles. "No, I'm fine."

I kept coming. "You don't have to be fine. No one is all of the time."

His breathing picked up, coming faster and faster. "I—I. No."

I gripped his shoulders. "Let it out."

He shook his head. "I'm not weak."

My gaze locked with Will's as I squeezed his shoulders harder. "Let it out. You're safe here."

He broke. Sobs wracked his body, and I pulled him into my arms. "Never be ashamed of feeling deeply. It doesn't make you weak. It makes you so incredibly strong."

He shook violently as he cried. "I hate her. Both Mom and Dad. For what they did to us. For everything." He sucked in air. "And it's all my fault."

I didn't let go. I held on as he wept. "What's your fault?"

"I knew they were messed up in bad stuff, but I didn't tell anyone. I just wanted Caelyn to finish school so she could get us out of there. I didn't want to go into foster care and maybe have to switch schools or be separated from my sisters. So, I kept my mouth shut. I almost got us killed."

My heart shattered at his words. The weight this boy was carrying was too much for anyone. "I need you to hear me, Will. None of this was your fault. Not a damn thing. You did everything you could to protect your sisters. You picked the wrong path. Everyone does. All you can do is learn from it and carry the lesson with you."

"But choosing the wrong path doesn't usually almost get your family killed."

I held him tighter. "But they didn't. They're alive and thriving. You guys are together, and your life is so good."

Will's sobbing slowed. "Caelyn works too hard. She doesn't think I see it, but until you came along, she was practically killing herself just so we could have anything we wanted."

I pulled back a little so I could see Will's face but kept a hold of his arms. "Is that why you give up everything you want?"

Wariness filled Will's expression. "What do you mean?"

"You play a sport you hate in the hopes of getting a scholarship. But you say you might not even go to college because Caelyn needs help. You don't take music lessons even though you love it. I'm guessing because they're expensive. What else are you giving up on because you think it might be a burden to your sister?"

He bit down on his bottom lip. "I just want to make things easier for her."

"You not being honest about who you are and what you want isn't going to make things easier on Caelyn. It's robbing her and the rest of the world of experiencing the real you. Name what you want. Chase it. We'll figure out how to support you, and I promise I won't let your sister hurt herself because of it."

Will was silent for a moment. "I want to play music. And I want to go to college. I want to take architecture classes and see if I like it. I want to see more of the world than this island."

I smiled and knew it stretched my face so wide it was probably scary. "Then let's chase those dreams."

Chapter Forty-Two

Caelyn

I HEADED UP THE STAIRS AND TOWARDS THE SOUNDS OF destruction, leaving Ava and Mia drawing on the back deck with Kenna. My muscles protested each step. The last couple of days had seemed like a lifetime, and all I wanted was a long bath and to sleep for at least twelve hours. Instead, I needed to have a long talk with Will.

I paused in the doorway, watching as Griffin and Will attacked a wall that separated two rooms. They seemed to move in tandem, a silent and invisible rhythm tying the two of them together. As Griffin pulled back for another swing, he spotted me in the doorway. He set his hammer down and pulled off his goggles.

As he strode towards me, my stomach hollowed. He radiated power and self-assurance as he moved through the space. Without a word, he pulled me towards him. The kiss he laid on me wasn't a casual hello. It was hungry and just a bit desperate. When I pulled back, I had to take a second to steady myself. "That was a heck of a hello."

"Missed you," he said as if that were the only reason necessary.

"Missed you, too. I'm ready for food, wine, and bed."

Griffin glanced over his shoulder at Will, who was still working away. A flicker of guilt passed over his features. "I think we need to talk before that happens."

My stomach pitched. "What now?" Had this week not rained down enough hardship?

Griffin grimaced but linked his fingers with mine, tugging me into the hallway. "Will and I had a talk this afternoon."

"A talk?" That wasn't exactly something to write home about. I often found Will and Griffin with their heads together, talking about the house or school or a million other topics.

"I pushed. I could tell he'd been holding a lot inside, and I didn't want that shit eating him up."

I tensed. My first instinct was to snap at Griffin that pushing Will wasn't his job. But I swallowed the words back. I'd known for a while now that Will was holding things back from me. Maybe they were things that he simply felt more comfortable sharing with a man. "What did he say?"

Griffin glanced over his shoulder towards the room where Will was working before returning his focus to me. "He blames himself for what happened that night."

"What night?"

"When that asshole broke in and terrorized him and his sisters. He knew things were off with your parents, but he didn't tell anyone. He's taking everything that happened on himself. And now he's doing everything he can to keep from being a burden."

"Oh, God." I felt sick to my stomach. "None of this was his fault. I can't—" Tears filled my eyes.

Griffin cupped my face, sweeping his roughened thumbs across my cheeks. "I know. And I told him that. But I think he could use hearing it from you, too. It's going to take some time for it to sink in."

I nodded woodenly. "Other than the night I picked them up at the sheriff's station he hasn't said a word about blaming himself."

"He's ashamed."

My insides gave a painful twist. My beautiful boy with the biggest of hearts. I couldn't handle the knowledge that he'd been carrying this around for so long. I took a shuddering breath, trying to get my emotions under control. Me crying all over him was not going to help the situation. "I need to see him."

Griffin pressed his lips to my forehead and then let me go. "He loves you."

"I know." I couldn't disguise the tremble in my voice, and I silently prayed that I could hold it together through this conversation.

Griffin led the way back into the construction zone and flagged Will down so that he stopped his demolition. Griffin inclined his head to me. "Your sister's home."

Will stiffened, and the action might as well have been a knife to the heart. When had Will ever been nervous to talk to me? Acid churned in my stomach. Always, I realized. We'd talked about so many things, but he'd never once shared what was deepest in his heart. I tried to smile. "Hey. This looks pretty impressive."

Will looked from me to Griffin and back again. "Griffin told you what we talked about, huh?"

Griffin gave Will a comforting slap on the back. "Just a little. But I think it's time that you and your sister really talk. Yeah?"

Will nodded. "Will you stay?"

Griffin looked to me as if for permission. I swallowed. "Of course, he can stay." I took a few more steps into the room, hesitant as first, but I couldn't stop once I started moving. I pulled Will into my arms, wrapping him in a hard hug. "I love you. None of this was your fault. Not a single thing. You got that?"

He nodded against my shoulder. "That's what Griffin said."

"Well, Griffin might be grumpy at times, but he's also really freaking smart, so I'd listen to him if I were you."

Will let out a little laugh and pulled back. "True."

Griffin scowled at both of us. "Who are you calling grumpy?"

Will and I grinned at each other. But after a moment, Will's smile slipped from his face. "I want to quit football."

My mouth opened and closed a few times. "But you love football."

He grimaced. "I hate it, actually. I'd rather take some music lessons instead. I can pay for them with what I make working for Griffin."

I gripped Will's arm, squeezing. "You don't have to pay for them yourself. I'd love to get you lessons." And thanks to Griffin's generosity, I didn't even have to check my bank account before I offered it. I surveyed my brother. "If you hated it so much, why did you keep playing?"

Will shrugged. "I was good at it. And Coach said I could probably get a scholarship for it."

"And you didn't want me to have to worry about college tuition." I couldn't believe I hadn't put the pieces together until now. Will was never jazzed on game days or overly excited when his team won a game. But I'd always thought it was simply his way of staying centered and focused. Meanwhile, he'd been spending hours on end every week doing something he hated, just to take some pressure off me.

"I didn't want you to have to worry about it."

"That's my job, Will. I'm the worrier here."

His eyes blazed. "It's not your job. It was Mom and Dad's job, but they failed, and it got dumped on you. It's not fair."

Anger flared to life inside me. At our dad. At our mom. At the drugs that'd destroyed everything in their path. But I couldn't rage against my parents or inanimate objects. So, my rage ate at me from the inside out. "It might not have been my job to take care of you from birth. But it's the job I've loved more than anything I've ever done. I wouldn't give it up if you paid me a million dollars. Sure, it's hard sometimes, but that just makes it all the more worth it when we succeed."

Will still looked skeptical. I pressed on. "We're a team. You, me, Ava, and Mia. We figure things out together. That means we'll figure college out, too. But I don't want you to hide your dreams from me because you think following them is asking too much. If you want to go to school to study music, we'll make it happen."

Will's gaze flicked briefly to Griffin. "I think I want to study architecture."

My chest burned. Architecture. Because he'd loved bringing this old house back to life. And Griffin had given him that. "I think you'd be an amazing architect. And look at all the experience you're already getting."

"You don't think it's dumb?" he asked hesitantly.

"Not dumb at all. And I'll do whatever I can to help you get there."

⌒◎

I set the final dish from dinner in the dishwasher and pressed the door closed. The machine whirred to life once I pressed the buttons. Bracing myself against the kitchen sink, I stared out at the night sky. Will, Griffin, and I had talked for hours. Well, Will had talked. Griffin and I had mostly listened. And I witnessed a side to my brother I'd never seen before. The things he wanted weren't extravagant. They were normal. But he'd been too afraid to reach for them.

There was heat at my back, and strong arms wrapped around me. "Are you okay?"

I leaned into Griffin's warmth, soaking up the comfort of his presence. "Would you be?"

He grunted. "You've had a rough few weeks."

Understatement of the century. "I feel like such a failure."

Griffin turned me to face him, searching my eyes. "Why?"

My breathing picked up speed as I tried in vain to shove the tears down. "He's been hurting, and I didn't even see it. What kind of pseudo-parent does that make me? Maybe Patti was right. I just don't have the right instincts."

Griffin's expression hardened. "Don't you dare agree with that woman. You are the best pseudo-parent I've ever seen. But growing up, it's messy and hard, and he's going to stumble along the way."

"But you saw it. You saw that he was holding back and knew you had to break through that wall."

Griffin brushed the hair away from my face. "I saw it because I've been there."

I twisted my fingers in his t-shirt. "I'm so sorry. For both of you. I hate that either of you were hurting. That you felt alone."

Griffin brushed his lips against my temple. "I don't feel alone anymore."

I tipped my face up to his, our lips a breath apart. "And you won't. Not ever again."

His mouth crashed down on mine. A searching hunger took over as I lost myself in Griffin's lips and tongue, in the feel of his body pressed against mine. I pulled back, breathing hard. "The kids are asleep." He nodded. "Take me to bed."

He searched my face, looking for something. That I was emotionally stable enough to make this decision perhaps. I fisted his shirt harder. "Please. I need to feel you. All of you." I wanted to get lost in this man who had come to mean comfort and safety, yet at the same time, could set my nerve endings on fire.

Whatever Griffin was looking for, he seemed to find it because he lifted me up in a flash. My legs encircled his waist, and I muffled my shriek in his neck as he took the stairs two at a time. When we reached the master bedroom, Griffin slowly lowered me. The friction as my center passed over the ridge in his jeans had me sucking in air.

As my feet hit the floor, Griffin framed my face with his hands. "You're so damn beautiful. I can't tell you how long I've wanted this moment. To know what your body feels like wrapped around mine. The taste of your skin. To be consumed by that light that flickers all around you."

The burning heat in Griffin's eyes lit me from the inside out. Never in my life had I felt more desired than in this moment. Wanted for my body and mind, my heart and soul. My hands went to the button on Griffin's jeans, popping it open and pulling down the zipper. I let out a strangled sound as my hand met the rigid line of him. I took him in my palm, and Griffin let out a groan. "You keep doing that, and we aren't going to get to have any fun."

I grinned. "This seems pretty fun to me."

"You don't know the meaning of the word." Griffin froze. "Shit."

I released my hold on him, looking up. "What?"

"I don't have any condoms." His gaze swept over my face. "I haven't been with anyone for a long time."

My stomach flipped. "I haven't either. And I'm on the pill."

He trailed a finger down my neck, hooking it in my sundress's strap and pulling it down. "Can I take you bare? Feel every inch of you?"

I shivered. "Yes."

Suddenly, my dress was in a pool at my feet, and Griffin's eyes flared. "No bra?"

My cheeks heated. "Can't really wear one with this dress."

His fingers hooked in the sides of my panties, and he slowly pulled them down my legs, each millimeter stoking the flame that had been lit in me. He lifted one leg and then the other, his eyes focused solely on the apex of my thighs. His thumb stroked my folds. "Shouldn't be surprised you're beautiful here, too."

"Please," I whimpered.

Griffin looked up at me through hooded eyes. "What do you need?"

"You." It was such a simple answer, but it was the only truth I had. I needed to feel him moving in me. To have him sear his essence into my bones so I'd never lose him.

Griffin pushed to his feet, pulling his shirt over his head and shucking his pants. He was in front of me in a flash, moving me back towards the bed. "You have me."

"Prove it."

As Griffin lowered me to the bed, I trembled. Not out of fear or nerves but because I knew this moment would change everything. I raised my knees, hooking my legs around him. His tip bumped against my entrance, but he stopped there, staring into my eyes.

Then, without a word, he slid inside, showing me everything I needed to know without another sound. In the gentle sweep of his rough fingers across my nipples. In the trail of his tongue down the column of my throat. In the slow, steady build of his thrusts.

I sucked in a sharp breath as he drove deeper. Griffin stilled. "You okay?"

"More. Please."

He grinned and began moving in earnest. Driving me higher with each thrust of his hips. The spot he reached inside twisted some invisible cord inside me so tight, I thought I'd surely snap, never to recover again.

Griffin's thumb found my clit, circling. Each tease and stroke stopped just shy of the place I knew would send me over the edge. With each pass, he came a little closer. Sparks of light danced across my vision as I reached for it, that invisible string holding us together, pulling us closer.

My fingers dug into his shoulders, my eyes locking with his, a million silent things passing between us. I could see it then. The love that shone there. And as Griffin swiped the pad of his thumb where I needed him most, I came apart. And I did it knowing he'd catch every piece of me.

Chapter Forty-Three

Griffin

THERE WAS NOTHING LIKE HOLDING CAELYN IN MY arms. The knowledge that she was wholly mine, and I was hers. The scent of her filling my senses, and the feel of her body cocooned by mine. It was like coming home. To a home that I'd been missing for so long, I'd lost any hope of finding it again.

I'd had her twice but still couldn't stop my fingers from wandering, from exploring every inch of her silken skin. She squirmed when I trailed a fingertip over the inside of her elbow. I grinned. "Ticklish?"

"Maybe…"

"Good to know." I wanted to make a note of every reaction she had. As if I could make a map of her body, discovering hidden paths and secret treasures.

Caelyn let out a little moan. "I'm so sleepy."

It was understandable. She'd been through the wringer today. I kept stroking her skin. "I should warn you, I have nightmares pretty often." The last thing I wanted was to terrify Caelyn because I was thrashing around. Worse, I could hurt her.

She turned in my arms so that we were face-to-face. "About your family?"

I nodded, my fingers tracing an invisible pattern on her bare shoulder. "About the boat sinking. My sister. It all plays back like a movie."

"I'm so sorry. That sounds trite. But I am. I can't imagine having to relive that over and over."

Normally, sympathy like Caelyn was showing felt too much like pity. But I knew that she didn't pity me. Caelyn simply had the largest heart I'd ever encountered. The empathy she felt for others made their pain hers. I pressed my lips to her temple. "Thank you."

She placed a palm on my chest, right over my heart. "Do you want me to leave?"

There was a flicker of pain in her voice that had me kicking myself and my demons. I searched her face. "Not if you don't want to. But if I start to talk in my sleep or move around, I want you to go. Don't try to wake me up. Okay?"

"I promise." She burrowed into my chest. "Why do I feel like we've been like this a million times before? That you've held me just like this? …And that sounded really silly."

I held her tighter against me. "No. I feel the same way. Like I've somehow always known you."

Her head tipped back so that she could see my face. "That's it exactly. How does that happen?"

"I don't know. I've never experienced it before."

Caelyn's fingers trailed across my chest. "Me either."

I watched as her thoughts seemed to drift. I wanted to see into that beautiful mind of hers and know every thought and dream. "If your life could look like anything, what would it be?"

Her mouth curved. "I love that game. I'd have my own little café. Something small where I could have a real connection with the patrons. A place where I was in charge of the menu but didn't feel like I had to be there from open to close every single day. I'd be married and have a slew of kids. Our house would be barely organized chaos but filled with so much joy. And Will, Ava, and Mia would love their honorary siblings. We'd have game nights and movie nights and a million different holiday traditions." She was quiet for a moment. "Everything I didn't have growing up."

I couldn't help seeing myself in the vision Caelyn painted. Chasing little ones with her green eyes around our yard. I wanted her to have it all. Every little piece that she'd envisioned for her life. I swept my lips across hers. "It'll happen. I know it will."

"I hope so."

We were both quiet for a while, but I couldn't stop thinking about Caelyn's dreams. About the family she was so desperate to create. About the one she'd already brought together in such a beautiful way. "I want to do something special for Will's birthday."

Caelyn's expression softened. "You're already letting us have a party here. And I'm making all of his favorite meals tomorrow. Breakfast, lunch, and dinner. None of which I should be doing because, technically, he's grounded."

I chuckled. "You know you'd never let Will's birthday pass without celebrating it."

"Fine," she huffed. "I'm a total pushover. Do whatever you want to make this day special for him."

I brushed my mouth against hers. "Thank you."

Caelyn looked as if she wanted to ask more but held herself back. "I guess we'll both be surprised then."

"I guess you will."

I gave a wave to the final delivery truck that had stopped at the workshop that afternoon. As I turned to take in the space, I couldn't believe I'd pulled it off. Crosby grinned at me. "Will is going to flip."

"I hope so." I winced. "I also hope Caelyn doesn't murder me."

Crosby chuckled. "It is going a tad overboard."

I scrubbed a hand over my jaw. "Maybe a little. But thanks for helping me make this happen." I'd called Ford and Crosby this morning and told them my plan. Ford had stayed with Will, keeping him busy while Crosby and I had transformed the workshop. Now, I couldn't wait to show him.

"Dinner's ready," Caelyn called from the back deck.

As Crosby and I headed back towards the house, I took in a sight I never thought I'd see at the farmhouse again. It was full of people. Hunter and Will manned the grill. Ford gave Mia a piggyback ride around the yard, while Kenna shouted for them to go faster. Ava helped Bell and Caelyn set serving platters on the overly decorated picnic table.

"I'm going to need more furniture out here," I muttered. As it was, we'd had to set up one of those folding tables and chairs for extra seating.

Crosby grinned. "Bet you never thought you'd be saying that."

"No kidding."

Caelyn motioned everyone towards the table. "All right, everyone, let's sit."

The meal was everything I'd grown to expect from these family dinners. Boisterous and full of laughter, though tonight had the added fun of celebrating Will's birthday. Everyone had brought him something. From a new video game to a gift card to the local hardware store to continue building his tool collection. Caelyn had somehow managed to get him both a book on architecture and a gift card for the music lessons of his choice in the past twelve hours. Will was beside himself.

Crosby cleared his throat. "Before Griffin gives you his present, I have something else for you."

Will's brows drew together. "But you and Kenna already gave me that game."

Crosby swallowed, looking at Kenna, who gave him an

encouraging smile. "This is actually from Harriet. When she had me draft her will, she asked for this to be given to you on your seventeenth birthday."

The table was instantly quiet. Mia looked at Caelyn. "Harriet sent him a present from heaven?"

Caelyn's eyes glistened. "It looks like she did."

Crosby handed a card to Will. Moving with care, Will opened the envelope. As he scanned the page, his body went rigid. When he looked up, his eyes were just a bit red. "She left me a college fund. It'll pay for wherever I want to go to school."

Caelyn gasped, her eyes filling with tears as she looked at Kenna. "Did you know about this?"

Kenna shook her head. "Not until today."

Will stared down at the paper. "I can't even thank her."

Caelyn wrapped an arm around him, but it was Kenna who spoke. "She knows, Will. That's why she gave it to you. Because she knew how much you'd cherish it."

God, I'd fallen into such a good group of people. One I probably didn't deserve but wasn't giving up for anything. I cleared my throat. "You can still tell her." Will met my gaze. "I talk to my parents and sister all the time. Maybe there's a place you felt close to her. Go there and tell her how grateful you are."

He nodded and looked at Kenna and Crosby. "The beach at The Gables. Maybe I could come by sometime and say thank you."

Kenna's smile was a bit wobbly, but she managed to hold back the tears. "You're welcome any time."

Ava looked at me. "What about Griffin? He still has something for Will."

I smiled at the girl whose comfort around me was one of the best gifts I'd ever received. "That's right, I do. We're going to have to take a field trip, though." And what I had couldn't exactly measure up to a full-ride to the college of one's choosing, but that didn't matter. What was important was that Will felt loved and cared for and seen.

I pushed up from the table and motioned for our group to follow me to the workshop. Caelyn found her way to my side, and I wrapped an arm around her. "You okay?" I whispered.

She nodded. "I can't believe Harriet did that. She's already done so much for us. Without her, I never would've gotten on my feet."

"She loved you, and this was just another way she could show you."

"You're right." Caelyn pressed a kiss to the underside of my jaw. "Now, are you going to tell me what you've been working on all day?"

"That would ruin the surprise."

"Oh, fine," she huffed.

As we reached the workshop, Crosby pushed Will to the front of our group and then joined me at the sliding barn doors. We each took hold of one. With a nod, we slid them open. There were a few gasps, and Mia let out a shriek. "Will! Look at all the instruments."

Will stood in stunned silence, gazing around the room. He took in the drum set and the baby grand piano. The electric guitar and the bass. The acoustic guitar and the banjo. There was some basic recording equipment, too. He slowly took one step forward and then another, his eyes jumping from one thing to another. Then he turned to me. "This—this is all for me?" I nodded. "Why?"

The single word broke something in me. "Because you should chase any dream you have."

He flew at me, his arms engulfing me in a fierce hug. "Love you, Griffin."

A burn took up root in the back of my throat. "Love you, too."

Caelyn

"**P**ANCAKES?" MIA ASKED HOPEFULLY AS SHE ENTERED the kitchen.

My mouth curved. Never had I been happier to get that question. Griffin and I had sat the girls down a few nights ago to tell them that Mom had passed away. Mia had been confused, but Ava had been angry, slamming doors until she finally broke down and had a good cry. They'd both been quiet since.

Nothing could break my heart more than knowing that my tiny terrors were hurting. Worse, there was nothing I could do to fix it. But Mia asking me for pancakes said that at least she was on her way back to life as normal.

"Sorry, Mi. You're going to have to settle for egg bake and muffins."

She eyed me suspiciously. "Bran muffins or yummy muffins?"

Griffin choked on a laugh as he lifted his glass of orange juice. I turned, pointing my spatula at him. "Don't encourage her."

"Wouldn't dream of it," he said, taking a swig of his juice.

Will grinned. "Yummy ones."

Mia let out a little squeal. "What kind?"

"My bran muffins taste yummy," I argued.

Ava appeared in the doorway. "Sorry, Cae Cae. They taste a little like cardboard."

I scowled at all of them. "If my muffins taste like cardboard, then maybe I shouldn't share these snickerdoodle ones with you."

"Snickerdoodle!" Mia shrieked.

"Did you go to The Mad Baker this morning?" Ava asked.

"Nope. Jules shared her recipe with me so I could make some for you hooligans. But I guess I'll just have to eat them all myself."

"No!" Mia cried, tugging on my free hand. "I'll eat all the vegetables you want if I can have one."

I grinned down at her. "I'm going to remember that at dinner tonight."

She scrunched up her face. "I shouldn't have said *all*. I should've said I'd eat one vegetable."

Will popped a piece of egg bake into his mouth. "Rookie mistake."

I huffed as I brought the basket of muffins to the table and took a seat. "You'd all probably be vitamin deficient if it wasn't for me." I handed the basket to Griffin. "And you'd probably be halfway to a heart attack with all the crud you put in your body."

He brushed his lips across mine as he took the basket. "Thank God I have you to keep me alive."

"Are you guys gonna get married?" Mia piped in.

Griffin and I both froze, our eyes widening. I cleared my throat and looked around the table. Will was turning red, trying to hold in his laughter. Ava simply looked curious. But Mia... she appeared hopeful. I took a quick sip of my juice. "Mia, people usually date for a long time before they get married. Griffin and I haven't known each other that long."

The words tasted like a lie. It felt as if Griffin and I had known each other forever. We'd fallen so easily into this pseudo-family life. But he'd not once brought up the future. Whether he wanted marriage and babies or if he was happy with things as they were now.

Mia looked back and forth between Griffin and me. "Well, if you do get married, I want to be a flower girl. Or a junior bridesmaid. Lisa's mom got married, and she got a really pretty new dress. It was all sparkly."

I couldn't hold in my laughter. Mia wasn't confused or worried about the relationship status of her sister or whether her life was about to change. She simply wanted a new sparkly dress. I glanced at Griffin, who was grinning down at his plate. "We'll keep that in mind."

"I think it would be nice," Ava said softly. "If we were always together like this."

I reached under the table and grabbed Griffin's thigh. My grip was so tight, I was surprised he didn't at least mutter a curse. Instead, he wrapped an arm around my shoulders and met Ava's gaze. "I like being together like this, too. You make this house a lot more fun."

"That's 'cause we're awesome," Mia added helpfully.

Will smiled. "She's not wrong. We are pretty rad."

I swallowed the emotions gathering in the back of my throat. "Well, my rad friends, hurry up and finish breakfast so we aren't late for school."

The kids hurried to finish up what they were eating, and Mia asked for a second muffin in her school lunch. I assured her there was already one in her rainbow lunchbox. As they ran to get their backpacks, I turned to face Griffin. "So, that was, um, interesting."

He trailed a hand down the column of my throat. "Mia's love of sparkly dresses knows no bounds."

I couldn't help the flicker of disappointment that rose at his words. Not that I expected him to drop to one knee, but a hint of what he saw for our future would've been nice. I stood, pushing my chair back. "That she does."

Griffin followed me, grabbing my hand. "Hey, is something wrong?"

I shook my head. "No. I'm just tired. My coffee hasn't kicked in yet."

He studied me carefully. "If you're sure."

"I'm sure." The last thing I wanted to do was put pressure on Griffin to name what this thing between us was. To promise me things he wasn't ready to give. I gave him a quick kiss. "I'll see you after work."

I started down the hallway and pulled open the front door. "Tiny terrors, I'll meet you in the car." A chorus of agreements met my ears, and I started towards my SUV parked in the drive behind Griffin's truck.

I came to a stop as I saw a paper fluttering against the windshield, held in place by only the windshield wiper. A chill skittered up my spine. It was probably just a drawing Mia had made me. I told myself that over and over as I walked slowly towards my SUV. There was no way someone had gotten onto the farmhouse property. There were locked gates and cameras and alarms.

My hand shook as I pulled the paper free. The blood drained from my head. There was a photo tacked to the note, one of me and the kids two Christmases ago in our matching PJs, but Will, Ava, and Mia's faces were all scratched out. And written in block letters was: *You stole my life from me. Now I'm going to take yours from you.*

Chapter Forty-five

Griffin

I CHUCKLED AS FOOTSTEPS THUNDERED DOWN THE STAIRS. You would've thought a herd of elephants was heading off to school instead of three kids. "Got everything you need?"

"Yep!" Mia called. Ava nodded, smiling. And Will offered me a fist bump.

I met his gaze. "Remember what we talked about?"

"Avoid Drew whenever I can."

"Good man."

Mia pulled open the front door, but was met by Caelyn barreling into the house as soon as she did. "No, go back inside right now."

Her sharp tone had Mia scrambling back, colliding with my body. I wrapped my arms around the little girl. "What is it? What's wrong?"

Caelyn slammed the door, locking it. "Are all the other doors locked?"

I quickly passed Mia off to a worried Will, who wrapped her in a hug. I strode to Caelyn. "I don't know. Tell me what's going on, right now."

She was pale, trembling, and her gaze jumped from child to child and then around the entry as if someone might pop out at any time. "We need to lock the doors." Her hand shook as she handed me a piece of paper. "It was on my car."

I scanned the page, my body locking. "Come with me right now." I hurried them into my office, pulling open the bookcase and heading for the panic room. I entered the code in a flash and turned on the lights. "Go downstairs. I'm going to lock you in until the sheriff's department can get here. Don't come out unless Parker or I come get you. Do you understand?"

Mia whimpered. "Luci. I don't have Luci."

"There she is," Will said, darting into the office to grab the kitten.

Mia kept shaking her head and tugged on my arm. "I want you to come with us."

I crouched, framing her face in my hands. "I need to wait for the sheriff, okay? Everything's going to be fine. And there are games down there. Will is going to play with you. Right, Will?"

He nodded, Luci squirming in his arms. "Yeah, Mi. Let's see what he's got." Will ushered Mia and Ava downstairs, but Caelyn remained.

She was still pale, but her jaw had tightened. "I'm staying with you."

"The hell you are. You're going down there and you're going to keep those kids calm."

Her hands fisted in my shirt. "What if something happens to you?"

I pulled her to me. "Nothing is going to happen to me."

"Swear it."

"I swear." I released her, heading to the gun safe on the wall. I punched in the code, and it unlocked. I grabbed my Glock and shut the door. "See, completely protected. Now, go downstairs. Keep them calm."

"Griffin?" she asked.

"Yes?"

"I love you."

I froze. The knowledge of her words seemed to zing through my body as if someone had lit a series of fireworks in my bloodstream. "What did you say?"

Caelyn pressed her lips together. "I love you. I just needed you to know that. I know you might not be ready—"

I kissed her, quick and fierce. "I love you. I think a part of me loved you from the first moment I saw you. Some part of me recognized that you were the one person who could understand me. Who could help me find my way back."

Caelyn's eyes filled with tears, but a sharp knock sounded on the front door. We froze. I brought a finger to my lips and then pointed down the stairs. She paused for a moment, but when I squeezed her arm, she followed my instructions. As quietly as possible, I closed the door to the panic room, then slid the bookcase back in place.

Another knock sounded. I eased towards the doorway of the office but stayed protected by the wall. "Who is it?"

"It's Parker."

The tension in my muscles eased a fraction. "You alone?"

"What the hell is going on?" he barked.

I quickly made my way to the door, unlocking it and creating just enough of an opening for Parker to slip inside. As soon as he passed the threshold, I shut and locked it behind him. He scanned me from head to toe, his gaze lingering on the gun in my hand. "What happened?"

I realized I'd let the note fall to the floor in the entryway in my rush to get Caelyn and the kids to safety. I bent, picking it up and handing it to Parker. He let out a litany of curses and then pulled out his phone, calling it in. "The Anchor deputies will be here in minutes. But more backup is coming. Where are the kids? Caelyn?"

I hesitated for the briefest moment. I didn't share with anyone that I had a panic room. They worked best when they were a secret no one knew about. "They're in my panic room."

Parker's eyes widened a fraction and then he nodded. "Think you can handle sweeping the house with me?"

I tightened the grip on my gun. "Let's go."

We moved from room to room on every floor, and it wasn't until we returned to the entryway and saw another sheriff's department vehicle racing up the drive that I relaxed a bit. I glanced at Parker. "Did you leave my gate open?"

He looked a little sheepish. "I didn't think I'd be here long."

I shook my head. I'd given him the code in case there was a true emergency. "I'm going to get Caelyn and the kids. Keep the deputies outside for now."

Parker nodded, heading out the front door. I strode back into my office, moving through the bookcase and to the reinforced steel door hidden behind it. I plugged in the code and called downstairs. "It's Griffin. You can come up now."

Caelyn was first up the stairs, practically tackling me. "You're okay? Tell me you're okay."

"I'm fine. Everything's fine. Parker's here with some other deputies." I looked at the kids. "You guys okay?" They nodded, but Ava and Mia appeared more than a little shaken up. I crouched, pulling them both into my arms. "Everything's okay." I held them for a long moment and then released them both. "Can you guys do me a favor?"

"Sure," Will answered.

"Don't tell anyone about that room. It's our secret hiding place, okay?"

Mia looked up at me thoughtfully. "Like a fort."

I forced myself to smile at her. "Exactly. Like a *secret* fort. Only we can know about it. Got it?"

"Got it," she agreed.

I looked to Ava, and she nodded.

"Okay, let's go talk to Parker." I ushered them out of the small space, closing the door behind us. The next hour flew by. We'd checked camera footage but didn't have the right angles to catch whoever had jumped the fence and left the note on Caelyn's SUV. Before long, what felt like the entire sheriff's department swarmed my property, looking for clues. Kenna, Bell, Crosby, and Ford showed up once Caelyn called to let them know what was going on. Kenna and Bell were a godsend, taking the kids upstairs to cuddle and watch a movie. Will hadn't wanted to go but when I mouthed, "*Please. Look out for them,*" he'd gone without another word of argument.

I kept Caelyn in my arms, unable to let her go. Somehow, I reasoned that if I just kept touching her, it would be impossible for her to come to any harm. She stood quietly, her back pressed to my front, and hadn't said more than a handful of words since we'd sent the kids upstairs. I pressed my lips to her hair, breathing her in. "Do you need anything?"

She shook her head, turning in my arms so her cheek was pressed to my chest. "Just you."

"You've got me. Always."

Her hands fisted in my shirt. "Thank you," she whispered.

Ford tapped away on the screen of his phone. "My friend's security company is supposed to do the install today, right?"

I muttered a curse. "Yeah." I'd completely forgotten.

"Do you still want him to come?" Ford asked.

I scanned the property around us, seeing most of the law enforcement officials heading for their vehicles. I couldn't imagine anyone would be working much longer. There couldn't be a piece of the property they hadn't investigated. I waved Parker over. "I'm supposed to have new security going in this afternoon. And given the circumstances, I really don't want to cancel that install."

Parker rubbed a hand over his jaw. "Understandable. It shouldn't be a problem. Unfortunately, we haven't found much."

A muscle in my cheek ticked. Were we going to find anything before it was too late? I held Caelyn a bit tighter but kept my gaze fixed on Parker. "What were you coming by for anyway?"

"Hell, I almost forgot. A print came back on the first note. The one Caelyn found on her SUV outside the store."

She stiffened in my arms. "Whose?"

Parker pulled out his phone and brought up a mug shot. "Darryl Kidman. He look familiar?"

Caelyn studied his face carefully, and I did the same. He was thin, cheeks almost sunken in but covered with a beard. Brown hair and eyes. Nothing about him was in any way remarkable. Nothing that said he was capable of threatening the people I loved most in this world.

Caelyn shook her head, letting out a frustrated growl. "I've never seen him before. Who is he?"

"He rolled with your dad's old crew. He's been popped for possession countless times, but nothing violent."

Caelyn's hands formed fists at her sides. "I don't even know him. Was he caught up in the bust seven years ago?"

"No," Parker answered. "That's what doesn't quite add up. He's never done hard time. There's only one thing I can think of."

"What's that?" I growled.

"Rumor has it he was your dad's right hand. Ran a lot of drugs for him."

Caelyn paled. "You think it's my dad pulling the strings."

Parker's jaw worked. "I think it's looking that way."

"Hasn't he done enough? He's already traumatized his children. Left them to almost get killed. And now this? What did we ever do to him other than ask him to love us?"

Parker looked from Caelyn to me and back again, unease filling his expression. "Because of you and your siblings, his face is in every police database. Because of you, he lost his entire network. I'm guessing that dealing made him feel like a big man even though he was the smallest of the small. You destroyed what he viewed as his kingdom. And that's enough for a twisted man to seek revenge."

Chapter Forty-Six

Caelyn

A S SOON AS PARKER AND THE REST OF THE OFFICERS left, I was moving, before I could even consider where I was going. I just needed to get away. From Parker's revelations about my father. From the worried, probing glances. Even from my friends. I rounded the house, heading for the woods. For the quiet peace of the pond.

I wasn't running exactly, it was more of a furious power walk. As the wind picked up, it stung my cheeks. That was the only way I even realized that I was crying. Tracks of silent tears ran down my face. Tears because the man who was supposed to love me simply because I was his daughter wanted to cause me the most pain imaginable.

As I reached the edge of the forest, I sank to the ground, leaning against the thick trunk of one of the trees and wrapping my arms around my legs as if somehow it could protect me from the knowledge that my father hated me down to his marrow.

Footsteps sounded, muted by the forest floor. I kept my gaze focused on the pond. The slight rippling of the water. A bird that swooped down hoping to spot a small fish.

Griffin lowered himself next to me. Without a word, he lifted me as if I weighed nothing and settled me in his lap. "I'm so sorry." He whispered the words against my temple, his lips brushing across the tender skin there.

I let myself melt into him, to try and soak up some of Griffin's strength. "Why does he hate me so much?"

"I wish I had the answer to that one. But some people just have ugly souls. I don't know if it's the life they've lived that rots their core, or if they were simply born that way."

I burrowed deeper into Griffin's hold. I knew he'd experienced more than his fair share of people with rotten cores. People who wanted to use him and betray him in the worst possible ways. Yet somehow, he'd managed to keep his good soul. He hadn't let the hurt that others had inflicted on him turn his core rotten.

I traced a finger over his heart as if the action would somehow allow me to soak up some of that goodness. I wanted to drown in the light that filled him. I tipped my face up to meet his gaze. "Make me forget." His brows drew together, puzzled. My hand slid up his chest to cup his jaw, and I brushed my lips against his. "Make me feel. Only the good." He studied my face as if he were trying to decide if this was a smart move. "Please." I wasn't above begging.

His hands skimmed down my body, sliding under the hem of my sundress. The glide of his palms against my skin created some sort of foreign energy that hummed around us. Something that would only ever belong to Griffin and me. I never wanted to lose it. It was safety and comfort, passion and want, hunger and complete satiation, all at the same time.

Griffin's fingers danced over my lace-covered core. I sucked in a sharp breath as he stroked me through my panties. I forced my eyes to stay open, to stay locked with Griffin's. I didn't want to miss a second of how his blue eyes seemed to change color in the late-morning light. How with each pass of his fingers, his gaze seemed to darken.

My breaths started to come quicker, my heart hammering against its cage as if it wanted to take flight, to get to the man who owned it entirely. "Please."

"What do you need?" Griffin asked, seeming in no hurry. As if he could simply stay like this all day.

"I need you."

His eyes flared, and his hand went to the side of his belt. To the multi-tool he always kept there. "Stay still."

I froze as he flicked open the knife and slipped it under my sundress. One flick of his wrist, and then another, and my lace panties were falling free. I gaped up at him. "That was a really nice pair of underwear."

Griffin grinned at me, holding the lace up triumphantly. "And I'll cherish them as the precious gift they are." He shoved the scrap of fabric into his pocket. "Come here." Griffin lifted me so I was straddling him, his fingers going to the button of his jeans. His cock sprang free, and I smiled. Apparently, he wasn't as unaffected as he appeared. "You're gonna ride me. And I'm going to make you feel only the good things."

My expression softened, and I took his mouth in a slow kiss as I lowered myself onto him. The stretch and fullness had my eyes fluttering. There was an undeniable sense of completeness. Not that I wasn't whole on my own, but that somehow with Griffin, I was so much more. My strengths were greater and my weaknesses not as noticeable. With him, I never felt alone.

I began to rock against him, slow, testing movements. Griffin's hands came to my hips, helping to guide my path. Together, we found a rhythm. The one we both needed. It was both tender and a little desperate. The need to know that the other was right here and that we were alive spurring us on.

Griffin snaked a hand under my dress, his thumb finding that bundle of nerves and circling, drawing ever closer to where I needed him the most. His other hand tangled in the back of my hair. "Look at me. Keep your eyes on me when you come. I want to see that green spark." Another pass of his thumb, and I was almost there. "I love you, Caelyn."

His words. His hands. His body. But most of all, the knowledge that I was wholly his. It was all I needed to fracture in his arms, the pieces of me splintering apart and reforming in a way that wasn't exactly the same person I was before. Because now I knew that I was loved so completely by this man.

Slowly, I came back to myself, my breaths steadying as my heart still struck out a staccato beat. "I love you, too. I wish you could reach inside my brain and heart so you could see how much."

Griffin's face softened. "I don't need to see it. I feel it every day."

My lip trembled. "Don't make me cry when you're still inside me."

He chuckled, sending delicious aftershocks through me. The tightening of my muscles had him groaning. "You are going to kill me."

"But it'll be a good way to go, right?"

Griffin brushed the hair back from my face. "The best." He carefully lifted me off of him and placed a kiss to the corner of my mouth before settling me in his lap again.

We were quiet for a moment, just enjoying the closeness and the peace. Griffin toyed with a lock of my hair. "I want you and the kids to move into the farmhouse permanently."

I froze. I'd held onto our little yellow house for so long. It was like a security blanket. For a long time, I'd thought if I just had that house, we were safe. But with Griffin, we'd found a whole new life. One that was even better than the one we'd created for ourselves in that little yellow home. I tipped my face up to his.

"Are you sure this isn't just sex endorphins? You did say it has been a while for you."

Griffin grinned and cupped my face. "Move in. Make this a real home. If you don't, I'm just going to come live in that tiny-ass loft with you."

I giggled at the image of Griffin climbing the ladder up to my bedroom loft. "Okay."

His eyes widened. "Okay?" I nodded. "I really thought I was going to have more of a fight on my hands."

I shrugged. "I like to keep you on your toes." I pressed a kiss to the underside of his jaw. "We're happy here. Even with all of the horrible things that have happened over the past few months, we're the happiest we've ever been. And isn't that what everyone hopes for? To have joy amidst all the trials. You give us joy, Griffin."

His gaze burned into me. "You have no idea the joy you give me. You made this wrecked palace a home."

Chapter Forty-Seven

Griffin

"WE HAVE ADDITIONAL CAMERAS SET UP NOW. They're placed at regular intervals over the entirety of the fence line. Now, you're going to get a fair number of false alarms from wildlife. Likely deer jumping over your fence. But we can adjust the cameras once you're not at a crisis point."

Crisis point was putting it mildly. I didn't think I'd slept for more than a few minutes last night. Even with a deputy in a car outside the house. I'd take a million false alarms if it allowed me to know what was happening on my property. "We can deal with that," I told the security expert, wrapping an arm around Caelyn.

Cain nodded. "Good. All the alerts will go straight to your phones. You'll be able to see live camera feeds and also rewind to see what triggered the alarm. There's also a button in the app that you can press to alert the sheriff's department immediately of an emergency."

Caelyn let out a shuddering breath. "Thank you. I hope we don't have to use it. But I appreciate knowing it's in place."

I reached out a hand to Cain, shaking his. "Thank you for hustling to get this all done so quickly."

Cain and his two-person crew had set up all the cameras and tweaked the security system in the house in a matter of hours yesterday. Now, it was all up and running. Cain released my hand. "No problem. I know what it's like to worry about the people you care about. I'm just glad there's something I can do to help you keep them safe."

Caelyn gave the gruff man a gentle smile. "It sounds like a good job to me. Are you going to get to stay on Anchor for a while, or do you have to head back to Oregon today?"

A smile that I hadn't seen in any of the hours I'd helped the man set up security stretched across his face. "I'm staying for a few days. As soon as my wife heard where I was going, she started planning a vacation."

"That's wonderful," Caelyn said. "Make sure you grab food at The Catch and Rocco's. And stop by Second Chances if your wife likes antiques and refurbished furniture pieces."

Cain shook his head. "If I take Kennedy to that shop, we're going to go home with a million little trinkets we don't need."

Caelyn chuckled. "You probably will, but it'll be worth it."

"Well, on that note, I better go find my wife. You have my cell number if you have any questions or issues." Cain met both of our gazes. "Stay safe."

"We will." I tightened my hold on Caelyn. "Thanks again, man."

"Anytime."

We waited as Cain climbed into his SUV and headed down the drive. When he disappeared from sight, Caelyn turned in my arms so she was facing me. Her smile was almost shy, but a little bit giddy, too. "Want to tell the kids we're moving in?"

I brushed the hair back from her face and pressed a kiss to her forehead. This was real. A fresh start. A family. "Let's go."

We headed back inside, towards the kitchen and the sounds of shrieking.

"The pink one's mine, Will," Mia cried.

"Will," Caelyn warned as she entered.

He shook his head but grinned. "I just wanted to see how much of a fit she'd throw if someone came between her and the pink donut."

Mia glared at him. "I'll put your hand in warm water while you're sleeping."

Will's eyes widened, handing over the donut. "Vicious, I like it."

Ava looked up from where she sat at the kitchen table, reading her book. "They've been like this since you started talking to Mr. Hale. But while they've been fighting, I've been eating."

"Hey," Will said, studying the box on the table. "Did you eat the Boston cream?"

She shrugged. "You snooze, you lose."

I held out a hand to Ava, and she gave me a high-five. Caelyn groaned. "You're all hopeless. A little sugar, and you turn into maniacs."

"What's a maniac?" Mia asked with a mouthful of donut.

"Someone who's just a little crazy," Caelyn answered.

Mia grinned, her teeth pink. "I'm crazy for donuts."

I wrapped an arm around Caelyn. "Give up now. You'll never win against sugar."

"Oh, fine," she huffed and then looked around at the kids. "Griffin and I have something to talk to you about."

"Okay…" Will said, looking a little wary.

"How would you feel about staying at the farmhouse? Not going back to our place?"

Mia's face looked as if it might crack in two, she was smiling so widely. "Stay here for good?"

Her sheer joy sent a burning sensation through my chest. "As long as you want."

"Forever!" she cheered.

"Forever it is, then." My gaze met Caelyn's in a silent promise. I might not be slipping a ring on her finger tomorrow, but I wouldn't hold back for long.

Mia launched herself at me, and I caught her with one arm, narrowly avoiding a donut to the face. I looked at Will, who was grinning. "Well, my music studio is here, so it is pretty convenient."

Caelyn rolled her eyes. "Easily bribed."

Our focus turned to Ava, who was quiet, her expression unreadable. I gave her a gentle smile. "What do you think, Avs?"

Her lips pressed together as if she were holding something back. "You want us?" she asked without meeting my eyes.

The burn in my chest intensified. I lowered Mia to the floor and crossed to Ava, crouching so that I was at eye-level with her. "I want you. All of you."

"Why?" she asked, her eyes filling with tears.

"Because I love you. And you make this house feel like a home."

She gave me a wobbly smile. "I think the farmhouse feels like home, too."

"So, you'll stay?" I asked. Ava nodded, and I scooped her up into my arms. "Then come on, tiny terrors. We need to decide what color to paint your rooms."

I led a parade of the people I loved most in this world up the stairs. We went from the girls' room to Will's, discussing what color options they wanted. Pink or blue for the girls. Green or gray for Will.

Mia tugged on my hand. "Can we paint it today?"

I chuckled. "I think we're going to need to test out our options first. But I can run to the hardware store and pick up some samples." I froze. In the joy of the moment, I'd forgotten what had happened yesterday. There was no way I was leaving them alone and unprotected.

Caelyn seemed to understand my battle and squeezed my free hand, whispering in my ear. "We're fine. We've got a security system that would make the White House jealous, and the panic room if anything goes wrong." A muscle along my jaw ticked, and Caelyn squeezed my hand again. "I promise. Nothing is going to happen. Go get some paint so we can keep this happy train rolling."

I pressed a quick kiss to Caelyn's mouth. "Okay, but keep your phone on you."

"Sir, yes, sir," she quipped.

My eyes narrowed at her. "I might be making you bring that back but in an entirely different context."

Caelyn blushed furiously and I chuckled. "Okay. I'll be back in an hour."

The girls were already chattering away about what they were going to do with their room, lost in their plans and dreams. Will gave me a mock salute, and Caelyn shooed me out of the room.

My trip to the hardware store had me adding all sorts of other things to my to-do list for the farmhouse. The kids needed a treehouse and a swing set. One that would make my little gymnast's eyes bug out. And something with a reading nook for Ava. As I made the drive back to the house with a dozen paint samples in hand, I started designing the structures in my head. It would be the perfect project to tackle with Will. He could be in charge of the design.

I rolled down my window to plug in the code for the gate. Just as I passed through, my phone beeped. An alert. Cain's security system. My blood turned to ice as I pulled up the camera feed and saw two figures running away from the fence. Towards the farmhouse.

Chapter Forty-Eight

Caelyn

I LEANED BACK, BRACING MY ELBOWS AGAINST ONE OF THE deck's steps, and tipped my face up to the sun. Breathing deeply, I took in the scent of the pines, the hint of salt in the air. The giggles from Ava and Mia as they chased Luci around the yard.

Will eased down next to me. "Happy?"

I smiled at my brother. "You know, despite all the crazy, terrifying moments of the past few months, I am."

"Good." There was a ferocity in his tone. As though if I weren't happy, he'd do everything in his power to make it so.

"What about you?"

Will's Adam's apple bobbed as he swallowed. "It's weird. But so much of what I was worried about…it just seems like it's all gone in the blink of an eye. Harriet taking care of college. Griffin taking care of you—"

"Hey, now," I said, giving his shoulder a slug. "I'm very capable of taking care of myself."

"I know you are, but someone needs to have your back."

"You've got a mighty big heart in there, you know that?"

Will's face flushed. "I get it from my big sister."

I pointed a finger at him. "Don't you make me cry."

"Oh, geez," he said, rolling his eyes.

My phone beeped, and I slid it from my pocket. An alert. The security system. My heartbeat picked up speed. It was a deer. It had to be. Or maybe Griffin had accidentally set off a sensor when he returned. I tapped a couple of icons on my phone.

"What is it?" Will asked, moving in close.

A camera view pulled up, and I caught just a flash of movement. A figure running out of frame. "Girls! Inside, now."

They both froze at my tone. But Luci, oblivious to it, kept right on bounding away towards the forest. Will grabbed my phone from my hand and pressed a button. "I sent the alert to the sheriff."

I ran to the girls. "Come on, hurry."

"Wait," Mia cried. "Luci."

"We'll get her later. She'll be fine." I prayed I was right. Whoever was here could care less about a cat. *We* were who they wanted to harm.

"No!" Mia tore from my grip and ran towards the woods where Luci had disappeared.

Panic swept over me, sharp and fierce. I pushed Ava to Will. "Take her inside to the panic room. You remember the code, right?"

"You go with Ava," he argued. "I'll find Mia and Luci."

"No. Will, I need you to do this. Please."

He nodded slowly, handing me back my phone. "Be careful. Stay in the woods until we call you with the all-clear."

"We will."

He was so smart, my brother. Because once I found Mia, we wouldn't be able to make it safely back to the house. Not with someone prowling the property. I ran towards the tree line and the sound of footsteps against the forest floor.

"Mia," I hissed, but she kept right on running. Finally, I caught up with her with a squirming Luci in her arms. "Mia, come here."

Her face was red and splotchy. "I'm sorry, Cae Cae, but I couldn't leave Luci."

My stomach twisted. My sweet girl. I pulled her and the cat into my arms. "It's okay. We're going to be okay, but we have to be very quiet. I'm going to find us a place to hide."

Mia nodded, clutching Luci tighter to her chest. I led them farther away from the farmhouse, constantly scanning the surrounding trees for any sign of movement, my ears primed for any hint of noise. There weren't any buildings out here, no place to truly hide. Only trees and the pond.

"Caelyn," a man called. "I know you're out here. That little girl, too. If you come out, I won't hurt the girl."

The voice was so familiar, but I couldn't place it. It sure as hell didn't sound like my father.

"What the hell, man? I'm not hurting some kid," another guy hissed. "And I already almost got caught when I tried to take them from the school."

"Shut up," the first man barked.

I urged Mia on, praying for her feet to move faster. We almost passed the large tree when I froze. There was a small opening in the trunk. Not big enough for me. But large enough for Mia.

I bent, motioning her over. "You're going to hide in here, okay? You stay here until I come get you. Promise? Only come out for someone you trust. Only our family, okay?"

Her lip trembled. "It's dark in there."

"I know, sweetie, but you're so brave. And you know who probably lives in there?"

"Who?"

I tried my best to force a smile. "Faeries. But you have to be very quiet. It's the only way they'll show themselves to you."

"Okay." Her voice trembled. "You'll come back for me, right?"

"I promise."

She slowly forced herself inside the tree trunk, Luci still in her arms. I tucked a hand inside and squeezed her knee. "I love you. I'll be back soon."

"Love you, Cae Cae."

I jogged away from the tree, hoping I hadn't lied. It didn't matter. All that mattered was leading the men away from Mia. I skirted the pond, remaining in the shelter of the trees. When I reached the other side, I knew I was running out of places to go. The rest of Griffin's land was far too open.

I scanned the trees around me. There was only one option. Up. I found a pine that had some branches low enough for me to reach. With a running jump, I hoisted myself up onto the lowest limb. The bark bit into my hands, but I didn't utter a sound.

With as much care as possible, I went from branch to branch until I could be sure I was at least somewhat hidden from any prying eyes below. I strained to hear anything, but only the wind sounded. Sliding my fingers into my back pocket, I pulled out my phone. Quickly, I turned it to silent and brought up a new text. I bit down on my bottom lip as I considered my options. I added Griffin and Parker to the chat.

I typed out a message, explaining that there were two intruders, where I'd hidden Mia, and roughly where I was located. Within seconds, there was a reply.

Griffin: *Stay where you are. I'm coming.*

Parker: *Griffin, do not engage. We're two minutes out.*

Griffin: *I'm armed. Let your officers know.*

The messages flew back and forth before I could interject a response. Help was coming. We would be okay.

Voices cut through the air. Footsteps came closer and closer. "I know you're here somewhere. There are only so many places you can go, Caelyn…"

I sucked in a sharp breath and gripped the branch I rested on. The pain of the bark slicing into my skin barely registered.

"Where the hell is she, boss? We gotta get her and go. The cops are gonna be here any minute."

"Shut up, Darryl. We're fine," the first man bit out.

Darryl. Darryl Kidman. The man whose fingerprints were on the first note I'd received. Why? What had I ever done to him? I leaned forward the slightest bit, trying to get a glimpse of the other man. His *boss.*

As I moved, my phone slipped from my grasp. I tried to grab it as it fell, but I couldn't make contact. It landed with a thump on the forest floor. The air seized in my lungs.

"Well, what do we have here?" the unidentified man said, picking up the device. "She falls right at our feet."

I wasn't at their feet, not yet. But there was nowhere else for me to go. My gaze zeroed in on the guns in their hands. Guns that could easily shoot me down if they so desired. But the police were here. They knew where I was. Where Mia was. Even if something happened to me, at least the kids would be safe. Tears burned the backs of my eyes. Ford and Bell or Kenna and Crosby would take them in.

"Get down here." The man looked straight at me, his face no longer concealed by shadows and the brim of his ballcap.

Max. The kind man who'd wanted a second job so he could try and get his son back. Max, who'd offered to walk me to my car after we got off work. My voice shook as I spoke. "If I come down there, you'll kill me."

Max swiped off his hat and pointed his gun in my direction. "If you don't come down here, I'll fucking kill you. How about that?"

"Jesus, Max. This wasn't the plan. We need money from her man. He'll give it to us to get her back," Darryl whined.

Max turned the gun on his friend. "Maybe I don't care about the money anymore."

"Shit, man. What's gotten into you?"

"Almost seven years locked up. That's what's gotten into me. My bitch of a wife thinking she could divorce me while I was inside. And take my fucking son with her when she went. *My* boy. And it's all this bitch's fault."

"Why?" I rasped.

His gaze shot to me, the gun along with it. "You put me away. You cost me *everything*."

"My dad put you away. He was the one who left his phone behind when he went on a drug binge." I held my tongue from adding that if Max hadn't done anything illegal, he wouldn't have gone to jail.

"And he paid the price. Him and your bitch of a mother."

"My dad?" I almost choked on the words.

"Gutted him like a fish. Had a little go-round with your mother before I killed her. You should've seen how she begged. Pathetic."

I swallowed back the bile rising up my throat. Sirens cut through the air.

"Shit!" Darryl cried. "I'm out of here. I'm not going down for this."

Without a second's hesitation, Max pointed his gun at Darryl and pulled the trigger, the bullet landing in his leg. "Good luck running on that." A second shot hit the hand holding the gun. "Just in case you were thinking of seeking retribution."

I didn't think, I simply jumped. I launched myself from the tree and towards Max. Maybe if I landed hard enough, I'd kill him. The only thing I knew for sure was that surprise was the only tool in my arsenal.

The force of my landing shocked all the air from my lungs. Pain flared in my ribs and cheek. My muscles from the dump of adrenaline. But the cursing and movement from the body below mine spurred me into motion. I struggled to grab hold of the gun, to point it away from me, towards Max.

"I'm going to kill you," he growled. "And I'm going to make it hurt."

"Caelyn!" The single word bellowed through the trees belonged to only one man. And hearing Griffin sent a rush of strength through me. I struggled harder, finally gaining purchase on the metal.

But it was too late. I heard a loud pop. Heat flared in my stomach, a burning pain unlike anything I'd ever experienced. My eyes widened as my body went limp. Too late.

Chapter Forty-Nine

Griffin

THE WORLD SEEMED TO SLOW AROUND ME, ALMOST AS IF I were moving through an invisible force field. A pressure keeping me from getting to Caelyn. Then a vicious pop. Her body going limp and rolling over, off the man who wanted to hurt her. To take her from me. The man raised his gun again, this time pointed at me. I didn't even think. I simply fired. Two shots as close to between the eyes as I could get.

The other man was screaming, but I could barely hear the words. I picked up the gun at his side and he crawled away as best he could. "D-d-don't shoot me."

"Then don't fucking move." I shoved the extra gun into the back of my jeans, running for Caelyn without waiting to see if the man obeyed.

Her eyes fluttered in a staccato rhythm. Open. Closed. Open. Closed. I crouched next to her. Blood seeped through the t-shirt she wore, staining the blue cotton. I lifted the fabric and cursed. There was too much blood. I pulled off my flannel and pressed it to the wound. Caelyn let out a low moan.

"I'm so sorry, but I have to stop the bleeding."

322 | CATHERINE COWLES

I could just make out voices on the other side of the pond. "We're over here," I shouted. "We need a medic."

Caelyn's eyes flared. "Mia."

"We're gonna get her. Don't worry. I just need you to focus on your breathing. Keep your eyes on me."

Her breaths were too shallow, and no matter how hard I pressed on her wound, the bleeding didn't seem to slow. Hell, I didn't even know if the bullet was still inside her body.

"Griffin," she wheezed.

"I'm right here."

Tears leaked out of the corners of her eyes. "Take care of them, my tiny terrors. Promise me you'll take care of them."

My heart spasmed in my chest. "No. Don't you talk like you're not going to be here. Help is on its way. It's only a matter of minutes."

"Promise me." Her eyes pleaded, tears glistening on her cheeks.

"I promise." The words ripped from my throat. It was a vow I never wanted to make.

"Love you," she whispered.

"I love you, too. And I'm going to show you every day for the rest of your life. You're the most important person in the world to me, and you're not going to leave us." Why had I waited to make her mine completely? To ask her to be my wife. To spend forever with me. It seemed so trivial now. The length of time we'd been together. None of that mattered when she and the kids were my whole heart. I pressed harder against the wound as blood began to seep through the gaps in my fingers. "Stay with me."

But there was no answer. Only silence.

I shifted Mia in my arms as I glanced around the waiting room. As soon as she arrived at the hospital, she'd flung herself from

Will to me. And she hadn't let go since. She'd finally fallen asleep about thirty minutes ago, but when Bell had offered to take her from me, I'd found it was me who couldn't let go.

These kids were the only pieces of Caelyn I had to hold onto. The one thing helping me hold onto hope. Because while Caelyn had been airlifted to Seattle, her heart had stopped. For two whole minutes, Caelyn had ceased to be. And I could feel every second of that time carved into my soul. As soon as we landed, the doctors and nurses had rushed her into surgery, and I was alone.

A kind nurse had offered me the use of their showers and a clean pair of scrubs. But as I looked down at my hands resting on Mia's back, I saw that there was still blood under my fingernails. How long would that last? Maybe forever. I swallowed down the scream that wanted to escape.

Crosby met my gaze from across the room. There was no signature smirk on his face now. Only lines of worry etched deep into his skin. His arm wrapped around his fiancée as she leaned against his chest. I couldn't help but wonder if I'd ever get to feel that weight again. The heaviness of Caelyn's head resting over my heart.

I forced myself to look away. But I was only met with more grief. Will and Ava next to me, his arm rubbing up and down her back as she stared off into space. Bell sat on their opposite side, gripping a water bottle so tightly, I was shocked it hadn't exploded all over her.

The visceral pain of every person in the room seemed to clog the air. Suddenly, I couldn't breathe. Kenna seemed to see my panic because she stood and held out her hands. "Let me take her for a little bit. You get some air."

"Thank you," I croaked, carefully handing Mia over. As soon as she rested in Kenna's arms, not waking, I bolted from the room. But I had nowhere to go. I didn't want to leave the floor, let alone the hospital. So I simply paced, up and down the short stretch of hallway, my feet squeaking against the linoleum each time I turned to head in the other direction. Just as I reached the opposite end for the fifth time, I almost collided with Ford.

He halted. "You okay?" I only grunted. "All right, that was a stupid question. Of course, you're not okay. What can I do?"

"Turn back the clock. Not allow me to leave them unprotected." Each of the words burned a trail of pain and guilt up my throat.

Ford's expression hardened. "You didn't leave them unprotected. You left them with a state-of-the-art security system in place."

"I shouldn't have left them at all," I bellowed. And I would never forgive myself for it.

Ford gripped my shoulders, his fingers digging into the muscles there and giving me a good shake. "Do not let yourself go there, man. It's not going to help the kids or Caelyn. You need to keep your head on straight. You can't lose it."

I gave a jerky nod. "I'm fucking terrified."

Ford pulled me into a hard hug. "I know. But Caelyn is strong. If anyone can beat this, it's her."

"Mr. Lockwood?"

I turned to face a doctor, who stood with the same nurse that had given me the clean scrubs. "Yes. How's Caelyn? Is she okay?"

I couldn't read a thing from the doctor's face. She looked to be in her fifties, the picture of professionalism with her braids woven into a tight bun atop her head and a carefully blank expression on her face. "She's being moved from recovery to ICU now."

ICU. That wasn't good. ICU was for people on the verge. The nurse took pity on me and added, "That's completely normal for patients coming out of a serious surgery."

The doctor nodded. "The bullet damaged a piece of Ms. O'Connor's liver. We performed a partial removal of the damaged area—"

"You took a part of her liver?" I barked. "She needs that to live, doesn't she?"

"The liver regenerates. She has the potential to make a full recovery," she explained.

"Potential?" My voice cracked on the single word.

"Ms. O'Connor had a second code during surgery. We were able to get her heart beating again, but we won't know if there has been any brain damage until she wakes up."

Brain damage. The words echoed around in my head. "But she's going to live?"

The doctor's lips pursed. "The first twenty-four hours are crucial, but we're optimistic."

I nodded my head slowly, having gone completely numb. The nurse took a step towards me. "I can take you up to her room if you'd like."

"Yes. Please."

Ford thumped my back. "I'm going to fill everyone in."

"Thanks." I didn't think I had it in me to repeat those words. I silently followed the nurse down the hall and to a bank of elevators. She didn't try and make idle chitchat as the elevator took us up five floors. I appreciated it. She led me down another hall and into a ward that was oval in shape. Individual rooms surrounded what appeared to be a nurses' station. It was clear that there were more nurses to patients here than on a regular floor.

The nurse moved towards a corner room and then paused. "She's going to look a little rough, but she's breathing on her own, and that's a great sign. Go on in."

"Thank you." I moved around her and through the door that was propped open. As soon as I caught sight of Caelyn, I froze. She was pale. Almost stark-white. And her face seemed swollen as if she'd been battered. A bruise bloomed across her cheek. I could only imagine what the rest of her body looked like.

This woman that was so full of life was far too still. I hated everything about it. I forced myself to step closer, one foot in front of the other as if they were weighed down with cement blocks. By the time I reached the bed, my breathing was labored, and my chest was so tight I thought I might be having a heart attack.

I lowered myself into the chair beside her bed. "Caelyn." Her name was a prayer. A plea for her to return to me. I slipped one hand under hers, placing the other on top, careful not to disrupt the oxygen monitor. "I'm here. And I'm not going anywhere. Not until you wake up."

There was no response. Only the constant beeping of her heart monitor, and the faint hum of the other machines. "I love you. More than I thought possible. I didn't think I could ever let anyone in again. But you and those tiny terrors... You wormed your way into my heart. So, you don't get to leave now."

A tear splashed against our joined hands; it was the only way I even knew I was crying. "I've lost too many people I've loved, Caelyn. Don't you leave me, too."

Chapter Fifty

Caelyn

I SEEMED TO DRIFT THROUGH FOGGY PAIN. OCCASIONALLY, voices pulled at me. Sounds I wanted to move towards, but I couldn't seem to find my way there.

"Come on, Caelyn. You can do it. The doctor says you're trying to wake up. Open those eyes."

Griffin. I wanted to see him. His blue eyes. Heck, I'd even take his scowl. I let out a groan.

"There you go. Keep fighting. Come back to me. I need you."

My eyelids fluttered. But they felt as if someone had tied tiny weights to my lashes. Griffin squeezed my hand, and I fought harder. Light flared, blinding me for a moment, and then my view was full of Griffin. Tears glistened in his eyes. "You're awake."

"Hi," I croaked.

He reached for a cup with a straw. "Here, take a small sip."

The water was like a balm to my throat, soothing the burn there. But before long, Griffin was pulling it away. "I don't want you getting sick. How do you feel?"

"Everything hurts." And my mind was muddied. I was in a

hospital, but why—? My eyes widened. "Mia, is she okay? Ava and Will?"

Griffin brought my hand to his chest. "They're fine. Everyone's fine. They're in the waiting room. When you're ready, we'll bring them in. But I want you to take it easy."

I sagged back against the bed. My side screamed in protest, hot, burning pain engulfing me. Griffin must have seen me wince because he pushed in even closer. "Are you okay? Do you want me to call the nurse?"

"No. No. I just want to be with you for a minute. Am I? Is everything okay?"

Griffin brushed the hair back from my face. "You're going to be fine. Now that you've woken up, they say you'll make a full recovery. But..."

"But what?" The stark fear on Griffin's face, the pain, it had me gripping his hand even harder.

"Your heart stopped twice. I almost lost you." His voice cracked, emotion leaking through his words. "I don't know what I would've done."

"I'm here. I'm right here." I pulled my hand from his grasp and framed his face with my hands, fingers rubbing against the stubble on his cheeks. "I'm not going anywhere."

His eyes drifted shut and he pressed a kiss to my forehead. "No. You're not. And you're stuck with me for life."

I let out a little laugh, instantly regretting it as pain flared to life throughout my middle. I let my hands fall back to my sides.

"What is it?"

I gave Griffin a weak smile. "I don't think laughing is on the docket quite yet."

He found my free hand again, holding it close. "It's going to take some time to recover. But we've got you every step of the way."

"The men? Are they...? Did Parker get them?"

Griffin's eyes shifted to the side. "One's in custody. The other's dead." He paused for a moment. "I shot him."

My hand spasmed in Griffin's. "I'm so sorry."

He looked back to me. "You're sorry?"

"That you had to do that. Even if he deserved it, I hate that you have to carry that weight."

He swallowed hard. "I'd do it a million times over if it meant keeping you safe."

"I love you," I whispered. "So much." I never thought I'd find someone who would love me enough to put me first. To stay by my side when times got tough. But in a matter of months, Griffin had proven to be that man and more. "I don't know how I got so lucky."

His gaze burned into mine. "I promised myself I'd wait. That I'd give you and the kids time to settle into the house and our new routine. But I don't want to wait. If the past few days have taught me anything, it's that we shouldn't waste any of the precious moments we're given. Marry me, Caelyn. Start forever with me right now."

My breathing had completely ceased as my heartbeat thundered in my ears. "Yes. It's totally and completely insane. But yes."

Griffin's lips found mine in the gentlest of kisses. But with that barest of touches, I felt everything. His love, protection, devotion. I knew, with him, I'd never doubt how cherished I was.

He pulled back, shaking his head. "I don't even have a ring to slip on your hand."

I linked my fingers with his. "I don't care about a ring. You've given me everything I could ever want. A home. A family. You."

"I love you, Caelyn."

A soft knock sounded on the door. It opened a fraction, and Will's face appeared. "I just wanted to—Caelyn! You're awake."

He bolted into the room and came skidding to a stop at the side of my bed. "You're really awake. They said if you woke up, you'd be okay." Tears filled his eyes.

"Come here," I said, waving him closer. Griffin released my hand so I could take Will's. "I'm fine. I promise."

"I was so scared," he said, his voice hoarse.

"But you were so brave. You kept Ava safe. You did what I asked."

He nodded slowly. "Are you hurting?"

I smiled. "A little. But seeing your face helps."

Griffin crossed to the door without another word as if he sensed I needed to see Ava and Mia, too. Within a matter of seconds, he'd returned with them—Mia curled in his arms, and Ava right beside them. As soon as they saw me, Mia burst into tears, and Ava ran to my bed.

"My girls. My beautiful girls."

Will wrapped an arm around Ava, bringing her closer to the bed. And Griffin sat in the chair next to my bed with Mia in his arms.

"I'm okay. I promise," I assured.

"I'm so sorry," Mia wailed. "I shouldn't have run away after Luci. Then you wouldn't have gotten hurt."

"Mia, no." I reached out and grabbed her knee, ignoring the flash of pain. "This isn't your fault. The only people responsible are the ones who did this and they aren't going to hurt us ever again."

"Promise?" she asked, voice wavering.

"We promise," Griffin said, holding her close.

I glanced at Ava. "You okay?"

"I'm okay if you are," she whispered.

"I'm better than okay," I said, looking at the people surrounding me. The love I felt for them, warming me from the inside out. "How about some happy news?"

Will gave a wobbly grin. "I think I've only got room for good news for about the next ten years."

"Sounds like a great rule to me." I looked at Mia. "Think you might be up for being a flower girl? Or a junior bridesmaid?"

Ava gasped, looking from me to Griffin and back again. "You guys are gonna get married?"

"We are," I said.

"What do you say?" Griffin asked. "How do you guys feel about being stuck with me forever?"

Will grinned. "I think I can struggle through it."

"You're already family," Ava said.

Mia beamed. "Do I get a sparkle dress?"

Griffin chuckled. "We'll get the sparkliest dress we can find."

"How about this summer?" I asked.

Griffin's eyes flared, a mixture of surprise and heat. "You want to do it that soon?"

"I don't want to miss a second of a life with you."

Epilogue

Caelyn

TWO MONTHS LATER

"THAT'S PERFECT." I SET DOWN THE END OF MY TABLE runner at the same time Bell set down hers. "I can't believe you made all this happen. Thank you."

She rounded to me and wrapped an arm around my shoulders. "I can't think of a better use for some of my furniture pieces."

I scanned the backyard of the farmhouse. It was dotted with a handful of mismatched tables and chairs with artful table runners and soon to be filled with flowers. Our friends had worked overtime to make this wedding happen.

Griffin had acquiesced to having a little more help on the house. And between him, Will, Crosby, and Ford, they'd completely finished the restoration just last week. Bell had offered to handle all of the furniture for our small affair. And Kenna was tackling flowers.

Just the thought of her seemed to will her into being. Kenna's rounded form came around the house with her fiancé hot on her heels. "Brown Eyes. Stop walking so fast. Something could happen to the baby."

She rolled her eyes. "Do you hear him? It's not like this little lady is going to just drop out of me."

"Little lady?" I squeaked.

She blushed. "Oops. I was going to keep that one a surprise. It's a girl."

I let out a squeal and flew in Kenna's direction, pulling her into a hug. "You realize this means we can start shopping for all the cute baby things now."

She grinned. "I like the way you think."

"Hey," Bell whined. "I want in on this."

We wrapped one another in one of our group hugs. "Love you, guys," I whispered. "Sisters of my heart."

"Always," Bell echoed.

Kenna sniffed. "You two are always making me cry now."

I chuckled. "Who would've thought we'd ever see the day where Kenna became a crier? I always thought that would be my role."

She straightened and brushed out invisible wrinkles in her sundress. "I'm pregnant. Which means, I have an excuse."

Crosby came to a stop outside our huddle. "You guys okay?"

"Oh, we're fine," Kenna griped. "Just like your progeny is fine."

Crosby grinned. "She tell you it's a girl? I'm gonna spoil her rotten."

"You will not," Kenna argued.

Crosby only smiled wider. "We'll just have to see." He turned to me. "We've got the flowers in the back of the truck. Ready for them to be put out on the tables?"

"We're ready," I said.

"Flowers!" Mia cried, leaping off the deck in a sparkly dress that might have blinded a few people as she spun in circles. One sparkly dress had not been enough for my Mi. She'd needed three. One for the bridal shower, one for tonight's rehearsal dinner, and one for the big day tomorrow.

"Mia, you look beautiful," Bell called.

Mia greeted her with a deep curtsey. "Thank you."

I choked on a laugh. "I'm pretty sure she thinks we're marrying into the royal family," I whispered.

"You might as well be," Kenna said.

We'd tried to keep our wedding off the radar. Only about twenty people were attending, in addition to the wedding party. But somehow, the danged reporter who never stopped harassing Griffin had gotten wind of our engagement. It might've been the massive rock Griffin had planted on my finger a week after my release from the hospital. Or, she might've started digging after the police report of my incident was released.

Griffin had been cleared of any wrongdoing, and Darryl Kidman would be in jail for a very long time. The police had found my father buried in Max's backyard, and we'd been able to put both my parents to rest in a cemetery on Shelter. There would never be simple feelings when it came to them and the events that had transpired, but we were healing together as a family. And having this wedding to focus on had helped so much.

Will opened up to Griffin as they worked on the house, letting his guilt and fear flow. Griffin was there every step of the way, encouraging and being a shoulder to lean on.

Mia had been struggling with nightmares, but we were there every time she called out. It helped that she and Ava shared a room, and that Luci never left her side. I swear that cat had become my little sister's fiercest defender.

Ava processed the way she usually did—quietly and with deep thought. We'd spent a lot of afternoons walking the property, just the two of us as I slowly got my strength back. And my girl opened up to me over time.

We were all going to be just fine.

Ava and Will bounded out of the house. "Hey," Crosby called, "we need your hands to unload flowers."

"I can help, too," I said, starting to head in that direction.

"Actually, Griffin wants to see you. He's in his office," Will said.

I stopped and turned back to the house. "All right. I'll be out to help as soon as I'm done."

I made my way inside, moving through the kitchen that had become my favorite place in the house and down the hall into Griffin's office. "Hey, handsome."

He looked up and grinned, those blue eyes sparkling. "Come here, gorgeous."

I crossed to him, and he tugged me onto his lap. "Have I told you lately that I love you?"

"Hmmmm," I said, tapping my lips with a finger. "I think you might've mentioned it once or twice. But I never get tired of hearing it."

He trailed his lips up the side of my neck. "I love you."

"Griffin." His name was more of a pant. "There are half a dozen people outside."

He chuckled, the sound sending shivers through me. "I'll be good. I promise."

"I hate that you have to be."

He squeezed my legs. "Trust me, I do, too."

"So," I said, twisting in his lap, "what did you need?"

"To give you this." He nodded to a long box on his desk. The piece that had once belonged to his father and had become his most prized possession.

"What is it?" I asked, sliding the box closer to me.

"Your wedding present. I wanted to give it to you before all the craziness began."

My mouth curved as I toyed with the ends of the ribbon. "You know you didn't have to get me anything. You've already given me so much."

He pressed his lips to my temple. "Open it."

I tugged on the ribbon, sliding the box out of its hold. I slowly lifted the lid. Inside were papers folded neatly in thirds. As I unfolded the stack, I gasped. "What in the world?" There were pictures and lists of places. Rome and the south of France. Mallorca, Spain and Mikonos, Greece.

"Next summer, you, me, and the kids are going to Europe. And every place we go, you're taking a cooking class."

Tears stung my eyes. "My dream."

His lips brushed my hair. "I love making each and every one come true."

I leapt from his lap, hurrying to a decorative box on his bookshelf. Griffin grunted. "That wasn't exactly the reaction I was expecting..."

I lifted the lid of the box and pulled out my own papers, but they were rolled into what looked like a scroll with a red ribbon tied around them. I turned, rushing back to Griffin and taking his mouth with mine in a hard kiss. "I love you so much. I never thought I could love a person as much as I love you."

He smiled. "Okay, that's a little better."

I handed him the scroll. "This is from me. And Will, Ava, and Mia."

Griffin quirked a brow but untied the bow. As he scanned the top page, his entire body locked. His gaze shot to mine. "This is paperwork to file with the court. To make me a guardian of the kids."

My tears spilled over, tracking down my cheeks. "We want to make it official in every way possible that we're family. Will, Ava, and Mia, too. Crosby can file them next week. If you want."

Griffin let the papers fall to his desk and framed my face with his hands. "I want." He slid his lips against mine in the most tender kiss. "You've given me my dream, too."

"What's that?" I asked.

"A family. Forever."

Acknowledgments

To my family and friends. Thank you for supporting me on this crazy journey, even if you don't read "kissing books."

Thank you to all the wonderful authors who have helped me along the way. From sharing wisdom and support to laughter when things get tough. You prove that the internet isn't always a scary place, after all. An extra special thank you to Emma and Grahame for walking with me through all of the ups and downs of this business. And to the Goldbricker ladies for all of the motivation and encouragement.

To my fearless beta readers: Angela, Crystal, Emily, and Trisha, thank you for reading this book in its roughest form and helping me to make it the best it could possibly be!

The crew that helps bring my words to life and gets them out into the world is pretty darn epic. Thank you to Susan, Chelle, Janice, Julie, Hang, Stacey, Jenn, and the rest of my team at Social Butterfly. Your hard work is so appreciated!

To all the bloggers who have taken a chance on my words… THANK YOU! Your championing of my stories means more than I can say. And to my launch and ARC teams, thank you for your kindness, support, and sharing my books with the world.

Ladies of Catherine Cowles Reader Group, you're my favorite place to hang out on the internet! Thank you for your support, encouragement, and willingness to always dish about your latest book boyfriends. You're the freaking best!

Lastly, thank YOU! Yes, YOU. I'm so grateful you're reading this book and making my author dreams come true. I love you for that. A whole lot!

Also Available from
CATHERINE COWLES

The Wrecked Series
Reckless Memories
Perfect Wreckage
Wrecked Palace
Reckless Refuge
Beneath the Wreckage

The Sutter Lake Series
Beautifully Broken Pieces
Beautifully Broken Life
Beautifully Broken Spirit
Beautifully Broken Control

Stand-alone Novels
Further To Fall

About

CATHERINE COWLES

Writer of words. Drinker of Diet Cokes. Lover of all things cute and furry, especially her dog. Catherine has had her nose in a book since the time she could read and finally decided to write down some of her own stories. When she's not writing, she can be found exploring her home state of Oregon, listening to true crime podcasts, or searching for her next book boyfriend.

Stay Connected

You can find Catherine in all the usual bookish places…

Website: catherinecowles.com

Facebook: www.facebook.com/catherinecowlesauthor

Catherine Cowles Facebook Reader Group: www.facebook.com/groups/CatherineCowlesReaderGroup

Instagram: instagram.com/catherinecowlesauthor
Goodreads: goodreads.com/catherinecowlesauthor

BookBub: bookbub.com/profile/catherine-cowles

Amazon: www.amazon.com/author/catherinecowles

Twitter: twitter.com/catherinecowles

Pinterest: pinterest.com/catherinecowlesauthor

Made in United States
North Haven, CT
18 January 2025